"The Ma~~" and
"The Golden Man"

TWO CLASSIC ADVENTURES OF

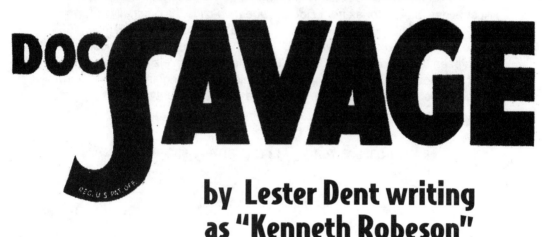

DOC

REG. U S PAT. OFF.

by Lester Dent writing as "Kenneth Robeson"

with new historical essays by Will Murray

Published by Sanctum Productions for
NOSTALGIA VENTURES, INC.
P.O. Box 231183; Encinitas, CA 92023-1183

Doc Savage Volume 9 copyright © 2007 by Sanctum Productions/Nostalgia Ventures, Inc.

This Nostalgia Ventures edition is an unabridged republication of the text and illustrations of two stories from *Doc Savage Magazine,* as originally published by Street & Smith Publications, Inc., N.Y.: *The Majii* from the September 1935 issue, and *The Golden Man* from the April 1941 issue. Typographical errors have been tacitly corrected in this edition. These two novels are works of their time. Consequently, the text is reprinted intact in its original historical form, including occasional out-of-date ethnic and cultural stereotyping.

ISBN 1-932806-76-8   13 DIGIT 978-1-932806-76-2

First printing: August 2007

Series editor: Anthony Tollin
P.O. Box 761474
San Antonio, TX 78245-1474
sanctumotr@earthlink.net

Contributing editor: Will Murray

Copy editor: Joseph Wrzos

Proofreader: Carl Gafford

The editor gratefully acknowledges the contributions of Tom Stephens, Scott Cranford, Kirk Kimball and John Petty of Heritage Auctions (www.ha.com).

Nostalgia Ventures, Inc.
P.O. Box 231183; Encinitas, CA 92023-1183

Visit Doc Savage at www.nostalgiatown.com and www.shadowsanctum.com

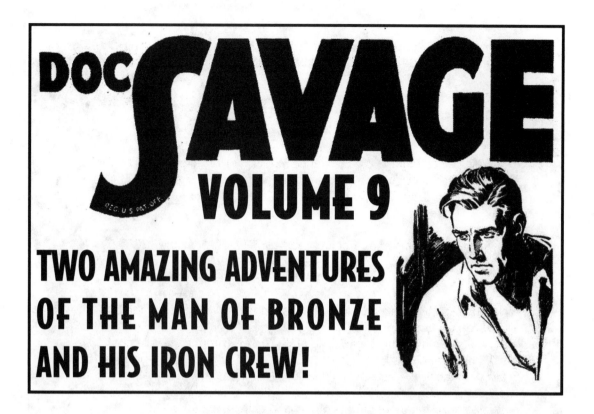

DOC SAVAGE
VOLUME 9

TWO AMAZING ADVENTURES OF THE MAN OF BRONZE AND HIS IRON CREW!

REG. U S PAT. OFF.

Thrilling Tales and Features

Cover art by Walter Baumhofer and Emery Clarke
Interior illustrations by Paul Orban

They couldn't believe the things he did; but no one could disprove them, until Doc Savage was plunged into the mystery of

THE MAJII

A book-length novel complete in this issue

By KENNETH ROBESON

Chapter I
MAKER OF JEWELS

"I AM about to be killed," the woman said.

The taxi driver whom she addressed had been half asleep behind the wheel of his parked cab, but the text of the woman's speech was not conducive to further slumber. He sat up straight.

The woman asked, "Have you ever heard of Doc Savage?"

"Who ain't?" growled the driver. "Say, what kind of a gag—"

"You will take us to Doc Savage," directed the woman. "And hurry."

The driver looked beyond the woman, after which his mouth fell open and his cigarette dropped off his lip and began to burn his coat front. The woman was veiled, but it was not that which shocked the hackman and scared him.

It was the four men behind the woman. They were four very tall men who had heads like cocoanuts in color, and who wore four of the most resplendent uniforms that the taxi driver had ever seen. Each of the four carried a modern automatic military rifle which was not much less than a portable machine gun.

"Well," snapped the woman. "Have you a tongue?"

"Sure." The driver swallowed twice. "I'll take you to Doc Savage." Then, under his breath,

"Ain't this a crackpot world!"

The woman spoke one ripping sentence which was absolutely unintelligible to the driver, but seemed to mean much to the four men with the uniforms and the rifles.

They all got in. The woman received much deference. She had bundled herself in a voluminous, shapeless cloak, but she had a nice ankle.

The cigarette burned through the hackman's trousers, scorched him and he jumped violently— then all but fainted, for, with a speed born of much practice, one of the brown men snapped up his rifle.

The woman cried out. Wildness, haste in her voice told the taximan the brown one was about to shoot. But she was in time. The automatic rifle lowered.

The driver found himself some blocks away, going in the wrong direction, before he got over his fright. He corrected his direction. The woman spoke to him.

"Is Doc Savage in New York?" she asked.

"Don't know," the driver said hoarsely. "He goes all over the world."

The cab was headed for a nest of buildings in the center of Manhattan, out of which towered one of the tallest skyscrapers in the metropolis.

"What," asked the woman, "does New York think of Doc Savage?"

"He's quite a guy," said the driver. "He helps people out of trouble. Does it for the excitement."

"Then he should be interested in saving my life, as well as others, including, very possibly, *his own*," the woman said.

"Yeah, I guess so," said the driver. He had already decided that the woman was some kind of nut.

The woman said no more, and the driver gave attention to his piloting, reflecting at the same time that the woman, while she spoke distinct and understandable English, had a pronounced foreign accent, but of what nation, the driver could not tell, he being no linguist.

They were down in the garment sector now, and the streets were comparatively deserted at this hour.

"Stop!" the woman commanded suddenly.

Her voice was shrill, tense. The driver swerved his machine in to the curb, then stared at his cargo as they unloaded hurriedly and scampered into a subway entrance. They disappeared.

The hackman had not been paid, but he only stared, for the truth was that he felt a relief at getting rid of his fares, for they were potential trouble, he felt.

But a low, coarse voice rumbled in the driver's ear in a manner to halt his feeling of relief.

"Where'd she go, buddy?" the voice demanded.

THE driver's head jerked around, and he saw that there was another taxi in the street behind him, with at least three men inside. The cab must have been following.

The man who had asked the question had a thick body and a hard manner—the manner of a man accustomed to treating other people as they do not want to be treated.

"Where'd they go?" the man growled. "Where were you takin' 'em?"

He twisted back his coat lapel to show something that the driver did not see distinctly but which he took to be a detective's badge.

"Doc Savage's office," gulped the driver, who had no love for trouble.

The thick-bodied man looked as if he had indigestion at the information, and he grimaced, seeming on the point of saying several things, none of them pleasant. Then he looked up and down the street furtively.

He dipped a hand in his pocket, brought it out palm down, but with a dollar bill held between the extended fingers. He passed the bill in to the driver, but when the latter reached for it, the hand slashed suddenly for the fellow's throat.

Awful horror came on the driver's face, and he threshed about, making gargling sounds, while a red flood bubbled and cascaded down his chest.

The thick-bodied man ran back to his waiting taxi, carefully wiping and pocketing the queer razor-blade affair with which he had cut the throat. He got into his machine.

"South," he said. "Give it all you got."

The driver was obviously no regular hackman. He looked as tough as the three in the rear.

"Well?" he said over his shoulder.

"The Ranee is heading for Doc Savage," said the thick-bodied man who had killed the taxi driver.

There was utter silence while the cab lunged along the gloomy streets, and inside it there was all of the cheer of a hearse interior.

"It ain't too late to get out of this thing," said one of the men. "We can grab a plane or a boat or something."

"Lingh may be able to handle Doc Savage," snapped the thick man.

"Yeah," grunted the other. "But let Lingh do it. I don't want none of this Doc Savage."

The thick man laughed, but not joyfully. "Get wise to yourself. Lingh probably has us covered."

They seemed to think that over, and, judging from the expression on their features, it was not pleasant thinking.

"Why'd you fix the hack driver?" one asked finally.

"He knew they were headed for Doc Savage," said the thick-bodied man. "He might have identified their bodies, and told what he knew, and that would have got to Doc Savage."

The cab took a corner, tires sizzling.

"Where to now?" asked the driver.

"Times Square subway station," said the thick-bodied man. "We're gonna head off the Ranee and her four boys with rifles."

THE Times Square subway station is possibly the busiest in the metropolis, but even it has quiet moments, of which the present happened to be one.

Cars of the train, as it rumbled and hissed to a stop in the station, were full of bright light and had only a few passengers.

The thick-bodied man and his companions were separated the length of the two-block long platform, and they got on the train without excitement, two at one end, three at the other, after which they walked through the train, looking carefully into each coach before they entered it.

Thus it was that they converged at the ends of one certain car which held their quarry.

The leader said to the two with him, "Lingh wants the Ranee alive. Remember that."

"Wonder why?" countered one of the pair.

"Don't know," said the man. "Doubt if Lingh knows. Think his orders come from someone else."

"Let's go," the other grunted.

They walked down the aisle, hands in bulging coat pockets.

Ranged side by side on the cane-bottomed seat running lengthwise of the subway coach, the veiled woman and her gaudy, dark riflemen escort were very quiet, watchful. They seemed a little confused, too, by the roar and shudder of the underground train.

They stood up suddenly before the thick man and his companions were near. The uniformed escort held the rifles across their chests, soldier fashion, alert.

"Easy does it," snapped the thick man.

He put a hand on the veiled woman's arm. That started it. Her escort clapped rifle stocks to shoulders.

The thick man yelled, "All but the Ranee, guys!"

Pockets split open to let out flame and noise. The thick man's aides were using sawed-off, hammerless revolvers which would not jam in cloth, and they shot as rapidly as fingers could work triggers, calmly, confidently.

It was plain they expected to blast down the uniformed opposition with the first volley. That did not happen. The tall, cocoanut-headed guards staggered, but did not fall.

"Watch it!" screamed the thick man. "They're wearing some kind of an armor!"

After that, there was screaming and noise and death in the moaning subway. Two of the tall men with the gaudy uniforms and the heads remindful of cocoanuts crumpled where they sat. The two others got in front of the veiled woman, shielding her, firing, screeching in their strange, foreign tongue.

Five men, altogether, were on the floor, badly wounded, when someone who knew a bit about the mechanics of the car managed to yank an emergency lever and the train ground to a stop, half inside of a lighted station.

The two uniformed men with the veiled woman got out on the platform and ran. The thick man tried to follow, with his single companion who had survived, but was shot at and, frightened, ducked back.

The wounded and dying screamed and groveled on the car floor, and that seemed to remind the thick man of something, for he turned deliberately, saw that one of the uniformed foreigners alone had a chance of living, and shot the man in the head. Then he ran, with his companion, out of the subway.

The veiled woman and her two escorts had vanished.

THE episode of the subway was newspaper headlines before the night was over, and it was a very mystifying matter to the police, who admitted they failed to make heads or tails of it, beyond the fact that they had identified three of the dead as local police characters known for their viciousness.

The desk clerk of the Hotel Vincent, a small but rather ornate hostelry which charged exorbitant rates and got the patronage of show-offs and people of importance, was reading the newspaper accounts of the subway slaughter. The hour was near midnight.

The clerk came out of the paper to an awareness of impatient fingers drumming the desk. It chanced that he noticed the fingernails on the drumming hand at first. It was a woman's hand and the nails were enameled blue. The clerk glanced up.

The woman before him was an unknown quantity inside the folds of a black veil and a voluminous cloak. When she spoke, it was in an accent distinctly foreign.

"I desire to see Rama Tura," she said.

The clerk lifted his brows, then made a show of sifting through the guest cards.

"Very sorry," he said. "We have no one by—"

The folds of the woman's cloak shook a little, and the clerk's eyes grew round, for she had exposed the business end of an automatic pistol.

"You will take me to Rama Tura's quarters," suggested the woman. "I know he directs you to say he is not here."

Two tall men wearing topcoats came in from where they had been waiting outside. They had heads which made the clerk think of cocoanuts.

The clerk sized up the situation, and since he was neither a hero nor a fool, he came from behind the desk, and the veiled woman and her two companions followed him into the elevator.

They rode to the sixteenth floor, where the clerk served as guide down a deeply carpeted Moorish hall to a door that was strapped with ornamental iron.

The clerk was on the point of knocking when one of the tall, dark men reached out and knocked him back of the ear with a revolver butt. The other dark man caught the clerk, and they held him while they knocked on the iron-strapped door.

"What is it?" queried a sleepy foreign voice from behind the panel.

"Cablegram," said the veiled woman, making her voice low and hoarse, so that it sounded remarkably like a boy's.

The man who opened the door certainly belonged to the same race as the veiled woman's two companions. His head had the identical hard round lines, the same fibrous brown hair.

He uttered the beginning of a cry when he saw his visitors. The sound did not get far, being stopped by a gun barrel which glanced off his head. He, too, was caught before he fell.

"Harm him not!" snapped the woman. "He is only a servant!"

She spoke in English, probably due to excitement, but was not too rattled to translate it into the tongue which the pair with her understood.

Three doors opened out of the room. The woman had not been there before, because she opened two and found closets, then tried the third, and discovered it led into what seemed to be the bedroom of a suite.

She went in with her small automatic pistol in hand, squinting in the luminance that came from a shaded bedside lamp.

The man who lay in the bed seemed, at first glance, to be dead.

HE was lean, this man in the bed, so lean that the coverlets seemed little more than wrinkled where they lay over his body. His head, however, was huge, a big and round brown globe that resembled something made out of mahogany and waxed over with shiny skin. His eyes were closed. He did not move. There was something unearthly about him.

The woman stood and stared at him through her veil.

Her two companions, having lowered the unconscious hotel clerk and the senseless man who had answered the door, and having locked the door, now came in. They stared at the man on the bed, and their eyes were as if they looked upon a deity.

Both got down on hands and knees and touched foreheads to the floor.

"Fools!" shrilled the woman.

"This man is Rama Tura, chosen disciple of the Majii," murmured one of the kowtowing pair in his native tongue.

"He is an old fakir," snapped the veiled woman.

The two guards seemed inclined to argue the point, but respectfully.

"He has the power of dying and returning to life when he so desires," one stated. "You can see now that he is dead. And was he not brought from our native land to this one in a coffin?"

The woman's cloak shook slightly, as if she had shuddered. She stepped forward and touched the weird form on the bed.

"You find him cold," said one of the guards. "He is a corpse. It is not good that we broke in here."

The woman's eyes became bright and distinct as seen through her veil.

"Is it that you no longer serve me?" she demanded.

The two got up off their hands and knees.

"Our lives, our bodies, are yours, Ranee," one said gloomily. "Our thoughts are birds that fly free. Is it your wish that we cage them?"

"You might clip their wings that they may walk on solid ground," said the Ranee. "You may also take your knives and cut off Rama Tura's big ears. It is my guess that he will revive from the dead in time to save them."

The men nodded, produced long shiny knives with black handles, and advanced upon the recumbent Rama Tura. Towering over him, they hesitated.

"He is chosen disciple of the Majii," gulped one. "Even the great American scientists have not been able to prove otherwise. For does he not take worthless glass and make it, by the touch of his power, into jewels for which men pay fortunes?"

"He is a fakir," repeated the woman. "He is a troublemaker. For years, he has been a nuisance. He is a common, ordinary beggar who for years made his living by performing street-corner tricks for tourists."

"He has powers no man understands," insisted the other stubbornly. "Out of worthless pebbles, he makes great jewels."

"Cut his ears off and see if he is magician enough to make them grow back again," the woman directed. "It is about those jewels that I wish him to explain."

The grotesque thing of bones on the bed opened its eyes.

"I am the dead who lives at will," he said. "What do you want?"

Chapter II
MAKER OF HORROR

THE veiled woman looked down at him and made some slight sound which in her land meant ridicule and disgust.

"You see," she said. "He awakened before he lost his ears."

There was absolutely no expression on the round, shiny head on the pillow. The eyes were open, but did not shift. The mouth was open, but the lips did not move when words came.

It was as if the weird-looking fellow were a corpse into the mouth of which a ventriloquist was throwing speech. He spoke English.

"To abuse the dead is sacrilege," he said. "But maybe your sin is mitigated because you do not have the mind to conceive my powers, my abilities and my condition. To you, I am the enigma of omnipotence, the—"

"You are a clever old fake," snapped the woman. "You are no different from other men, except certainly, more ugly. Now, you will tell me about those jewels, or my men will take your ears, after the fashion in my land."

"You are from Jondore?" asked Rama Tura.

"I," said the woman, "am the Ranee, the widow of the Nizam, ruler of all Jondore, descendant of rulers."

"Your voice had a familiar sound," murmured the strange-looking being on the bed. "Why are you here?"

"I will tell you, old fakir," the woman said angrily. "I am in New York by chance. I was making a trip around the world. And here I heard of this jewel-making séance of yours. I cabled my late husband's brother, Kadir Lingh, present ruler of Jondore, that I intended to investigate you."

She hesitated.

"I have a hideous suspicion," she said.

Rama Tura showed a slight sign of life. "What suspicion?"

The woman did not answer directly, but snapped. "Your organization is wide. I have reason to think my cable did not reach Jondore. I have been followed, my movements checked by men of Jondore. Your men! Once, they shot at me!"

"This cannot be true," murmured Rama Tura.

"Tonight I started to see a man who can handle things like this," snapped the woman. "I was attacked. Later, I found watchers about the headquarters of the man I wanted to see. They were your men."

"Who is this one you intended to see?" Rama Tura queried.

"Doc Savage," said the Ranee. "But you know that."

"Ah," murmured Rama Tura.

"You are a devil incarnate," the Ranee told Rama Tura grimly. "You are scheming to take the lives of many people, in order to accomplish an insane scheme."

But Rama Tura seemed interested in Doc Savage.

"Of living men," he said tonelessly, "it may be that Doc Savage has greatest knowledge, but his learning is of the material and the so-called scientific. He has not touched the abstract and invisible, the real power of concentrated thought as a concrete entity."

"Drivel," said the Ranee.

"Can Doc Savage make jewels of pebbles?" queried Rama Tura.

"You cannot, either," snapped the veiled woman. "And you are going to stop it! Otherwise, I am going to put Doc Savage and the police both upon your trail. I am going to tell them what is behind your actions."

"And what is behind it?" Rama Tura queried.

The woman swallowed. She seemed to brace herself.

"The Majii," she said.

Rama Tura looked very much as if he had been struck.

"So you have fathomed it," he mumbled hoarsely.

That, in turn, had a profound effect on the Ranee, for it was obvious now that her early conception had been only a grisly suspicion, but that Rama Tura's words had convinced her that she had guessed the sinister truth.

"Seize him!" she shrilled at her two companions. "If he is put out of the way now, it will save countless lives!"

Rama Tura sat bolt upright in his bed. His body was a pitiful string of bones. His chest resembled a gnarled, thin brown root. He was entirely hideous to the eye.

"I fear," he said, "that I shall have to demonstrate."

HE sat perfectly still after that, and if at first he had been unwholesome, a brown, lecherous harridan, he was more so now, seeming to emanate an aura of the indescribable.

There came into the room the feeling of a tomb, the very real yet somewhat impossible sensation which comes upon those who stand in the presence of those that no longer live.

The Ranee struggled visibly against the feeling. "Old buzzard!" she snapped. "You have practiced these tricks all of your life. Of course you are good at them!"

Rama Tura said nothing. His eyes had not moved. His mouth had not closed.

Suddenly, there appeared in the far side of the room an incredible thing, a monster of shapelessness, a fantastic ogre of a thing.

The Ranee, her two guards, stared at it. The light from the bedlamp hardly reached that far, and they could not make out the exact identity of the thing, except that it was a creature possessing eyes, and so large that it might have difficulty getting entirely into the room.

The air in the room began to change, to take on a definite odor, vague, repulsive, a bit warm, as if it might be the breath of the horror which had appeared so weirdly and was watching them.

"It is my servant," the death-faced Rama Tura said tonelessly. "It is here for a purpose."

The Ranee continued to stare.

"It is my guard," said the man in the bed again, referring to the thing in the door. "It is lent to me by my master, the Majii. It does strange things to men."

As if in verification to his words, both the guards now did an incredible an unbelievable thing. They presented their own guns to their own heads and calmly committed suicide. A single long breath could have been drawn between the time the first hit the floor and the other followed him.

The Ranee made a hissing sound of horror, spun and ran wildly. She did not go toward the door and the thing she could see there, but toward another door, and tore it open wildly, finding beyond a sitting room, a luxurious parlor of a place.

She plunged on and slammed against another door, which was unlocked and let her, luckily, out into the corridor, from which a passing elevator cage carried her, silent and quivering, to the street.

The night swallowed her.

Chapter III
CHOSEN OF THE MAJII

THE newspapers made a big splurge next morning. The headlines said:

THIEVES ATTACK RAMA TURA

Raid on Quarters of Mysterious Mystic
Results in Death of Pair

Two alleged robbers were killed in the hotel apartment of Rama Tura, man of amazing powers, last night. According to Rama Tura, the slaying followed a terrific hand-to-hand fight with three assailants, one a woman, who escaped.

This story was corroborated by Rama Tura's servant, and the hotel clerk, who was himself forced to guide the thieves to Rama Tura's quarters.

There was more of it, a detailed resumé of the banditry efforts as told by Rama Tura, and it was a convincing yarn, perfectly logical.

The motive, according to Rama Tura, had been a desire on the part of the thieves to force him to reveal how he made jewels out of worthless pebbles and bits of glass.

In the center of the front page of one newspaper was a box, editorial in nature, discussing the mysterious Rama Tura and his powers. It was headed:

WHAT IS HE?

Rama Tura came to the United States from the Orient, from a wild mountain province called Jondore.

Rama Tura takes pebbles and makes diamonds, rubies, emeralds. Jewel experts say they are genuine beyond doubt. They back their judgment by purchasing the stones.

One third of the selling price of these stones goes to American charity. Two thirds goes to a fund for charity administration in Jondore, Rama Tura's native land. Rama Tura himself takes no money.

What manner of being is this Rama Tura? Is he a faker? This paper had three of the greatest jewel experts pass on Rama Tura's products as genuine.

How does Rama Tura make his jewels? If he uses fakery, the most intense skeptics are baffled.

Rama Tura claims to be a disciple of the Majii. The Majii was a horrendous war chief who lived thirty centuries ago and conquered much of the Oriental world of that day. The Majii was a magician who could bring himself to life after being killed on the field of battle. He could slay thousands with a stare. He was cruel.

The Majii is believed by historians to be only a myth.

But Rama Tura is no myth. Just what is he?

Some other newspapers carried yarns along the same vein, elaborating on the queer personality of Rama Tura, and one even went over the strange fact that Rama Tura apparently had actually been brought from Jondore to the United States in a coffin.

One paper further stated that Rama Tura slept in his coffin, and was said to come alive only on special occasions, but the police disproved this by stating that Rama Tura had been in his bed when the thieves walked in on him.

Another journal hooked the robbery in with the slaughter in the subway, pointing out that the two thieves killed in Rama Tura's apartment were of the same nationality as some of those killed in the subway, namely Jondoreans.

The police hinted there might have been a quarrel prior to the robbery, but failed to indicate how such a thing might have come about.

Several newspapers bore quiet advertisements that afternoon.

RAMA TURA WILL APPEAR TONIGHT IN TEMPLE NAVA

To those who read this, and who had been following the affair in the newspapers, the item meant that Rama Tura would that night make jewels out of worthless articles in Temple Nava.

TEMPLE NAVA was not a building by itself, but an establishment on the upper floor of a Park Avenue building which was nothing if not exclusive.

It had been installed by a cult of wealthy thrill-seekers who had, after the Depression came along, been too busy to indulge in whimsies.

The furnishings, very rich, had been intact—no one could be found with enough money to buy such costly gimcracks—when Rama Tura leased it and began to set New Yorkers by the ears.

The swanky Temple Nava was the gathering place of many of the nabobs of the metropolis that night. There were many scientists and jewel experts. Rama Tura invited efforts to prove himself a fake.

There were many sensation-seekers, also, but those fry were not even permitted into the building. Policemen handled the traffic, and to enter the premises, one had to exhibit a bit of cardboard bearing cabilistic symbols. These were issued to the proper persons by detective agencies hired by Rama Tura.

It is a common thing for ladies to wear gloves the year around, so the presence of such covering on the hands of one woman who presented a card attracted no undue attention. No one, of course, imagined the gloves covered blue fingernails.

The lady herself did get a good deal of attention. A formal gown of black set off a remarkable figure, and her wide brown eyes stared aloofly from a face that would have been perfection except for a certain grimness about the mouth.

Her manner suggested someone bent on a mission that might not be exactly pleasant. She had an olive skin.

Her card was satisfactory, and she was admitted.

Not long after, a choleric dowager complained that she had lost her card of invitation, perhaps to a thief. She happened to be well known, and she was admitted anyway.

Straight into Temple Nava stalked the woman with the remarkable figure and the determined manner.

Many men saw her and admired her. Others saw her and looked as if a hungry tiger had walked into their midst. These latter were aides of Rama Tura. He seemed to have an incredible

number of them. One hurried to present himself before Rama Tura.

Rama Tura had just been carried into Temple Nava in a plain black coffin, and he was being photographed by newspaper cameramen.

It was plain to see that the cameramen considered the coffin business ridiculous fakery, but it made good stuff for their papers, and they had orders to get the photographs.

The messenger made signals furtively, and the cameramen were bustled out.

Rama Tura had lain in the coffin all of the time, very much like a dead man. Some of the photographers had touched him and he had seemed quite cold and lifeless.

The messenger leaned over the casket and said, "The Ranee is here."

RAMA TURA opened his eyes. He opened his mouth and it stayed open.

"I know it," he said in the tongue of Jondore.

"Someone told you first," gulped the messenger.

"No," said Rama Tura. "I know all things."

There seemed no way of refuting this, so the messenger swallowed several times.

"We did not scare her into leaving New York," he pointed out. "She is here because she intends to make more trouble."

"She had nerve to walk in boldly," said Rama Tura.

"There are police," reminded the other. "She will expect them to save her."

"She will be mistaken," intoned the other.

The messenger squirmed uneasily. "But she is the Ranee—"

"The Majii, my master, has waited thirty centuries for what he is now preparing to do," murmured Rama Tura. "The Majii has a plan of such vast size that you would not even understand it, my servant. If the Ranee insists on meddling, she must be put out of the way. No one must interfere."

The messenger nodded, then asked a very natural question. "How?"

"My magic will take care of that," Rama Tura advised him.

A little later, Rama Tura was carried out on the floor of Temple Nava by six big men of Jondore who were naked above the waist. It was a very effective entrance.

Rama Tura, it developed, was not to perform his feats on anything so prosaic as a stage, but in the center of the floor. Comfortable seats for the spectators—who would later be customers, perhaps—had been arrayed about the open space.

A large circular cloth of scarlet was carried in and placed on the floor, and Rama Tura was lifted from his coffin-like box and placed on this.

Very slowly, like something arising from the dead, Rama Tura got to his feet. He began to speak in a hollow, macabre voice. He did, however, use excellent English.

"I am not going to bore you with a mystic monologue," he told those present. "You probably would not believe me, anyway. I care not whether you think I am a fakir and a showman, for it is not important."

He turned slowly, like a machine, to survey those assembled in Temple Nava. His eyes were weird brown disks in his big, shiny skull. Several people shuddered.

"Perhaps," Rama Tura continued, "it has occurred to some of you to wonder why India has always been the world's treasure house of precious stones, for you all must have heard of the fabulous collections of the Rajahs. It is because jewels have a significance in the Orient, a significance that goes back some thirty centuries to a fabulous being known as the Majii. The Majii could do anything."

He paused as if for that to sink.

"Anything," he repeated. "It is my opinion that the Majii was the basis for the well-known story of Aladdin and the lamp. The Majii was really the Genie who appeared when Aladdin rubbed the lamp. In other words, this tale which is thought to be fiction is true."

He paused again.

"But that is neither here nor there. I do not attempt to explain my methods, except to tell you something I know your minds are too undeveloped to grasp. You will not believe that thought can be converted into matter, that the essence of the mind is supreme over all things. Yet this is quite true and the foundation of all so-called miracles.

"You find this hard to believe. All right—do not try. The primitive native cannot understand how an admixture of yellow and blue paints will produce a green paint, not knowing aught of the science of light. He knows that it does. You will watch me and know that I do produce jewels in a way you cannot understand."

This lengthy harangue was received with great interest, and while it was going on, Rama Tura's assistants had been circulating through the crowd, eyes alert, and had found two persons surreptitiously trying to use miniature cameras.

These individuals had been conducted to the front row and, to their embarrassment, requested to use the cameras openly.

Something vague and heavy came into the atmosphere of the room. An odor it was, with a tomblike mustiness. The audience tensed.

"Will someone bring an object forward for me to convert into a gem?" Rama Tura requested.

"Hard, crystalline substances are the most suitable. Artificial jewels are excellent. Other things require too much time and effort."

Someone got up hurriedly and offered a large red imitation stone. The bearer admitted this had been purchased in the dime store that afternoon.

"MAKE a pearl out of it," someone shouted.

Rama Tura was cupping the paste stone in the basket of bones that was his hands.

"No," he said. "Pearls are an animal product, rather, the secretion of a sick oyster, and not true jewels."

Rama Tura now went into action. Those in the audience who had been there before began to whisper to their companions, giving advance information on what was to happen. A woman or two complained uneasily to an escort of the indefinable odor that weighted the air.

Two big, dark Jondoreans brought in a cube of substance that resembled ordinary fire brick and sat it down on a metal tripod about level with Rama Tura's waist. On this, the worthless jewel was placed.

Rama Tura began to stare at the paste gem. The manner of this staring was somewhat unnerving. His eyes seemed about to come out of his head. His paper-thin lips writhed over a few ugly teeth which were plainly in the last stages of decay.

Some wag in the audience whispered, "If he's such a whiz, why don't he think himself into a new set of choppers."

If Rama Tura heard this reference to his teeth, he gave no signs. He was going through all the motions of a man in terrific agony. He groaned, mumbled, grimaced. He picked up the fake gem repeatedly and warmed it in his palms.

Suddenly he emitted a rasping whine.

The audience became aware that streamers of strange-looking vapor were gathering in various parts of the room, and floating toward Rama Tura. The things looked like wisps of colored fog.

The streamers began to gather about the black cube on which the stone lay. They bundled, thickened there. An awful cracking and popping filled all of the room.

Those who had miniature cameras began to take pictures madly.

The bundle of vapor about the gem began to glow. It grew hotter and hotter, giving off a light as blinding as the glow of an electric arc. Everyone in the room distinctly felt the frightful heat.

Then the heat died away, the glow disappeared, and aching eyes could make out the block of the fire brick on the stand.

A beautiful uncut diamond, as large as a pigeon egg, lay on the fire brick.

... streamers of strange-looking vapor were gathering ... floating toward Rama Tura ... An awful cracking and popping filled all of the room.

Rama Tura said calmly, "Such is the power of concentrated thought."

A man of Jondore in a silken robe placed the gem in a satin-lined box and passed through the audience showing it, making little speeches indicating that it was for sale, and that a third of the proceeds would go to American charity, two thirds to the fund for administering charity in Jondore.

The latter fund, it was explained, was directed by prominent individuals in Jondore.

SEVERAL jewel experts were present. They gave the gem a thorough test. They all passed the same opinion.

"Genuine, undoubtedly," they admitted. "Blue-white, and nearly perfect."

Unexpectedly, a woman stood erect in the audience.

"Let me see that jewel!" she commanded loudly.

It was the Ranee. The man with the gem bowed and came over. He let the woman examine the bauble. This she did with a magnifying glass.

The scrutiny had a remarkable effect upon her. She waved her arms and cried out for attention.

"Police!" she shrilled. "Arrest this Rama Tura!"

Every eye in Temple Nava was now on her.

"He is a fiend!" the woman shrieked. "He is doing something that menaces your very lives! He is plotting wholesale murder!"

"It is unfortunate and I apologize for her," he said. "She is suffering from a form of madness of the mind prevalent among the people of my country."

Rama Tura now advanced. He came slowly, and he was very much like a hideous corpse walking through the medium of manipulated strings.

The Ranee watched him. There was horror in her eyes. She trembled. She still held the jewel, but it dropped out of her hands, rolled under the seat and there was a scramble as several tried to get it.

Unexpectedly, the Ranee screamed, and every muscle in her slender frame seemed to loosen and she fell flat in the aisle.

Rama Tura stopped where he was.

"It is too bad," he said in English. "Her ailment is far advanced and she will now die."

She looked over the crowd, and what she saw there did not satisfy her. Expressions on most of the faces said they thought that she was just an hysterical woman.

"Fools!" she screamed. "Rama Tura is doing something which may cause many in this very room to die!"

From where he stood in the center of the open space, Rama Tura began to intone timbreless words.

Chapter IV
THE MAN ON THE STRETCHER

THE afternoon of the day following, two men were bending over the Ranee. One was small, gray, wearing all-white clothes. The other was a lumpish man with a kindly, doggish face.

The woman lay in a rather bare room, spotlessly clean, all remarkably white in color. Her bed was high off the floor. She pitched from time to time.

The men seemed to be administering stimulants in an endeavor to make her speak. They bent forward as the woman made some vocal noises.

"Doc Savage." Only the two words were distinguishable, and a moment later, she said them again, "Doc Savage."

The small grayish man straightened.

"You have sent for him?" he asked the other.

The plump man nodded. "By telephone. He is on his way."

They exchanged nods, and when the woman did not speak again, they drew aside, as if it were possible for their voices to disturb her.

"It is strange, this case," one said.

The other grunted. "She's calling for the right fellow to find out what is really wrong with her."

The small grayish man smiled at his companion. "You had a part in his education, did you not?"

The plump man nodded. He was head of the institution, one of the largest hospitals devoted to psychiatric work in the city, possibly the world.

"Doc Savage studied under me," he admitted. "But that was years ago. The man has far outstripped me—outstripped anyone I know, for that matter. He is a mental wizard."

An orderly appeared with word, "Doc Savage has arrived."

"Ever seen him?" the plump man asked the grayish one.

"No."

"Get set for a surprise then. He is one man who looks his part."

The man who entered the room shortly afterward seemed of gigantic size when he was in the door, but there was the remarkable illusion of growing smaller as he advanced.

This was due to the symmetry of a remarkable muscular development, an even construction which seemed to make him a man of ordinary size until he was near an object to which his stature might be compared.

Even more unusual was the man's skin, finely textured and of a bronze color. His eyes ran a close third in the summary of his unique characteristics—they were like pools of flake gold, never still.

He was a man who by his appearance alone would stand out instantly in a multitude. Yet his clothing was quiet, showing not the slightest suspicion of showmanship.

"There is something wrong?" asked the newcomer in a voice of warmth and modulation.

"This woman, Doctor Savage." The plump man pointed. "She has spoken your name a few times."

Both the lumpish man and the small gray man launched into a detailed account of their observations of the case. The woman had been brought in the night before from Temple Nava, where she had collapsed in the middle of a tirade against the mysterious Rama Tura, who was getting columns of newspaper publicity by making diamonds out of less-valuable things.

The woman had at first been thought to suffer from an ordinary fainting spell, but then it had been discovered that she did not respond to the usual reactions and stimulants.

"There seems to be nothing organically wrong," the lumpish man explained. "To tell the truth, it has me baffled."

From that point, the discussion went entirely technical, entering terminology which would have been utterly Greek to an unversed listener.

"I will examine her," Doc Savage said.

EXACTLY one hour and twenty-eight minutes later, he was finishing a microscopic analysis of spinal fluid, doing the work in the finely equipped laboratory which was a part of the hospital.

The bronze man had as observers some half a dozen men, specialists in that line, who were seizing an opportunity to observe a master at work.

Completing his own examination, Doc Savage permitted each of the spectators to scrutinize the extraction.

"You have seen this and the other tests," he said. "What do you make of it?"

"Practically normal," one said.

"Exactly," the bronze man agreed. "According to all conventional tests, there is absolutely nothing wrong with the woman."

One began, "Her heart and respiration—"

"Symptoms," Doc told him. "She breathes slowly because she is not moving, and her heart beat is accelerated a trifle due to her mental state."

"Then you think—"

"Her trouble is entirely mental," Doc said. "At least, the seat of it is in her brain."

"A mental disorder—"

"Not in the conventional sense," Doc replied. "Our tests would have shown that. It is something else."

The bronze man moved away from the microscope.

"This woman was brought from Temple Nava, I understand," he said. "She repeated my name, so I was called. Is that right."

"Correct," he was told.

"Has anyone tried to see her?"

"No one."

"I see."

A moment later, a small sound became audible, a low, mellow trilling, the pulsations of which ran eerily up and down the musical scale and seemed to come from no definite spot.

Some of those present showed surprise. They did not know that this was the sound of Doc Savage, a small unconscious thing which he did in moments of mental stress.

"You have some thought?" asked one who had heard the sound before—it was the lumpish man—and knew what it meant.

"I have," the bronze man admitted. "It is rather fantastic, but it is possible."

"Do you mind explaining?" he was asked.

"The thing is hardly in keeping with medical theory," the bronze man said slowly. "It is only a theory, a rather wild one, based on studies which I once made in the Orient. If it is true, it is a thing rather hideous to contemplate."

The listeners looked disappointed.

"We will examine the woman again," Doc said.

They went into the remarkably white bedroom which had held the woman.

The male intern who had been attending the patient lay on the floor. It was plain to be seen that he had been knocked over the head.

The woman was gone.

IT was nearly nightfall when Doc Savage crossed the ornate modernistic lobby of the skyscraper which housed his New York headquarters and entered, through what appeared to be a section of wall panel, his private elevator.

The conveyance lifted him with terrific speed for a time, then stopped so abruptly that the bronze man continued upward a few inches, then dropped back to the floor. He stepped out on the eighty-sixth floor, and approached a plain door which bore, in small bronze lettering:

CLARK SAVAGE, JR.

Before Doc Savage reached the door, it opened without visible aid—a mechanical phenomenon which was accomplished through the medium of radioactive discs in his pocket and a sensitive electroscope connected to relays.

The opening of the door let out sounds that resembled a miniature riot.

"You'll eat the rest of that apple, or I'll skin you alive!" labored a squeaky, enraged voice.

Chairs upset. Blows whacked. There were gasps, grunts, much puffing.

Doc walked in.

The combatants were circling each other warily. Each had done some damage on the other. This might have seemed strange, in view of the fact that one was slender, lean of waist, while the other was a two-hundred-and-sixty-pound colossus who might conceivably be mistaken for a bull ape.

The slender man was "Ham," sometimes designated as Brigadier General Theodore Marley Brooks, cleverest lawyer and snappiest dresser ever turned out by Harvard.

The human ape was Lieutenant Colonel Andrew Blodgett Mayfair, world-famed industrial chemist, better known as "Monk."

These two were members of a group of five remarkable men who had long been associated with Doc Savage in his remarkable career of helping those in trouble and righting wrongs.

To all appearances, Monk and Ham were going through one of the more violent stages of their eternal quarrel. No one could recall one having spoken a civil word to the other, but it was only occasionally that they came to blows.

"What now?" Doc Savage asked in a tone which showed no particular interest.

"This shyster!" Monk jerked a thumb at Ham. "He tried to feed Habeas another one of them apples filled with pepper."

"I'll break Habeas of robbing my coat pockets!" Ham gritted.

"You'll eat the apple yourself!" Monk assured him.

Habeas Corpus, object of the melee, was under a chair, long snout and enormous ears protruding. Habeas' ears were so huge that it was doubtful if he could have gotten them under the chair without difficulty. Habeas was Monk's pet pig.

Doc Savage said, "Would a little excitement interest you fellows?"

The abruptness with which Monk and Ham put aside their private quarrel was a giveaway. Their scrapping was nothing more than a habitual amusement, even if it did seem that they often earnestly endeavored to murder each other.

DOC SAVAGE explained about the woman in the hospital, repeating exactly what he had been told.

"It *is* strange," Monk muttered when the bronze man finished.

"It is," Doc agreed, "more than that. Someone did something to that woman, did something horrible. Perhaps it was done to shut her mouth. It might conceivably be done to kill her."

"What was it?" Monk asked. Monk had a small, childlike voice which sounded ridiculous for a being of such homely bulk.

"Rather not say yet," Doc told him. "In fact, it is doubtful if my explanation could be put clearly enough for you to exactly agree that the thing I think happened is possible."

"Um," said Monk.

Ham murmured. "I gather we are going to mix in this affair?"

"We are," Doc told him. "Did you notice, until last night, various strange-looking brown men were loitering in the streets about this building?"

"Huh?" Monk exploded.

"They were," Doc said. "I watched them for some time, secretly, but there was nothing to show that they were observing us. They disappeared last night, about an hour after the time this woman was stricken at the gem-making séance of the mysterious Rama Tura."

Ham went over to the massive inlaid table which was a part of the reception room furniture, and picked up an innocent-looking black cane. He separated this near the handle sufficiently to show that it was in reality a sword cane.

"Brown men," he said. "From the newspaper accounts, this Rama Tura is also a brown man."

"Exactly," Doc agreed.

"It begins to smell like a shenanigan of some kind," Monk said, small-voiced.

MONK came near not getting into Rama Tura's Temple Nava jewel-making séance that night, simply because he had garbed himself, largely to disgust Ham, as disreputably as he could.

His suit was a horrible, baggy-checkered thing which had been faded and burned by laboratory chemicals during the course of his experiments. He had not shaved.

They had secured entrance cards indirectly, through wealthy persons whom Doc Savage knew. Monk argued. Finally, he was admitted.

Ham had no trouble whatever. Ham was his usual sartorial perfection. He wore full dress, and more than one man with an eye for dress eyed him enviously. He carried his plain black sword cane.

They waited with the crowd at the elevators, and neither glanced through the door. Had they done so, they might have seen Doc Savage in the crowd of curious who were not being admitted.

The bronze man did not stand out from the crowd in his usual fashion. He wore a light, enveloping topcoat, a snap brim hat and spectacles. He walked with a stoop. There was not enough light to show the bronze color of his skin.

Doc moved away from the vicinity, and shortly afterward, was probing into the back of a large, plain roadster. When he left the machine, he had secured a metal box larger than a suitcase.

He went to the rear of the building which housed Temple Nava. As he expected, it had a freight entrance, which was deserted at this hour. The job of picking the ponderous lock delayed him some little time.

He closed the door carefully behind him, still carrying his metal case, and one of the freight elevators carried him up to Temple Nava. He operated the controls himself.

The freight elevator admitted Doc into a rough corridor, which in turn gave into Temple Nava. There was a guard at the door, a lean, swart man of Jondore.

He was standing where he could not see the freight elevators, and there was so much noise in Temple Nava—the jabbering of the crowd—that he had not heard the cage arrive.

Doc Savage moved through the darkness until he stood close to the lookout. Then Doc set his

Doc

throat and chest muscles carefully. He had practiced ventriloquism until he was fairly adept. He also spoke the language of Jondore, which was a rather common one in the Orient.

The lookout seemed quite surprised when a guttural voice from inside the temple seemed to call, "You at the back door—over here a moment."

The guard walked away in obedience to the summons. Doc ducked inside. When the guard returned, looking baffled, Doc Savage was on the stage which stood at one end of the temple, but which Rama Tura was not using for his present purpose. The stage was dark, deserted, with the curtains down.

Doc Savage climbed with his metal box. A few minutes later he was high off the floor, crouched precariously, cutting a round hole in the curtain.

He had tied the metal box to the perch with a stout cord, and now he opened it and drew out a small cinema camera which differed from other cameras in that it had a lens of several times the usual size.

Doc suspended this in front of the hole, lashing it there. It made almost no noise when he started it. The film magazines were very large, and would run more than an hour, taking pictures through a lens so fast that it would function in light little stronger than that given off by a candle.

Doc next cut a peephole for his own eye.

RAMA TURA was just beginning the discourse that preceded his performance, using the same trend of statements, if not the same words that he had employed the previous night.

Monk and Ham—Monk had managed that—occupied adjacent seats. As was to be expected, Rama Tura's line of talk did not register on Ham. It struck him as little better than the sales patter of a street corner astrologer. Ham curled a lip.

"It seems to appeal to the rest of these stuffed shirts," Monk told him in a stage whisper. "You oughta like it."

Ham brought a foot down sharply on Monk's instep. Ordinarily, Monk would have suffered in silence. This time he did not. He let out a bawl of pain that caused at least a dozen people to jump out of their comfortable chairs.

Immediately, two turbaned men of Jondore approached Monk, wearing disapproving frowns.

"Gonna try to throw me out," Monk surmised.

"Hope they do," Ham replied grimly.

But the two men of Jondore only took up a position near Monk and Ham and stood there.

Rama Tura went on with his monologue. The white lights in the place had been switched off and red ones turned on, lending a more weird atmosphere.

Rama Tura was not quite on the point of calling for imitation gems to turn into genuine stones when there was a commotion across the temple.

Four men of Jondore, turbaned, appeared, bearing a stretcher on which was a form swathed in a cloth which looked like a piece of the temple drapery. The stretcher was carried toward the exit.

"A thousand pardons," intoned Rama Tura. "It is merely one who has fainted and will be taken to a hospital."

Monk gripped Ham's arm, breathed, "Hey! They carried that from back toward the stage! Doc was back there."

"We had better look into it," Ham said grimly.

They craned their necks—and saw something. A naked male elbow was partially visible under the drapery that covered the form on the stretcher. The skin of this elbow had a pronounced bronze tint.

"Doc!" Monk gulped.

Both the homely chemist and the dapper lawyer arose and moved toward the door. They kept hands close to their armpits, where nestled little machine pistols which were charged with so-called "mercy" bullets, slugs which produced quick unconsciousness without making more than minor wounds.

THEY were not molested. They shoved into the elevator into which the stretcher had been taken. Other than themselves and the form on the stretcher, there were only the four men of Jondore.

Monk hauled out his machine pistol and waved it carelessly.

"Get 'em up!" he told the men of Jondore.

They glared at him. But they lifted their hands.

Ham closed the elevator door, operated the controls so that the cage sank several floors, then stopped it.

"Now we'll see what has happened to Doc," he said grimly.

He whipped back the drapery.

The man on the stretcher was not Doc Savage, but a lean-faced, wolfish Jondorean, and he held in either hand a water pistol of the ordinary dime store variety.

The instant he was uncovered, he pointed one water pistol at Ham, the other at Monk, and tightened down the triggers.

Hissing streams of some pungent, burning liquid hit Monk and Ham in the face, splattered, vaporized. Too late, they jumped backward. The stuff had blinded them agonizingly.

Monk tried to use his machine pistol. It made an unearthly bullfiddle roar. But Monk was unable to see a target, and the slugs went wild. Then Monk fell down, groveling, as consciousness went from him, and Ham did the same thing a moment later.

One of the men of Jondore said dryly, in his own tongue, "It was said to us that they were foxes, but they are indeed but puppies with pointed ears."

Monk's finger, tightening by some unconscious reflex, caused his machine pistol to moan briefly, after which Monk became quite still.

Chapter V
THE CAUTIOUS FOE

THE moan of Monk's machine pistol was by no means a small sound, and it carried up the elevator shaft, and muffled somewhat, drifted into Temple Nava, where Doc Savage heard it.

The bronze man had heard the first burst of the rapid-firer, and was already on his way to investigate. The second burst hurried him.

Coat collar turned up, hat down, stooping so as not to seem so tall, Doc whipped around the fringe of the spectators, heading for the door. He did not expect to depart undetected, nor did he.

Rama Tura had sharp eyes. He saw Doc. For once, Rama Tura's dead face showed alarm. He crackled a few words in his dialect.

Turbaned men of Jondore instantly converged on Doc. Doc quickened his pace. They raced to head him off. Doc picked up a chair, shied it at the first. The man upset.

A woman screamed. The temple became a bedlam. With his fists, Doc dropped two assailants. A gun went off somewhere. A woman fell on the floor and tried to crawl under chairs, squawling at the top of her lungs, then fainted into silence.

Rama Tura was whooping in English.

"Thieves!" he screamed. "This man stole some of the jewels I have made!"

It was a lie, pure and simple, but it served the purpose of setting the detectives present, and there were several, after Doc. Some of the officers drew guns.

Doc doubled low on the floor. He had a lot of respect for the shooting of New York policemen. And they did not know his identity.

Men were ahead of Doc, and there was a long thin Oriental rug on which they stood, and the bronze man yanked this. He did not spill them, but they were very busy for a few moments keeping their balance, and the bronze man got past them.

He was in the front corridor now. He knew the general layout of these buildings, how the electrical wiring was brought up through a shaft, and branched off at each floor through power boxes.

It took him only a moment to find the box and get it open. He unscrewed fuses, jerked switches and the premises went dark.

The stairway was dark also, down to the first landing, where there was light. He did not pause there, but went on. Five flights down he paused, and thumbed an elevator call button vigorously. The cage came shortly.

On the street, there was excitement. It centered about a policeman who wallowed in a spreading puddle of red on the sidewalk. It was not necessary to ask questions. Bits of excited talk told what had happened.

Brown men had dashed out carrying two unconscious captives—Monk and Ham. A policeman—the one on the walk—had tried to interfere. He had been shot in his chest for his pains.

The assailants had escaped in a car with their two captives.

Doc Savage ran for the spot where he had left his roadster. It was a little more than possible that he did not have much time to lose.

THERE were five men in the group who aided Doc Savage, and each was an expert in some particular profession, at which he worked during odd times. Two of the five were absent from New York.

Colonel John "Renny" Renwick, engineer, was in Germany, attending an international association of engineers conclave. William Harper "Johnny" Littlejohn, was also abroad, in Central America, heading a bit of archaeological research.

Major Thomas J. "Long Tom" Roberts was the only other of Doc's group in New York.

Doc's roadster was fitted with a shortwave radio transmitter and receiver. Long Tom Roberts, who was an electrical expert of note, would probably be in his laboratory, and would have a receiver turned on, tuned to the wavelength which Doc's outfit used as a matter of course. Doc raised Long Tom on the first call.

Long Tom had a rather quarrelsome voice.

"I'm packing," he said. "An electrical outfit made me a fat offer to go to South America and superintend some construction. I stand to make fifty thousand out of it."

"Then you would not be interested in some excitement?" Doc queried.

"What kind?" Long Tom countered. The radio loudspeaker did not improve the natural sourness of his voice.

"Rama Tura, the jewel maker, has something up his sleeve," Doc said.

"Of course he has," Long Tom snorted. "But let him trim the suckers. He's only going after the rich ones."

"Rama Tura's men just seized Monk and Ham," Doc said. "There is also a matter of a woman to whom something mysterious and terrible happened, who kept calling my name, and who has now disappeared rather queerly."

"This electrical concern offered me fifty thousand and a bonus," Long Tom said.

"All right," Doc said. "Take it."

"I will not," Long Tom said contrarily. "Where'll I meet you?"

"Rama Tura's apartment," Doc Savage said, and gave the address.

Where Rama Tura resided was no secret. The matter of the two men killed in the attempted jewel robbery had spread that over the newspapers.

The subdued lobby of the Hotel Vincent, in which Rama Tura had been residing, was quiet and only partially saturated with pale light when Doc Savage drove past. The bronze man parked in a spot where he could keep a watch on the place, and waited for Long Tom to appear.

A newsboy passed, crying his wares. Doc bought a late edition.

There was no mention of the excitement at Rama Tura's latest jewel-making séance, which was not surprising, since it had occurred only a few minutes ago. He glanced over the paper. Two items caught his attention.

Except for a difference in names and addresses, they might have been identical.

Two men had been murdered. Both murders had been committed by robbers. Knives had been the death weapons in each case. Both victims had been fairly wealthy. Both men had been avid amateur photographers.

DOC SAVAGE got out of his roadster, went to a telephone and called the detective agency which had charge of issuing the tickets to Rama Tura's jewel-making séances. The agency was a perfectly honest one.

He requested the night operative on duty to check the list of persons to whom cards had been issued for Rama Tura's previous night's performance.

Both murdered men were on the list of ticket recipients.

There was no definite proof, but it was possible that Rama Tura had taken measures to see that the pictures of his performance were never developed.

Doc Savage went back to his roadster. Long Tom should have arrived by now. He was not in evidence.

Long Tom's car was equipped with a radio. Doc, adjusting his own receiver carefully, got the carrier wavelength of Long Tom's transmitter distinctly. Evidently it was switched on. It did not sound far away.

Doc tried repeatedly, but did not raise Long Tom. Something, it seemed, had happened to the electrical wizard.

Doc Savage walked into the Hotel Vincent, strode across the dim, empty lobby, and noted that the clerk seemed to be asleep with his head on the desk. Doc did not address him, but walked around and shook him.

The clerk was evidently drugged. He was slightly disheveled, as if he had been held, and there was a prick on his arm where a hypo needle had probably entered.

DOC made, with a pen, certain strange-looking marks on the desk blotter. These were hieroglyphics of the ancient Mayans, and could be read by very few men in the civilized world. Long Tom could read them, having acquired the ability during the course of a certain Central American adventure.*

Long Tom, should he arrive, would be certain to see the symbols and know Doc was upstairs.

Scrutiny of the registration cards told Doc the floor of Rama Tura's suite. The bronze man went to an elevator. The operator was slumbering inside—drugged. Doc ran the cage up himself.

There was no sound outside the door of Rama Tura's suite. Doc tried the knob, found it unlocked, and walked in. The lights were burning. There was flame in the fireplace, rather low. The ashes looked unnatural. Doc went over.

Documents had been burned recently in the fireplace, and the ashes mashed into millions of indecipherable fragments. No hope of learning anything there.

Doc went on into the other rooms. Dresser drawers were upset on the floor. Coat hangers were strewn about opened closet doors. Everywhere were these signs of a hasty departure.

A wastebasket held newspapers, wrapping papers, bits of cord—and a crumpled ball of white cloth. Doc got the cloth. It was a hospital frock, and bore the name of the hospital from which the mysterious woman of the blue fingernails had escaped.

There was a damp spot on the gown, on one arm, and it gave off a strong scent of toilet water.

In the bathroom, a bottle of toilet water had been broken, and was still wet on the floor.

Doc Savage studied this fairly conclusive proof that the mysterious woman had been in the suite recently, then made another round of the place, found nothing of interest, and went downstairs.

The Hotel Vincent telephone operator occupied a small room by herself, and was evidently not a very energetic young woman, because she was placidly reading, unaware that anything out of the ordinary had happened.

After a little argument, Doc got a look at her call charge slips. Since every call made by a guest was charged for at ten cents each, a record was kept.

One call had been made from Rama Tura's suite that night. It was timed less than an hour previously. Doc studied the number, made his small, fantastic trilling sound briefly, while the operator gaped wonderingly, then called the same number himself.

He got the office of a transcontinental airline. There happened to be an alert young man on the desk, and he distinctly remembered a call at the time Doc mentioned.

It had been made by a voice with a distinctly foreign accent, and the inquirer had desired to know whether the plane due in from San Francisco at midnight carried as a passenger one Kadir Lingh.

"Naturally, we do not give out such information," said the young man at the airline office.

Doc Savage made his identity known, and requested speech with an official of the concern who happened to know his voice.

"What about this Kadir Lingh?" he asked, when he was sure of getting the information.

"Kadir Lingh is aboard the midnight plane," Doc was told. "Not only that, but we have a request from the American government to show him every courtesy. It seems that Kadir Lingh is the ruler of some country in the Orient."

"He is the Nizam of Jondore," Doc Savage replied. "Jondore happens to be a province, under British protectorate, with a population only a little smaller than the United States. Should something happen to Jondore, it is pretty logical to think the same thing would happen to the rest of the Far East."

"What makes you say that?" the other asked curiously.

Doc Savage hung up without answering.

NO one around the Hotel Vincent knew anything about the exodus of Rama Tura's retinue, so Doc Savage left the place.

The bronze man's roadster was fitted with spare equipment for almost any emergency, including a length of electric wire and a trouble lamp.

Out of the wire he improvised a simple radio loop aerial. His receiving set was especially sensitive to directional loop reception when certain terminals were used.

He tuned in on Long Tom's transmitter. Then he drove toward it. This was no simple task, since the presence of large buildings at times completely distorted the loop indications.

Long Tom's car stood in a dark side street, askew of the sidewalk, one wheel smashed off, the radiator partially caved in by a telegraph pole. Water still drooled from the radiator.

A few spectators were staring sleepily. Doc's questioning elicited word that no one knew what had caused the wreck or what had happened to the occupant of the car. The machine had simply been found.

Doc circled the machine. His identity became known and several persons began to whisper excitedly and point him out. He carefully paid no attention to this. He had never become so blasé that public attention did not embarrass him. It was for this reason that he avoided the public eye whenever possible.

Finding nothing in or on the machine, he withdrew and circled the spot, still continuing his scrutiny. The crowd followed him wonderingly, still whispering.

Fifty feet down the street, Doc found a smear of dampness on the pavement which, when he turned a light upon it closely, had a distinct reddish cast. Seepage from a wound! And it had been wiped up. It was very fresh.

Whether the stain had been made by fluid from Long Tom's body, or not, there was no way of telling. But something had certainly happened to Long Tom Roberts, the electrical wizard.

Doc Savage went to his roadster and consulted the dash clock. It was ten minutes past midnight. He knew his own driving ability.

His best effort would not get him to the airport in time to meet the midnight plane from San Francisco in which Rama Tura had been interested—the plane bearing Kadir Lingh, potentate of Jondore.

But there was always the chance the plane might be late.

Chapter VI
MURDER ON THE LOOSE

POSSIBLY because land is somewhat appallingly expensive in the vicinity of New York City, and because aviation in its infancy had not the funds of a Midas to expend, rather cheap sites were frequently selected for airports.

Cheap land meant land away from other habitation, frequently in or near a marsh. The airport used by the transcontinental line in which Doc Savage was interested was in such a location, and it was surrounded by brushland.

Doc Savage was half a mile away from the airport when he heard the shooting. There were four measured shots that might have come from a revolver. Then something that sounded like a shotgun went off. A man shrieked. All of these noises were sufficient to carry over the idling of a plane engine.

Doc Savage bore down heavily on the accelerator. The heavy roadster began to cover ground in a slightly eerie manner. Doc kept a close watch, half expecting to meet a machine or machines, but nothing appeared and he swerved into the airport.

There was much excitement. Men ran across the tarmac from various directions, converging on the hangars. The floodlights were on. At least two bodies lay in their glow. Doc ran forward.

"Damned gang raided the midnight plane!" he was told. "After one of the passengers."

"They get him?" Doc asked.

"Heck no. The passenger had a bodyguard. Boy, you never saw such shooting."

"Who got killed?"

"The assistant pilot, poor sap. He tried to be a hero. The other stiff is one of the raiders. Shot through the thinking box."

Doc Savage nodded, asked, "Anyone else?"

"Sure," said the informer. "The guy they are questioning."

"Who is he?"

"Another one of the raiders. Man, did he get it! One of the passenger's bodyguards swiped him with a knife, right across the lamps. Fixed 'em both."

"Put his eyes out?"

"You said it."

"Where is the passenger and his bodyguard?"

"Skipped. Grabbed a car and chased the other birds. Stole a hack from a poor driver to do it."

The informant could give information precisely and quickly.

"How long have they been gone?" Doc demanded.

"Long enough so that you can't catch 'em. Five minutes ago. These Long Island roads go every which way."

Doc Savage considered briefly.

"Do not let it be known that I am here," he directed. "But tell whoever is in charge that I want to see him privately."

"O.K."

THE member of the raiding party who had been left behind was horribly blinded, thanks to the knife cut which he had sustained across the eyes.

The blade had all but separated his eyeballs as a sharp knife would a pair of apples. He was moaning and blubbering and it was quite certain he would never look upon the world again.

The airport attendant stood around and looked sorry, for it was a pitiful thing.

They might not have looked so sorry had they known this man who was blinded was the same one who had pursued the Ranee the night before and had so callously killed a taxi driver, simply because the poor fellow had known the Ranee was endeavoring to get to Doc Savage. He was a cold slayer and he had probably gotten less than he deserved.

They were trying to question him. The man moaned and blubbered and screamed. The questioners were not experts enough on wounds to know the man was suffering no very intense pain as yet, and that he was setting up a howl to make it seem he was in no shape to answer questions.

The questioning had gotten nowhere when a rasping, coarse voice said from the door:

"The first man who moves won't move again!"

Everyone spun. What they saw inspired neither mirth nor a wish to move too quickly. There was a man in the door, shrouded in a black raincoat, an aviator's helmet and mask. He held two revolvers as huge as anyone present had ever seen.

"Get your hands up!" the newcomer snarled. "Back against the wall, then turn around."

They did so and he searched them. Such weapons as he found, he smashed on the concrete floor, after unloading them.

He walked over and grabbed the blinded man by an arm.

"I'm gettin' you outta this, buddy!" he growled. "Let's blow!"

They went out swiftly, the masked man guiding the blinded one.

"Stick in here five minutes and be healthy," advised the masked man to those left behind.

One pilot did not take the advice, and thrust his head out, with the result that a gun banged and plaster jumped off the stucco wall well above his head. Everyone remained out of sight after that, and they heard a car go moaning away into the night.

The masked man drove the car furiously, hit the main highway, swung left, took the first right turn, and held the machine at seventy.

Later, he turned into a winding lane which crossed the island and slowed the pace, on the principle that nothing is more suspicious than a car traveling at an unnatural speed.

The blinded man had been silent with his agony, but now he spoke.

"Thanks, pal," he said. "Who are you?"

The masked man said nothing.

"You done me a turn," grumbled the blinded one. "Any reason why we can't knock ourselves down to each other?"

"No reason," said the masked man. "How's the lamps?"

"Not bad," said the other. "Take a gander at 'em, will you."

The masked man stopped the car, removed the emergency bandage and scrutinized the sliced eyeballs. There was not the remote chance of the eyesight being saved.

"Whatcha think?" the blinded man gulped eagerly.

"Could be worse," said the other.

"Sure. I'll be up and lookin' at the dames in a week." The sightless one settled back on the cushions with a sigh. "Say, where'd you come from? I don't know that voice."

"New man," said the other. "I just mixed up in it."

"Hot stuff, what?"

"You said it."

"Think it's worth the trouble?"

"Sure thing. Biggest the world has seen."

"You must know more about it than I do," said the blind man. "I don't even know what it's all about."

"It's big," said the masked man dryly.

THE car went over a stretch that needed repaving, bucking and swaying, the headlights jumping up and down far ahead. The engine ran quietly, however, and the springs did not need oiling.

"You on the payroll?" the masked man asked curiously. "Or do you get a share?"

"Payroll. You?"

"Same. Who hired you?"

"Guy named Kadir Lingh," grunted the blinded man.

"Hm-m-m!" the other said explosively. "That's funny. Kadir Lingh was the bird who came in on the plane tonight, the lad you fellows were to get."

The other was holding his eyes and wincing.

"That *is* funny," he mumbled. "We only had his description. We were to grab him and take him to the guy who hired us. Only it didn't go off."

The car sailed over a very steep hill in easy high gear.

"Describe the man who hired you," requested the driver.

The blinded man would miss his eyes. He had been very observant. True, he had a character easy to describe, for he was painting a word picture of the maker of jewels, Rama Tura.

The masked man laughed shortly when the description ended.

"That," he said, "is Rama Tura, the man who makes diamonds and other jewels out of pebbles and imitation jewels."

"He hired you?"

"I left him," said the masked man, "not more than an hour ago."

"I don't understand it," mumbled the one who did not have his eyes. "He said he was named Kadir Lingh, and that he was the big-shot in some province in or around India."

"Rama Tura is a slick egg," advised the pilot of the car. "No doubt he told you he was Kadir Lingh so that the police would look for the wrong man in case they caught you and you talked."

"I wouldn't talk."

"Sure, sure. Rama Tura, maker of jewels, just wasn't taking any chances."

The blinded man groaned. "I wonder what the whole game is?"

"Don't *you* know?" the masked one exploded.

"Heck no. I was told it was big, and that it would mean millions of dollars and involve most of Asia before it was over. That's everything I know. Rama Tura, if that's really who hired me, don't tell much."

"How did he come to contact you?"

"Oh, I belong to a mob that does little jobs," said the blinded man. "It wouldn't be hard for a guy who wanted a job done to hear of us. The boss—Rama Tura—had some of them guys he brought from Jondore, but he needed some Americans to kinda help out. That's where we came in."

"That," queried the masked man, "is all you know?"

There was something queer about his voice. It had changed, changed remarkably. It was not at all like it had been a moment ago. The blinded man realized that.

"Say!" he exploded. "Who are you, anyway? What's your name?"

"Doc Savage," said the masked man.

Chapter VII
SUSPICIONS

DOC SAVAGE, having learned disgustingly little by his role of pretended rescuer of the blinded man, drove into the city and directly to a concern which made a business of supplying ambulances for long hauls.

He delivered the blinded man to them, along with an order for a doctor, and certain instructions. Then he made a long-distance telephone call.

The sightless one would then be taken upstate, where another ambulance would meet the first, and the patient would be transferred. That was the last his old haunts would ever hear of the patient.

The fellow would go, as a matter of fact, to an institution which Doc Savage maintained in the mountains, an elaborate place, where the man's brain would be operated upon in such a delicate manner that all memory of his past would be wiped out, after which he would receive a course of training in upright citizenship, and learn a trade by which he could make a living without his eyes.

Doc Savage had maintained this unique "college" for a long time, and its existence was known to almost no one outside the specialists who worked there, and Doc's group of aides.

Even the "graduates" were delivered in such a manner that they did not know where it was. No "graduate" had ever been known to return to crooked ways.

Returning to his skyscraper headquarters, Doc Savage found that the device which recorded all telephone calls during his absence held an unpleasant and shocking message. The mechanical device on the telephone consisted of a phonographic device which said, through a loudspeaker, "This is a mechanical robot in Doc Savage's office which will record for his attention any message you care to speak," after which the communication of the caller was placed on another record.

There were really two calls of importance.

The first was from the hospital to which Doc Savage had gone to visit the woman who had disappeared, and it advised that three men—the two doctors and the intern who had attended the woman—had been found with knives sticking in their hearts.

The bronze man made his weird, small trilling sound for some moments after he heard that, and the note was as chill, as eerie as a frigid wind trickling through the frozen pillars of some polar ice field. For once, it was not pleasant to hear.

First the men who had taken pictures. Now the doctors and the intern.

Rama Tura was wiping out everyone who might possibly have learned anything about him.

The second important call was in the dead voice of Rama Tura.

"Long Tom, Monk and Ham wish to send you a message," the mechanism had recorded Rama Tura as saying. "They say that they do not think you will or should accede to a certain demand which I am going to make. But first, let me prove that I have them."

Following that, Ham's voice said, "Doc, they're planning—" after which his voice ended suddenly, as if a hand had been slapped over his mouth. Then came Long Tom's sour voice, not speaking words, but remonstrating angrily close to the telephone transmitter. It sounded as if he were being abused.

It was apish, stupid-looking Monk who made best use of the opportunity. He spoke Mayan, and said, "See a man called Kadir Lingh—" before he was shut off violently.

"I do not believe they had time to tell you anything of value," Rama Tura's lifeless voice continued. "It was necessary to let you know they were with me."

The voice might have been coming from a phonograph which was incapable of registering tonal differences.

"You see," Rama Tura said, "within the next twelve hours, you will receive a box. This box will be a reminder to attend to your own business. It will contain the head of one of these friends of yours."

THE bronze man's features held no visible emotion as he put the recordings aside and set the machine for future operation. That did not mean, however, that he was unconcerned.

There was a grim speed in his movements as he passed into an adjacent room, which held a scientific library of great completeness, thence into his unusual laboratory.

From a cabinet he took a vest which consisted of a light, bulletproof chain mail, to which was attached rows of small pockets, these padded so that, once the vest was donned, its presence was hardly noticeable. The pockets held innumerable gadgets which, on occasion, served for some rather strange uses.

The bronze man left his headquarters this time by descending in the speed elevator to the basement level, and stepping into a passage which led some scores of yards to a metal door that admitted into the Broadway subway tunnel. He walked, crowding aside as trains passed, to the nearest station, and from there took a taxi.

There was quiet in the vicinity of the building housing the Temple Nava. Police guards were gone from in front, although a few curious loitered quietly in the lobby, talking. No brown men of Jondore were in evidence.

Doc Savage went up to Temple Nava exactly as he had earlier in the night, using the freight elevator in the rear.

The Temple Nava had a disheveled aspect. Rama Tura apparently had not gone on with his jewel-making séance after the excitement. Chairs were upset and scattered about.

Doc Savage moved back to the stage, alert, and climbed to where he had left the motion picture camera. It was still in the obscure hiding place, sensitive lens through the curtain.

Producing a flashlight which spiked a stream of intense white light scarcely thicker than a pencil, Doc went over the camera.

What he found did not seem to satisfy him. He clambered down, and studied the floor beneath, and examined the film of dust, microscopic in places, on the braces and struts.

Someone had climbed to the camera, other than himself.

He removed the camera with the greatest of care, not opening it, not even touching it, but wrapping it in a tapestry which he yanked from the wall.

Twenty minutes later, he had the camera under a strong X ray in his laboratory.

The film magazine was empty. Whatever had been photographed would serve no purpose, for Rama Tura or his men had obviously taken the film.

Certain of the fastenings and hand grips on the camera seemed to bear a thin coating of oil. It might have seeped from the mechanism.

Doc Savage used chemicals to analyze the oil film. It was a potent toxic and an acid in solution—the acid to burn the skin and admit the poison into the system.

Touching the stuff would have been an excellent bid for death.

Doc went over the camera for fingerprints, and was not surprised at finding none.

GOING back into the reception room, Doc Savage used the telephone. His first call was to the police, an inquiry as to whether any trace had been found of Kadir Lingh, ruler of Jondore, who had managed to escape the reception at the airport. There was some news.

The taxicab seized by Kadir Lingh and his bodyguard had been found in Brooklyn, deserted except for one brown man, probably a Jondorean, who had been sitting in the back seat, suffering the unavoidable after effects of a bullet through the brain.

The police official had an additional word.

"This fellow Rama Tura has dropped out of sight," he said. "We wanted to question him about that fracas at Temple Nava tonight, and about the two alleged robbers who were killed in his apartment. He has checked out of his diggings. No one has an idea where he went."

Doc gave courteous thanks and hung up.

THE recording device showed no calls during the bronze man's absence at Temple Nava, which was good evidence that Monk, Ham and Long Tom had not escaped.

Doc now proceeded to make a series of telephone calls. He got some sharp answers from persons who did not like the idea of being aroused at this hour of the night. Simple statement of his identity, however, was in each case sufficient to stem the complaints.

Monk's pet pig, Habeas Corpus, was in Doc Savage's office. During the telephoning, the porker came out of the library, where he had been staying, and stood and eyed Doc Savage intently, grunting several times in a vague way.

The shote gave every evidence of becoming concerned about Monk's continued absence. Doc interrupted his telephoning to give Habeas an apple, which the diminutive porker ignored.

From an executive of the Better Business Bureau, Doc Savage secured the information he was seeking. It is one of the purposes of Better Business Bureaus to investigate unusual enterprises and ascertain, if possible, whether they are fakes designed to gyp someone. Rama Tura and his fantastic jewel-making séance had not escaped this one.

"It is, of course, incredible that the jewels are being made by hocus pocus," the executive of the bureau told Doc. "But the jewels produced are unquestionably genuine. Hard-headed buyers have paid enormous sums for some of them. One third of the money goes to American charity, and the other two thirds to a charity in Jondore."

"That," Doc said quickly, "is what interests me. What about this charity in Jondore?"

"It is a fund to be administered by prominent persons in Jondore," the other explained.

"Has the money been sent to Jondore?"

"No. We took care of that."

"What do you mean?" Doc demanded.

"We suggested that the money be kept here in the United States for a few weeks, until it was quite certain that Rama Tura had a legitimate right to sell those jewels," said the Better Business Bureau man.

"Your theory was that they might be stolen jewels which Rama Tura was disposing?"

"Exactly."

"It is hardly likely they are stolen jewels," Doc said. "Stones the size of those Rama Tura has been producing have a character all of their own, even if recut. Had they been stolen, someone would have recognized them."

"Well, where in the devil are they coming from?" the other demanded. "I don't know how Rama Tura does that ball of fire stunt. But damned if I'm gullible enough to think he stands there and makes diamonds."

Doc Savage asked, "Where is the two thirds of the Jondore proceeds?"

"In cash in the Oriental National Bank," said the man from the Better Business Bureau.

"Cash?"

"Yes."

"Why?"

"Darned if I know. It's in a safety-deposit box, or rather, a whole series of boxes. I saw it myself."

"Rather a strange business," Doc Savage said dryly.

"You said it."

They terminated the conversation.

Doc Savage made arrangements to have a heavy police guard placed over the Jondore charity funds in the Oriental National Bank. This was simply accomplished, since the bronze man held a high honorary commission.

While Doc Savage was still talking about that matter, the second of his bank of telephones—he had several—rang. He picked up the instrument.

"I think," said a voice in almost unnaturally precise English, "that you might save my life if you care to hurry."

Doc demanded, "Just what is the idea?"

"I am the Nizam, Kadir Lingh, of Jondore," said the precise voice. "I am at present holding them off. But I shall not be able to accomplish this much longer."

Quite distinctly over the telephone wire came the bang of several shots, followed by two more much closer to the transmitter.

"Where are you?" Doc asked.

"I was too busy getting here to notice," said the other.

"What can you see from your windows?" Doc questioned.

There were two more shots.

"I am in a boathouse," said the man. His voice was calm. "I cannot see anything but woods and the occasional flash of a gun and the car which I abandoned."

Doc suggested, "Look out on the water and see what you observe."

Another shot.

"I see a green light," said the man. "It flashes once every ten seconds. There is a white light beyond it which blinks about once every second. Perhaps you could look at a chart—"

"I will be right out," Doc said.

DOC SAVAGE was a disciple of the theory that the various abilities of the human animal, memory among other things, can be developed by careful practice and concentration.

For this reason, he took two full hours of various exercises daily, and had taken them since childhood. These exercises were remarkable and covered not only the building of his physical body, but the development of sight, hearing, touch, olfactory organs, and the rest.

There was also a routine for memory, although perhaps the more important side of the memory training was back in the bronze man's childhood. In the cradle stage, he had been broken of forgetting things, just as other children are broken of the thumb-sucking habit.

From the very date of his birth, the bronze man had been trained for the strange career which he now followed.

That explained how he knew, without consulting a marine chart, that there was a ten-second green blinker and a one-second white blinker in Long Island Sound off High Point.

High Point was a spot unpopular with suburbanites, due to the fact that there was a marsh to the west of the high ground, a smelly marsh which made High Point a malodorous place when the wind was in certain directions.

The road was bad. Doc's roadster pitched, swayed and jarred, despite its excellent springing. There was a heavy dew, and that made the road slippery, for it was asphalt.

Doc kept the car's radio tuned to the wavelength of the police broadcasting system, listening for anything that might be important. There were innumerable reports of fights, prowlers, and suspected burglars, a number of lost persons. Following, there was a list of stolen cars.

The bronze man seemed to pay them no particular attention, and made no note, yet, hours later, he would be able to recall any of the stuff that he might find useful.

He found some of it useful when he neared High Point.

There was a car in the ditch. A roadster, it looked as if it had tried a turn too fast and skidded. Both front wheels were smashed and the radiator was back around the engine. Doc looked at the license tags.

The car had been reported in the police broadcast as stolen that night.

The engine was still warm. There was one bullet hole in the rear of the body, two more through the glass. Doc Savage left his roadster, glided into the brush, and worked forward without much noise.

He found a dead man. The fellow was brown; a voluminous turban lay beyond, as if it had fallen off his head when he went down. He had been shot in the back.

A gun went off somewhere ahead. Echoes rompled hollowly through the darkness.

Doc whipped forward. The dew was very heavy. When he disturbed bushes, it showered down on him. He heard another shot, much closer.

Doc circled widely so as to approach the scene of the shooting, not from the road, but along the beach. It was the direction from which a new arrival would least be expected.

There were several shots in quick succession. The flash was no more than fifty feet from the bronze man.

Doc waited. The gunman was shooting at what, in the moonlight, seemed to be a boathouse. A moment later, a replying shot came from the structure. Doc waited a bit longer. There were no more shots. He reared up and advanced.

His advance was remarkably silent—until he encountered the unexpected. A bush to the left gave a noisy shake. Doc knew instantly that the gunman had been canny enough to tie a string from one shrub to another by way of guaranteeing a warning should anyone try to stalk him from the rear.

The gunman heaved up. He looked thin and gigantic in the moonlight. He had a rifle. It let out noise and fire without coming to his shoulder.

DOC SAVAGE got down in time to let the bullet pass. While the shot echoes still whooped, he rolled, got the string into which he had moved, and broke it, retaining one end. Then he crawled rapidly to the left.

Silence fell. A gun smashed from the boathouse. That commotion died. Waves made noise on the nearby beach.

Doc jerked the string. It fluttered the bush. The gunman, excited, cut loose with three shots. Doc jerked the string and the bush made much noise, and the gunman cut loose again, after which he could be heard clicking the magazine out of his rifle. He was reloading.

Doc thumbed on his flashlight, hurtling forward as he did so.

The beam disclosed a lean brown man who had been one of Rama Tura's assistants at the jewel-making séance earlier in the night.

He goggled briefly into the light, let out a squawk, spun, and tried to run and reload his rifle at the same time. It was the wisest thing he could have done under the circumstances.

He might even have succeeded, except that a single shot smacked from the boathouse, after which the man gave a rabbit hop, hit squarely on his head and went on over in a somersault an acrobat would have envied, ran a dozen paces, then fell flat on the wet grass and did not move afterward.

Doc made only the briefest of examinations. The man in the boathouse had killed the fellow.

There was noise of a door being unbarred over at the boathouse. A rather small man came out.

"Careful!" Doc called.

"There were only three of them," said the small man. "I got the other two."

He came up.

"I," he added, "am Kadir Lingh, a Nizam, although I may not look it."

Chapter VIII
THE NIZAM'S STORY

"A NIZAM," Doc Savage said, "is the equivalent of a king."

The small man showed white teeth in the moonlight.

"The equivalent of more than a king, with the king business what it is today," he replied cheerfully. "But I trust that will not embarrass you."

Doc turned the light on him. He was attired in a business suit which must have cost several hundred dollars. Even the sartorially perfect Ham had never worn anything to exceed it.

The man had shoved a turban inside his coat and now he drew this out and pulled it on. On the front of the turban was an emerald which looked as if it might be as valuable as a diamond of equivalent size.

"Just how did you come to call me?" Doc asked dryly.

"Ten days ago, in Jondore, I got a cable from the Ranee, widow of my dead brother, the Son of the Tiger, former Nizam of Jondore," the man said. "The contents of that cable caused me to make what you must admit was a remarkably quick trip to New York.

"Arriving tonight, I was met with a rather violent reception. I had much trouble, and my bodyguards were all killed. I ended up in that boathouse, after having wrecked a car which I appropriated. There was a telephone. I had heard of you."

"Heard of me where?" Doc demanded.

"Jondore," said the other. "You have quite a reputation."

The man was highly educated. He spoke English easily, rather than in the bookish, stilted manner common to educated foreigners.

Doc asked him, "Where are the men who pursued you?"

"Their bodies?" The other gestured. "Over here."

They were two of Rama Tura's satellites, and they were quite dead, one behind a tree, the other back of a bush. Both had been shot.

"I am not a bad marksman," said the small man in the turban.

Doc Savage replied nothing, but thought of the running man who had been shot. The bullet was in the fellow's brain, and some peculiarity of reflex had kept him going for a bit after he was struck.

The turbaned man queried anxiously, "Do you think I shall have trouble with the American police over this?"

Doc seemed to consider.

"It might not be necessary that they know," he said.

"I see," smiled the other. "What they do not know will not hurt them. Thank you."

"Do you," Doc demanded, "know what this is all about?"

The small man nodded. "Everything."

Doc said, "Mind telling me?"

"I," said the small man, "am supposed to be the richest individual in the world. You have heard, of course, that the richest man in the world is not Rockefeller, Ford or Mellon, but is the—"

"Nizam of Jondore," Doc said.

"So you knew it."

"It has been in the newspapers. It has been mentioned in magazine articles."

"Did the reading matter state in what form the wealth was kept?" the turbaned man demanded.

"Gold and jewels," Doc replied. "Mostly jewels."

"Very accurate," the other agreed. "The fortune is something of a ruling family affair, inherited from one generation to the next. My brother, the dead Nizam, known as the Son of the Tiger, was the last possessor. Mind you, I say the *last*."

"Meaning?"

"Meaning that the fortune, some billions of dollars, has vanished into thin air."

DOC SAVAGE was silent. He might have been digesting the information; he might have been studying the character of the other.

"There has been nothing in the newspapers of this," he reminded.

"Naturally not," said the informant. "And for some very good reasons. First, the fortune is to a certain extent a symbol of my prestige over my people. Should it become known that I had lost it, I naturally would not be thought such a remarkable fellow. There are certain tribesmen in Jondore who are all too willing to jump on the Nizam at the slightest excuse."

Doc Savage began searching the followers of Rama Tura who were dead in the vicinity. He found nothing in their pockets. The small, dark man bobbed alongside, talking rapidly.

"The jewels and gold were kept in my palace in Jondore, in modern vaults and under heavy military guard," he said. "The stuff simply disappeared."

"Guards bribed?" Doc suggested.

"Unlikely. They were the royal guard of the Nizam. A Jondorean would rather belong to that than be the chief of a tribe of his own." The turbaned man smiled slightly. "We have always arranged for members of the guard to be treated as princes, for the very good psychological reason that it makes them like their jobs."

Doc Savage began stripping outer garments from the dead Rama Tura follower.

"What about the thieves entering the vaults?" he asked. "They use cutting torches or explosive?"

"They used nothing as far as we can see," said the small man. "The vaults were intact—and empty. That is somewhat incredible, because only one living man knows the combinations."

"Who is that?"

"Myself."

Doc Savage was taking shoes, trousers, coats and turbans from the slain Jondoreans. He turned each garment inside out and rolled it separately, then tied them all together with a length of silken cord.

"The Nizam, Son of the Tiger, my brother who died, knew the combination," continued the alert dark man. "Before his death, he gave it to me."

"Your brother, the previous Nizam, died naturally?" Doc queried.

"He was shot," said the other, "by a fellow who has always been a source of trouble in Jondore."

"Rama Tura?" Doc asked.

"Rama Tura it was." The turbaned man blinked. "But how did you know?"

BY the time they had reached Doc Savage's skyscraper headquarters, the bronze man had also explained about the Ranee.

"Will you describe that woman again," requested Doc's companion.

The bronze man did so.

"That," declared the turbaned man, "is undoubtedly my brother's widow, the Ranee."

Doc Savage had the bundle of clothing which he had moved from the slain men, and he deposited this in the laboratory. Then he came back into the library and began glancing through scrapbooks of newspaper clippings.

There were hundreds of these. Doc did not prepare them. They were furnished by an agency which was in that business. They covered every political development reported by the press of the world, among other things.

Doc found a picture. He compared it with the visage of the man he had found in the boathouse on Long Island Sound. The legend below the picture said:

The New Nizam of Jondore

The small, dark man came over, glanced at the picture, and showed his amazingly white teeth in a quick smile.

"You are cautious, and there is a saying that the cautious tiger lives long," he murmured. "It is not a bad likeness of me, do you think?"

"Not bad," Doc said and put the clipping volume away.

The bronze man went back into the laboratory. He took off his coat and donned a rubber frock and rubber gloves, then pulled on a hood which had very large goggles built into it. Before going to work, he asked one question.

"What is behind all of this?"

The other seemed surprised. "But it is simple. Rama Tura stole the jewels. He is disposing of them."

"I suspect," Doc told him, "that there is much more to it than that."

Since Doc Savage's life was devoted to the strange pursuit of righting wrongs and punishing evildoers, he had devoted much time to the study of detective methods.

He had originated scientific procedures of his own, some of which had been adopted by police departments, but many of which were a bit too complicated for universal use.

Among other things, he had perfected a electrospectroscopic analysis contrivance which, in the course of a very few seconds, would give him the chemical elements composing almost any given substance. This device further more had the advantage of being able to handle particles of microscopic smallness.

Doc spent almost an hour on the garments taken from the slain men.

"I should think," said the turbaned man, "that you would be worried over your three aides, Long Tom, Monk and Ham."

"I am," Doc Savage said quietly. "And I am doing everything possible to find them."

AFTER the hour had passed, the bronze man knew much about the clothing. He knew where the cotton had been grown, what mills had woven the garments, what clothing concern had made them. But to find where they had been sold would take time and might conceivably be valueless.

In each garment, there was dust. Doc concentrated on that. There was more than one kind of dust. The ordinary street variety, Doc dismissed.

There was a peculiar whitish dust. He put it under a strong microscope, studied it, then consulted geologic charts. In the laboratory storeroom were thousands of tiny phials holding ores, rock samples, soils, clays. All were labeled. Doc consulted these also.

The dust came from a rock strata that underlay by some thirty feet the downtown east side of New York City.

Doc Savage telephoned, got a man out of bed, and learned there was a building under construction on the east side. A huge, slum-clearance project, it was now in the excavation stage.

"You will stay here," Doc told his turbaned visitor.

The other blinked. "Why?"

"Rama Tura's men are quartered somewhere

near that excavation," the bronze man said. "Otherwise, the dust would not be in their clothing, even the inside of their garments, in such quantity. It has been dry, very dusty weather for excavating."

The other nodded, murmured, "Truly you amaze me," and seemed content to remain behind.

DOC SAVAGE stripped off the rubber laboratory smock and hood and gloves. He substituted certain small containers for others in the pockets of his unusual vest. He drew on his coat.

"You should understand you will be virtually a prisoner here," he said. "The door has no lock, and will only open, thanks to a certain mechanical device, for myself and my men."

The turbaned man hesitated. "I suppose I will be safest here."

Doc gave him one of the machine pistols, and showed him how it operated.

"Thank you," said the dark man.

Doc Savage went out, the door opening weirdly for him, and closing when he had left the vicinity of it.

The bronze man now did something an observer would not have expected. He whipped down the corridor, around a corner, and put both palms against the solid wall.

He held them there for a count of ten, removed them for another ten count, and put them against the wall again.

A few feet away, the wall opened soundlessly. Its mechanism was a combination actuated from a thermostatic device buried in the wall plaster. Heat from the hands was enough to work the combination.

There was a hollow wall space beyond. It held much apparatus. At one point, a tiny red light glowed. Doc went to it, unhooked a telephone handset and plugged the cord into a jack below the light. He had tapped one of his telephone lines which was being used.

He listened a moment. His trilling noise, very vague, with an undertone of grimness, seeped through the confines of the hidden runway. It died quickly.

He threw a switch. It opened the telephone line, cutting it off from the outside.

Another door, cleverly concealed, admitted the bronze man into the laboratory. Soundlessly, he whipped into the library and across it into the reception room.

The small brown man in the turban was holding one of the telephones, impatiently clicking the hook in an effort to raise an operator on the dead wire. He seemed to think that the connection had only failed.

The brown man did not move until Doc Savage

took him by the throat with both hands. Then it was too late. He could only writhe and kick and make croakings.

"I suspected you," Doc Savage told him, "all along."

Chapter IX
DOC HAS A WATERLOO

THE brown man's feet and hands made mad motions; he gargled and hacked; his tongue ran out and so did his eyes. The brown of his face became a purplish black.

"You were trying to warn them," Doc told him quietly. "It was likely that you would do that."

The bronze man slackened his grip, and the captive sank down in a chair, pumping air madly with his lungs, and did not resist being searched. His face faded back to brown.

"Would you care to know when you first gave yourself away?" Doc asked.

The man let out several words of the vile profanity of Jondore. His brown visage was an evil map of hate, fear, disappointment.

"When you killed your friend who was pretending to besiege you in the boathouse," Doc told him. "You were afraid I would capture him, and he would talk."

The brown man glared wordlessly.

"It was good acting," Doc Savage told him. "Overdone only in spots. But I had expected you to try for my life earlier. Why did you not?"

The man said, in the tongue of Jondore, more that was uncomplimentary.

"Had I been aware of how little you know of what it is actually all about, I would have killed you," he gritted.

The bronze man studied the other.

"Of course, the idea was to learn how much of your scheme was known, and what measures were being taken against you," he said. "It was not a bad move. But it seems to have backfired."

The turbaned one spoke English.

"What do you mean?" he asked.

"You," Doc informed him, "are going to talk. You probably can tell just about everything. A clever fellow like you would occupy a high position in the organization."

The other grinned. It was an altogether hideous grin.

"I would like to wager that even you cannot get anything out of me," he mumbled.

"You told me that jewel thievery is behind this," Doc reminded him. "That in itself proves the jewel theft is not the motive. It is something possibly much more—horrible."

The brown man sat perfectly still in his chair and stared. His eyes seemed to grow bigger, his mouth warped down at the ends; after a little, a wetness came into his eyes. He sobbed once.

"This is horrible," he choked.

Then he leaned forward and buried his face in his hands, making bubbling noises, shoulders heaving.

It was rarely that an actor fooled Doc Savage. But this one was good. He put across his deception—for all of ten seconds.

Suddenly realizing, Doc Savage whipped forward, grabbed the man and straightened him. Too late. There was a wet, chewed spot on the fellow's immaculate sleeve. Doc held him and turned the sleeve back.

On the inside, between the lining and sleeve cloth, there was a smear of greenish-yellow stuff. Chewing and sucking, the man had gotten it into his mouth through the cloth.

The fellow's eyes were already taking on a dullness.

"It will not kill me," he mumbled. "It will make me unconscious for hours. Nothing can revive me."

He went to sleep.

HE was right, although Doc Savage did not surrender to the certainty until he had worked over the man for some twenty minutes. That state was not insensibility of the common order, but more of a semi-suspension of animation. No known stimulant brought appreciable results.

Doc filled a hypo needle in the laboratory and administered its contents to the fellow. He watched the results closely to be sure of no fatal reaction. The stuff he had given was a drug which would keep the man senseless for days—or until the proper reactant was applied.

Satisfied, Doc put the brown man in a ventilated wall compartment where he would be unearthed by nothing less than a virtual wrecking of the place.

Doc went into the laboratory and consulted a weather chart, automatically recorded by his own instruments. It showed a prevailing northeasterly wind during the past few days.

The bronze man used another of the cars from a concealed garage which he maintained in the skyscraper basement. It was a small, plain delivery truck, and he chose it because more delivery trucks were abroad on the streets at this hour than any other vehicle.

He left the truck a short distance from the new slum clearance project excavation.

It was still dark, and the wetness of the heavy dew lay on the streets very much as if it had rained. Out on the river, tugs hooted, and on Brooklyn Bridge, street cars made noise.

The excavation was near the foreign quarters, and some rather strangely-garbed persons were abroad. It was an excellent hiding region for the men of Jondore, a spot where their queer garb, their dark skins, would be unlikely to attract attention.

Knowing that the prevailing northeasterly wind would have carried dust from the excavation in a certain direction, Doc began his search.

He worked swiftly, for he held no doubts about Monk, Ham and Long Tom being in deadly peril. It was entirely possible that they might not be alive even now.

The most likely spot was a row of ancient tenements, most of them vacant, buildings of exactly the same kind the slum clearance project was trying to eliminate.

Doc found a fire escape at one end of the block, made sure no one was in sight of the gloomy spot, and climbed to the roof—or almost to the roof.

He did not go over the parapet which surrounded the roof immediately. He clung to the fire escape and used a diminutive periscope of a device to look the roof over.

THE move paid dividends. Two men were lying atop the roof on cots. This in itself was not unusual, as tenement inhabitants often slept on the roofs. But these fellows had brown skins—that became evident when one struck a match to light an American cigarette.

They were near a roof hatch, and there were no chimneys or ventilators near them. It would be impossible to approach them without being observed.

Doc Savage picked his chance, whipped over onto the roof, and managed to travel thirty feet toward the men and to the left, and got into the shelter of a large chimney without being observed.

Concealed there, he faced the street, set his throat muscles, and began to speak Jondorean in ventriloquial voice which made the words seem to come from a considerable distance. They were loud, alarmed words. It sounded very much as if an excited Jondorean were shouting a warning from the street.

The two lookouts swallowed it. They popped off their cots, clucking excitedly at each other, and sprinted for the roof edge to look over. They passed Doc Savage without once glancing behind the chimney.

Doc had his shoes off. His charge was silent lightning. He got the first from behind. He did not strike a blow, for blows make noise. He simply seized the fellow by the nape, and put strength and knowledge to work. The victim made no sound before he went limp.

Doc had to hit the second man. He struck him in the throat, more of a hard grasp than a blow. He held the man's windpipe closed, reached around, and found the spinal nerve centers. The fellow stopped struggling.

Doc put them side by side in the gloom near the chimney. They carried revolvers. He used the barrel of each to break off the tempered firing pin in the other; then he placed the weapons behind an adjacent chimney, where it would look as if they had been hidden, but where they would not be too hard to find.

He went to the roof hatch.

THERE was darkness down in the house, and smells of the Orient, incense and the residue odors of cooked spiced foods. Doc descended, not on the steps, but on the banister, slowly, sliding, feeling ahead.

Ordinary corn flakes had been sprinkled on the steps, stuff that would crunch noisily if stepped upon. There was a bottle, delicately balanced, on the post at the foot of the banister.

Down the hallway, a man coughed. He coughed very hard.

Monk's childlike voice said distinctly, "I wish you'd choke."

Ham said, "Shut up, simple."

Monk grumbled, "Between you and this guy coughing—"

Doc Savage was whipping forward—and the last thing he expected happened. A dog came at him, barking, setting up a fabulous noise.

Dynamite exploding could not have touched off things more abruptly. Men began to shout in various parts of the place. A gun went off, apparently accidentally.

Doc hurtled forward. The dog barked, snapped, and its claws made frantic scratchy noises as it tried to keep up.

A brown man came out of the room from which Monk's voice had emanated. He had a revolver, a flashlight. He got no chance to use either.

Doc ran an arm, stiff as a ramrod, into the man's stringy middle. Air came out of him with a force that threatened to bring up the man's insides. Doc went over him and on.

There was light in the room, an oil lamp. These tenements were frequently not wired for electricity. Monk, Ham and Long Tom were all three there, tightly bound.

Monk let out a pleased howl, rolled over and kicked up his tied ankles where Doc could get at them with a knife. The bronze man whipped out a blade, slashed hurriedly, got Monk free. The homely chemist came up on his feet, began to jump up and down to restore circulation.

The dog came in, skidded to a stop, eyes on Doc Savage. A long moment, and the canine lowered the hair along its back, half wagged its tail.

Monk stamped his feet. More than ever, he resembled a bull ape.

"Scat, bowser!" he howled.

The dog yelped and ran.

"They stole the pooch off the street," Monk said irrelevantly. "Some watchdog."

Doc got Ham free. The dapper lawyer's clothing had suffered during the night. He ran to a litter of duffel near the door and came up with his sword cane, looking triumphant.

Long Tom, released, said, "They were going to kill us."

Doc ran to the door, whipped small glass balls out of his vest and hurled them. They were tear gas. It spread in the corridor. Men squawked.

Back to the window, Doc moved. It was boarded up on the outside. He retreated from it, backing.

"How many of them here?" he demanded.

"Twenty," Monk said. "And maybe more."

"Watch it!" Doc warned.

He got another ball from the vest, this one of metal, not much larger than a good-sized bird egg. He did something to it, threw it at the window.

Came flash, roar, dust, flying wood and plaster. Part of the ceiling, lath and plaster, came down on their heads. But there was a gaping aperture where the window had been. Two floors down was the street. Doc went over and dashed his flash beam out.

"You can drop, down," he said.

Ham, looking very glad for the chance, hopped through. Then Long Tom went.

Monk started to leap, thought of something, nearly fell out trying to keep from jumping, and managed to stay in.

"That woman!" Monk exploded. "She's here! A prisoner!"

"Where?" Doc asked.

Monk waved an arm generally.

"Around somewhere," he said. "Dunno where, exactly. That lug, Rama Tura, came and got her."

"Out," Doc told him.

Monk gulped, "But ain't you gonna go and—"

"Out," Doc said.

Monk went out. He grunted loudly as he hit the sidewalk, then squawked that he had broken both legs, but using a voice which showed he had not.

Instead of following them, Doc Savage turned back.

THE tenement was full of shouts, and much vituperation in the rather strange-sounding tongue of Jondore. The tear gas, however, was keeping Rama Tura's men back.

Doc fished goggles out of a pocket of the

Came flash, roar, dust, flying wood and plaster. Part of the ceiling, lath and plaster came down on their heads.

special vest. They had many uses, those goggles. They were excellent for diving. They were a protection against tear gas, as long as one held his breath.

Doc put them on, drew several deep breaths, then held a normal one in his lungs—after the fashion of pearl divers of the South Seas—and whipped out into the corridor.

A bullet came down the passageway, probably fired at random. Several more followed it, as if other gunners thought it an excellent idea.

Blows were crashing. Squeaking noises sounded as if laths were being pulled off a wall. The noises were in a room opening off the corridor. The door was closed. Cloth, which had been stuffed in the crack at the bottom to shut out the gas, projected into the hall.

Doc veered, hit the door. Panels, crosspiece, fell out, letting him in, although the frame stayed. He ran out of the shower of splintered fragments.

Four men were in the room. Three were tearing at a wall, obviously endeavoring to get into another hallway without entering the one which held the tear gas.

The fourth man was small, wiry, immaculately clad. He reminded Doc of Ham, except that his skin was brown, and his features Asiatic. His mouth was taped. Cords secured his wrists and ankles.

The three men had put their guns in their

pockets while they worked at the wall. They tried to get them out as Doc charged. Only one of them, who danced away cunningly, had time, and he was upset by the bound man, who whipped against his legs.

The other two, with Doc upon them, did not try blows. They grasped frenziedly for holds and showed they knew much of jiujitsu.

Doc let one get an arm hold, then used him as a ram to upset the other. He swooped, got them both in his arms, and their heads made a *bonk!* of a noise coming together.

The man with the gun had disengaged himself, was trying to kick the bound man away and at the same time aim at Doc. The combined effort took time, of which there was little. He tried to run just as Doc reached him, and Doc put a fist back of his ear with a force that caused him to turn a handspring without using his hands. He lay very still after he fell.

Doc scooped up the prisoner.

"Shut your eyes. Hold your breath," he ordered.

They went out into the corridor, escaped two bullets blindly aimed at their noise, and got into the room where Doc had found his men.

Monk, Ham and Long Tom were below the window, whooping at the top of their lungs for Doc, for police.

"Where is the woman?" Doc asked the bound man, tearing off the adhesive gag. "The one who is a prisoner."

"Downstairs," said the captive in utterly precise English.

"Who," Doc demanded, "are you?"

"Kadir Lingh, Nizam of Jondore," said the man.

Doc Savage tossed him through the window. Monk caught him.

MORE bullets were in the corridor when Doc went back. They came from above and below, and part of them were coming from what sounded like an automatic rifle.

Doc kept close to the wall and low, reached the stairs, and rode the banister down because it was quicker and more silent. He hit a man at the bottom. The man struck him. Doc struck back, hit a throat and the man fell down, gagging. Doc went on.

There was a weird odor in the air down here, the same one which had been in the atmosphere of Temple Nava, during the jewel-making séance. It must not have been present long, or it would have penetrated upstairs.

Ahead was a door. It glowed red from light within. Doc reached it, hesitated, then popped his head forward to look within. On the face of it, that looked reckless, but as a matter of plain fact, he had long ago learned that he could take a chance such as this, see what was within, and get back before a gunman could shoot accurately.

There was no one with a gun in the room.

Rama Tura's casket stood on one end a little beyond the middle of the floor, and within it, lying as if dead, except that his eyes were open, was Rama Tura, he who claimed to be a worker of miracles.

Doc stared for a long moment, half of his attention on the shouting, the shooting, in other parts of the tenement. The brown men of Jondore must be shooting at every shadow.

Doc entered the room alertly. It was somewhat unbelievable that Rama Tura would be here, like a corpse in his box, in the thick of the excitement. It was strange. The fellow was capable of movement, even if he did indeed look dead. He had moved about in Temple Nava séances.

The bronze man's flake-gold eyes roved, examining the floor, the bare walls. There was nothing suspicious. He reached the coffin and the fantastic man who half stood, half reclined in it.

RAMA TURA spoke.

"Bronze man," he said. "You are tampering with things which you, with all of your learning, know nothing."

His words were a hollow breath, so low that Doc barely caught them.

Doc said nothing in reply. He reached out to lift Rama Tura from his macabre receptacle.

"No," Rama Tura warned faintly. "Do you want to die?"

Doc changed his mind. There might be poison on the man's garments. Doc whipped off his coat, threw it against Rama Tura, and prepared to grasp the scrawny body through the folds of the garment.

Then came the phenomenon. Rama Tura, the man who looked like a corpse, seemed to fade, to become a wraith. He seemed, in the casket, exactly like the images which movie cameramen secure by trick double exposures when they want to portray ghosts on the screen.

It was incredible. Doc grabbed furiously. He got hold of something—something horrible, for a stinging, not unlike an electric shock, slammed up his arms. It seemed to spread over his body. It was as if he had taken hold of something poisonous, something that could kill instantly.

He backed away. The room, its contents, had become shadows in front of his eyes, as if his pupils were out of focus. The stinging had gone all over his body. He shook his head. He slapped his face.

Standing there slapping his face, he ceased to remember.

Chapter X
LADY OF TRICKS

OUT in the dingy street, where the faint light of dawn was appearing, Monk, Ham, Long Tom and the brown man who had said he was Kadir Lingh, Nizam of Jondore, stood and tried to think of something to do. They had cut Kadir Lingh loose, and he was kneading his legs and arms.

The howling for the police had gotten results. Police sirens were moaning not far away.

Monk jumped, howled, as a bullet cut his clothing and gullied his right side slightly. The shot had come from a window of the tenement. Others followed. Monk was running, and they missed.

The others followed Monk's example. Across the street, the houses had ventilating shafts for cellars in the sidewalks, with gratings over them. They wrenched up a grating and got down in the pit. It was like a trench.

Monk had no more than hit the pit and he squawked, "I'm goin' back in there!"

"Dope," Ham told him. "Doc wants to handle these things his own way."

Monk contrarily put his head up. Jacketed lead made an ugly sound on the concrete walk. Brick dust fell out of the wall behind them. Monk sat down sheepishly and examined a neat part in his bristling, rust-colored hair.

Ham searched around, found the bullet which had so nearly split Monk's skull, and patted the distorted bit of lead lovingly.

"My friend," he told the bullet. "You nearly did the world a great service."

Monk told Ham, "I oughta kick you out of here!" and sounded very earnest.

Kadir Lingh, Nizam of Jondore, said nervously, "Please, gentlemen! It is really nothing to fight about!"

"They don't need anything to fight about," Long Tom said gloomily. "Listen!"

They could hear cars. The shooting had stopped. They thrust up their heads, and these excellent targets drew no bullets.

An instant later, a car leaped into the street from a driveway that entered the row of tenements halfway down the block. Another machine followed. A third. When they passed under the street light at the corner, Monk made out the occupants.

"Rama Tura's men!" he bellowed. "They're gettin' away!"

"Doc!" Ham exploded. "What became of Doc?"

They were still trying to learn that half an hour later, after the police had arrived and the row of tenements had been searched from top to bottom. Absolutely no one was found. Doc had vanished.

Rama Tura's men had not only escaped themselves, but had made off with such of their fellows as had been put out of commission during Doc's raid.

Monk and his companions roamed the vicinity, searching, and eventually found Doc's small delivery truck where he had left it. They spent an hour in the vicinity before they concluded there was nothing they could do. Then they headed uptown in the delivery truck.

"You got a story to tell?" Monk asked Kadir Lingh, Nizam of Jondore.

The brown man told them his story. He had a cultured voice. His recital was almost identical with the one told Doc Savage by the clever individual who had pretended to be the Nizam. It differed only in the ending.

"A gang attacked me at the airport when I arrived," said the Nizam. "I managed to escape, but only for a time. They overhauled me, killed my guards, captured me, and took me to that room where Doc Savage found me."

"Why?" Monk demanded, not unreasonably.

"To keep me from launching an investigation of Rama Tura, obviously," replied the Nizam.

Ham studied the brown man. The Nizam seemed to interest the dapper lawyer, or perhaps it was the Nizam's undeniably perfect garments. Ham had a mania for clothing.

"Scarborough and Son, on Bond Street," Ham said. "Right?"

The Nizam was puzzled at first, then smiled.

"My tailors," he said. "Yes. Excellent, I think."

Monk's snort conveyed infinite disgust.

LONG TOM was driving, and doing it a bit recklessly. He popped the delivery truck between two meeting street cars, and the squeeze was so close that both trolleys stood still fully five minutes before their conductors recovered their aplomb.

"You got less sense than Ham," Monk complained. "Such driving!"

Long Tom said nothing. In the next block, he gave a road hog taxi driver the scare of his life.

Monk swallowed several times and began to question the Nizam industriously to keep his mind off the ride.

"So you are the richest man in the world?" he told the Nizam, in a tone which insinuated it was something of a crime.

"*Was*," corrected the Nizam. "I have been thoroughly robbed."

"How long after the death of your brother, the previous Nizam, did this happen?" Monk queried.

"Six weeks," replied the brown man.

"And you have been trying to find your wealth?"

"Trying is a mild word for it," said the Nizam. "We have moved heaven and earth. My entire—you would call them the treasure house guard—is in prison, awaiting execution."

"Nice," Monk murmured in a way that said it was not.

"Oh, I merely hoped to frighten one of them into telling something of value as a clue," said the Nizam. "They will not be executed, although life is not held as dearly in my land as in yours."

Monk considered, then began, "This woman—"

"The Ranee, my dead brother's widow," supplied the brown man.

"The Ranee," Monk said. "She was on a cruise around the world. Right?"

"Right."

"A measure to make her grief more bearable," Ham put in suggestively.

The Nizam looked uncomfortable.

"As a matter of fact, I think not," he said. "The Ranee probably went abroad to forget what a thorough cad my brother had been."

"What do you mean?" Monk demanded, interested.

"My brother—actually my half brother—was something of a bad boy of Asia," said the Nizam. "He had a good deal of trouble, not only with various Rajahs in his empire, but with the British government. To be frank, he tried a number of times to throw the British and their protectorate out of Jondore. But that all died—with the death of my brother."

MONK thought that over.

"Getting back to what I started to ask," he said. "Could the departure of the Ranee have anything to do with the disappearance of the jewels and gold?"

The Nizam flushed quite distinctly. He did not answer.

"Well?" Monk grunted.

"As a matter of fact, that is why I came to New York," the Nizam said with visible reluctance.

"Any proof?" Monk questioned.

"None," the Nizam replied, and sounded relieved. "The Ranee has always been a glorious woman."

Long Tom saw a car coming toward him in the center of the street, started to bluff the driver, saw at the last moment that it was a police squad car, and was almost chased onto the sidewalk. He craned his neck.

"Looks like some excitement ahead," he said.

He drove more rapidly. They could make out a crowd, ambulances, squad cars and many policemen in blue.

"In front of a bank," Long Tom vouchsafed. "Bet the thing has been robbed."

They stopped the delivery truck and unloaded to ask curious questions. A policeman, when Long Tom had made his identity known, gave them information.

"Doc Savage suggested having a guard put over this bank this morning," he said. "It was a swell idea, only the guard wasn't big enough. Four of our men got shot, and the bank vaults were cleaned, out—the safety-deposit vaults, I mean."

"Know who done it?" Long Tom queried.

"Rama Tura's men," said the cop. He looked at the Nizam. "Ain't no doubt of it. They looked like this guy you've got with you."

"He's all right," Long Tom said. "Just what was in the bank?"

"The cash from those jewels Rama Tura has been selling," replied the officer. "I mean, the two thirds that was to go into that charity fund. Somebody said there was more than two millions."

MONK had thought the new development over by the time they reached Doc Savage's skyscraper office, and he had an idea formulated.

"You say this treasure of yours amounted to billions?" he asked the Nizam.

The brown man nodded. "Yes."

Monk scratched his nubbin of a head. "Then the jewels Rama Tura had produced here in New York, if they really are yours, are only a drop in the bucket. I've got an idea."

He went to the telephone and put in calls for London, Antwerp, Paris and Berlin. That the calls all got through within the course of the next hour was a tribute to modern transatlantic telephone efficiency.

"That," Monk said when the last call was completed, "will cost Doc about three hundred bucks."

"You get your money's worth?" Ham asked sarcastically.

"Well," Monk scratched his head again. "New York isn't the first place Rama Tura has worked. He was in London a month ago, Paris a little before that. He pulled the same gag that he did here. He sold a lot of jewels that were undoubtedly genuine."

"What about the proceeds?" Ham demanded.

"The money went one third to local charity, two thirds to a Jondorean charity fund, like it did here," Monk said.

The Nizam asked suddenly, "Just who administers that Jondorean charity?"

Monk consulted a bit of paper on which he had written. The names were Jondorean, and he did not try to pronounce them, but spelled each out.

The Nizam made a startled hissing sound.

"Something funny about them names?" Monk demanded.

"All of those men," the Nizam said grimly, "have died within the last month."

"Natural deaths?"

"In some cases, apparently. Two were killed hunting. Others died of ailments diagnosed as natural."

"Were they prominent?"

"Rajahs, all of them," said the Nizam. "In the United States, their position would correspond to that of governor of a state, although they have powers a good deal more absolute."

Monk grimaced and yanked several stiff red bristles from his nubbin of a head, then eyed them intently.

"This thing, whatever it is, is infernally big," he muttered.

Ham added, "And if you ask me, there is something more behind it than the theft of the Nizam's wealth."

Monk scowled at him. "And what makes you say that?"

"The fact that those Rajahs have died," Ham said.

Monk grunted, "I still don't get what you—"

The door buzzer whined.

Monk shrugged, got up and walked to the panel, so that it opened when he drew near, due to the influence of the radioactive plaque which he carried, upon the electroscope mechanism.

Monk peered at the person who stood in the corridor outside.

"Blazes!" the homely chemist gasped.

SHE was not especially tall, and a soiled dark cloak and a crumpled black hat and a dark veil hid her attractiveness, if any, but she had a nice ankle. She looked at Monk, then past him, and saw the Nizam.

"Kadir!" she gasped, and darted forward, arms outstretched.

Monk stepped aside, as if to let her pass. Then he tripped her, but caught her before she fell entirely to the floor. He turned her with lightning speed and shucked off her hat, the veil.

The Nizam made a snarling sound, sprang forward, swung a fist, and knocked Monk down as beautifully as he had ever been knocked down in his life.

"She is the Ranee!" the Nizam gritted. "In Jondore, you would die a thousand deaths for laying a hand upon her!"

Ham looked at Monk on the floor and said, "He never did have any manners."

Monk got up. His neck was red. Hard tendons made four white lines down the back of each hairy fist.

And then—no one exactly saw it—the Nizam was flat on the floor and the noise of a blow was resounding from the walls, and Monk was over the fallen one, grasping him by the collar. Lifting the Nizam, Monk shook him as if trying to ascertain if his teeth would come out.

"This is the United States," Monk said grimly. "And when you sock a guy, you oughta be sure he stays socked."

The apish chemist tossed the Nizam into a chair, where the brown man lay limp and gasping. Monk waited until he could understand things.

"I stopped her," Monk told the Nizam, "because I thought she might be a dame sent by Rama Tura to stick a poisoned needle into you or something."

The Nizam thought that over. Then he got shakily out of the chair, clicked his heels and bowed.

"I am sorry," he said.

Long Tom grunted, not unreasonably, "This kind of thing is only killing time and maybe causing hard feelings."

The Ranee had stood aside during the excitement, saying nothing, and now they gave her their attention.

She was worth attention. Women of the Orient have the reputation of losing their beauty in their early twenties, and especially does this apply to the women of Jondore. This woman must be near thirty. She had the complexion and delicacy of features of sixteen.

Monk, who had a true appreciation of feminine pulchritude, sighed audibly.

"To a true flower of the East, I offer humble apologies," he told the woman.

It was gallantry so unexpected on Monk's part that Ham all but gulped his surprise.

Monk accompanied his delivery with a bow which could not have been exceeded for courtliness by a knight of old. It seemed to go over.

The Ranee gave the homely chemist a brilliant smile.

"You are forgiven," she said. "Not many men would have displayed such quick thinking."

Monk had a way with women, even if he did have the pulchritude of a gorilla. Perhaps it was his very homeliness.

"Will you tell us your story?" he suggested.

They all saw the Ranee's shudder. She replaced the hat, the veil, as if to conceal from them the horror on her face.

"I was wrong," she said in a dry voice. "Rama Tura is no faker. I thought he was."

Monk squinted. "You mean that he really makes those jewels with his hocus pocus?"

The Ranee was slow answering. She did not nod. She did not shake her head.

"I do not know," she said. "Rama Tura has horrible powers. He does things that seem impossible."

HER voice was more dry, and she seemed to have difficulty with her words. Monk brought her ice water from the cooler. It was distilled water made in the laboratory—an enemy had once tried to poison Doc Savage and his aides by tapping the city water main which supplied the bronze man's headquarters.

The fake Nizam whom Doc had overpowered, and who had drugged himself to prevent being questioned, was still in the secret runway behind the laboratory wall. But his presence remained unknown to Doc's aides, there being no reason for them to examine the hidden space.

The Ranee took the ice water gratefully.

Ham suavely took charge of interrogating the Ranee. It went against Ham's grain to see Monk, his arch rival, holding the center of any stage.

"We have a suspicion that there is something besides stealing jewels behind this affair," said the dapper lawyer. "Have you any thought on that score?"

Effect of the query upon the Ranee was marked, even though they could not see her features. She half turned, as if contemplating flight. Then she faced them, and her eyes were very wide back of the veil.

"There is—more back of it," she said, and her voice was so small that they barely heard.

"What?" Ham rapped.

She tied her small hands together in a hard knot.

"You will think me insane," she said. "But I cannot tell you."

"Why not?" Ham exploded.

"It is impossible for me to tell you that—either," the Ranee replied. She seemed to have difficulty with the words.

THE woman's actions seemed to amaze the Nizam more than anyone. He darted forward, grasped the Ranee's arm, and rattled words in the tongue of Jondore.

The Ranee shook her head and replied in the same tongue. The Nizam spoke snappishly now. The woman still shook her head.

Doc Savage's three aides, not understanding the language, could only look puzzled.

The Nizam gave an exaggerated shrug.

"Rama Tura is up to something horrible," he said. "She will not explain what it is. That is not like the Ranee."

"Rama Tura has some hold over her," Ham suggested.

The Nizam and the Ranee went through another exchange in the language of Jondore. The Nizam

moistened his lips and looked amazed.

"It is not Rama Tura," he gulped. "It is the mastermind who is directing Rama Tura."

Ham did something that was rare for him. He dropped his sword cane.

"Rama Tura is not the real brains!" he exploded. "Then who is this real chief?"

"That, the Ranee also refuses to tell," said the Nizam. "She says we will understand her reasons when we learn who he is—if we do learn."

Monk growled, "This is a fine run-around!"

Long Tom snapped peevishly, "What I want to know is what became of Doc?"

The Ranee spoke Jondorean. Her words caused the Nizam to all but jump up and down.

"Doc Savage is a prisoner!" he shouted. "The Ranee saw him brought into Rama Tura's new hideout."

The Ranee interposed, speaking rapid English.

"You can rescue him," she said.

"But your getting away will cause Rama Tura to change his location," Long Tom barked. "Or did they turn you loose?" The last was sarcastic.

"Perhaps they have not discovered my escape," the Ranee told him. "They gave me a tablet to make me sleep. I got rid of it without their discovering. When I pretended to sleep, they left me, and I escaped."

"Can you show us this place?" Long Tom rapped.

"I can."

Monk grabbed up his pig, Habeas Corpus, by one big ear, and lumbered for the door.

"We're off," he grunted.

IT was a shabby section occupied by warehouses, small factories, wholesale firms. It was a very busy section, with trucks rumbling, sidewalk carts being wheeled along full of small merchandise, and busy throngs hurrying.

Talk on the sidewalks was of money, contracts, grosses, bills of lading, orders. No one paid attention to anyone else.

Long Tom tooled their car in to the curb at the Ranee's direction.

"It is the building in the middle of the block," she said.

The building was big, eight stories. The windows were dirty, but so were the windows of all the other buildings in the block. There was one battered doorway, wide enough to drive a car through—it had been constructed for the purpose of admitting cars, obviously. But it was closed by a sheet metal door which might or might not be solid.

"Sure that's the place?" Monk asked.

"Certain," said the Ranee. "I can guide you up by the rear route by which I escaped."

"You know exactly where Doc is?" Monk asked.

She shook her head. "No."

Monk looked at the others. "I vote for fireworks."

Long Tom, who despite his somewhat fragile appearance, was as much of a fire-eater as the homely Monk, nodded vehemently. Ham shook his head, more as a policy of disagreeing with Monk than anything else.

Long Tom backed the car into traffic, stopped beside the cop at the corner, then drove on around the block slowly, by which time the cop had gone up and moved a parked car out of the driveway into the building.

Long Tom got an opening in traffic, and bore on the accelerator. The car—it was Doc's special limousine—leaped as if in a navy plane catapult. Rubber tire treads screamed as it arched in toward the door.

The Ranee got out one startled shriek. Monk wrapped her face protectingly in his arms. The car hit with a sound like a boilerplate factory blowing up. The door caved. The car went inside.

Monk and the others remained in the car, looking about. They were about as safe as they could be. The car was a rolling fortress of armor plate and bulletproof glass. It was even gas-tight—if the crash had not opened it somewhere.

A gun went off. The bullet glanced off the car top. It had come from a tiny balcony along the rear wall.

Monk opened the limousine door, holding a supermachine pistol. It moaned. The man who had fired the shot fired two more, then seemed to go to sleep on his feet and came tumbling down steps that led to the balcony.

Monk piled out of the car.

"Let's take this place!" he howled.

THEY spilled out on each side of the car, all with the machine pistols. There was a door on the balcony, and that seemed the only way up into the building. They ran for it.

The Ranee was last out of the limousine. She started after them, hesitated, spun and got back into the car.

Monk noted her actions over his shoulder.

"She's got sense," he grunted. "This won't be no woman's brawl."

A brown man jumped out on the balcony as they came up the steps; they shot him with mercy bullets, and he whirled and ran back out of sight. The chemical in the bullets required a moment to function.

The stairs were wide, so they got onto the balcony almost together.

"Spread!" Monk warned. "We don't all wanna get swatted at once."

They plunged through a door, clattered up more stairs that led to the upper regions. A door gaped at the top. Monk barged into it.

Then excitement really let loose. A long, guttering red spark appeared in the darkened room beyond the door. It was accompanied by a noise as of a thousand big firecrackers going off in machine-like succession.

Monk got down. He never did quite understand how he managed it so quickly. The slug stream from the machine gun banged the door casing apart, like something hungry.

"Blazes!" Monk squawked. "They're set for us!"

He knew that, because this was a heavy machine gun which required a tripod emplacement. Such guns are not lugged around at random.

Ploom! It was a strange, wet sounding explosion. It mystified Monk for a moment. Then he got the smart of tear gas.

Crack! That one was like lightning striking. With it came a flash as of lightning, too. Monk was conscious of a great force slamming against his chest—a timber of some kind, blown from the top of the stairway by a grenade.

There was debris, dust and smoke. And Monk toppled down the stairs and out on the balcony. Ham, Long Tom and the Nizam were beside him, bruised, cut a little, but still under their own power.

Surprising things had happened to the big room into which they had rammed their car. For one thing, half a dozen patches of plaster had fallen off the ceiling, and through these freshly made holes, gun snouts nosed.

The door was barricaded now, by a huge grille affair of iron bars which must have been intended for burglar protection.

A gun whacked, and the bullet came close enough to Monk to cause him to all but fall down in dodging. He, along with the others, got back into the ruined stairway. But that would be shelter only for split-seconds.

Monk nudged Ham, said, "Them blackies, you fashion plate!"

The "blackies" were compact smoke bombs, and Ham now yanked them out of his pocket and lobbed them. They ripened into a pall of dense black smoke that all but filled the room below.

Under cover of that, they went down the stairs. Gun noise made their ears ache; powder-driven metal made brief, awful noises on floor, walls.

They reached the limousine. Monk wrenched at the door handle.

"Blazes!" he howled. "Try the other doors! This one must have locked accidentally!"

Ham, Long Tom, ran around the car. Their startled yells sounded an instant later.

"Doors locked!" they barked.

Monk yanked at the door, struck with his fist, knowing the while that he was a fool, because even acetylene and dynamite would have difficulty affording entrance to this rolling citadel.

Then Monk sensed movement in the car and jammed his homely face close to the glass.

The Ranee was inside.

"Open!" Monk squawked. "It's us!"

The woman heard him. She saw him. She looked right into his eyes. But she made no move to let them in.

It was a moment or two before Monk let himself believe the grisly truth.

"Tricked!" he howled wrathfully. "She led us into a trap!"

He roared and wrenched at the door and generally gave the impression of a gorilla in a fit of rage.

"I'll bet," he squawked, "the Ranee is the big brain back of the whole blasted business!"

THERE was no getting into the limousine. Doc Savage had arranged its construction too well for that. Nor was there any escape by the door. They tried that. The bars were chained, padlocked in place.

Bullets had continued to search through the room, but thanks to the sepia oozings of the smoke bombs, none of the slugs had damaged anything but nerves.

"Under the car!" Ham rapped from somewhere in the murky void.

"That," Monk said, "is an idea, much as I hate to admit it."

The limousine had a long wheelbase; it was a big car, but its size seemed none too adequate, now that they crawled under it. The headroom was nothing to speak of, either. They made themselves as compact as possible and peered out gloomily.

Monk rubbed a hand over the hard concrete floor.

"I hope they don't start trying to put bullets under here like billiard shots," he grumbled.

The Nizam sneezed, coughed, from the effects of tear gas which had seeped down from the upper regions. Their foes were also doing much gagging and hacking.

Monk, wrinkling his nostrils, wondering just how long it would be before the stuff got strong enough to affect their eyes, was suddenly aware of another odor. It was quite distinct. It had just arrived. He would have noticed it earlier, had it been present.

The scent puzzled Monk for a moment, for it was familiar. Then he remembered. Rama Tura's jewel-making séance! The aroma had been there, had filled the place like an incense.

Monk suddenly thought of something else—the crowds in the street.

"Police!" he squawled at the top of his shrill voice. "Help! I'm being murdered!"

THE shooting might conceivably have been mistaken, by the unsuspecting on the street, as the noise of a stationary engine; the explosion might have been misconstrued as some natural uproar. But Monk's shrieks could hardly be misunderstood.

"Help!" Monk whooped. "Help! Help!—"

He ended it suddenly. A new voice had penetrated Monk's self-made bedlam—a voice that was commanding because of its very harridan unreality. Rama Tura's voice!

"To hope that the police may arrive in time to aid you must be a pleasant hope," Rama Tura said. "But it is a waste of time."

The voice was uncanny. It reminded Monk of the results one got when dragging the sharpened point of a playing card over a rotating phonograph record.

Monk gritted, "Can you guys tell where he's callin' from? I'll slip him some bullets!"

"No," said Ham. "Don't you feel slightly strange?"

Monk thought at first that was some kind of crack, then realized Ham was in earnest, and that he, Monk, was feeling a bit queer. Then—he was suddenly very dizzy.

The voice of Rama Tura, much louder, filled the room with a big droning.

"Doubtless you think it is impossible for me to stand back in safety and transform you into unconsciousness by the literal application of my powers of concentration," Rama Tura intoned. "Yet you are going to experience just that."

Long Tom barked, "Say, my head—my head—"

He did not finish, and Monk knew by the sounds that he was trying to crawl out from under the car. He seemed to have trouble making it.

Monk gave Long Tom a shove, with the idea of aiding him. Rather, it developed, Monk's shove was only an effort. Something had happened to his simian frame. There was a tingling in his sinews, as of tiny electric shocks progressing. There was numbness, also. And he had no strength.

Monk tried to say something, to warn the others, to even speak to them, demanding to know their condition, but words would not come, and he could hear no sounds from them to indicate how they were faring.

He tried again to cry out, but did not succeed, after which, like an echo, Rama Tura's hollow voice intoned words that seemed to be coming from a well of small diameter and great depth.

"You are becoming unconscious," Rama Tura was saying.

He was still saying that, the last thing Monk remembered.

Chapter XI
STAMPEDE

DOC SAVAGE regained his consciousness with those same words of Rama Tura booming against his eardrums. The voice sounded much louder than it was, at first, for there was something askew in the bronze man's mental processes.

He shook his head violently, and that made it ache violently, but after the pounding of pain subsided, he could think more clearly.

The last thing he could recall was his weird encounter with Rama Tura. At least, that was the last thing he could recall distinctly. There were other vague things, like a dream all but forgotten. Shots. An explosion. Men shouting.

The bronze man concluded that these vague things which he could remember were recent occurrences, and it was possible they had contributed to his awakening.

His feet were fastened in a remarkably effective manner. They had used a long, stout iron bar with an eye in each end. An ankle was wired to each eye in the rod, holding his legs apart, where the smallest possible strength could be brought to play.

His wrists were handcuffed behind him. He tested the links. He could often break ordinary ones, but he did not break these.

The effort put the terrible banging ache back in his head, so he set his teeth, and with a violent wrench, threw an arm out of joint—a feat he had acquired for just such occasions as this—and got the handcuffs around in front of him.

With his fingertips, Doc put violent pressure on such nerve centers as were accessible, and succeeded in dulling the larger part of the headache.

He had grasped the iron bar which held his feet apart and was ascertaining the chances of bending it upward when there was noise of many feet on the stairs.

Brown men of Jondore flocked into the room, which was a large, long one, with doors at either end. The Jondoreans looked worried.

They glared at Doc Savage, but the bronze man was lying back, his handcuffed wrists again behind him, as if he had never regained his senses.

The man said, "The only safe tiger is a dead tiger. Why do we keep this man and the others alive?"

"It is the wish of the Majii, master of all things," another replied.

"Rama Tura would have them dead," the first muttered.

"The kitten does not eat the mouse of the tomcat, his father, if he is wise," snorted the second. "Rama Tura is but a servant, even as you and I."

"Not as you and I," the other corrected. "He has those strange powers which were bestowed upon him by the Majii."

Six men came in then, scampering along under the burden of Rama Tura and his strange casket which seemed to serve as resting place and litter.

Behind them came other brown men, carrying Monk, Ham, Long Tom and the Nizam, all of whom were obviously unaware of what was happening.

The Ranee walked among them, unguarded, any expression that might have been upon her face hidden by the veil, which she still wore.

Rama Tura must have given the necessary orders earlier. Doc Savage was gathered up off the floor, slung over the shoulder of two men, who managed his weight with difficulty, and all filed out through the opposite door in a procession.

They crossed another room, waded through a litter of brick and mortar, and scrambled into an aperture recently opened in a wall. This let them into another building, apparently empty. They descended stairs.

Four large trucks were parked in the alley. They scrambled into these. Doc Savage could hear police sirens in front of the building and in nearby streets. Then the rumble of the truck engines drowned that out.

They drove away without being molested, which was not surprising, since there were hundreds of just such trucks as these in this part of the city.

DOC SAVAGE managed to keep track of what was going on, although he was handicapped somewhat by pretending to be unconscious.

Rama Tura and the Ranee were riding in another machine, as were the other prisoners. Doc was alone with a swarm of Jondoreans who quite patently wanted his life, and discussed ways of taking it without getting themselves in wrong with their master.

"Guns are exploded by accident," one man suggested.

"A gun would be heard on the street," it was pointed out.

"Then if I should walk, with my knife in my hand, and a lurch of the truck should throw me off balance, would that be my fault?" the first demanded.

"It would be if Rama Tura thought so," he was told.

Rama Tura must have given orders shortly after that, because the trucks separated. The one bearing Doc Savage rumbled on interminably.

The bronze man, checking its turns, its probable speed, and taking into consideration the decrease of other traffic noises, concluded they were in the country. The machines eventually hit a very rough road.

The driver muttered at the road. Rasping and scraping noises came from the sides of the truck. Branches dragging, no doubt. Finally, the truck stopped.

Doc lay in it nearly an hour. Then other trucks arrived. He was hauled out.

Monk and the other prisoners were there, all bound and gagged. Among them, Ham alone seemed to be conscious.

More time passed. Everyone seemed to be waiting for something. Then Rama Tura came, borne in his box by four stalwart Jondoreans.

With Tura was the Ranee, still veiled.

Rama Tura gestured at the woman, indicating, it seemed, that she should go to the west. That interested Doc, for during the past hour he had heard sounds of airplanes. There was an airport in that direction.

But the Ranee seemed to have something on her mind. She gestured, said something in a vehement manner. Her words did not reach Doc. But she was standing so that he could read her lips.

"Doc Savage and his men, and Kadir Lingh, are to be kept prisoners," she was saying in Jondorean.

Rama Tura spoke in his characteristic manner, without moving his lips noticeably, so Doc failed to get his reply. Evidently, however, he had assured the Ranee the captives were to meet no harm.

"They are not to be killed!" the Ranee insisted.

Doc was certain of Rama Tura's reply to that, because he nodded.

The Ranee departed, two men with her.

Rama Tura came over to Doc Savage. He kicked the bronze man in the side. His strength was little short of astounding, considering his corpse-like appearance.

"You," Rama Tura told Doc, "are to die at once."

THE bronze man had been feigning senselessness, but the kick had been painful enough to make him conclude to assume a slight revival. He said nothing. Rama Tura apparently gave his promises little consideration—at least, the one he had made the Ranee.

Rama Tura hunkered down to bring his macabre mask of a face close to Doc's features. And with that, Doc suddenly perceived that the man was not what he seemed. The death mask aspect of his features was a clever make-up. Rama Tura, the real man, was vastly different. Just what he would look like, it was impossible to tell.

"You have mixed in something which does not concern you, bronze man," Rama Tura said hollowly.

Doc said nothing.

"You do not even know what the affair is all about," Rama Tura continued. "And it is my thought that, before you die, you would like to know just what it is."

Doc deliberately registered great interest.

Rama Tura, seeming gratified at the display, ground out, "It is big, bronze man, this thing. It is bigger than anything you have ever encountered. I might even add that it is as big as anything you have read about in your history books."

Doc, just on the chance that it would goad the weird fellow into revealing more, jeered, "Any fool with a tongue can make talk."

Rama Tura shook his head.

"You think I am lying," he murmured. "I am a conceited man, for I have the right to be, and, strange as it seems, your not believing me injures my vanity."

Doc only watched him.

Rama Tura intoned, "You have guessed that jewel thievery is not the big thing behind my actions. That was clever. But you did not guess my real scheme, the plan of myself and the Majii, my master."

Doc kept an intense stare on Rama Tura's face, trying to hold the brown, evil eyes with his own flake-gold ones. Rama Tura was glaring back.

"It is, or would be, almost fantastic to you, this thing we are doing," Rama Tura continued. "You would think it quite horrible, no doubt, because it involves the taking of a few hundred lives, and later, perhaps many more than that."

He squinted at Doc.

"The thought horrifies you, does it not?" he demanded.

Doc said nothing—only stared.

"The thing behind my actions is—something I shall, of course, not tell you," Rama Tura said, and looked very pleased with himself.

Doc continued to stare at him. And suddenly Rama Tura cried out and bounced frantically backward, his face averted. He had suddenly realized what Doc was trying to do by his staring—trying to hypnotize him.

RAMA Tura leaped about as if he had something hot on the soles of his feet, and he beat his head, his face, as if to awaken himself.

Doc had very nearly gotten him, and the fact had thrown the weird brown man—if he was brown—into a wild rage.

"You are able to do things which the world thinks are amazing!" Rama Tura sneered and snapped his fingers. "They are nothing. You have been a child in my hands. You would not even be a child in the hands of the Majii, my master."

Doc said dryly, "It is possible we have learned more than you think."

Rama Tura made a jeering noise.

"I have gotten the money from the sale of those jewels, which you tried to keep from me," he said. "It is even now in a truck headed for—"

He stopped, for it apparently dawned on him that he was making a fool of himself. He straightened, shouted to his men. "We will not delay longer. You will use knives on them—all but the Nizam, whom we are by all means to keep alive."

The brown men came forward, as if they had been waiting for just that. The favorite place for carrying their knives seemed to be in sheaths strapped to their shins. Several were pulling up their trouser legs to get these weapons.

Doc Savage proceeded to demonstrate that he could move, manacled though he was. An acrobat would have envied the series of flips which he now did. He moved with all the vigor of a bass freshly yanked out of the water, and he had just as much at stake.

The bronze man was seeking a position where the wind would blow over him, then upon his foes. There was not much wind, but it would not take much.

Doc gained his position. He managed to get hold of one trouser cuff, then the other, and wrench them open—not merely turning them down, but tearing open the entire hem.

A yellow powder came out of one cuff, a blue one out of the other. Doc twisted and managed to get the powders to fall in the same pile.

The results were remarkable. There was a *whoosh!* of sound, as if flashlight powder had gone off, except that the flame was green and not very bright. A cloud of bilious-looking smoke arose and spread.

The foremost knifeman plunged into the smoke, and immediately let out a bawl of agony. He fell headlong. The skin on his visage and hands appeared to have been suddenly blistered.

The man's knife flew out of his hand and landed near Doc Savage. Doc had rolled to get away from the smoke cloud, for it was a gaseous combination of acids capable of producing a most agonizing burn.

Doc got the knife and threw it to Monk, who was alert and caught it, then slashed his legs loose with all the speed he could manage.

A BROWN man rushed Monk with a knife, and the homely chemist, with no regard whatever for the fine points of fighting, all but kicked the fellow's jaw off.

Monk then freed Ham, Long Tom and the Nizam. It was not quite as simple as that, however, for he was rushed twice, and knocked down both assailants, then had to throw a convenient stick at a man who was about to use a gun.

Doc Savage, in the meantime, had continued his flipping manner of flight, and was behind a tree. He tried to break the handcuff links, but they were too much for him.

He eyed them closely. They were made of alloy, the first pair he had ever seen made of such material.

Doc shouted, his trained voice carrying over the uproar, and directed his men to run around the cloud of acid vapor, seeking to draw their pursuers into it. He made the suggestion in the Mayan tongue which they used when not wishing to be understood by listeners.

Monk and the others did so. Several pursuers, overanxious to seize them, got into the burning, stinging vapor. Three, however, rounded the outskirts of the cloud. They had drawn their guns.

Doc Savage, kicking about in dead leaves near his tree, had uncovered a heavy fallen limb. He got his manacled wrists in front of him.

The limb appeared too thick for any man to break, and it was not rotten. Doc got leverage upon it and snapped it in three pieces with an ease that made the feat seem trivial.

About this time, the three men who had rounded the acid cloud were preparing to shoot. Doc lobbed his sticks, one at each gunman. He made what, under the conditions, looked like a good average—two out of three—but nonetheless, he seemed disappointed.

Long Tom and Ham took a reckless chance, charged the third gunman. They would probably have been shot. But Monk threw the knife in a way which showed he had practiced the art, and put the blade in the gunman's chest, not far from the heart.

The man upset.

Rama Tura's other men ran wildly away, pursued by the cloud of vapor, which the wind was carrying. They outdistanced it, then turned around and began shooting.

"Run for it!" Doc called.

The bronze man was working at the wire which held his ankles to the eyes in the ends of the iron bar. Monk stopped to help. The others ran on, retreating, at Doc's rapped command.

Doc said grimly, "Monk, you threw that knife at the man's heart."

Monk took pains not to look at Doc. The homely chemist was well acquainted with the rule of Doc's that at no time was life to be taken if it could possibly be avoided.

Monk began, "Aw, I didn't—" Then he changed his mind, being fairly sure he was not an accomplished enough liar to fool Doc.

"Heck!" he grunted sheepishly. "I was excited."

Doc's ankles came free, and he got up and ran. Bark, chopped off trees by bullets, was falling about them. There was enough gun noise for a pitched battle.

"We're gonna—make it," Monk puffed.

They did. The men of Jondore were either not good runners, or they did not take the pursuit wholeheartedly.

THEY ran approximately a mile, and came to a busy highway, where they waited for a motorist. Long Tom contributed the mainspring of his wrist watch, which his captors had not taken, since it was plainly not a valuable one, and Doc picked the lock on his wrist manacles.

A motorist who would not stop nearly ran over Monk, but the next one stopped and agreed to give them a lift. Doc Savage did not enter the machine.

"You fellows be careful," he directed. "This Rama Tura and the Majii, whoever that is, are clever. Next time, they will probably kill you the instant they get their hands on you."

Monk growled, "Next time, it'll be us gettin' our hands on them."

Ham said, "Don't brag, stupid."

Long Tom demanded, "Doc, what are you going to do?"

Doc Savage did not answer that.

"You will see me down at headquarters shortly," he said.

He watched the motorist drive out of sight bearing Monk, Ham, Long Tom and the Nizam. The bronze man then plunged back into the timberland.

He heard shots when he had covered half a mile. They were ahead, and also to the westward. There was about twenty of them. Doc began running with a speed that would have given a college sprinter much to think about.

Next, Doc heard plane motors. There must have been about sixteen motors, but the way they were grouped indicated they were in four planes.

Doc saw the planes shortly, peering out at them from under a tree, so that they did not see him.

There were four very big ships, and they bore the markings of a transcontinental airline.

They were exactly the same type of planes which held the commercial speed records for the flight from New York to Los Angeles.

Doc went on, with a good idea of what he would find.

He found one dead man. He had feared there would be more. There were seven others who had been slightly wounded. All were the personnel at the chief passenger airport of New York City.

What had happened was bloody, violent and simple. Rama Tura's men had simply raided the airport in force and taken what planes they wanted.

One of the planes had been loaded with the contents of a small truck—packages bearing the stamped paper wrappers of a bank. That was enough to tell Doc it had been the money, proceeds of the sale of Rama Tura's séance jewels.

Doc Savage made a few suggestions about organization of the hunt for the planes. Then he returned to the city. He entered the skyscraper which housed his establishment by the secret garage and the private elevator.

The instant he was in the eighty-sixth floor corridor, he could see that something was wrong. The reception room door was open, and Ham, Long Tom and the Nizam stood just inside, looking very worried.

"What is it?" Doc asked.

"Now Monk has disappeared!" Ham gasped.

Chapter XII
THE NIZAM SURPRISE

THE anxiety in Ham's voice as he announced that Monk was missing was striking considering the fact that he and the absent chemist had never within the memory of anyone presented each other with a civil word.

It proved that Ham considered Monk his closest friend, even though they did squabble. The truth was that either Ham or Monk would have risked his life to save the other. They had done so, on occasions.

"How did it happen?" Doc asked.

"He just disappeared," Ham groaned.

"Call his penthouse laboratory," Doc suggested.

"We did," Ham said slowly. "Jove! I hope nothing happened to that homely ape."

Long Tom grunted, "You two guys give me a pain. You put in your time trying to kill each other. And the minute one of you thinks the other is in a jam, you bust out in tears."

Ham snapped, "I'm going out and hunt Monk! Something terrible has happened to him. I know it has!"

Doc Savage said quietly, "Hunting would be worthless unless we have a clue to go on. Wait around. We will see what turns up."

The bronze man eyed the Nizam. "Rama Tura admitted there was some big plot behind what is happening. I do not think he was lying. Can you give us any hint which might help us learn what it is?"

The Nizam gave that some moments of thought. The Nizam had been very dapperly clad indeed when Doc first encountered him, but the violence of the night had put him in a rather disheveled condition.

"My fortune which disappeared is the only angle I can think of," he said. "I have told you of that."

"It looks as if your fortune was merely used to get cash for the bigger scheme, whatever it is," Doc said. "That is, of course, merely theory. We have not yet proved that Rama Tura and his Majii robbed you."

The Nizam shrugged. "It has me baffled."

Doc Savage now went into the laboratory, opened the door into the hidden space between the walls, and dragged out a bound, gagged and sleeping figure.

They all noted the Nizam's reaction when he saw the prisoner—and had reason to remember it later. The Nizam, who had been as cold and calm as any of them so far, gave a great start and began to tremble violently.

"Who is that?" he almost screamed. And he spoke his native Jondorese, apparently forgetting his English in his excitement.

"This," Doc Savage told him, "is the fellow who tried to trick me by pretending to be you. You will recall that this happened immediately after you arrived by plane and they seized you."

The Nizam continued to tremble violently. His brown skin had become the color of lead.

"Do you know him?" Doc Savage asked.

The Nizam's answer was to keel over in a dead faint.

DOC SAVAGE studied the inert figure of the man who was ruler of Jondore, and until lately the richest of living men.

The bronze man's small, fantastic trilling noise became quite distinctly audible, an eerie cadence that rose and fell, and might have been the song of some exotic-feathered thing of the jungle.

"This is something new," he said.

Long Tom squinted and pulled at an ear which was rather large and only slightly less transparent than a sheet of oiled silk. He said nothing.

Ham, while looking at the unconscious Nizam, said, "I do wish we had some idea of where Monk is."

Doc Savage administered stimulants to the Nizam, and the fellow responded enough to give some foundation for believing that he would revive completely within a few minutes.

Doc next went to work on the false Nizam. Using a hypo needle, he injected the concoction of drugs which nullified the effects of the stuff he had used to make the man helpless.

"The fellow sucked some stuff out of his sleeve to make himself unconscious so that he could not be questioned," Doc reminded. "Perhaps he has recovered from that by now. We will see if he is conscious when he comes out of the shot I administered."

While they were waiting for the systems of the two Jondoreans to absorb the various mixtures of chemicals, Doc Savage stripped the coat off the fake Nizam, so that the man would not have the opportunity to again make himself senseless. He also removed the gag. But he left the man's arms and legs fastened by handcuffs.

Ham paced slow circles and waited, "Drat it! What about Monk?"

Doc said, "There is nothing to go on yet."

Ham headed for the reception room.

"What now?" Doc asked him.

"I'm gonna hunt Monk!" Ham barked.

"Do not leave," Doc requested.

Ham nodded. "I will use the telephone."

Ham disappeared into the reception room.

Doc Savage and Long Tom watched the Nizams, fake and genuine, closely, noting that both were reviving with about the same slowness. They would regain consciousness almost together.

Reactions of the two Nizams, on recovering, were, strangely enough, almost the same. Both opened their eyes, blinked, and looked about. They were fully conscious. But neither said anything.

Doc was about to put a question when a terrific howl came from the reception room. It was Ham, and he was shrieking.

"Doc!" he roared. "Look at this!"

Doc Savage whipped out of the laboratory, across the library and into the reception room.

Long Tom was close behind Doc.

Ham stood in the middle of the reception room. He pointed at the door.

Monk stood in the opening, and under one furry arm was his pet pig, Habeas Corpus.

"Where have you been?" Doc demanded.

"Why," Monk said innocently, "I just went downtown to that place where we had the fight to see if I could find Habeas. I found 'im, all O. K."

HAM, who had shown such anxiety, now gave every indication of having a stroke. He made gargling rage seconds, and rushed to the corner beside the big office safe, to come back flourishing one of his sword canes, which he had evidently cached there some time ago.

"I oughta trim your toenails right off next to your ears!" he screeched at Monk.

"What's the idea of this?" Monk demanded, bewilderedly.

Long Tom supplied the answer. "You went off without saying anything and Ham has been shedding tears all over the place."

Ham looked very red and angry and groped for something to say, but apparently could think of nothing properly expressive of his state of mind.

Monk smiled blissfully and murmured, "So Ham was worried. I always did know he loved—"

Ham shrilled, "Shut up, if you don't want to be dissected!"

A voice behind them in the library door said, "And you will all put up your hands, unless you want to be autopsied."

It was the Nizam, the real one. He held a gun—one of the supermachine pistols which Doc Savage had given him to use in case they encountered Rama Tura's men.

He was carrying the man who had tried to pass himself off as the Nizam upon Doc Savage. The latter was still handcuffed. He said nothing.

No one moved. No hands went up.

"Something has happened which changes the situation greatly for me," said the genuine Nizam. "You will put your hands up and permit me and my companion to leave. I assure you that I mean business."

The sensible thing to do was to get hands up, and Doc Savage did so. But not Ham. He was already in a blind rage over the Monk incident, which he well knew would furnish Monk something to rib him about.

Ham would almost have parted with an arm rather than have Monk know he had expressed fondness for him.

So Ham snarled and hurtled forward, flinging his sword cane spear fashion. The tip of the blade was coated with a chemical, akin to the one in the mercy bullets, which would produce swift senselessness, once it were introduced into a wound, however small. But the sword cane missed, due to Ham's haste.

The Nizam tightened on the supermachine pistol. The gun let out its bullfiddle moan. Ham went down.

The superfirer continued to hoot, and Long Tom and Doc Savage went down in quick succession. They moved only a little after they fell.

IT was night, with the lights of the city a magnificent spectacle from the skyscraper windows, when Doc Savage and his aides revived.

The squealing of Habeas Corpus, a plaintive sound, was the first noise that Doc Savage heard. The bronze man awakened first. After a while, the others were up.

They held a somewhat gloomy discussion, which consisted largely of Monk, Ham and Long Tom advancing various theories, none of which exactly explained what had happened.

"It was that fake Nizam!" Long Tom complained. "Just seeing him went all over the real Nizam. I wonder what caused it."

"That," Ham said, "is just another black spot in the whole very dark mystery."

They telephoned the police, and learned no trace had been found of Rama Tura or any of his men.

Doc had the police put out a pick-up order for the Nizams, real and fake.

They sent out for papers, the late editions. The sheets were full of the murders, with the usual wild speculations, and an occasional fiery editorial accusing the police department of inefficiency—a stock procedure, incidentally, which had about gone out of style in New York City.

About that time, Doc Savage chanced to find, in his coat pocket, a business card which he had not put there. It was embossed with the royal emblem of Jondore, an affair of a tiger head and spears, entwined by a serpent. The card also bore the simple lettering:

KADIR LINGH

There were words printed on the back in a stilted but precise hand which might have been trained to print the rather unusual letters which formed the Jondore alphabet. The message was to the point:

PLEASE DROP YOUR INTEREST IN THIS AFFAIR. IT WILL SAVE MANY LIVES FOR YOU TO DO SO.
                              KADIR LINGH

Monk did some very vehement muttering when he had perused the scroll. Then he looked at Doc Savage.

"What about it?" he asked. "Do we drop it?"

Doc asked dryly, "Would you like to?"

"Heck no," Monk grinned. "I've been havin' the time of my life."

"There is something behind all this," Doc Savage said. "Something large and terrible. We will go on, get to the bottom of it."

"Swell," Monk grunted. "That guy Rama Tura needs a good squashing, and I'm in favor of our doing it, even if the job takes us clear to Jondore."

"Even if it takes us to Jondore," Doc Savage agreed.

Chapter XIII
THE LOOMING TERROR

IT took them to Jondore.

They arrived three weeks later—arrived in Benares, which is not in Jondore, or even very near it, but is in India, south of Nepal, an independent state somewhat similar in set-up to Jondore, politically. Benares is possibly the best hopping-off place for Jondore—Jondore not being among the most accessible places in the world.

In those three weeks there had been nothing whatever to show what might have happened to Rama Tura and his organization, or to the Nizam of Jondore, former richest man in the world, or to the mysterious man who had pretended to be the Nizam. The Ranee, widow of the dead ruler of Jondore, had also dropped from sight.

Not that Doc Savage had not searched for them. The bronze man had expended money and influence in an effort to get a trace of his quarry, and he had been given access to the police reports, which were indicative of a thorough search officially, Rama Tura being wanted for a score of murders, more or less.

Nor had anyone uncovered a clue which had proved of value in solving the mystery of just what was behind the entire grisly affair.

Rama Tura and the rest had simply dropped out of sight as completely as if Rama Tura had worked some of the ability at miracles which he seemed and claimed to possess, and had removed everyone into the spirit world.

Monk even commented to that effect.

"Dope," Ham snapped back at him. "There is no such thing as a mug like Rama Tura performing miracles."

It was when they sought the usual clearance papers to enter Jondore that Doc Savage and his three aides encountered the first—and a very minor example—of the difficulties that lay ahead. They were refused admittance.

The refusal was simple, to the point, and simply explained. The Kadir Lingh, Nizam of Jondore, had notified the British Foreign Office and his own consular representative that Doc Savage was under no circumstances to be admitted to Jondore.

There was the further simple statement that Doc Savage and his aides would be officially executed if caught in Jondore. The statement indicated that the Nizam considered Doc and his men public enemies of Jondore. The Nizam came near enough to being an absolute monarch that he could order such executions.

Doc Savage talked the matter over at length with the British officials, and, although the bronze man had a certain amount of drag, he having been of service to John Bull in an official way on other occasions, he was advised to drop the matter and return to the United States.

Doc read between the lines and concluded that the British considered Jondore the powder keg of their Asiatic possessions, and feared the bronze man might be the spark which would ignite it.

The British put agents to watching Doc and his men. The shadowing was open, and Doc agreeably invited the agents to accompany him about, even to dine with him.

That was how it happened that British agents were with Doc Savage when he purchased airplane passage to the coast, and were with him when he and his three aides boarded a liner sailing directly for the United States.

The agents were not along when the liner lowered Doc and his three aides over the side in a power launch that night, some distance off the coast. Habeas stayed aboard, on his way to New York.

It was not entirely by chance that Doc had picked this particular liner, because it happened that the concern which owned it was one of the bronze man's wide commercial holdings.

So when the British radioed in midocean, querying whether or not Doc Savage was aboard, they were informed Doc and his men were on the passenger list. This was not, technically, a lie. Their names had simply not been erased from the list.

JONDORE was, in effect, a great, fertile valley, which was accessible by air and by three mountain passes which were sheer gorges through which narrow trails had been constructed.

There was no railway, and no way by which an automobile could enter Jondore, except by being taken apart and packed in on the backs of yaks, donkeys, and the tough little Himalayan ponies.

The guards at one of the mountain passes into Jondore failed to notice anything peculiar in the fact that within a space of two days, four different donkey merchants were admitted.

Donkey merchants, itinerant peddlers, were quite common, and also welcome, because they were taxed heavily. Barefoot, rather ragged, these particular hucksters differed little from the average run.

The night after the admission of the last of these four specific merchants found all four of them hunkered about the tiny blue flame of a fire in a small canyon. The nights were very cold in the mountains surrounding Jondore.

One of the hucksters began the conversation. He was a big fellow with a hump on his back and a limp in his right leg. His skin was almost black, his hair was short, jet-black, and so curly it was like a mass of tiny coil springs.

He wore a turban which was remarkably new and clean, and a robe which seemed about to fall to pieces in spite of many patches.

He spoke to a squat, broad, bald-headed fellow who had a yellow skin, teeth blackened from betel chewing, and who wore enormous spectacles and rather untidy garments.

"Did you have any trouble, Monk?" he asked.

"No, Doc," replied Monk. "Them Jondorean words you taught me were enough to get me by."

Shaving all of the coarse, rusty hair from Monk's apish frame had made a startling difference in his appearance.

Doc said, "How about you, Ham? And you, Long Tom?"

Ham and Long Tom had both turned into fat Hindus, through the medium of body pads, plastic make-up, and body stain. The disguises were perfect enough that it was doubtful if they would have recognized each other.

"What is our next move?" Ham wanted to know.

"We will work toward Dacal, capital city of Jondore," Doc said. "And we will see what we can pick up on the way."

Just what Doc Savage meant by saying they would try to pick up information on the way became apparent the following afternoon, when they entered a small village.

It was not unusual for merchants to travel together in Jondore, for the hillmen were chronic bandits.

The town consisted of rows of stone huts facing a lane of dust which must have been a remarkable mudhole on the rare occasion when it rained.

There were skin *yurts* of hillmen and herdsmen pitched around the outskirts, and the inevitable combination of temple and monastery was the most pretentious structure in town.

THERE were several inns, and they selected one which seemed to boast the least dirt and the fewest smells, although it was a close choice.

Ham, the fastidious, did considerable grumbling over the quaint and malodorous custom of keeping the animals in a yard under the inn windows.

"That is so the owners can look out occasionally and make sure their animals have not been stolen," Doc told him.

"A fine country!" Ham sniffed.

The inn food was too much for them. They cooked their own over a small fire in the yard, bothered by inquisitive donkeys and yaks. Other travelers were doing the same thing.

They kept their eyes open, and noted that many of the travelers were leaving immediately after they had eaten. Doc Savage ambled over to one who was preparing to depart.

"Truly this place pleases not even a yak, O brother," he said in Jondorean. "Can it be that you leave to find other and more pleasant lodgings?"

The traveler eyed Doc, and apparently saw nothing but a kinky-haired, hump-backed Jondorean with a limp, a fellow who looked quite harmless.

"It is indeed a foolish lamb which goes into the den of the lion, sees the lion and yet lies down there to sleep," replied the traveler.

"What have you seen here?" Doc asked.

"The lamb might see the lion, and yet not know it was a lion, never having seen one before," said the other. "Perhaps it is that you are new in Jondore."

He whacked his pony lustily and rode off.

Doc Savage went back to his aides.

"THERE is something happening in this village," he informed them. "Remain here, keep close to your donkeys, and watch."

Doc Savage moved away, affecting the bow-legged, shuffling gait of one who had spent much of his life astride ponies and donkeys. He had not gone far before he saw that there was indeed something brewing.

Armed men were the rule rather than the exception in Jondore, for it was a wild, untamed land, but men abroad in the streets were much too heavily weighted with weapons, and they frequently walked in groups, muttering in low, excited voices. Doc tried to get close to one of the groups and was cursed and had sticks thrown at him.

Merchants, especially those who carried their wares on donkeys, were not held in much esteem in Jondore.

There is one spot where information can usually be picked up—the drinking places. Doc sought one which served not only the strong-buttered tea popular through the Himalayas, but also a potent beverage derived from fermented maize.

By the simple process of loosening his purse strings, Doc became a very popular fellow. He consumed nothing but the strong-buttered tea himself, and cheese, which no one considered in the least strange. An hour thus expended got him some information.

The head men of the village and the army—each village in Jondore had its private-armed force—were that night holding a meeting in the council house near the monastery.

"Whispers say it has to do with the return of the Majii," someone stated, then shut up suddenly, as if having let slip a matter that it was not healthy to discuss.

That was enough for Doc Savage, and as soon as he could manage without exciting suspicion, he left the drinking place and worked toward the monastery. He haunted shadows when he got near the place.

The monastery was a large structure, by far the most elaborate in town, which did not make it exactly a breathtaking bit of architecture, and the doorway was small, arched and near one end.

The patch of murk around the corner might have been made for eavesdropping. Ensconced there, Doc managed to overhear two men in the entrance, probably guards, as they talked.

"It is truly a great thing for Jondore, this return of the Majii," one murmured.

"You speak words of truth and wisdom," the other agreed. "Yet there are some dogs who sit back and yap, even after they have been shown a bone. They do not want to follow the Majii, master of marvels, ocean of wisdom though he is."

"There are many of those dogs," agreed the first.

"Many, truly," said the second. "But the word of the Majii will prevail, even if those who dissent have to die, so that—"

There was a yell inside the meeting hall. A shot. Another.

A man popped out of the door. He was white, nattily attired in whipcord-laced breeches, riding boots, a leather blazer and—incongruous touch—a beret of leather which matched his jacket. He wore two big revolvers, cowboy fashion, in low-slung holsters.

The two door guards, startled, let the white man whip past them. Then they lifted their rifles.

The white man looked back over his shoulder, saw the rifles being raised, and drew both of his revolvers. He stopped, spun, and both his guns went off.

The two guards collapsed.

THE village had been quiet. But now it exploded. Armed men popped, howling, from houses. A flood of gesticulating, screeching figures poured from the meeting hall.

Doc Savage mingled with them, galloping along with them after the madly fleeing white man. It was a bloodthirsty mob, out to slaughter the fugitive.

The white man ran fleetly, keeping his guns in his hands. He was an uncanny marksman. Three times, enraged villagers tried to head him off, and he used his weapons with effect. Then he came to

a point where a throng of foes literally blocked the street.

His guns made a great deal of noise. His foes made almost as much. But the odds were too great. The white man backed, spun, tried to flee, but the avalanche of Jondoreans from the meeting hall headed him off. An instant later, there was a tremendous melee.

Doc Savage was in the thick of it, making a great pretense of trying to get the fugitive, but actually putting himself in the way of the villagers as much as possible. Now he went into action, using fists, knees, furiously.

Seizing his chance, he got one of the small smoke bombs out of his pocket, dropped it, and an inky fog promptly enveloped the fray. That did the trick.

Seconds later, Doc appeared on the edge of the battle. He was dragging the white man, who was badly battered. The fellow was thin, almost fragile. Doc shouldered him. Then he ran.

Twice, they were shot at. One of the marksmen used a modern rifle and missed; the other fired with what must have been a homemade muzzle loader charged with pebbles, bits of iron and whatever else was handy. The miscellaneous missiles broke Doc's skin in four different places, but he was not damaged seriously.

The white man did not speak. He was holding his head, and scarlet from a cut crawled through his fingers.

Ham, Monk and Long Tom met Doc, riding their donkeys. They had started toward the sound of the fighting.

Doc put the white man on his feet, signaled his aides, and warned them not to speak. He did not want their unfamiliarity with the Jondorean tongue to reveal they were not the itinerant merchants that they seemed.

They persuaded the donkeys into a run and left the village.

THE white man spoke at last.

"Bally decent of you chaps," he said. "You jolly well took my iron out of the fire."

Doc kept silent.

"Jove," murmured the white man. "I hope you speak English. My Jondorean is rotten. What about it—savvy English?"

"Lizzle," Doc Savage said, giving the word "little" the mutilation of a Jondorean who knew only a few words of that tongue.

The white man asked curiously, "Just why did you aid me, old fellow?"

Doc feigned a groping for the proper English words.

"Mebbeso money," he managed finally.

The white man laughed, as if not at all surprised. "You'll jolly well get paid for it," he informed them. "Say, how would you like a bit of a job?"

Doc again paused before speaking.

"No savvy," he said. "You talk. Mebbeso savvy."

"I am a British secret agent," said the white man. "You savvy same?"

"Uh," Doc agreed.

"I was sent in here to investigate this business of the Majii," announced the man they had rescued. "You savvy Majii?"

"Uh!" Doc said with great vehemence.

"What do you know about him?"

"Vezzy lizzle." Doc paused as if groping for a very big word, his prize piece of the English language. "Vezzy mistiliffilulous."

"Very mysterious, is right," the other chuckled. "Is that all you know?"

"Uh," Doc nodded.

"I do not know a dratted bit more than that myself," said the white man. "I just got into Jondore, and heard there was something going on in that village meeting hall, and tried to get in to eavesdrop a bit. They caught me, the beggars."

"Job," Doc said. "No savvy."

"Oh, you want to know about the blooming job." The man was riding ahead of Doc on the donkey, and he carefully adjusted his position. "I want to get to Dacal, capital city of Jondore. I am going to have some very firm words with the Nizam. I shall bally well put a bee in his turban. I will remind him what a fleet of British bombing planes could do to his palace and to Dacal."

"Uh," Doc said agreeably.

"I want you to escort me to Dacal," said the white man anxiously. "I need a bodyguard. I will pay handsomely. Do you want the job?"

Doc let enough silence elapse to make it seem he was thinking it over thoroughly.

"Uh," he agreed finally.

They rode on, keeping to rocky ground, seeking the fastest traveling. For a time, they heard pursuit behind them.

The baying of dogs, evidently on their trail, gave them some bad moments, until Doc Savage dropped back and distributed common pepper—the stuff was in their packs of merchandise—over their trail.

After that, they lost pursuit.

It was some two hours before the white man made a remark concerning Doc's three aides, who had not said a word.

"They are very quiet," he remarked. "Can't the chaps talk?"

"Talk vezzy good way lose head," Doc reminded.

MORNING sun was soaking into the cracklike canyons of the mountains when they sighted Dacal, capital of Jondore. It was distant, a strange, unreal image in a gray, woolly mist.

Dacal was a jumble of tightly packed buildings, many having colors so bright as to be perceptible even from the mountain heights from which they were viewing it.

The city lay in the center of a valley, and near it was an almost emerald-green lake. The valley itself was entrancing, even from a distance; sight of it alone was enough to cause them to stand there for a long time, silent and admiring.

Nor were they the first to be stricken speechless by this vale of Jondore. Songs had been written about it, and poems, based on the ecstasizing of travelers who had been so fortunate as to see the rare spot.

The white man whom Doc had rescued finally sighed.

"They jolly well say the sharpest thorns grow on the prettiest flowers," he murmured. "Let us be toddling."

Hours later, as they rode through a land that was a paradise of beauty and luxuriance, munching delicious fruits plucked from trees along the road, they heard hoofbeats. A sizable squad of riders came into view.

The horsemen were tall, lean, with a hungrily alert look.

"Look kinda like they was out huntin' a square meal," muttered Monk, who was bringing up the rear, far enough back that their "employer" could not hear.

The riders were soldiers, it developed, for their attire was uniform; plumed turbans, long loose tunics of bright blue, and baggy trousers that were bunched into low felt boots.

Each man wore short sword and pistol; rifles were holstered on the front part of each saddle, dangling down the fore quarters of the horses.

Doc Savage studied them through an ancient telescope such as donkey traders carried for scrutinizing mountain passes in search of bandits.

"No wise traveler enters a sandstorm when he may go around it," he murmured in Jondorean.

Then he absently stuck the telescope in the saddle pocket.

The white man they had rescued from the villagers squinted at Doc, as if trying to fathom what the words meant. Then he peered at the soldiers, who were still too distant for close study with the naked eye.

"Mind lending me your telescope, chappie?" he suggested.

Doc guided his donkey close to the white man,

… Doc appeared on the edge of the battle. He was dragging the white man, who was badly battered.

extended the telescope—and something seemed to go wrong. Doc's donkey gave a great jump, crashed into the other's mount.

Doc, apparently to keep from falling, flung out his arms and grasped the white man, and in an instant, they had both crashed to the hard road.

Doc lay where he had dropped, emitting grunts that sounded very pained.

The white man bounded up, grimacing, and clutched his sleeve. The fabric of his shirt, the leather of his blazer, was cut. He shucked off the blazer, rolled up his sleeve and examined his arm.

A trickle of scarlet was coming from a small cut.

"Your deuced knife!" he exploded. "It might have cut me badly."

Doc Savage was fumbling inside his voluminous garment, and unobserved by the other, managed to free his knife of its sheath and thrust it through his robe. He stood up, contriving so that the other would be certain it was the knife which had cut him.

"Sorrow is a vast sea about me, out of which I shall never be able to swim," he said in Jondorean.

THE white man took the telescope and studied the gaudily caparisoned band of horsemen.

"Soldiers of Kadir Lingh, the Nizam," he said. "That is jolly fortunate for us."

Doc, registering alarm, grunted, "Mebbeso bad," in the bad English he was affecting.

"No, no," the other said hastily. "They will not dare molest me, and I will see that they do not touch you. We will hail them."

Doc and his three aides waited, playing their parts as rather-frightened traders in a wild country where anything might happen, and their "employer" rode forward grandly and hailed the approaching squad of horsemen.

The meeting occurred some distance down the road, and Doc and his companions could not hear what was said. They could, however, see that the conversation seemed to elate the white man. He waved at them, then advanced, riding with the uniformed squad.

"Everything is jolly," he hailed them. "One of these soldier chaps speaks English."

The horsemen surrounded them. They were a grim-visaged gang. No one spoke.

The white man cracked out words—words in perfect Jondorean, which he had professed himself unable to speak.

With hair-lifting speed, the soldiers whipped out their guns and covered Doc Savage, Monk, Ham and Long Tom.

The white man said in English, "Doc Savage, you and your three men will surrender if you have the least idea of what is good for you."

Long Tom gulped, "Well, for—double-crossed!"

Monk glared at the white man and gritted, "The rat flea!"

Ham murmured, "I fail to understand this at all!"

Doc Savage said nothing, nor was he showing any evidence of surprise.

Menaced by numerous guns, they did the sensible thing and let themselves be relieved of weapons, and permitted their wrists to be bound, after which preparations were made to lead them by ropes about their necks.

The white man rode over and looked down at them. He had exchanged with one of the soldiers and was riding a fine saddle mount.

"He who is wise and patient knows that all trails have an ending," he said in a totally different voice.

The hollow, deathlike quality of that voice he had used, the absolute absence of tonal difference, caused Monk and the others to give a tremendous start of surprise.

"Blazes!" Monk squawked. "Did you get that?"

Monk started forward, reckless of the guns which covered him, trying to reach the white man, but the latter spurred his mount and got clear.

Monk retreated disgustedly, and eyed Doc Savage.

"That hollow voice!" he exploded. "That guy isn't a white man! He's Rama Tura, the lug who made those jewels in the séances!"

The white man laughed at them.

"I am Rama Tura," he agreed. "And possibly you will admit Rama Tura is something of an actor, eh?"

DOC SAVAGE studied Rama Tura with no perceptible fear or anxiety.

"You are very clever, but we already knew that," he said slowly. "But one part of this affair was not staged—your flight from those villagers in the meeting house."

Rama Tura scowled, swore in Jondorese, violently, abusively—not at Doc, but at the villagers who had tried to kill him.

"I was there to persuade them to accept the leadership of the Majii," he grated. "The offspring of swine turned upon me."

"I wondered about that," Doc told him.

Rama Tura smiled thinly. He certainly bore little resemblance to the corpse figure which he had pretended to be in New York.

"You truly saved my life," he said. "For that, I owe you something. Only, I do not pay debts."

"You owe us more than you think," Doc Savage said.

Rama Tura looked interested, but Doc did not elaborate.

Chapter XIV
BLACK HOLE

IT was dark. Somewhere, it must be light, because it was daytime—the following day. But it was dark where Doc Savage and his three aides spent time—time that was beginning to drag.

It was also quite hideous where they were. The things on the floor made it that way. Not that the things on the floor were menacing. They had no matches, but they had felt over them.

They were bones, human, they knew by the skulls; on the floor also was a dust that was not pleasant to think about, although Monk, undoubtedly to get Ham's goat, had at one time gone into a lengthy monologue about how long it took a human body to turn into dust in a dry place such as this was.

The place was round, wide enough that two of them could barely span it by joining hands with outstretched arms. The walls were of stone, but they might as well have been of glass, for they had been polished to an incredible slickness.

Somewhere above—too high for them to reach it by forming a pyramid—was a door. Fortunately, they had not been kicked through, but had been permitted to slide down a rope.

They had talked—and talked. Possibilities suggested that might explain what was behind the machinations of the Majii and his disciple, Rama Tura, had been numerous, but based on no foundation sufficiently solid to warrant them being regarded as fact.

They had decided on one point.

"Is Rama Tura a Jondorean or a European?" Monk had pondered.

"A part of each," Doc Savage had said. "A half-breed, in my opinion."

Monk and Ham were quarreling to kill time, Monk berating Ham for using his robe to spread over the dust as a pallet, and Ham denying wrathfully that he had employed the homely chemist's garb thusly. The squabble lacked its usual entertaining angles. It sounded forced.

Long Tom said gloomily, "They're gonna let us stay here until we croak!"

The garments they wore were cheap, ragged, and had been given them by their captors. Their own clothing, including Doc Savage's vest with its remarkable assortment of gadgets, had been taken from them. They had, indeed, been stripped to the skin, and even give a bath—thrown into a horse trough, rather.

Doc Savage had been listening. To their ears came the erratic noises made by a guard pacing somewhere above and outside, and another sound, fainter, a murmuring intonation from a considerable distance, that was probably the noise of a temple.

There were chimes from time to time, and gongs, and once strains of the exotic music of the Orient, all rather pleasant.

There was a clanking above, and the outer door opened, letting very weak light through big iron bars. A brown face pressed to the bars, peering downward, and an arm came in with a burning brand—a bit of wood with an end cut into shavings—fell downward, and its light illuminated the prisoners. The face withdrew and the door grated shut.

"He does that about once every two hours," Monk grunted.

"All right," Doc said. "Now we go into action."

Monk made a surprise sound in the darkness. "So you got a scheme! But why wait this long?"

"It is now almost dark," Doc told him. "It is difficult to prowl during the daytime. Last night, we were tired. The rest did us good."

"How you gonna get out?" Monk grunted.

"With your aid," Doc told him.

THEY spoke in very low voices, for it was not beyond possibility that there might be a microphone, perhaps of supersensitive parabolic type, concealed above them. Rama Tura was, they had reason to believe, no stranger to modern devices.

To cover any sounds, such as a microphone might pick up, if one were there, Ham and Long Tom now began to sing. They rendered roistering chanteys of the sea, and there was much more volume than music.

Doc Savage and Monk faced each other in the center of the round cistern of a cell. They joined hands firmly above their heads.

Then, keeping a tight grip on each other's hands, they walked backward until each had gotten his feet against the wall. Thus, their bodies formed a bridge from one wall of the cistern cell to another.

It was no easy thing they were seeking to accomplish. Nor was it impossible. They had their shoes off, and the walls of the prison, while glass smooth, were entirely dry. They began to walk up the wall, maintaining their human bridge.

They lost out and fell back exactly eleven times in the next forty-five minutes. Then they got up to the opening. The next part was ticklish. Doc Savage felt with his feet, found the bars, and hooked toes around them.

"All right, Monk," he said. "I'll try to hold you if you say so."

"I'll take my chances on dropping," Monk muttered. "I've fell so danged often I'm wrecked, anyhow."

Down below, Ham and Long Tom made noise with their singing. They were, however, standing well clear.

Doc relaxed tense back muscles, their pressure bridge collapsed, and Monk went down to land with a loud thump and a tremendous grunt. Doc held the door bars with his toes. An instant later, he was clinging to the bars.

The whole performance, for all the trouble it had given them, possibly could have been duplicated by any accomplished team of circus or vaudeville acrobats.

Doc waited. His watch, of course, had been taken. But he had cultivated a fair ability at judging time, which was as effective as anything for the work at hand. Their guard might not wait the full hour, anyhow, or he might wait more.

Possibly seven minutes passed. Then the heavy bars on the outer door grated, and the panel—it was of timbers, iron strapped—opened and the guard did exactly what he had done before; the fellow put his face to the bars to look down.

The guard stood there very still, except that his hands came loose from the bars and dangled on the ends of limp arms. It was doubtful if anyone standing behind him, and there was no one, would have noted anything peculiar.

Doc, clinging to the bars with his feet, had the man by face and neck. The neck grip—fingers on nerve centers—did the trick.

The man senseless, Doc went through his clothing. There was a very modern padlock, American made, on the inner door of bars. The guard carried the key.

Some two seconds later, Doc Savage was outside.

It was dark in the passage, which was underground and below the north wing of the castle of the Nizam, the ruler of Jondore. The chanting which they had heard throughout the day was still going on.

It was not an unusual sound in Oriental cities, especially in the wilder interior. Occasionally, there were voices or the clatter of a bullock cart. One significant thing, however: they had heard no laughter on the streets.

The overpowered guard was a three-hundred-pound ball of blubber with a stunted knot of a face. His robe, not unlike an Arab burnoose, contained enough cloth to fashion a small circus tent. Doc relieved him of both robe and turban.

Doc tied an end of the robe around the man's ankle, then grabbed the fellow by the wrists and dangled man and robe, rope fashion, into the circular cell.

"Monk, up," he called softly.

Shortly, Monk arrived, clambering up the rope and the guard, grunting and groaning as if he were about to die.

Doc then hauled up prisoner and robe.

Monk stopped groaning, exploded, "Hey! Ham and Long Tom figured on comin' up, too!"

"They are going to remain in the cell," Doc said quietly.

MONK swallowed several times, then gulped, "But I don't get this! We've all got a chance to get out of the town!"

"We do not want to get out of the town," Doc told him. "Not after the trouble we had getting here."

Monk thought that over. "Then you—"

"I am going to look around," Doc explained. "One person can do that much better than four. This palace is probably the center of things. At least, if that Nizam can be gotten hold of, he can be made to talk—and clear up this whole mystery."

"Um-m-m," said Monk in a tone that was not too enthusiastic.

"Put on this fellow's robe and turban," Doc directed. "You will take his place as sentry. Your skin is still dyed, and you are big enough to get by, providing it is not too dark."

Monk began thinking of objections. "But what if someone comes along and looks down through the bars into the cell? They'll see two missing—"

"They will see the senseless guard, dressed in your robe. Ham and Long Tom will see that he stays senseless," Doc interposed. "A bundle of spare underclothing can be arranged to look like another sleeping person. That completes the list of four, does it not?"

Monk said, "But I can't speak this cackle they call a language."

"Just nod and grunt if you are spoken to," Doc suggested. "This guard is a surly fellow, if you noticed. It will seem natural."

Monk was trying to think of a further argument when Doc Savage left him.

Doc moved swiftly and, since he wore no shoes, silently. The absence of shoes would not draw attention, since many Jondoreans went barefoot.

There were two guards, soldiers, at the end of the passage. They looked very alert, and there seemed no possible chance of passing them, because a large lantern stood near them.

Doc crept to the edge of the lantern light. He could see into the lighted room beyond the guards. It was circular, and there were plenty of columns supporting the roof. There was an open door.

Silence was pronounced as Doc waited.

"Guards!" rapped a voice in Jondorean. "Over here a moment, quickly."

The voice sounded as if the speaker were beyond the open door, and it had an imperative rap of authority.

The guards snapped their rifles across their chests and advanced toward the distant door on the double quick.

"Never mind!" clipped the authoritative voice. "It was only a shadow."

The guards saluted, turned and came back.

Doc Savage watched them closely. He was no longer in the passage, but inside the large room, behind a pillar, well into the shadows.

The guards gave no sign of suspecting that it was a ventriloquial voice thrown by Doc Savage, and not one in authority, as they had imagined, that they had heard.

They did, however, keep a closer watch than before, but after a few minutes, relaxed, and Doc managed to creep away.

The big room had two doors other than the first one Doc had seen; both being open, Doc eased through one, and through a walled channel of darkness. The passage ended, and he stepped into another large room—and suddenly ducked back.

He had heard marching men. They came into view a moment later, four abreast, moving with a military tread. Two bearers were in advance with resin-knot torches.

Rama Tura led the procession.

Kadir Lingh, Nizam of Jondore, strode next.

THE parade—some fifty armed men, not all of them soldiers—were in the party. Those who were not uniformed wore expensive robes and had the air of men of importance.

The parade crossed the chamber with the air of having some very definite place to go.

Doc Savage had quitted his prison cell for the very specific purpose of finding the Nizam and learning, by one means or another, just what was behind that gentleman's unusual behavior in New York City. So Doc joined the parade—at a safe distance.

The group went directly to what was evidently the palace stables, where grooms had horses waiting. Mounted, the squad seemed much larger, almost a young army. They rode away, and rode fairly hard.

Doc Savage had heard of the claim sometimes made that if a man and a horse engage in a walking contest, the man can outlast the horse.

The bronze man was a physical marvel, thanks to training which had started in the cradle, and his two hours of exercise taken every day. He had never engaged in public athletic contests, simply because it was best in view of the unusual career for which he was training that he should not get any newspaper publicity that was avoidable.

However, these horses were not walking. They trotted, galloped, and ran some of the time. Moreover, they were fine mounts.

Three hours later, Doc was a mile behind. Had it been daylight, when the mounted men would undoubtedly have traveled faster, he might have been farther back.

Five hours later, he had lost another half mile—or thought he had, until he came upon the horses, reins held by soldiers, most unexpectedly.

Several minutes must have been lost by the party in dismounting, because Doc could hear them in the distance, walking. Climbing, rather.

The horses had been left in a canyon, with walls of rock on two sides that, as far as the eye could tell in the deceptive darkness, were vertical.

The rock was hard; it cut even Doc's bare feet, which were not tender. At times, there seemed to be a path, but more often progress was a matter of scrambling from one crack to another.

The air was cold. Such dust as Doc's fingers touched was so frigid it felt like snow. In the distance, and now Doc knew he was out of the canyon and mounting on up, could be seen the lights of the capital.

They were not like the lights of an American or European city; there were no street lamps. Doc gave all of his attention to the trail—it was a trail—and to the jagged peak above. Attention there was necessary.

Jagged peak above—no! Its contour had changed abruptly, perhaps due to an altered viewpoint. Doc paused to study it.

IT was like a black cube, a giant spotless dice, standing on the vast hump of stone. It was hardly on a peak, for there was higher ground back of it.

The bronze man's low, mellow trilling note which meant always some moment of mental excitement, came, persisted briefly, then was gone.

He knew what this thing was. He had not seen it; so far as he knew, no pictures of it were in existence, although at least two men had been executed for trying to smuggle pictures out of Jondore. But tongues cannot be censored, and travelers had told and written of it.

The block of stone—it was black, and no white man had ever gotten close enough to it to tell what it was made of, although undoubtedly some stone foreign to the immediate region—was the tomb of the Majii!

Tomb of the Majii—the fantastic master of miracles, mythology had it, who had lived innumerable centuries ago, just how many centuries, mythology was uncertain. The Majii! This was the English spelling of a word that sounded similar in Jondorese.

Dialects differed in Jondore, and the name was not Majii everywhere. In the north, it was Jagee, and in the south, it was Genee, or Gini.

But no white man had ever touched this tomb. It was one of the mysteries of the world. The cult of the Majii, and much of the Jondorean population worshipped the Majii, had guarded it always from defiling hands.

Doc Savage advanced, and the block of black loomed larger. It was shiny, so marvelously made that it resembled—there was moonlight here—a great block of black glass.

The party the bronze man was following was entering the tomb by a small, almost round doorway. Rama Tura and the Nizam were already inside. Indeed, the last of the squad was just filing in.

Doc darted forward, haunting shadows. Reaching the round aperture, which looked modernistic, he listened. No sound.

He entered—of a fair certainty the first white man ever to cross that fantastic threshold.

Chapter XV
MAGIC OF THE MAJII

THE passage seemed warmer, and the smoke of resin-knot torches was distinctly irritating to the throat. Small sounds, exaggerated by the acoustics of the corridor, must be coughing of the men ahead.

There was an almost geometrical straightness to the passage, and at times there were other corridors leading off, always at exact right angles.

Doc, however, kept on the trail of those ahead. It was not a long trail. He glided to an arched doorway and peered through.

The room beyond was tremendous, somehow remindful of the dome inside the capitol at Washington, except that the interior was almost starkly plain. The resin-knot torches, four of them, did not give more than a fitful light.

There were two things in the center of the room.

The first was a gigantic affair which resembled a vase. It had one enormous handle—entirely too big for even a score of men to employ in lifting the object, even if they could reach it, which they could not without scaffolding. Out of the top of this came a steady blue flame, evidently fed by some kind of an oil reservoir.

The second object was behind the first, a plain oblong perhaps four feet wide, the same in height, and ten feet long.

Both objects certainly looked as if they were made of solid gold.

The crowd which had entered the tomb of the Majii now gathered around the rectangular block of yellow metal.

Rama Tura—he had removed the white shading from his skin and looked almost pure Jondorean—stepped forward, then lifted what developed to be a lid on the box. The instant he had the lid up, he bounced back and sank to his knees.

Everyone else fell to their knees. They also put their foreheads on the floor repeatedly, then lifted their eyes to stare at the long yellow box.

Several fantastic things happened. First, a weird and not unpleasant odor came into the room. Doc recognized it promptly as the same aroma which had always accompanied Rama Tura's apparent miracles in New York City.

After the scent had been present some minutes, no one making the slightest sound in the meantime, Rama Tura began to murmur slowly and monotonously. His words were almost a chant.

A mist arose from the hollow interior of the yellow block. It was an incredible yellow. It thickened, arose in a long cloud. The fantastic aroma in the room was stronger.

Unexpectedly, a volley of gasps came from the kneeling spectators.

A figure was rising with uncanny slowness from the block interior. It was, to every outward appearance, the figure of an embalmed dead man.

The unearthly apparition poised there a moment, then sank back and disappeared.

Rama Tura got to his feet, walked to the tall urn from the top of which came the blue flame, and gave it a brisk stroking with both hands. Results were instantaneous.

There was a flash of astounding brilliance, a crash as if the earth had come apart. The flash blinded Doc momentarily. When he could see again—excellent as was his emotional control—he started when he looked at the yellow block.

A figure was standing erect there. It bore some resemblance to the embalmed thing which had arisen before—it had on the same garments.

The garments consisted of a cloak, shoulders to ankles, some cloth which seemed partially woven of gold; and there was also a turban and a mask, the latter a death-mask affair of gold leaf.

"I am the Majii," said the apparition in Jondorean. "What is it that you wish here?"

TO say that the spectators, with the exception of Rama Tura, were tongue-tied was expressing it mildly. Fully two minutes elapsed and no one vouchsafed a word.

Rama Tura stepped forward finally.

"These are ones who doubted that you, O Majii, master of all that breathes and grows, all that is fluid and all that is solid, could return to life," he said elaborately. "I brought them here that they might see for themselves."

"Horses that are led to water do not always drink," said the Majii in a rumbling, impressive voice. Indeed, the voice was almost thunder.

"No!" Rama Tura exploded hastily. "These men are glad to be your servants, O Majii. But they wanted to be sure it was you they served. You see, this world has gotten full of trickery, and things are not always what they seem."

There was silence. Then came the thunder of the Majii.

"I have arisen from the tomb in which I have lain two score and ten centuries and more," said the great voice. "Do any of you doubt that?"

No one apparently did, or if they did, neglected the moment to say so.

Without looking the group over in a manner that was apparent, the Majii boomed, "I see among you the Nizam present ruler of my ancient homeland of Jondore. Will he step forward?"

Kadir Lingh, Nizam of Jondore since the death of his half brother, shuffled out a few paces from the group. He showed no great enthusiasm.

"You are of my blood," said the Majii.

Kadir Lingh was in no hurry in replying.

"So it is said," he agreed finally.

"You are my servant?" queried the huge voice.

Again Kadir Lingh hesitated.

"I am," he said.

"It is well," boomed the Majii. "As one who does what I decree, you will have riches and more power than ever a ruler before you, and everlasting life."

The Nizam bowed and said, "I am glad."

But he did not sound glad.

"From my tomb, here, I have sent my other self, my mind, out from time to time to observe the world, and my mind came back to me very depressed," said the Majii. "It is not well, the things which happen in this world, and least well of all is the manner in which the white man oppresses the brown. And now, lately, my mind has returned, telling me it is time that I arose and led my people to the place they deserve."

At this point came a pause for the listeners to digest the words.

"To those who help me, riches and power and life always," continued the Majii. "Will you all help me?"

Every man in the strange tomb room nodded.

"It is well," rumbled the Majii "You may go, all but the Nizam, to whom I wish to talk."

All but Kadir Lingh filed out, plainly a bit anxious to get out of the awful presence. Rama Tura, maker of jewels, was last to go.

Kadir Lingh turned and made sure they were all gone. Then he stamped over in front of the Majii and spoke angry English.

"This damned mumbo-jumbo has gone far enough!" he snapped. "You can't fool them always with your fakery!"

DOC SAVAGE had retreated to a cross passage when the men left, and he had returned in time to witness and hear what was now happening in the huge-domed chamber.

The Majii's face was expressionless behind the gold leaf. But he laughed.

"You still insist that I have no powers not held by an ordinary man," he said.

Kadir Lingh resorted to Jondorean, saying, "I know who you are. I know you are not—"

"Speak English!" snapped the other. "Some fool might overhear us, and few in Jondore can speak English."

Kadir Lingh changed to English and said, "I have been aiding you in your deception, at least to the extent that I helped you deceive Doc Savage in New York. In return for that, you promised to give up this insane thing which you contemplate."

The Majii made no reply to that.

"I will give you funds that you may live the rest of your days in luxury," Kadir Lingh continued. "That is the best way out."

The Majii rumbled, "You fool! You are not the one to dictate to me!"

"I have aided you that disgrace might not come upon the kingdom of Jondore!" Kadir Lingh shouted angrily. "I will aid you no more. That is final!"

Laughter came from the Majii. Great, ribald, crashing laughter it was, with a very perceptible undertone of viciousness.

"You will do what I say," he thundered. "I have increased my power in your land until now I am even stronger than you. Only a few of your villages are still faithful, among them the one where my good servant Rama Tura so nearly met his end, only to have Doc Savage rescue him. And that is another thing. Doc Savage and his aides must die!"

Kadir Lingh put out his jaw and said, "They will not!"

The Majii rocked on his heels and intoned, "You will have to obey me!"

"No," Kadir Lingh said with finality. "I will broadcast to the world your identity, and the thing you are trying to do, and what you have done."

Kadir Lingh paused, scowled darkly at the other, and suddenly seemed to come to a snap decision.

"Better than that," he barked, "I shall seize you and take you with me and unmask you now. I shall tell how you worked the whole incredible scheme!"

Kadir Lingh sprang forward as he spoke. He was attempting to seize the other.

But the Majii must have been expecting something similar, for he dodged the groping hands, and countered with a vicious kick to Kadir Lingh's middle which sent the ruler of Jondore, gasping and grimacing, to the floor.

Then the Majii whipped out a great, jeweled knife and descended upon the fallen potentate.

DOC SAVAGE pitched from his concealment. He ran as he had run on few other occasions. But the floor was slick, and the distance was great. He would never make it before the Nizam was knifed by the fiendish one in the golden robes and the weird gilt face.

Doc shouted. A crashing, imperative sound. It had to be.

The Majii glanced up, then gave a great leap, not toward Doc, nor exactly away from him, but toward the yellow block from which he had come. He stood erect in the block.

There was a flash, completely blinding. Simultaneously, there was a crash as if a field gun had gone off. It left Doc's eyes aching and his ears ringing.

And the Majii was nowhere to be seen. He had disappeared. Just how, it was impossible to tell.

Kadir Lingh, Nizam of Jondore, sprang erect from where he had been knocked. But he seemed too dazed to say anything.

Doc Savage ran to the golden block, and looked inside. Strong as was his self-control, he all but recoiled, for there lay in the sarcophagus the same grisly embalmed body which had earlier risen in such uncanny fashion.

There was a death mask of gold leaf over the features, but the visage bore a marked likeness to that of the Majii.

No living body was this thing in the gilt container. That was sure.

Doc Savage drew from his robe a rock which he had brought along as a weapon, and used a sharp edge of this to scrape the yellow block. The huge urn of a thing gave light enough to observe the truth about the block.

It was not gold. It was lead, or a similar substance, gilded.

Then a swarm of brown men came rushing into the place.

THE newcomers were robed in scarlet, and the cut of their garb indicated they were members of some cult, probably the attendants of the tomb.

They carried no firearms, but they did wield knives, very thin-bladed things, literally razor-edged thorns of steel. And there were scores of them.

Kadir Lingh, Nizam of Jondore, came close to Doc Savage.

"Death is before us," he said. "Be it said that I shall die in company befitting a Nizam."

Doc said, "Take off your robe and try to whip it into the eyes of the first to arrive, blinding them, and giving you a chance."

An instant later, the horde was upon them. Strangely enough, the knives were not used, except as a threat to drive them into a corner, after which the blades were unexpectedly put away, and it became a hand-to-hand affair. Such a melee was Doc Savage's specialty.

But specialty or not, there was a limit to the bronze man's capabilities. Two score men—his foes numbered that at least—could conceivably bring down an elephant, or the most vicious lion, providing they made the attempt with reckless lack of fear, as these fellows did. Moreover, Doc did not have any of the gadgets which he usually employed with such effectiveness.

They buried him, like ants upon a drop of syrup, and he fought tirelessly, until he was layered over with the bodies of the senseless, but for one that dropped, a dozen seemed to appear—more men were running into the domed chamber from the passages. It was hopeless.

Doc did not exactly give up. They finally got him worn down to the point where they could hold him, by the aid of thongs which they had managed to loop over his limbs.

The room seemed to be full of men, not only the tomb attendants, but the party which Doc had followed here. The latter must have heard the uproar and come back—all but Rama Tura.

One man—he seemed to have higher rank than the others of the tomb guards—sidled to the big yellow metal vase out of which the blue flame came steadily.

He rubbed the vase, somewhat fearfully.

The flash and crash came, and there was standing, as if by magic, the Majii in his yellow casket.

"What is wanted of me?" boomed the great voice of the Majii.

"This prisoner," a man mumbled. "What shall we do with him?"

"Determine," commanded the Majii, "just how many knives his body will hold."

They gathered around the bronze man, crowding somewhat as if anxious to be first to use their knives.

"Place yourselves in line, all but those needed to hold the bronze man," commanded the Majii. "There is no honor in being first."

They formed a procession of sorts, all with sharp blades. Carrying knives seemed to be in as much fashion in Jondore as was carrying watches in America.

The first man came to Doc's tightly held figure. The fellow took his time, studying the bronze man.

"Is there honor in being first to kill him?" he queried.

That particular question never did receive an answer. There was a loud clatter of running feet, and a man came tearing wildly into the domed tomb.

This fellow was highly excited. He tried to go to his knees in front of the Majii, and because he did not slacken his speed in time, toppled over and skated along on his nose, then tumbled on his back.

The performance would have been laughable, except that the messenger was undoubtedly bearing some terrible tidings.

The messenger said something in Jondorean. His voice was low, guttural and furiously rapid.

The Majii plainly did not like the news. He gave the bearer of it a resounding kick in the ribs, then came stamping over to Doc Savage.

"What have you done to Rama Tura?" he gritted.

"Made a move," Doc Savage said, "to make my own life worthwhile to you, and to put a value to you upon the lives of my three aides."

"Your friends!" the Majii snapped. "Orders have been given that they be executed!"

"I think," Doc Savage said, "that they can take care of themselves."

Chapter XVI
THE AIDING LADY

MONK thought the same thing—that he, and Long Tom and Ham in the cistern of a cell which he was guarding, could take care of themselves.

They had been managing it rather credibly, although it was true that there had only been one tense moment, and that when some beetle-browed officer, evidently a captain of the guard or something equivalent, had stalked up and glared down into the cell.

He had, fortunately, been either too proud, or too ugly-tempered to favor Monk with a word, for which Monk had been extraordinarily grateful.

Confidence is a great elixir, especially to those who do not keep too close a guard against its intoxicating qualities. And Monk had never been noted as the possessor of even the minor subduings of an inferiority complex.

That got him a crack over the head. It happened at the end of the passage, when he was spinning to march back in his regular pacing past the cell.

He never did see, until some five minutes later, the thing which had hit him, for the reason that the blow came from behind, and was hard.

The one who had struck Monk down was almost shapeless in an enveloping robe. The attacker now glided down the passage, after securing the padlock key from Monk's prone form—largely by the sense of touch, for it was dark in the underground place.

Reaching the locked door, the assailant opened it, and sent a rope snaking down.

"For the love of mud!" exploded Long Tom, when the rope hit him.

"Well, don't stand there!" snapped Ham. "Obviously, the rope is for us to climb."

They clambered up, not having much difficulty with the job. So dark was the passage that they did not know their rescuer was not Monk, until the individual spoke.

"Where are the two others?" asked the rescuer. "Doc Savage and the one called Monk?"

Had they been hit with hammers, Ham and Long Tom would not have been a great deal more surprised.

"It's a woman!" Ham gasped.

Long Tom, going on the principle that it was best to move and ask questions afterward, suddenly seized the feminine figure. He dragged her toward the nearest light, which happened to be beyond the corner where Monk had been struck down.

They saw Monk, and Ham leaped to his side and started to feel his pulse. Monk sat up, took his wrist out of Ham's fingers, and felt tenderly of his cranium.

"Something's wrong with my head," he mumbled, not yet revived enough to realize what had occurred. "Something is wrong with my head."

"You are finding out about it awfully late in life," Ham told him unkindly.

Long Tom had gotten the woman into the light.

"Hey!" he exploded. "Look who it is!"

Monk peered at his attacker.

"The Ranee," he gulped.

THE Ranee's rather entrancing features showed marks of some weeks of worry, as well as the stamp of genuine fear.

"Where is Doc Savage?" she asked.

"Search me," Monk told her. "He went prowling to see what he could find out."

"You see," Ham told the woman dryly, "we are still trying to find out what this is all about."

"He—Doc—was going to find Kadir Lingh and ask him plenty of questions," Long Tom contributed.

"If Doc Savage followed Kadir Lingh—" The Ranee wrung her hands instead of finishing. "Then he is at the tomb of the Majii. And no telling what will happen to him there."

She tugged at their arms, and because there seemed nothing else to do, they followed her. They did not entirely trust the woman, for she had double-crossed them in New York, but she seemed earnest enough now, and she had gotten them from the cistern of a cell, although they could have done that themselves at any time.

"Hurry!" she urged. "Orders came from the tomb of the Majii that you were to be executed immediately. We must get away before the executioners come."

That put willingness in their legs, and they raced along the passage, keeping up with the woman. They came to the exit, and two unconscious uniformed men were lying there. The Ranee pointed at them.

"They did not suspect me," she said. "I was able to knock them unconscious."

They went out into the darkness, and heard horses champing and moving about. The Ranee escorted them directly to the mounts.

"They are fast," she said. "I intended to have

you use them to escape from Jondore. But now we will use them to hunt Doc Savage."

Monk, mounting his animal, discovered a sizable pack on the back of the rather uncomfortable Jondorean saddle.

"What's this stuff?" he demanded. "Grub?"

"Partially," replied the Ranee. "In it, you will also find your belongings which were taken from you when you were captured."

"You think of everything, don't you?" Monk told her admiringly.

They mounted and rode, rather slowly at first, taking back streets, then, once they had left the capital city, more swiftly, running their animals whenever the trails permitted.

"You know the way to this Majii's tomb?" Monk demanded.

"Very well," the Ranee replied.

Ham spurred up until he was beside the Ranee, and began to put questions to her.

"Just what is behind all of this?" he demanded. "We know it is pretty bad, something that is liable to get a lot of people killed. But beyond that, we're stumped."

"I cannot tell you," the Ranee said promptly.

Ham's voice took on a sharpness. "But that does not make sense!"

"I will explain," the Ranee told him. "My explanation may not seem sufficient to you, but to me it is an ample reason."

"Go ahead," Ham said with bad grace.

"I love Jondore," said the Ranee. "I do not want the country disgraced. I do not want—well, certain people also disgraced."

"That's no reason," Ham said.

"The present Nizam, Kadir Lingh, and myself believe we can settle this affair by ourselves, or we have believed it, although I am becoming doubtful," the Ranee continued, heedless of the interruption. "We deceived you to keep you from learning the real truth which would disgrace us—Jondore."

"As a reason, that is very thin," Ham told her.

"I knew you would think that," she replied. "But if you knew the truth, you would understand."

There was a certain tenseness, plainly noticeable, in her voice.

Ham began, "But if you would tell us—"

"I will talk no more about it!" she snapped.

And she did not, although Ham did his best to provoke her to speech as they rode through the night. She had not disclosed anything further when they came into a region of rocky peaks and canyons of rather frightening depths.

At last the Ranee pointed to a square block of stone atop a high ridge and said, "There is the tomb of the Majii."

Monk squinted upward. "Looks kind of spooky."

"It is probably the most fantastic thing in the world," the Ranee replied.

"What do you mean?" Ham asked.

"I hope you will never know," the Ranee told him.

THEY left their horses and climbed, using every precaution toward silence, until at last the block of the tomb towered above them to surprising height, at which point the Ranee stopped them.

"There is one door into the place," she said. "Sometimes it is guarded, sometimes not. But there are always men inside, men who are descendants of men who have devoted their lives to attending the tomb, to guarding it."

"The idea is to be careful," Monk grunted.

"Exactly," she told them.

They advanced with infinite care, and fifty feet from the circular entrance, discovered two guards at the opening.

"Let me handle this," Ham breathed.

Ham had brought with him to Jondore two of his sword canes, which were custom made for him abroad. They had been in his pack which had ostensibly contained trade goods, and the Ranee had returned them to him. He carried one as he crept forward.

But, after covering several paces, he got another idea and came back to secure the second sword cane. They were his favorite weapons and he had brought both of them along.

He advanced again, but not too closely. Poising one cane in his arm, he threw it, javelin fashion. He followed it instantly with the second blade. He had carried these weapons in his hands for years; he had practiced countless hours with them. He could do some amazing things with them.

Each lookout was impaled in a leg. Each emitted a startled grunt, which was not extremely loud. Each man bent over to see what had hit him. And both fell over on their faces and apparently went to sleep.

Ham listened for some moments. The grunts had not attracted attention. Monk and the others appeared beside him, and they went in.

Their advance was without incident, and they reached the great-domed room which held the gilt block and the big urn from the top of which played the steady blue flame. They looked the place over, saw no one, and advanced.

The casket was closed, and so fine was the workmanship on it that their first hurried inspection failed to discern the lid.

They went to the big urn, which was far more spectacular.

"What's this?" Monk demanded.

"It is the lamp of the Majii," the Ranee breathed hoarsely. "Keep away from it. The horrible thing has burned for centuries. It was built by the Majii himself."

Monk sniffed.

"I'm chemist enough to know an ordinary vegetable oil flame when I see it," he said. "That's some kind of local alcohol burning through a wick."

He scowled at the big urn.

"And I'm gonna find out what this thing is made of," he added. "Looks like gold."

He went over and rubbed the vase vigorously, scratched it with a fingernail.

He got results. There was a flash, an ear-splitting report.

Monk was a score of feet from the vase, running, when his eyes returned to normal after the flash. He peered about. The others had likewise retreated, thinking at first that the blast was some kind of a bomb.

Monk sniffed. The air was filling with an odor. It was not the smell of any burned explosive, but a totally different aroma.

The scent which had accompanied Rama Tura's jewel-making séances!

THE Ranee cried out, "Flee from this place! That perfume always accompanies the magic of the Majii!"

Doc Savage's three aides hesitated. They had come this far, and did not wish to depart without learning something.

Then, abruptly, it was too late. Brown men, the tomb attendants and uniformed soldiers of the Nizam, came rushing into the vaulted room.

They were armed, but it must have been some superstitious belief on their part that to fire guns would desecrate the tomb, for they attacked with their bare hands, a procedure that might have been their waterloo, except that they greatly outnumbered those they sought to capture.

As it was, Monk, Ham and Long Tom cut loose with their supermachine pistols—they had been in the group of things returned by the Ranee—and filled the chamber with thunder and metallic capsules containing the chemical that produced senselessness.

Men yelled out. The mercy bullets stung a little when they struck. The machine pistols moaned by spurts, like angry animals. For a moment, the attackers were driven back, completely stopped.

Then there was another of the weird, frightening flash-bang combinations—and the weird figure of the Majii was suddenly standing in his gilt casket, which was now open.

The Majii was an imposing spectacle, especially as he leveled an arm at Monk and the others and held it there. Silence fell for some moments.

Then came the thunderous voice of the strange individual.

"You will become helpless!" boomed the Majii.

What happened then was quite the most astounding thing that ever occurred to Monk, Ham and Long Tom.

They became helpless!

Monk in particular fought vigorously to lift his arms, and getting no response, looked down at them in a futile anger. He tried to get his machine pistol up, tried with all of his will power. The arm moved all of an inch.

"Blazes!" Monk exploded.

Ham said in a strained voice, "This just *couldn't* happen!"

They felt no pain, no discomfort, except the cloying odor of the room in their nostrils. They could think clearly, could understand each other. But they could not make an offensive move.

Behind them, the Ranee choked, "I knew something horrible would happen if we came here. This is the tomb of the Majii."

The fantastic figure with the thundering voice boomed, "I am the Majii!"

Then the horde of brown men was upon them.

Chapter XVII
ALADDIN'S CAVERN

MONK and his companions were genuinely surprised when they were not killed instantly. But a shout from the Majii saved them, and they were bound securely.

After this, the soldiers were ordered to leave the domed chamber, and they did so, leaving only the regular tomb attendants.

Those who remained seemed quite familiar with the place, and what would come next, for they gathered up Monk, Ham, Long Tom and the Ranee and carried them over to where the Majii stood.

The Majii was not a very distinct figure in the eerie blue light. He leveled an arm at the Ranee.

"For what you have done tonight, you shall die," he boomed. "You have been important to me, and you could have been important in the future, and profited thereby, but you have forfeited that right."

The Ranee said nothing.

The Majii spoke in Jondorean, which Doc's three aides could not understand, and one of the tomb attendants moved forward, somewhat fearfully, and gave the vase of the blue light a gingerly rub.

There was the usual prompt flash and crash.

This time, no unexpected figures appeared. Instead, the floor a few yards distant split open—a slab seemed to have fallen out of it. The blue flame showed steps leading downward. They were well-worn steps.

The Majii led the way, and they descended into as remarkable a series of rooms as Monk had ever seen. It was not a cavern, in that it was probably part of the foundation for the big black block that was the tomb.

They first noticed that the rooms were of tremendous size. Then they perceived other things which interested them much more.

The chambers were storerooms. And they were filled almost to capacity.

Monk peered in amazement at the objects.

There were crated airplanes, dismantled, speedy fighting ships—the utmost in modernity, every one. There were guns—light, dangerous field pieces. There were rifles, machine guns, bayonets, small arms. And there were an incredible number of cases of ammunition.

"A regular arsenal," Monk gulped.

"You will not look at these things," the Majii commanded.

Monk was baffled, no little scared, when he now found himself unable to examine the objects stored in the stone rooms. It was an inexplicable feeling. He had never obeyed a command so completely before.

They came into a small chamber which was empty, except for two prisoners. Monk peered at these two, and recognized them.

Doc Savage and Kadir Lingh.

DOC SAVAGE, it was starkly evident, had gone through a process of torture. His marvelous body had not been damaged seriously, but he had been beaten, his skin cut and salt rubbed into the wounds, and he had been burned with irons, if the blisters were any indication.

Monk and the others were deposited roughly on the floor, after which the Majii swung over and stood before Doc Savage.

"You will now help Rama Tura!" he grated.

Doc Savage said, "You know what I want first."

The Majii bowed slightly.

"You want the release of your aides and the Ranee," he said. "It shall be done. You, yourself will remain here, a hostage, for a period of one year."

Doc Savage said nothing.

"I will go and have Rama Tura brought to you," boomed the Majii. "After you help him, your friends will be freed, and escorted to the border."

The Majii went out, and the tomb attendants accompanied him, closing a heavy iron door behind them.

Doc Savage was bound tightly. It was with difficulty that he managed to roll over and face Monk.

"Can you roll over here, Monk?" he demanded.

Monk put forth a tremendous effort, and hardly stirred.

"I can't, Doc," he groaned. "That guy put the jinx on me, or something."

"How about the rest of you?" Doc demanded.

The others were in the same predicament as Monk.

Doc Savage now began the laborious task of changing his position. It became apparent that he was almost exhausted physically by the torture he had undergone. He took all of three minutes in moving a dozen feet.

But he could now look into Monk's eyes.

"Monk!" he said sharply. "You are all right now."

He held Monk's small eyes for some moments, steadily. Then he repeated his words.

Monk blinked. He managed to sit up.

"Blazes!" he exploded. "You took the jinx off!"

"You were hypnotized," Doc said. "Roll over here and we will see if we can untie each other."

Monk hurriedly complied.

"Hypnotized!" he gulped. "Man, oh man! And I was really beginning to think that Majii was some kind of a miracle worker."

"He comes near being that," Doc said grimly. "He is a master of hypnotism."

Monk was working at the bindings.

"But guys have tried to hypnotize me before and didn't have any luck," he muttered. "Hypnosis won't work on anybody who don't want to be hypnotized."

"It was that aroma, that vapor in the air," Doc told him. "You always caught it before Rama Tura and the Majii performed their feats."

Monk said, "I don't see what that had to do with it."

"It is a drug in vapor form," Doc told him. "It affects the brain like—well, you have seen truth serum render a man incapable of thinking up lies. This stuff renders the brain incapable of resisting hypnotic suggestion."

Monk's stubby fingers were strong—he was able, when in form, to accomplish the feat of circus strong men, the bending of silver half dollars in his hands. He was getting the ropes off Doc's wrists now.

"Hypnotism!" he growled. "That explains a lot of things."

DOC SAVAGE shook off the ropes, and began to work on his own ankles, while Monk rolled to Long Tom.

"That jewel-making business," Monk demanded. "Was that hypnotism?"

"It is a wild story," Doc Savage said. "The Nizam, here, Kadir Lingh, has told me much of it."

The bronze man spoke rapidly as he freed himself.

"The Majii is trying to stir Jondore into an uprising against the British," he said. "He has a fanatical hatred of the British. To buy arms and ammunition, he took the wealth of the Nizam. But he dared not sell the jewels in open market, because it would have come to the attention of the British, so he recut them, or ground off the previous cuttings, and sent his lieutenant, Rama Tura, abroad to dispose of them. They chose the fake jewel-making séances as the method."

Doc got up, began untying Kadir Lingh. Long Tom was free, but unable to move, not yet having been brought out of the Majii's hypnotic spell.

"Rama Tura used the aromatic vaporized drug," Doc continued. "With it, he could hypnotize an entire crowd. Rama Tura is also a skilled hypnotist. The ability is not uncommon in this part of the Orient. Rama Tura's audiences simply believed they saw anything they were told they were seeing. You remember the men who took pictures of the jewel-making séances? They were killed because they had taken pictures that would show Rama Tura as a trickster."

"But what about the two hospital doctors who were killed in New York?" Monk demanded.

"Rama Tura got rid of everyone who might have an idea of what was back of his actions," Doc replied. "The two physicians, Rama Tura feared, might have learned something from the Ranee."

Everyone was untied now.

Doc Savage aroused Long Tom, Ham and the Ranee simply by telling them they were out from under the spell.

The Ranee gasped, "But I do not understand how you can revive us!"

"You are still hypnotized," Doc told them. "But this time, you are under my spell."

Ham added, for the Ranee's benefit, "Doc studied hypnotism himself. He spent some time in India doing it."

"Oh." She seemed slightly dazed. "But in New York, in Rama Tura's quarters, I saw a horrible monster of a thing—"

"A product of Rama Tura's hypnotic hold over you," Doc assured her. "That is one of the possibilities of advanced hypnotism—making the subjects see things which actually do not exist."

Monk growled, "I'll make this Majii see things that *do* exist when I get hold of 'im!"

"You had best stay away from him," Doc advised.

"Huh?"

"You are still under the effects of that drug," Doc announced. "Mere contact with the Majii's presence will put you back in his power."

"Whew!" Monk exploded. "This *is* a predicament!"

They moved toward the door.

Ham thought of something.

"Doc," he said rapidly. "What was that stuff about you doing something for Rama Tura?"

Doc Savage did a rare thing; he almost smiled.

"You recall when Rama Tura was playing the part of the white man, and my donkey jumped against his, and we both fell to the ground, and Rama Tura got up with a cut on his arm, which he thought had been made by my knife?" Doc asked.

"Sure," said Ham.

"The cut was really the mark of a hypo needle, the scratch of its sharp point," Doc explained. "The needle administered to Rama Tura a concoction which has caused him to become blind. They have failed to cure him. I happened to be able to do so, knowing what is wrong with him."

They reached the door.

"So you knew the white man was Rama Tura all the time!" Ham murmured.

"His disguise was not quite perfect enough to get by," Doc said grimly. "And it was necessary to do something to make those fellows want to keep us alive. Control of Rama Tura's eyesight did the trick."

They opened the door.

PANDEMONIUM let loose. The two guards were alert, and the fact that Doc Savage yelled in a perfect imitation of Rama Tura's voice that seemed to come from behind them, telling them not to fire, delayed them hardly at all.

Long Tom got a bullet through the shoulder. The noise of the shot really did more damage than the bullet itself, for it set off a bedlam of shouting all through the stone rooms.

"Place is alive with 'em!" Monk exploded.

"We'll try to make it out!" Doc barked.

The two guards were unconscious now. Monk appropriated one of their guns, Long Tom the other. They raced for the steps that led upward to the great-vaulted room.

"This place has been here a long time," Ham clipped, noting the depth to which the tread of feet had worn the stone steps.

"There is a rather remarkable story behind this place," Doc told him. "Tell you about it when we have time."

A squad of three tomb attendants appeared above, and there was a brief exchange of shots and a charge, after which the four were groaning on the floor, wounded, but not fatally, and Doc Savage was running somewhat unsteadily, due to a puncture in his left leg, above the knee. He said nothing of the wound, and the others did not notice in the excitement.

They gained the final steps which led up into the vaulted room.

Doc stopped. He pointed to an elaborate mechanism above.

"The device which opens that crack in the floor," he said. "You will notice over here, under the block of a coffin, there is another device, by which the Majii moved the embalmed body and got up through. The slab on which the body lies simply drops down."

Monk exploded, "We hardly got time for details—"

"Wait!" Doc rapped. "In behind somewhere, probably around that corner, must be the apparatus which discharges the vaporized drug into the domed chamber. We want that put out of commission."

Monk began, "I don't see—"

"We will come back here with soldiers faithful to Kadir Lingh," Doc said. "We want to raid the place without danger from that stuff."

The bronze man started forward. His wounded leg was giving him weakness and agony, and try though he would not to show it, he weaved slightly.

"Doc!" Monk exploded. "You've been shot."

Doc said, "That vapor apparatus must be—"

"I'll get it," Monk barked. "I know enough chemistry to recognize the thing when I see it."

Ham and Long Tom took the two rifles and dashed up into the domed room.

Monk ran in search of the device which dispensed the potent vapor that rendered the minds of victims susceptible to bulldozing by others—which was what it amounted to.

Doc Savage, the Ranee and Kadir Lingh awaited Monk's return. They could not have stood there more than seconds, but it seemed an age.

Then Monk came galloping back.

"Found it!" he squeaked.

Doc began, "Did you—"

"I sure did," Monk grinned. "That thing won't work again for a long time! But we gotta blow!"

They "blew." Up the stairs, into the domed room, which was, to their infinite relief, empty, and across that into the passage that led to the outer darkness. Or perhaps it was dawn now.

They were shot at when they appeared in the round door.

HAM and Long Tom threw themselves flat to return the fire, which was coming from three riflemen in the boulders outside, near the edge of the eminence upon which the black tomb stood. The riflemen, vastly surprised, retreated to the trail and down it to what was evidently a more secure entrenchment.

Doc and his party raced into the boulders—and found themselves stuck there. No other trail, explained Kadir Lingh, led down from the tomb. And the riflemen had blocked this one thoroughly.

They did the only thing left for them to do. They waited.

Back in the tomb, there was a guttural roaring. That would be the pursuit. Before long, it would learn they had gotten out of the tomb, and would converge upon them.

Doc crept to the trail lip, and down it, carrying in his hands two large stones. He had the idea of dislodging the riflemen, but that proved futile, for there was an open stretch in front of them, on which moonlight shone quite brilliantly.

Doc threw the stones, and drew lead unpleasantly close, then crept back to the others. He told them how it stood.

Monk suggested, "Maybe I can get down the cliff. I'll try it, anyhow, because it's our—"

"Wait," Doc said abruptly. "Listen!"

They listened, and heard nothing—which was the important point.

"That noise inside!" Monk barked. "It's stopped. Them guys are quiet."

Doc held brief silence, during which his trilling, small and eerie in the moonlight, was audible.

"Monk!" he said sharply.

"Yeah," said Monk, who was preparing to try the cliff descent.

"That vaporizing drug, unless carefully administered, will undoubtedly cause death," the bronze man explained. "That is the way of most substances as strong as it must be. If a quantity of it were released at once, it would probably kill all of those in the tomb."

"Um-m," Monk muttered.

"What did you do when you found the containers of the stuff and the apparatus for putting small amounts of it into the domed room?" Doc asked.

"Why," Monk said, "I just busted the jars and let the dope spill out on the floor."

"You undoubtedly killed them all," Doc said grimly.

"Uh-huh." Monk did not manage to sound very sorry. "You gotta admit it was kind of an accident, though."

Chapter XVIII
THE DEAD MAJII

JUST what had happened inside the tomb was something they evinced no desire to learn immediately, after Doc Savage explained that it would probably take hours for the vapor to drift out.

In the meantime, they sniped with the riflemen

on the trail below, and, although they could not get down, neither could any foes come up.

The sun came up in a blaze of blood-red light that was remindful of the events of the night, and from bitter cold, the air turned unpleasantly hot.

"We will go in now," Doc Savage announced. "At least, we can smell the stuff if it is still there."

Long Tom and Ham were left with the rifles to hold the trail. Doc, Monk, Kadir Lingh and the Ranee entered the tomb of the Majii.

And tomb it was, for it had been constructed for death, and it held nothing but death. Some of the Majii's men had almost reached the outer air, for there were bodies along the passage, numbers of them in the vaulted room, and the others below. Even Monk, who really held some bloodthirsty ideas where enemies such as these were concerned, was appalled somewhat.

"Tough I had to have that accident," he mumbled.

The Majii and Rama Tura had been together in life; so were they together in death, lying with no more than the length of an arm between their bodies.

The Ranee got in front of the body of the Majii.

"It is better that you do not know," she said wildly.

Doc Savage spoke to her gently.

"Kadir Lingh has already told me," he said. "And my men will not talk where it would be better if they kept still. The world will know nothing of this, other than what it already knows."

The Ranee seemed to think that over. Then she stood aside.

Monk stepped close to the Majii, bent and removed the golden tint on the dead man's skin. It was not gold leaf, but gilt grease paint, and it came off with some rubbing.

Monk squinted at the visage of the Majii. He scratched his nubbin of a head.

"Huh!" he grunted. "This guy is the fake Nizam who tried to put up a job on us in New York."

Kadir Lingh spoke up suddenly.

"It is the same man who tried to trap you in New York," he agreed. "But do not call him the fake Nizam. He was the *real* Nizam of Jondore."

Monk had the expression of a man trying to swallow a pill too big for his throat.

"But *you* are the Nizam," he said.

Kadir Lingh shook his head. "I was not as long as that man lived."

"Listen, fellow," Monk told him. "You're making me dizzy."

"That man," Kadir Lingh pointed at the dead Majii, "was my half brother, the Nizam of Jondore whom the world thought had died, but who did not die."

Monk's mouth fell open. Without closing it, he said, "I begin to get it."

"My half brother hated the English, who really control Jondore, because we must have their permission before making any important move," said Kadir Lingh. "He wanted to revolt against the English. But they watched him. He needed money to buy arms, and, although he was the richest man in the world, he could do nothing, because the British made him account for his wealth, knowing very well what he wanted to do. So he hit on the very brilliant plan—"

"Of faking his death and stealing his own fortune and converting it for revolt money," Monk finished. "I see it, all right."

Doc Savage moved away, leaving Kadir Lingh and the Ranee explaining that they had given in for a time to the wishes of the dead man because of various reasons—he was the Ranee's husband, whom she had thought for a time that she still loved, and because the custom of the Orient decrees that a wife shall always subjugate herself to her husband.

Kadir Lingh had his reasons also, and he had made the mistake of trusting his half brother's word. In Doc Savage's New York headquarters, when Kadir Lingh had come upon his half brother a prisoner in Doc's secret laboratory room, the half brother had promised to drop the whole thing if Kadir Lingh would get him back to Jondore. He had not kept his word.

All of that, Doc had heard before, from the lips of Kadir Lingh, while they were both prisoners of the Majii. It was not pleasant listening, and he cared for no second telling.

He could hear occasional shots as Ham and Long Tom held the trail.

Doc hurried down to the rooms in which the arms were stored and broke open a box, stirring up grayish dust on the floor in the process. The stuff settled on his hands, a grayish film.

It might have been an omen, that gray dust. That, and the sound of distant shots.

As omens, they pointed to the next mystery which was to involve Doc Savage and his aides, an adventure that was to take them into one of the least known and most incredible sections of South America. A region in which war, modern, bloody, had raged for years almost unknown to the world.

But that was a war between nations. The war which Doc Savage was to wage was against an unknown horror, a fantastic thing which preyed upon both warring enemies—and upon those whom Doc Savage knew, his friends. And always was the work of this horror marked in a way that was unmistakable—upon the bodies of the victims was always a gray dust.

Where that gray dust of death came from, no one knew. What it was—that was a problem that led Doc Savage, in its solving, face to face with things such as he had never dreamed existed.

DOC SAVAGE carried a light machine gun and ammunition out to the edge of the trail, and they set it up, fed the belt into the block, and let loose a burst.

Results were much more than they had hoped for. The riflemen fled—whether from fear, or because their ammunition was low was unimportant.

It became evident that, with the aid of the arms from the tomb, they would be able to fight their way to the capital city, where help from reliable soldiers was certain.

Monk contemplated the black tomb of the Majii before they started down the trail.

"Doc," he said. "You made a crack about there being a remarkable story behind this place. What is it?"

"The theory came from Kadir Lingh," Doc said.

"Yeah?" Monk looked interested. "What is it?"

"Remember the story of Aladdin and the Lamp," Doc asked. "Aladdin rubbed the lamp and a genie appeared and opened a treasure cave."

Monk said, "But what's that—" and thought of something and did not finish.

"This tomb of the Majii and its contents are centuries old," Doc reminded. "Much older than the story of Aladdin and the Lamp. This ancient Majii, ruler of Jondore, is said to have been able to rub that big lamp in the tomb and cause a treasure cave to open."

"Sure!" Monk exploded. "It was hocus-pocus! That stuff in this tomb *did* look old—the mechanism, I mean. And the rooms underneath might be called a cave."

"Kadir Lingh feels sure this is the real cave of Aladdin," Doc said.

"We might have trouble proving it," Monk said.

He scratched his nubbin head.

"Let the dang genie have Aladdin's cave!" he finished.

THE END

Coming in DOC SAVAGE Volume 10:

After Long Tom is arrested on spying charges, Doc Savage intervenes in an Amazon border war and battles the mysterious Inca in Gray in

DUST OF DEATH

An unusual story of high adventure, danger, politics and deadly peril—and of Doc Savage and his intrepid companions in adventure.

Then, what could freeze men in the middle of summer? There was no ice; no freezing machinery; yet men were frozen into solid rock. The Man of Bronze and his Iron Crew journey to the Arizona Badlands and discover a lost race and a strange mist that can transform a human being into

THE STONE MAN

What is the strange mystery that so baffles everyone, and requires all the skills and abilities of Doc Savage and his brain trust?

Don't miss these two thrill-packed novels in DOC SAVAGE #10!

INTERMISSION by Will Murray

The Shadow's Walter Gibson once remarked that Street & Smith had a way of taking a classic like *Lorna Doone* and turning it into a Western.

Our lead story in this Doc Savage volume owes its premise, if not its plot, to a famous tale out of *The Thousand and One Nights*. The reader has to read deep into *The Majii* before he realizes that Lester Dent had backed Doc Savage into a modern retelling of the tale of Aladdin's Lamp.

Although nominally set in China, the original story of Aladdin actually took place in some Muslim never-never land, analogous to Dent's mythical Jondore.

"Aladdin and the Wonderful Lamp" is the fable of a Chinese tailor's lazy son who is tricked by a Moroccan magician to retrieve a magic lamp from a cave. There, he finds not only the rusty lamp, but jewels growing on trees. Refusing to surrender the lamp, Aladdin is locked in the cavern, entombed until he decides to rub a magic ring given him by the wicked magician as a protective talisman. A spirit thus summoned restores him to the surface. Later, he discovers that the old lamp contains a powerful wish-granting jinni.

Lester Dent wove key elements of this tale into the fabric of *The Majii*. In fact, it was written under the working title of "Genie." But at the end of *The Roar Devil,* he blurbed it under a very different title:

> Doc Savage did not, of course, know of the shadow that even now loomed over his New York headquarters—a shadow that had stretched all the way from the far-off Orient—*The Shadow of the Crescent.* Nor did he know, not being a mind reader, that…he was to be plunged too swiftly into a swirl of terror and death and intrigue that haunted *The Shadow of the Crescent.*
>
> Out of the Orient came he who was a servant of *The Shadow of the Crescent.* He was a strange being, this servant, a being who wrought horror and wonders that men said were impossible. His word was death, and with his alchemy he could do the incredible. He took a piece of worthless glass, and before the eyes of the greatest chemists in the world, turned it into a diamond worth a quarter of a million, American money.
>
> And he was only a servant of the master of knowledge.
>
> Strange, impossible things happened to Doc Savage and his aides when fate pitted them against *The Shadow of the Crescent.* For they fought a creature such as they had never dreamed existed.

The Majii was written during the hectic spring of 1935, when Dent was under great pressure to step up his Doc output. Street & Smith hoped to publish *Doc Savage Magazine* twice a month in the Fall. Dent was in the Caribbean, seeking lost treasure. S&S wanted him in New York, writing with a top speed.

Under pressure, Dent would start one novel, hit a plot snag and, in frustration, move on to another. As Walter Gibson explained: "Les Dent wrote a very breezy outline because his stories weren't as complex. But he would bring in different things that would happen. Every now and then he'd find himself out on a limb; something that he'd figured on wasn't jelling well enough. So Les used to have his troubles in the middle of the story…"

While in Florida, Dent started *The Quest of Qui,* got hung up, and moved on to *Spook Hole,* then *The Roar Devil.* Next, he tackled *The Majii* and hit a snag there as well. So he put this story aside and returned to finish *The Quest of Qui* instead. When Lester blurbed it again at the end of that story, its final title was in place:

> The Majii, men said, was living again. The most hideous creature of history, a being whose powers were beyond the human, was this Majii. He had done things so incredible that historians had refused to chronicle, designating the deeds as too much for sane belief.
>
> The Majii had been in his tomb a dozen centuries. The historians were sure of that, even if they did not credit the legends of his horror and his power.
>
> Which explains why the appearance of the Majii in America was not taken seriously—until uncanny things began to happen—and Doc Savage became involved.
>
> Monk, at first, thought the Majii was a clever fakir.
>
> "That guy," he goaded Ham, "might make you a swell valet."
>
> Monk was to regret that crack.

Dent finally gave in to his editor's demand that he return to New York in April. He departed Miami at month's end, just after finishing *The Majii.*

There's a mystery surrounding the exact authorship of *The Majii.* Certainly Lester Dent penned the final draft. But his manuscript includes a surviving page of an alternate ending that doesn't quite read like his work. Suspects range from his secretary at that time, Tulsan Martin E. Baker, whom Dent was grooming to be a Doc Savage writer, to seasoned pulp veteran J. Allan Dunn, with whom Dent was friendly.

The Majii outline does not survive, so we have no insights into Dent's plans for this story. But for a locale, Dent selected the now defunct princely state of Hyderabad, ruled in 1935 by the potentate popularly called "The Richest Man in the World," Lieutenant General His Exalted Highness Sir Mir Osman Ali Khan, the Nizam of Hyderabad and Berar.

Dent kept the title and changed his name, of course. He turned Hyderabad into Jondore, and took other liberties. For example, the true Nizam had never set foot outside of India by the time of his silver jubilee in 1937. He was the last of a long line of Nizams, his reign ending after India achieved independance from Great Britain after World War II. Historically, Hyderabad was a part of India.

The black cube Dent calls the Tomb of the Majii appeared to have been modeled after the Kaaba at Mecca. The Kaaba is a cube-shaped granite building housing the so-called Black Stone, thought to be a meteor fragment. Muslims revere the Kaaba, which is their destination during the annual pilgrimage called the Hadj. Dent obviously juggled the details to arrive at his conception as well.

The Majii also owes a debt to Walter Gibson's pioneering work in *The Shadow.* Going back to the 1932 Shadow novel *The Ghost Makers,* Gibson periodically pitted the Dark Avenger against fraudulent spiritualists, whose tricks the writer was very familiar with as an expert in stage magic and illusion. *The Majii* borrows this Gibsonian premise and takes it further than The Shadow's reconteur ever dreamed of going. But then the Man of Bronze operated on a far broader scale than did the Master of Darkness.

Our second story unquestionably was inspired by a Shadow novel *The Veiled Prophet.* This was another variation on the fraudulent mystical cult racket that flourished in the Roaring Twenties and to a lesser degree in the Depression era. It was published in 1940, and in plotting *The Golden Man,* Dent specifically referenced the Shadow tale, marking one of the few recorded examples of a direct synergy between the two great Street & Smith series.

Not referenced, but probably influencing this story, was the so-called Sleeping Prophet of Virginia Beach, Edgar Cayce. Dent had an interest in ESP, and may have borrowed Cayce's trait of going into sleep trances while doing his readings in depicting the Golden Man. Beyond that, the story seems to parallel in strange ways the unexplained flight of Nazi Deputy Fuhrer Rudolph Hess in May 1941, on a unauthorized peace mission to Scotland. But to say more would spoil the story. *The Golden Man* appeared in the April, 1941 issue of *Doc Savage.*

Dent turned in *The Golden Man* under the title "The Wizard." It was almost certainly retitled because Street & Smith was gearing up to publish a new magazine called *The Wizard. The Golden Man* was a more appropriate title anyway. The action takes place on the eve of America's entry

Lester Dent

into World War II, and reflects Dent's pacifistic leanings as various forces attempted to draw the US into the global conflict. All that changed with Pearl Harbor, as it did for most Americans.

In keeping with Street & Smith policy, the warring nations are not explicitly named. Written in the summer of 1940, during the bloody period when German U-boats were harassing Atlantic shipping, *The Golden Man* captures the unsettling period immediately after France and the Low Countries fell to the Nazis, and many feared lone holdout England would ultimately lose the war.

Stylistically, *The Golden Man* differs from *The Majii*. It was one of the first wherein Dent shifted to a less pulpy writing style. For a new trend was sweeping the pulp field. As Robert Turner explained in his autobiography *Some of My Best Friends are Writers... But I Wouldn't Want My Daughter to Marry One:*

> The trend was away from the fast-paced, hard-boiled, action-for-action's sake type of thing and was leaning more and more toward better characterization, less pulpy writing, and more emotional impact, involving real people in crime rather than the stock private investigators, although these were still in demand if they had something special to distinguish them.

Competition from comic books and other media forced the pulps to grow up just a little bit. The hardboiled objective approach, as practiced by Dashiell Hammett, was out. A more subjective storytelling tone came into vogue. As a fan of Hammett, Dent preferred the objective approach, which writer Steve Fisher once described this way: "You *saw* what happened from the outside but were never permitted inside a fictional character." Now Dent had to retool.

The trend had started in *Black Mask* shortly after Dent stopped writing for it in 1936. But disintegrating pulp sales in 1940 prompted the entire field to adopt it. In *Doc Savage,* Dent dropped his trademark exaggerated characterizations in favor of realistic depictions of people and places. His writing smoothed out, reflecting a different tone.

While *The Golden Man* marks a slow maturing on the part of the themes explored in the pages of *Doc Savage,* it's famous among Doc readers due to the glimpse it gives into his mysterious origins.

The Andros Island mentioned in Chapter XIII is almost certainly the big barrier island in the Bahamas. But it must be noted that there is another Andros Island, in the Agean Sea near Greece. What personal significance the Atlantic Andros Island had to Lester Dent is unknown. It's not mentioned in the logs of Dent's schooner *Albatross.*

James Bama's cover for Bantam's 1971 reprint of *The Majii*.

The largest of the Bahamas group, Andros even today is not much of a tourist destination. Presumably, Dent visited it during his Caribbean days, and selected it storywise for its isolation.

Lastly, *The Golden Man* fell victim to the overzealous Street & Smith copy editor named Morris Ogden Jones who cut any fat from a Doc story he could find. In this one, he excised Doc Savage's signature trilling from two key scenes, as well as the ending. Through the courtesy of the Norma Dent Estate, we've restored those passages for this edition, and in our next issue we will be presenting the 1935 Doc Savage story *Dust of Death,* uncut for the first time ever.

Will Murray is the literary agent for the Estate of Lester Dent, and collaborated posthumously with the Man of Bronze's principal writer on eight Doc Savage *novels, including* Python Isle, The Jade Ogre, Flight Into Fear *and* The Forgotten Realm.

BATMAN'S SHADOWY ORIGIN!

"With this astonishing discovery, Anthony Tollin and Will Murray have REWRITTEN the history of BATMAN!" – ROY THOMAS

"This is one of the most important DISCOVERIES ever made on BATMAN'S creation!" –TONY ISABELLA

$12.95

THE Shadow
by Maxwell Grant

Who is LINGO?

plus the novel that inspired BATMAN!
PARTNERS OF PERIL
Foreword by JOKER creator Jerry Robinson

On Sale Now!

"My first [BATMAN] script was a take-off on a Shadow story." — BILL FINGER

Now reprinted for the first time ever!

THE SHADOW NOVEL THAT BECAME THE FIRST BATMAN STORY

THE SHADOW #9

The Golden Man

A Complete Book-length Novel

by KENNETH ROBESON

Who was this man who said the sea was his mother and the night his father and who could tell to the minute when vessels would be submarined? Doc Savage and his aides had to find out fast—and stop the march of tragedy!

Chapter I
THE SUPERNATURAL

It began on the American passenger steamer *Virginia Dare,* while the vessel was en route from Portugal to New York with a load of war refugees. It was at night.

Mr. Sam Gallehue, in spite of the full-bodied Irish of his name, his West Tulsa, Oklahoma, birthplace, his American passport, was really quite English. Quite.

Referring to the incidents of that night, "Disturbing," Sam Gallehue said. "Disturbing—Yes, definitely."

But *disturbing* was hardly a strong enough word.

DOC SAVAGE AND HIS AIDES

Doc Savage—Clark, Jr.—is beyond question one of the most outstanding personalities in the world today. He travels from one end of the world to the other, righting wrongs, helping the oppressed, giving good guys the break, always, but never taking a life, if there's any other way out. Doc's "college," for instance, is a scientific institution in upper New York where he sends all captured crooks, who, through expert treatment, and sometimes involved operations—for Doc Savage is one of the world's most skilled surgeons—are made to forget all about their vicious past and start life anew useful and decent citizens. Doc's companions couldn't be better if they'd been made to order. HAM—Brigadier General Theodore Marley Brooks, the shrewdest lawyer Harvard ever turned out, a faultless dresser, and an efficient fighter with his unusual drug-tipped sword cane. MONK—Lieutenant Colonel Andrew Blodgett Mayfair, one of the world's foremost chemists, and tougher than tough in a scrap. RENNY—Colonel John Renwick, at the top of the engineering profession. LONG TOM—Major Thomas J. Roberts, a veritable wizard in the field of electricity. JOHNNY—William Harper Littlejohn, renowned geologist and archeologist. They're the perfect group of altruistic adventurers. You'll never meet their like again!

Lieutenant Colonel Andrew Blodgett Monk Mayfair had a word—several words, in fact. But his words were not from Sunday school, or from any respectable dictionary, although expressive. Unfortunately, they were not printable.

Brigadier General Theodore Marley Ham Brooks had no word whatever—the thing left him speechless. Ham Brooks was a noted lawyer who could talk a jury out of its eyeteeth, and it took a lot to make him speechless. But, as everyone admitted, what happened that night was a lot.

First, there was the star.

It was a clear night and the usual number of ordinary stars were visible—the Encyclopedia Britannica states the unaided human eye can see about six thousand stars on a clear night—in the crystal dome of a tropical heavens. The sea, with no more waves than a mirror, was darkly royal-blue, except where now and then a porpoise or a shark broke surface and caused a momentary eruption of phosphorescence that was like spilling sparks.

As to who first saw the star, there was some question whether that honor fell to Ham Brooks or Monk Mayfair.

Both these men were standing on the starboard boat deck, where there was a nice breeze. It was a hot night; it had been hot since the *Virginia Dare* had left Portugal, and Monk and Ham—so had everyone else, too—had grumbled extensively about the heat, although there were scores of Americans on the ship who should have been overjoyed to be there instead of in Europe, dodging bombs, bullets and blitzkriegs.

The truth was: Monk and Ham were irked because they were leaving Europe by request. Not at the request of anybody in Europe; they would have ignored such urging. The request had come from Doc Savage, who was their chief, and who meant what he said.

The mess in Europe had looked enticing—Monk and Ham liked excitement the way bears like honey—and they had slipped off with the idea of getting their feet wet. Doc Savage had cabled them to come back—quick—before they got in trouble.

"Trouble!" Monk snorted. "Compared to the kind of things Doc gets mixed up in, Europe is peaceful. Hey, look!"

"Look at what?" Ham asked.

"Over there." Monk pointed out over the sea.

THEY could see the star plainly. It was not a star in the sense of being a planet or a heavenly body twinkling far off in outer space. This was an actual star; a five-cornered one.

The star was black. In the dark night—this fact was a little confusing to newspaper reporters later—the star could be readily distinguished in spite of its blackness. This black star could be seen in the black sky because, around its edges, and particularly at its five tips, it had a definitely reddish, luminous complexion. As Monk expressed it later—Monk's descriptions were inclined to be grisly—the star looked somewhat as if it had been dipped in red blood. The star was high and far away in the night sky.

"Hey, you on the bridge!" Monk yelled. "Hey, whoever's on watch!"

Monk's speaking voice was the small, ludicrous tone of a child, but when he turned loose a yell, the seagulls got scared a mile away. An officer put his head over the bridge railing.

"What the blankety-blank goes on?" the officer asked. "Don't you know people are trying to sleep on this boat? You'll wake up the whole ship."

"Look at that star!" Monk said. "What the dickens is it?"

The officer stared, finally said he would be damned if that wasn't a funny-looking thing, and pointed a pair of strong night glasses—the night glasses being binoculars with an extraordinary amount of luminosity—at the star. He handed the glasses to Monk, then Ham. The consensus was that they didn't know what the thing might be. Something strange, though.

The steamer *Virginia Dare* was commanded by Captain Harley Kirman, a seaman of the modern school, with looks, dress and manners of a man behind a desk in an insurance office, although he loved his ship, as much as any cussing, barnacle-coated bully of the old windjammer school.

Captain Kirman was summoned from a game of contract bridge. Another participant in the card game, a Mr. Sam Gallehue, accompanied the skipper when he reached the bridge.

The captain stared at the star. He unlimbered a telescope as large as a cannon—inherited from his seafaring grandfather, he explained—and peered through that. He took off his hat and scratched his bald spot. The bald spot was crossed from right front to left rear by a scar, that was a souvenir of a World War mine. Captain Kirman's bald-spot scar always itched when he got excited.

"Change course to west, quarter south," Captain Kirman ordered. "We'll have a look."

Monk propped elbows on the bridge rail and contemplated the five-pointed thing in the sky.

"What do you suppose it is?"

Ham shrugged. "Search me. Never saw anything like it before."

MONK MAYFAIR was a short man, and wide. His long arms—his hands dangled to his knees—were covered with a growth of what appeared to be rusty shingle nails. His mouth had a startling size, the corners terminating against his tufted ears; his eyes were small and twinkling, and his nose was a mistreated ruin. The narrowness of his forehead conveyed the impression there was not room for a spoonful of brains, which was deceptive, since he was one of the world's leading industrial chemists. In general, his appearance was something to scare babies.

Ham Brooks has good shoulders, medium height, a wide, orator's mouth in a not unhandsome face. His clothing was sartorial perfection; in addition to being one of New York's best lawyers, he was its best-dressed man. He carried an innocent-looking dark cane which was a sword cane, tipped with a chemical that could produce quick unconsciousness.

They watched the star.

"Blazes!" Monk said suddenly. "Look at the ocean. Right under that thing!"

Mr. Sam Gallehue hurried over to stand beside them. Gallehue was a lean man with some slight roundness in his shoulders that was either a habitual stoop or a sign of unusual muscular strength. His face was long, his jaw prominent, a combination which expressed sadness.

Mr. Sam Gallehue wore his usual ingratiating smile. He was a man who invariably agreed with anything and everything anyone said. If anyone should state the ship was sailing upside down, Mr. Gallehue would agree profusely in a phony English accent.

"That's puzzling," Monk said.

"Yes, puzzling, definitely," agreed Mr. Gallehue. "Very puzzling. You're right. Very puzzling."

They meant the sea. It had become—the phenomenon was confined to one spot directly beneath the luminous-rimmed black star—filled with a fiery brilliance that was astounding, because it could hardly be the natural phosphorescence of the sea. Phosphorescence like a multitude of sparks pouring through the water in momentary existence was visible here and there, but this was different. It was not like sparks, but a steady luminance, quite bright.

"It covers," Ham decided aloud, "less than an acre."

"Yes, you're right," agreed Mr. Sam Gallehue. "Less than an acre. Exactly."

The steamer plowed through the dark sea, with the only sounds the faint steady rushing of water cut by the bows, and tendrils of music amidships that escaped from the first-class lounge where there was dancing. But on the bridge there was breathless quiet, expectancy, and eyes strained ahead. The luminous area was still on the sea, the black star steady in the sky.

The lookout in the crow's-nest gave a cry.

"Man swimming!" the lookout yelled. "Off the starboard bow. Middle of that glowing patch of water. Man swimming!"

Captain Kirman leveled his granddad of a telescope and stared for a while. Then he scratched his bald-spot scar.

"What's wrong?" Monk asked.

Wordlessly, Captain Kirman passed the big telescope. Monk discovered that the instrument was one of the most efficient he had ever used.

The crow's-nest lookout had been wrong on one point—the man in the sea was not swimming. The man lay perfectly still. On his back, with arms and legs outflung. He was a large, golden man. There was something unusual about him, a quality distinguishable even from that distance— something about him that was hard to define, yet definite. He was not unconscious, but merely floating there.

Monk lowered the telescope.

"Well?" demanded Ham impatiently.

"It's kind of indecent," Monk explained. "He ain't got on a darned stitch!"

THE *Virginia Dare* lowered a lifeboat with speed which demonstrated the efficiency of modern davit machinery. Captain Kirman dashed into his cabin and came back with a blanket and a pair of trousers. "Put the pants on him before you bring him in," he said.

The modern steel lifeboat had a motor which, gobbling like a turkey, drove the craft across the sea into the luminous area, and, guided by searchlights that stuck straight white whiskers from the liner bridge, reached the floating golden man.

The bright area in the sea slowly gathered itself around the lifeboat. A phenomenon so startling that Monk and Ham stared at each other, blinked, then peered at the sea again. "D' you see what I do?" Monk demanded.

"The phosphorescence is gathering around the lifeboat," Ham said.

"Yeah. Only I don't think it's phosphorescence. The stuff glows too steadily, and the color ain't like phosphorescence."

They stared, dumbfounded as the glowing patch in the sea followed the lifeboat to the steamer. When some fifty or sixty yards separated the lifeboat and ship, the luminous area rapidly left the smaller craft and surrounded the liner. The *Virginia Dare* was much larger, and the glowing mass spread out thinly to entirely surround the vessel.

Monk grunted suddenly. "Where's a bucket, a rope, and a jug?"

Ham said, "I know where there's a jug. I'll get it. You find the rope and the bucket."

The dapper lawyer secured from the bar a clear glass jug which had contained foundation syrup for a soft drink. He rinsed it hurriedly.

They hauled up a bucket of sea water, poured it into the jug, and inserted a cork.

"I swear I never saw water shine like that before," Monk declared. "I'm gonna analyze it."

Ham held the jug up to the light. He shook it briskly, and the water charged back and forth against the glass with bubble-filled fury.

"Kinda spooky," Ham said in an awed voice.

Monk carried the jug to a darkened part of the deck, and held a hand close to it. His palm was bathed in reflected magenta radiance.

"What *is* that stuff?" Ham asked.

"I'll have to analyze it," Monk said. He sounded puzzled.

HAM rubbed his jaw, his expression thoughtful. "You ever hear of ectoplasm?" he asked.

"Eh?"

"Ectoplasm," Ham said. "The stuff spiritualists and mediums talk about. When they perform, or pretend to perform, the feat known as telekinesis, or locomotion of objects at a distance—such as making a table lift, or causing rappings on a table—they claim the phenomenon is the work of ectoplasm."

"Hey, wait a minute," Monk said. "What're you talking about?"

"Ectoplasm. E-c-t-o-p-l-a-s-m, like in a ghost. It is supposed to be a material of living or protoplasmic nature, drawn either from the medium or from some other presence, which is independently manipulated after being drawn."

Monk considered this.

"Nuts!" he said finally.

Ham shrugged. "Ectoplasmic material is supposed to be manipulated or controlled through an etheric connecting link, so that a tremor or vibration in the ether, such as a light wave which normally excites the retina of the eye, is detrimental to its activity."

"Where the hell'd you get that stuff?"

"Out of an encyclopedia one time."

Monk snorted. "Oh, be reasonable. This stuff is just something in the water that happens to glow."

"Then what made it follow the lifeboat?"

"I don't know."

"The golden man was in the lifeboat. It followed *him.*"

"Huh?"

"And, when the golden man was taken aboard the steamer, why did it surround the bigger ship?"

Monk peered at the jug of luminous water with a mixture of emotion. "I got half a notion to throw this overboard and get rid of the whole mystery."

Ham strode out on the open deck and looked upward, craning his neck.

"That black star is gone," he announced.

Chapter II
THINGS TO WONDER ABOUT

THE rescued golden man had been taken to the ship's hospital. Monk and Ham accompanied Captain Kirman to the hospital, and the agreeable Mr. Sam Gallehue brought up the rear, being stickily polite whenever they gave him a chance.

Monk carried the jug of luminous water under his arm until he passed his cabin, where he paused to deposit the jug on the table. After he had left the jug, Monk hurried forward and touched Ham's elbow.

"Hey, what got you started on that talk about ectoplasm?" he wanted to know.

"It just occurred to me," Ham said.

"But that's spook stuff."

"Sure."

"There ain't no such animals as spooks."

"You'll find a lot of people," Ham said, "that will argue there is such a thing as spiritualism."

"Yeah," Monk agreed. "And you'll find in the United States about five hundred institutions for treating insane people."

The hospital was situated in the midships section of the liner on B deck. They found the officer who had been in charge of the lifeboat standing outside the hospital door, which was closed.

Captain Kirman asked the officer, "Was he conscious when you picked him up?"

"Yes, indeed, sir."

"Was he injured in any way?"

"He did not appear to be."

"Who is he?"

The officer looked somewhat queer. "He said that he did not have a name."

Captain Kirman frowned. "That's a strange thing for him to say."

"I know, sir. And that wasn't the strangest thing he said, either. He said his name might be a problem, because parents usually named their children, but, since the sea was his mother and the night was his father, and neither parent could talk, getting him named might be a problem."

Captain Kirman scowled. "Are you drunk, mister?"

The officer smiled. "It did not make sense to me, either."

CAPTAIN KIRMAN rubbed his scar, chewed his lower lip in exasperation, and finally knocked on the hospital door, which was opened by a genial gentleman—he was looking bewildered just now—who was the ship's doctor.

"How is he, John?" Captain Kirman asked.

The doctor looked at Captain Kirman steadily for almost a minute. "What *is* this?" he asked finally. "A rib?"

"Eh?" Captain Kirman was surprised.

"This man your sailor just hauled out of the ocean." The doctor jerked a thumb over his shoulder at the hospital door.

"What about him?" Captain Kirman asked.

"He looked me in the eye," the doctor growled, "and he said, 'How are you, John Parson? I believe you will enjoy living in that little villa in Maderia. It is very peaceful there.'"

"Oh," said Captain Kirman. "An old friend of yours, is he?"

The surgeon swallowed.

"No."

Captain Kirman peered sharply at the doctor. "Hey, wait a minute! *You don't know him?*"

"Never saw him before in my life. So help me!"

"But you just said he called you by name."

"That's exactly what I did just say."

"But—"

"And that isn't the half of it," added the doctor. "You heard me say he mentioned that villa in Maderia."

"What about the villa?"

"Nobody on this green earth but myself and the man who owns the villa knows I have been dickering to buy it. And here is something else! *I don't know myself whether I have bought it yet.* The man had to talk to his daughter about selling, and she was going to visit him last week, and he was going to cable me in New York, and the cable would cinch the deal."

Captain Kirman's laugh was a humorless spurt of breath past his teeth. "And you never saw this man we rescued before?"

"Never."

"Somebody around here must be crazy."

Monk Mayfair had been taking in the conversation so earnestly that he had his head cocked to one side. Now he interrupted. "Dr. Parsons," he said. "I'm Mr. Mayfair—Monk Mayfair."

"Yes. I've heard of you." Dr. Parsons smiled. "But I'll confess I've heard more about the man with whom you are associated—Clark Savage, Jr. Or Doc Savage, as he's better known. I've always hoped I would someday meet him. I've seen him demonstrate surgery."

Monk said, "Let's try something, just for fun, doctor."

"What do you mean?" Dr. Parsons asked.

"Just for fun," Monk said, "let's send a radiogram to that man you were going to buy the villa from. Ask him if he really sold it to you."

The ship's physician gave Monk a queer look. "So you've sensed it, too."

"Sensed what?"

"That this man we rescued tonight may not be—well, may be different from other men, somehow."

Monk said, "I haven't even seen the guy, except through a telescope. What do you mean—different?"

The physician examined his fingernails for a moment.

"You know, I think I'll take you up. I'll send that radiogram about the villa," he said.

Captain Kirman snorted, shoved open the hospital door, and entered. Monk was about to follow the skipper when Ham tapped the homely chemist on the shoulder. Monk turned. Ham said, "Aren't you the guy who was sneering at spiritualism a while ago? Now you want radiograms sent."

"I just want to satisfy my curiosity," Monk explained sheepishly.

"You saw the golden man through the telescope," Ham said. "Have you ever seen him before?"

"I'm sure I haven't," Monk declared.

"What if he knows all about *us,* too?"

"Don't be silly," Monk said, somewhat uneasily.

THEY entered the hospital, a white room with square windows, modern fluorescent lighting, and neat equipment which included a nurse who was eye-filling.

The golden man lay on the white sheets on a chrome-and-white examination table. He was not as large as Monk had somehow expected him to be—he was very little above average size, in fact. His shoulders were good, but not enormous; the rest of his muscular development, while above average, was not spectacular. His body did give the impression of perfect health and magnetic energy.

Monk decided—he checked on this afterward with Ham, Mr. Sam Gallehue, Captain Kirman and others, and they agreed with him—that the golden man's face was the most outstanding of his features. It was hard to explain why it should be outstanding. The face was not a spectacularly ugly one, nor a breathlessly handsome one; it was just a face, but there was kindliness about it, and strength, and power, in addition to something that could hardly be defined.

The golden man spoke in a voice which was the most completely pleasant sound Monk had ever heard.

"Good evening, Captain Kirman," he said.

Astonishment jerked Captain Kirman rigid. The golden man seemed not to notice. He turned to Monk and Ham.

"Good evening, Mr. Mayfair and Mr. Brooks,"

he said. He contemplated them and seemed to radiate approval. "It is too bad the human race does not produce more men like you two and like the man with whom you work, Doc Savage."

Monk became speechless. Ham, fighting down astonishment, asked, "Who are you?"

For a moment, the golden man seemed slightly disturbed; then he smiled. "I have no name, as yet."

"Where'd you come from? How did you get in the water?"

The golden man hesitated, and said finally, "The sea was my mother and the night was my father, but you will not believe that, so perhaps we should not discuss it."

Ham—he confessed later that his hair was nearer to standing on end than it had ever been—persisted. "There was a black star in the sky," he said, "and there is something that glows, a kind of radiance, that is following the ship. What are those things?"

The golden man sighed peacefully. "Do not be afraid of them," he said. "They will go away, now that I am safe, and you will not see them again."

He leaned back, closed his eyes, and, although Ham asked him more questions—Monk also tried his hand at inquiring—they got no results. The golden man simply lying, conscious and composed, seeming to care nothing about them or their questions. The nurse finally shooed them out of the hospital, saying, "After all, no telling how long he had been swimming in the sea before we found him."

In the corridor, Ham asked, "What do you think, Monk?"

Monk became indignant. "How the hell do I know what to think?" he growled.

THE sea next morning was calm, so Monk and Ham breakfasted on the private sun deck—they had one of the high-priced suites, with a private enclosed sun deck adjoining—under a sky that was the deep, cloudless, blue color of steel. They could look out over a sea of navy corduroy to the horizon. Smoke from the funnels trailed back like a black tail astern, and there was a lean, mile-long wedge of wake.

Ham had orange juice, toast, delicate marmalade, a kipper. Monk had a steak, eggs, hot biscuits, four kinds of jam. The breakfast steward was pouring coffee when Dr. John Parsons, the ship physician, arrived.

Dr. Parsons grinned wryly. "Remember that radiogram we talked about last night?"

Monk nodded.

"Well, I sent it," the physician said. "And I got an answer a few minutes ago."

"What did the answer say?" Monk asked seriously.

"I had bought the villa."

Monk peered at his coffee cup as if it was a strange animal. "Now—how do you figure this man we found in the ocean knew that?"

The physician jerked at his coat lapels impatiently. "I wish *you* would figure that out," he said.

After Dr. Parsons had gone, Monk and Ham drank coffee in silence. There seemed to be no words. This verbal drought persisted while they fed their pets. The pets were a pig and a chimpanzee. The pig, named Habeas Corpus, was Monk's pet; the chimp, Chemistry, belonged to Ham. Both animals were freaks of their respective species, Habeas Corpus being mostly snout, ears, legs and an inquiring disposition. Chemistry did not look like chimp, ape, baboon, orang, or monkey—he was an anthropological freak. Chemistry did look remarkably like Monk, which was one of the reasons why Monk did not care for the animal.

Ham broke the silence. "How long did you hang your head out of the porthole after I went to bed last night?"

"Last night—you mean when I was looking at that glowing stuff in the water?" Monk asked.

"Yes. How long did the glow stay in the water around the ship?"

"Until about an hour before dawn," Monk confessed.

"It followed the ship all the time up until then?" Ham demanded.

"Yes."

"How did it disappear?"

"It just faded away."

"How fast was the ship going all that time?"

"Over twenty knots. Practically top speed."

"How do you explain that?"

"The top speed, you mean?"

"No, the luminous stuff following the ship."

Monk grimaced, and did not answer. He never liked things he could not understand.

IT was ten-o'clock-beef-tea time that morning—the *Virginia Dare* was a Yankee ship, but Captain Kirman liked the English custom of serving beef tea at ten in the morning, and tea and crumpets about four in the afternoon, so he had instituted the practice on his vessel—when the golden man appeared.

The golden man joined Monk, Ham and Captain Kirman, who were on the promenade deck, sprawled in deck chairs, balancing napkins and cups.

The golden man approached them with a firm, purposeful stride. Monk noted that, although the suit the man wore was a spare from somebody's supply and did not fit him, yet the fellow had a kind of majestic dignity. Monk noted also that Mr. Sam Gallehue was trailing along behind the golden man, but that was not unusual. Mr. Sam Gallehue almost invariably trailed along behind people.

None of them ever forgot what the golden man said. It was a verbal bombshell.

"This ship is going to be destroyed at about eleven o'clock this morning," he said.

Then he turned and walked away, leaving his listeners to stare at each other. Monk started to get out of his chair and follow the man. But Captain Kirman dropped a hand on his arm and halted him.

"The poor devil is crazy," Captain Kirman said.

Monk, although he nodded his head, was not so sure.

Chapter III
THE WEIRD

THE ship did not sink at eleven.

It sank at seven minutes past eleven.

The explosion took about half the bottom out of Hold 2, ripped a little less of the bottom out of Hold 3, and tore approximately eleven by twenty-eight feet of steel plates off the side of the ship above the waterline. There was no panic. Alarm bells rang throughout the vessel for a moment, then became silent. Thereafter, they rang at intervals of two minutes, short warnings. There was very little excited dashing about. Unruffled officers appeared at strategic points and began steering passengers to their boat stations.

Ham Brooks was knocked down by the explosion. He was not hurt, and he was slightly indignant when Monk solicitously helped him to his feet. He had lost his sword cane, however, and he spent some time hunting it. After he found the cane, he and Monk went to the bridge to offer their services, but it developed that these were not needed.

Captain Kirman and his crew were almost monotonously efficient in abandoning the ship. It was necessary to abandon the ship, of course. The *Virginia Dare* was sinking, and fast.

"What was it?" Monk asked. "A boiler let go?"

"Torpedo," Captain Kirman replied cryptically.

"What?" Monk ejaculated.

Ham put in, "But we're not yet at war!"

Captain Kirman shrugged. "I saw the torpedo wake. So did my officers. It was a torpedo, all right."

"But anybody could see this is an American vessel."

The liner, as was the custom for the last year or two, had huge American flags emblazoned, two on each side of the hull, and large stationary flags painted on the deck, fore and aft.

Monk said, "I can't think a sub would be crazy enough to torpedo an American ship."

Captain Kirman shrugged. "We got torpedoed, anyhow."

An officer walked up, saluted with smartness. "Submarine has appeared off the port quarter," he reported.

They crowded to the rail and strained their eyes, then used binoculars. The submarine was there, plain for anyone to see. There was no doubt about her identity. Numerals and letters were painted on the conning tower, and the design of the craft was itself distinctive enough to answer all questions of nationality.

The sub belonged to a country presumably friendly with America.

"I'll be damned!" said Captain Kirman fiercely. "This is going to cause plenty of complications."

The sub apparently satisfied itself that a mortal blow had been struck, then submerged and did not appear again. It had not offered help.

The *Virginia Dare* sank.

Captain Kirman was, in the tradition of the sea, the last man to leave his vessel. In the lifeboat with him were Monk, Ham, Sam Gallehue, and the strange golden man who had predicted this disaster. Captain Kirman cried a little when the blue-green sea swallowed his ship.

MONK and Ham—they had brought their pets—were not excited. Excitement was their business, in a manner of speaking. For a number of years they had been associated with Doc Savage in his strange career, and it was an existence that had accustomed them to trouble.

They were, however, puzzled. Puzzled by the golden man, who had such a strange personality. Circumstances under which the fellow had been found—the black star, the strange luminosity in the sea—had been startling, even weird. The fact that he had calmly predicted disaster to the ship, and the disaster had materialized, was something to wonder about. Monk stole a glance at the fellow.

The golden man lay relaxed on a thwart of the boat, his manner so completely calm that his presence seemed to have a soothing effect on those around him.

Monk moved back to the strange man.

"Mind answering a question?" Monk asked him.

The golden man smiled placidly and nodded.

**Ham Brooks was knocked down by the explosion—
and Monk tried to help him to his feet.**

"How did you know our ship was going to get torpedoed?" Monk asked bluntly.

The golden man's smile went away for a moment, then came back. "I suppose I was looking at my mother, and the knowledge came to me," he said. "I guess one would say that my mother told me."

"Your mother?"

"The sea."

This was too much for Monk; he gave it up. He went back, sat down beside Ham. "He's a goof," Monk whispered. "He says the sea told him the ship was going to be torpedoed!"

Ham absently scratched the back of his chimp, Chemistry. "I wish I had something to tell *me* such things," he said. "For instance, I could use some nice advance information about what the stock market is going to do."

Monk growled, "Listen, you overdressed shyster—you don't believe that guy can *really* foretell the future."

Ham shrugged. "If he didn't, what *did* he do?" he demanded.

Monk gave up, and lay back, eyelids half-closed against the noonday sun. He spent a long time furtively examining the golden man. There *was* something a little inhuman about the man's appearance, Monk decided.

The breeze dropped. By two o'clock, the sea was glassy, the heat was irritating. Future prospects were none too good, for the nearest land was some hundreds of miles away, and the lifeboats were hardly capable of making such a distance. To further darken the situation, the radio operator was not sure that his S O S signal had been received by anyone. The torpedo had damaged the current supply to such an extent that the radio had been able to put out only a weak signal.

Captain Kirman, his face showing a little of the strain, got out his navigational instruments, current tables, and charts, and began calculating.

The golden man looked at him. Then spoke quietly. He said, "You are preparing to plot a course to the nearest mainland. It would be better not to do so. We should remain here."

"Remain here?" Captain Kirman lifted his head to stare at him.

"At six o'clock this evening," the golden man said, "a steamer will arrive at this spot. It will be the Brazilian freighter *Palomino.*"

Captain Kirman became pale. He sat very still. Finally he put away his charts and instruments. "Pass word to the other boats to remain here, in a close cluster," he ordered.

THE steamer *Palomino*—she gave the first impression of being mostly rust, but she floated, so she was welcome—arrived on the horizon a few minutes before six o'clock.

The effect the appearance of the *Palomino* had upon passengers and crew of the sunken *Virginia Dare,* adrift in lifeboats, was inspiring. There were cheers, shaking of hands, kissing.

Stronger than these emotions, however, was stark amazement. The story of the golden man's predictions had gone from boat to boat during the afternoon. Of course there had been profound skepticism. More than one passenger had voiced an opinion that Captain Kirman must be touched, or he wouldn't have taken the word of a half-stupefied castaway that rescue would turn up if they waited.

Most affected of all was Captain Kirman. He lost his temper, sprang to his feet, and collared the golden man. "How the hell did you know that ship was coming?" Captain Kirman yelled. "And if you say your mother, the sea, told you, damn me I'll throw you overboard for the sharks to eat!"

The golden man replied nothing whatever to this outburst. His face was placid; his smile, although slight, was unconcerned. The composed confidence of the fellow, and his strangeness, further enraged Captain Kirman. The captain whirled on the radio operator. "You sure no ship acknowledged your S O S?"

"Positive, sir," declared the radio operator.

"Was this"—Captain Kirman jerked his thumb at the golden man—"fellow hanging around the radio room at the time?"

"No, sir."

"Have you seen him near the radio room?"

"No, sir."

Captain Kirman gave up, red-faced, and bellowed greetings to the steamer *Palomino.* The sailors on the rusty hulk bellowed back in their native language, which was Portuguese, then rigged davit falls and hoisted the lifeboats of the *Virginia Dare* on deck. There were blankets for everybody, food and hot wine.

IT was soon learned that the *Palomino* would put the rescued passengers and crew of the *Virginia Dare* ashore in Buenos Aires, South America, but first the vessel would have to go directly to another port, not so large, in another South American republic, to take on fuel and deliver cargo.

The captain of the *Palomino* made this very clear in a little speech he delivered through an interpreter.

Monk asked Ham, "Do you speak Portuguese?"

"Sure," Ham said.

"How much?"

"I used to know a Portuguese girl," Ham said, "and I learned enough that we got along."

"That'll probably be a big help," Monk muttered. "But come on over anyway. Let's brace this skipper." He hauled Ham across the room. "Ask him how his ship happened to show up where we had been torpedoed. He was off his course. How come?"

Ham put this query to the *Palomino* commander. Monk's conjecture about Ham's ability with the Portuguese must have been approximately correct, since the palaver went on for some time, with much grimacing and shaking of heads. Finally Ham turned to Monk.

"He ees say that she very fonny business," Ham said.

"You can skip the accent," Monk growled. "What does he mean—funny?"

"It seems," Ham elaborated, "that the captain of the *Palomino* got a radiogram today about noon that caused him to change his course and head for this spot. The radiogram was an S O S from the *Virginia Dare.*"

"Oh, so they heard our S O S, after all. That's fine—" Monk's jaw fell until his mouth was roundly open. "When did you say that radiogram came?"

"About noon today."

"Noon!"

"Yes."

"But the *Virginia Dare* sank at eleven!"

"Uh-huh."

"Hell, the ship couldn't send an S O S after it sank."

"Sure," Ham said. "Sure it did. But that isn't all."

Monk got out a handkerchief and wiped his face. "If that radiogram was sent at noon—who sent it? There was no radio in any of our lifeboats. How in the dickens—" He fell silent, pondering.

"I said that wasn't all," Ham reminded.

"Huh?"

"They have just discovered in the last half hour that the radio operator of the *Palomino* never received such a message," Ham explained.

Monk gaped at him. "No?"

"The message never came over the radio."

"Say, what is this?" Monk growled. "The *Palomino* skipper says there was a message, then he says there wasn't! Is that it?"

Ham explained patiently, "Here is what happened. The message was handed to the captain of the *Palomino,* on the bridge, shortly after noon. The message was brought by a man who wore a radio operator's uniform, but at the time the captain was figuring out his midday position, and didn't pay too much attention to the man."

"When the skipper read an S O S message, he surely called the radio room to check on its authenticity," Monk said.

"Yes, he did. But there is a speaking tube that leads from the bridge to the radio room, and the skipper used that. He says a voice answered him, and it sounded like the regular radio operator. The operator—or this voice through the speaking tube—told the skipper that there was no doubt about the message being genuine, and to go ahead and steam full speed to help the ship. That satisfied the skipper. Incidentally, if it hadn't been for that radiogram, we would probably never been found. This is a mighty deserted stretch of ocean."

Bewildered, Monk asked, "Where was the radio operator when all this was going on?"

"In a trance."

"Eh?"

"The radio operator's story is queer. He says that, a little before twelve, he felt strangely drowsy. This drowsiness came on all of a sudden, and he dropped off to sleep. He claims now that it wasn't exactly like dropping off in a nap—he says it was different, kind of like a trance. And during this trance, he remembers just one thing, a black star."

Astonishment yanked at Monk's face. "Now wait a minute! What was that he remembered?"

"A black star."

"You kidding me?"

"I know it's crazy," Ham admitted. "A black star. The radio operator says it was on his mind when he came out of this so-called trance—he came out of it incidentally, about one o'clock—but he doesn't know whether he saw a black star, or had it impressed on his subconscious somehow, or what made him have it on his mind."

Without a word, Monk wheeled and walked out of the cabin. He strode on deck, where he leaned against the rusty rail and let the wind whip his face.

"When we found that guy swimming in the sea," he muttered, "I wonder *just what we did find.*"

THERE was one more incident. This occurred when the golden man unexpectedly approached Captain Kirman that afternoon. About the golden man was his typical impassive calm, dignity, and power of character that seemed to give him a hypnotic influence over those with whom he came in contact.

He said, "The submarine which torpedoed your vessel should be punished, Captain Kirman."

Captain Kirman swore until he ran out of breath, then sucked in air and said, with careful self-control, that he wished to all that was holy that he knew some way of seeing that the job got done.

The golden man stated quietly, "The submarine will be meeting a supply ship." He named a latitude and longitude. "You can radio the American navy to send a cruiser to the spot."

Captain Kirman blinked. "Why not a British boat? There may not be an American cruiser in this part of the ocean."

"One is now less than seventy miles to the west of the spot where the submarine will meet the supply ship," the strange golden man said peacefully. He started to move away, then paused to add, "The submarine is not actually the nationality which she pretended to be."

Captain Kirman could only gape at him. Later, Captain Kirman found Monk and Ham. The captain gave the scar on the top of his head a furious massaging with his palms as he told about the conversation.

"This thing's got my goat," he confessed. "I'm not a man who believes in spooks, but I'm beginning to wonder if we didn't find one swimming in the ocean."

Monk asked, "You going to notify the American navy?"

"Would you?"

"I believe I would," Monk said.

Captain Kirman grinned. "I guess you're getting as crazy as the rest of us."

THE matter of the torpedoing of the American liner *Virginia Dare* became, in diplomatic parlance, what was termed an incident, which was another way of saying that it came within a shade of plunging the United States into a conflict.

The American cruiser, as a result of a radiogram which Captain Kirman sent, at sunset that evening came upon a freight steamer and a submarine holding a midsea rendezvous. The cruiser came up quietly in the dusk, and very fast. It put off a plane, and the plane dived upon the unsuspecting freighter and submarine without warning.

The observer of the plane used a good camera, getting enough pictures to tell a story—the photographs showed sailors at work with paint brushes, wrenches and welding torches, changing the appearance of the submarine back to normal. The pictures proved beyond a shadow of a doubt that the submarine belonged to one European power, but had been masquerading as belonging to another.

The sub made a frantic effort to submerge when discovered. This caused a disaster. Someone forgot to close the hatch, and the U-boat never came up again. There was, of course, no actual proof that the submersible accidentally destroyed

itself, but there was never any doubt in the minds of pilot and observer of the U. S. navy plane.

As for the freighter, it got away. It was not the ponderous hulk it appeared to be, and it left the vicinity at a speed which almost equaled that of the navy cruiser. It managed to escape in the extremely black night.

Washington diplomats—largely because they did not have absolute proof—decided to softpedal the incident somewhat. There was never any doubt, however, that a European power had made an attempt to arouse American public sentiment against another nation by trying to make the public think one of that nation's submarines had torpedoed an American liner without warning.

Chapter IV
THE UPSET PITCHER

THE steamer *Palomino* was a slow hooker. Days elapsed before she drew near the small South American seaport where she was to refuel before continuing to Buenos Aires. Eventually, the South American coastline did appear like a black string lying on the western horizon.

That night, Ham came upon Monk in the bow. Monk was pulling the large ears of his pet pig, Habeas Corpus, and staring at the deck.

"Ham, I been thinking," Monk muttered.

"What with?"

"Oh, cut out the sass," Monk grumbled. "You go around claiming I'm dumb, and personally, I'm convinced you're so stupid you think the eternal triangle is something babies wear. The point is, maybe we're both kind of dumb."

"How do you mean?"

"About this fellow they found in the ocean—this golden man," Monk said thoughtfully. "I've been studying him. And I can't make up my mind."

Ham nodded soberly. "I've been doing the same thing."

"Apparently," Monk said, "he has some kind of power. Apparently he knows about things that are going to happen before they happen. Apparently such things ain't possible."

Ham grimaced. "It's crazy, and we both know it," he said.

"Sure—it's impossible," Monk agreed. "But just the same, what are we going to do about the evidence that is in front of our eyes?"

Ham said abruptly, "I'll bet we've both thought of the same thing."

"Doc Savage?"

Ham nodded.

"Well, it's the smartest idea you've had recently, because it's the same as mine," Monk declared. "If Doc Savage could talk to this golden mystery guy, and examine him, we would know for sure whether he has some kind of supernatural power."

Ham said, "There's another angle to it, too."

"How do you mean?"

"This will sound crazy."

"Well, what is it?"

"If this fellow they found in the sea *does* have supernatural power, he ought to be protected. It would be too bad if he had a power like that, and crooks got hold of him."

Monk pulled at one of his tufted ears. "I thought of that, too."

"A bunch of crooks, if they got something like that," Ham said, "could cause a lot of trouble. Think of what you could accomplish if you *knew what was going to happen in the future.*"

Monk grinned. "That does sound crazy."

Ham scowled. "Well, we better take this man to Doc, anyway."

"He may not want to go."

"We can ask him."

"And if he don't say yes?"

Monk grinned. "Then," he said, "he can look into the future and see that we'll take him whether he wants to go or not."

THE golden man had one particular trait which by now had been noticed by everyone. This was his preference for solitude. He never took part in conversation, and when spoken to about some trivial matter, did not trouble to answer. He had placed a deck chair on the top deck in a lonesome spot where the wind blew the strongest, and he spent long hours there, lying relaxed with his eyes half closed, as if in inner contemplation.

Monk and Ham found him there. They explained that they wished to converse privately.

"It's important," Monk said.

"If you wish," the golden man replied placidly.

They could not help being impressed by his calmness. Neither Monk nor Ham was easily awed, for they themselves were famous men in their professions, besides being additionally noted because of their association with Doc Savage. The feeling that the golden man was an extraordinary individual disturbed them.

For the conference, they selected deck chairs under their windows. It was rather hot to retire to a stateroom, and there was no one in view on deck.

Ham, who was more silver-tongued than Monk, took the burden of explanation. He did a good job of it, using a normal but earnest tone, speaking simple-worded sentences that were effective. As he talked, he watched the face of his listener, distinguishable in the glow from an electric deck light nearby. He got the idea his talk was

doing no good, and after he finished, he was surprised to receive a lecture in return.

"Clark Savage," said the golden man, "is, as you have just told me, a great man, and a kind one. He follows a strange career, and in being fitted for this career, he was placed in the hands of scientists at childhood, and trained by those scientists until he came to the estate of man. Because of this, many people do not understand him, and accordingly regard him as a kind of inhuman combination of scientific wizardry, muscular marvel, and mental genius. Those who are close to him know differently—they know that he has strength of character and genuine goodness. They know that he would have been a great man without the training of those scientists." The golden man sat silent for a moment, as if musing. "It is unfortunate for humanity that the world does not have many such as Doc Savage," he continued. "If ever the world needed men who combine scientific ability and moral character, it is now."

Monk took in a deep breath. "How about going with us to talk to Doc Savage?" he asked.

"Of course."

"You'll go!" Monk exclaimed, delighted.

"Yes."

"That's swell!"

Apparently feeling the matter was satisfactorily settled, the golden man got to his feet and walked away. The placidity of his going kept his departure from seeming curt.

Monk and Ham were silent for a while. Then, "He knew all about Doc," Monk ventured.

"Yes, seemed to," Ham admitted. "But that's just another of the strange things about him. Incidentally, I sent Doc a radiogram, describing this fellow fully, and asking Doc if he had ever heard of him. Doc radioed back that he had no knowledge of such a man."

"Well, we got him to agree to see Doc," Monk remarked.

They still sat there when the noise came from behind them. A noise from their stateroom. The sound of something upsetting, breaking with a crunching shatter.

They exchanged stares.

"Stay here," Monk breathed.

The homely chemist whipped out of his deck chair, got up on tiptoes, ran to a door, veered through it, took a turn into a corridor, and reached their stateroom. The door was closed. He put an ear to it, heard no sound. He hesitated, then entered.

When he rejoined Ham a few minutes afterward, Monk was calm.

Ham was excited. "What was it?"

"The jug of water was on the floor," Monk

**Ham and Monk were bumped into and shoved
about by the wildly excited crowd!**

said. "I guess it rolled off the table, or something. It broke."

"You mean that jug of glowing water?"

"Yes."

"Broke?"

"Yes."

"But the boat hasn't been rolling."

"I didn't think it had, either," Monk admitted.

They were both rather silent.

Chapter V
THE FIFTH COLUMN

THE name of the town was not *La Corneja,* but that was what Monk always called it. The name *la Corneja* was Spanish for crow, and the place was a crow among towns, far the most drab and shabby seaport on that coast of South America, so the name Monk applied was not inappropriate. *La Corneja* was not the principal seaport of the republic; the republic itself was one of the smaller ones in South America. Certainly the town had none of the beauty and prosperity which marks—to the astonishment of American tourists—much of South America.

Monk and Ham went ashore as soon as the steamer *Palomino* tied up to a dock for coaling, to stretch their legs. Later they had a surprisingly good luncheon. Then they took a stroll.

The stroll accounted for two things. First, it enabled them by chance to see the thin man with the scar under his left eye. The man was talking to Captain Kirman of the *Virginia Dare.* The two men were conversing in a small bar. Monk and Ham placed no significance in the incidence then, although later they attached a great deal.

The second incident of the stroll was a street fight which they witnessed. This occurred later in the afternoon. The fight broke out suddenly in a market where they were standing.

One native hit another with a ripe and squashy fruit, at the same time calling the man a crawling dog, and adding colored information about his ancestors. The fight spread like flame after a match is dropped in a gasoline barrel. There was suddenly excitement all around Monk and Ham.

They were bumped into, jolted, shoved about, although no one swung any blows at them. After being jammed in a struggling group for a while, they extricated themselves. Once clear, they stood, well on the outskirts of the fight, and watched the melee. It was good entertainment.

Then someone yelled, "The police!" in Spanish. The fight ended more suddenly than it had started. Participants scattered in all directions. One moment, they were there; the next they were gone. Monk and Ham prudently took to their heels also.

"Wonder what they were fighting about?" Ham pondered. "Didn't seem to start over anything."

Ham shrugged. "Search me. They wanted the exercise, maybe. I've seen times when I just felt like starting a scrap."

They dismissed the fight as a welcome piece of entertainment they had witnessed, and wandered along the streets, examining the shop windows.

They were on a side street when the thin man with the scar below his left eye approached them. He had a bundle under his arm. He was excessively polite, and nervous.

His English was good enough. "Señors," he said, "I saw you back yonder, looking at that fight. It later occurred to me that you kind Americans might help a poor man who is in trouble. I was the cause of that fight. A man and his relatives hate me because of … er … a matter about a woman. I have married the woman, their sister, and they do not like that. I love Carlita, and she loves me, but if we stay here, there will be *much* trouble. We want to leave, to go to some other place, and be happy by ourselves. But we have no money. I have only some fine silken shawls which cost me much money, but which I will sell very cheap. Could you good Americans help out a poor man by buying my shawls?" He said all this in one rush of words, tinged with frantic haste.

Monk and Ham exchanged amused glances. This was an old gag. It was an old trick for selling shoddy merchandise. Gyp artists in New York often used it. The fellow must take them for suckers. The shawls would be shoddy.

But, to their astonishment, upon examining the man's shawls, they found them of exquisite workmanship and quality. The price named was a fraction of their real value.

"Bargain!" Monk whispered.

Ham agreed. He appreciated a bargain.

They bought the shawls.

The thin man with the scar under his eyes almost sobbed as he parted with the merchandise. Then he fled down an alley with his money.

Monk and Ham, feeling proud of themselves, walked along the street.

"You know, these are darn fine shawls," Monk said. "They must be worth a hundred bucks apiece."

"Much as I hate to agree with you," Ham said, "we did get a buy."

They were arrested on the town's main street.

Nearly a dozen neatly uniformed officers—it developed that they were Federal police—closed in. Monk and Ham were handcuffed, searched. Howling protests were ignored. They were dragged off to the city hall, which also contained the jail, and stood before an officer.

"What's the meaning of this?" Ham demanded indignantly.

The officer in charge spread the shawls out on a table. He examined them, then grunted angrily. He indicated the unusual design.

"These shawls," he said in a grim voice, "are actually maps of this country's fortified zones. In other words, you two men seem to be spies. Fifth columnists, I believe is the term."

Both prisoners protested a mistake.

The officer shrugged. "The commandant will arrive shortly. He will hear your stories."

THEIR jail cell turned out to have one window, size eight-by-ten inches, a wooden frame on the floor filled with straw for a bunk, and walls over two feet thick of stone. There were other inhabitants in the form of bugs of assorted sizes.

"No wonder that guy sold the shawls so cheap!" Monk growled.

Ham nodded. "It was a frame-up. We took the bait clear up to the pole."

They moved to the window, tested the bars. These were as thick as their wrists, of steel, and solid.

Monk said, "Say, earlier in the afternoon, I remember seeing that thin guy with the scar under his eye talking to Captain Kirman."

"I saw him, too."

"You suppose there's any connection?"

Ham scowled. "There's sure something phony about this."

The door of the cell was unlocked shortly, flung open, and policemen entered with guns and grim expressions. The officers proceeded to strip all the clothing off Monk and Ham, and take the garments away. The two prisoners were left naked.

"A fine out!" Ham yelled, almost hysterical with rage. "There'll be international complications over this!"

"Oh, shut up!" Monk grumbled. "You don't really get mad until somebody steals your clothes."

Ham had an hour in which to fume. Then the police were back again, and with them, the commandant. The commandant was an athletic man of middle age, efficient, speaking English smoothly.

He had their clothing.

"You two men," he said, "became very careless."

"We're getting mad, too," Monk assured him. "Or at least one of us is."

The commandant indicated their clothing. "In the pockets of your garments, we found incriminating documents. In one was a forged passport. In another suit, there were letters which you had already decoded, that proves conclusively that you are spies of a European power."

An indignant protest from the two captives led the commandant to exhibit the evidence. It was exactly what he had said it was.

"How did your men come to arrest us?" Ham demanded, his voice ominously calm.

"We received a telephone tip."

Ham turned to Monk. "That fight we saw was part of the frame-up. Remember how they crowded against us, and shoved us around? The passport and these letters were planted on us then."

"Yes," Monk said. "And you remember last night, in our cabin—I bet somebody was eavesdropping."

The commandant smiled, but with no humor. "So you claim you were framed?"

Indignantly, Monk announced his identity, and added further that they were survivors of the torpedoed American liner, *Virginia Dare*.

The commandant was slightly impressed. "We will check that story," he said. "We wish to be perfectly fair."

The commandant then went away.

He was back before dark. His face was not pleasant.

"Captain Kirman," the commandant informed them grimly, "declares that he never heard of you."

Monk was stunned. "You're *sure* of that?"

"There is no doubt."

"You really saw Captain Kirman?"

"Yes."

"He has a scar on his head. Are you sure—"

"A scar that was the result of a mine fragment in the World War," the commandant said impatiently. "Yes, we discussed the captain's scar."

Monk and Ham had been reluctant to capitalize on the name of Doc Savage, and their association with him. But now the situation demanded that. With earnestness, they told the commandant that they were associated with Doc Savage, and that, if he would radio Doc, he would receive confirmation of the fact.

The commandant crisply agreed to send the radiogram.

The answer came the following afternoon. By that time, the *Palomino* finished fueling and had sailed for Buenos Aires.

The radiogram was to the point.

TWO MEN YOU HAVE IN CUSTODY ARE IMPOSTERS. MY AIDES MONK MAYFAIR AND HAM BROOKS ARE IN MY NEW YORK HEADQUARTERS NOW.

DOC SAVAGE.

Monk became pale.

THEY were court-martialed that afternoon. They were convicted. They received the traditional funny-paper sentence—but there was nothing funny about it.

They were sentenced to be stood against the stone prison wall at dawn and shot. The sentence prescribed the size of the firing squad which was to do the job—it was to contain eleven riflemen, and one rifle to be loaded with a blank, so that no member of the squad need be absolutely sure that his bullet was a deadly one.

Chapter VI
THE BROKEN FRAME

FOURTEEN weeks later, Monk and Ham were still in jail. Same jail. Same cell. Fourteen weeks was a long time, about as long as fourteen years, but that was about all they had learned. They had lost weight, had become prospective mental wrecks. They had even stopped quarreling.

It had been two weeks before they learned why they had not been shot immediately. The commandant was convinced they were Fifth Columnists and he was trying to break their nerve and get a confession that would involve associates. The commandant hoped to clean out the hotbed of foreign agents and saboteurs which had descended like a locust swarm upon South American republics with the advent of the European fracas. Since they had nothing to confess, Monk and Ham were under unearthly strain, expecting each dawn to stand in front of the firing squad.

The commandant had adopted their two pets, Habeas Corpus and Chemistry, but that was vague consolation.

They were held incommunicado, as far as the public was concerned. In fact, no word of print had appeared in the newspapers concerning their arrest.

Ham kept a calendar by scratching marks in the cell wall. "Three months and two weeks," he said one morning.

That was the day the commandant unlocked their cell, gave them their clothes, and a profuse apology.

Said the commandant, "There is something very strange about this matter. We now discover that you two men are actually the men you claimed you were—Ham Brooks and Monk Mayfair, aides of Doc Savage."

"A fine time to be finding that out!" Monk said.

The commandant was genuinely regretful, he said. He added, "Only because Doc Savage began an investigation to determine your whereabouts did we learn the truth." The commandant then exhibited a radiogram which had been exchanged between himself and Doc Savage in New York, and between himself and the American State Department.

Monk was convinced the commandant had really been fair. He controlled his rage and demanded, "But what about that radiogram you first sent to Doc? How come you got a faked answer?"

"I am sorry to say," the commandant explained, "that we have discovered an operator of the local commercial radio station was bribed to supply the fake message."

"Who did the bribing?"

"A man," said the commandant, "who told the radio operator his name was Captain Harley Kirman of the torpedoed ship, *Virginia Dare.*"

"You met Captain Kirman," Monk said. "Was it the same man?"

"According to the description—yes."

"Then Captain Kirman got us in this mess?"

"Yes."

Monk gave his belt an angry hitch. "How soon," he asked, "can we charter a plane that will fly us to a place where we can catch a Pan-American plane north?"

"I will see that you are furnished with an army plane," the commandant volunteered.

THE taxicab which took Monk and Ham to the airport was trailed. The hack Monk and Ham took was a secondhand yellow cab imported from the north, but it was called a *fotingo.* All cabs in the town were called *fotingos,* for some reason or other.

The man who did the trailing also rode a *fotingo.* The man had lived for the past fourteen weeks in an apartment across the street from the jail. He and a partner had managed to keep almost continuous watch on the jail. Always close at hand, they had kept a high-powered rifle equipped with a telescopic sight. Unfortunately—or fortunately, depending on the viewpoint—Monk and Ham had not come in range of window or rifle. And a few minutes ago, when the pair had left the jail, there had been too many police around.

The shadow watched Monk and Ham depart from the airport in an army pursuit ship. Then he lost no time getting to the telephone office and putting in a long-distance call.

He called a number in New York City.

"Pollo?" he asked.

"Yes," said the New York voice.

"Juan speaking."

"Yes, Juan."

"I have bad news," said Juan. "The truth was found out about them today. They have left the prison. They have also left the city—in an army plane."

"You fool!" said Pollo. "You stupid idiot! If you think you are going to get paid for failing to do the job, you're crazy."

Juan jammed his mouth close to the transmitter and said, "Perhaps you would prefer me to sell certain information to the police? Or to the man called Doc Savage."

"Now," Pollo said hastily. "We can settle this without unpleasantness, I am sure."

"Of course, we can settle it," Juan assured him. "You have my money cabled down here by tomorrow morning. That will settle it."

Pollo was silent for a while. "Yes, I guess that is the way to do it," he surrendered reluctantly.

AT the New York end of the wire, Pollo put the telephone receiver on its hook. He was a thin man with a scar under his left eye. He took hold of his face with his left hand, and the enraged clenching grip of the fingers twisted that side of his face and made more unpleasant the scar below his eye. His thin body shook with rage. Great feeling was in the flow of profanity which he kept up for about a minute and a half.

The telephone rang, and the operator said, "The other party wishes to reverse charges on the call you just received from South America. Will you accept the charges? They are thirty-six dollars and eighty-seven cents, tax included."

"Yes," Pollo said through his teeth. "I'll pay it." The swearing he did afterward eclipsed the streak he had just finished. "Fall down on the job, will he!" he gritted. "And then it costs me thirty-six dollars and eighty-seven cents to find out about it." His face was purple.

When his rage had simmered to a point where it was only heat that whitened his face, he got up and went into another room. The place was an apartment, and large, located in the busy downtown section where comings and goings did not attract too much attention.

Four men were seated at a table, giving their attention to a bottle, a pack of cards and stacks of chips. They looked, in the tobacco smoke that was a hades-blue haze in the room, a little like four well-dressed devils. The police had fairly complete histories of three of them. The fourth had been lucky thus far.

Pollo growled at them, and they looked up.

"Things went wrong in South America," Pollo explained. "Those two men, Monk and Ham, got away in spite of that fool Juan I had hired to see that they remained there. Now Monk and Ham are probably on their way up here. I imagine they will come by plane."

The four men looked at each other. One of them, who had been about to deal, laid down his cards.

"Which adds up to what?" he asked.

"When Monk and Ham get here, we will have to get rid of them." Pollo made a pistol shape with his right hand, and moved the thumb to indicate the imaginary gun was going off. "Like that."

Then the man who had put down the deck asked, "Do you know about this Doc Savage?"

"What has that to do with it?" snapped the thin man with the scarred face.

"For me personally, it has right considerable to do with it," the other man said dryly. "I have had certain parties who were friends of mine, and who went up against this Doc Savage, and I have not heard from them since. I know other parties who have had friends, and the same thing happened to the friends. Also I have heard rumors about Savage, and I have heard the rumors are not exaggerated."

"Who's afraid of this Doc Savage?"

"I am." The man got up from the table and put his hat on his head. He said, "Well, goodbye. I may see you again, but I doubt it, particularly if you go up against Savage."

His three companions also got up and put on their hats. They walked to the door.

"What in the hell are you doing?" Pollo demanded angrily.

"Savage scares us, too," a man explained. "We think we'll leave with Jed, here."

"But damn you," Pollo yelled, "I'm paying you big money."

"They don't make money that big," Jed said.

He left, and the other three with him.

POLLO felt like swearing some more, but he had another feeling, a cold one in the pit of his stomach, that kept him silent. He went to a telephone, dialed, but got no answer. He sat before the telephone for something over an hour, dialing at intervals of fifteen minutes, until finally his party came in.

"Hello. Pollo speaking, chief. I thought Jed and those other three men you sent me were supposed to be tough."

A voice in the telephone assured him, "They do not come any tougher."

"When I mentioned Doc Savage, they got up and walked out. Quit cold."

There was a silence of some duration, and more meaning, at the other end of the line. *"Who* did you say you mentioned to them?"

"Doc Savage."

Over the wire came a sound that was not coherent.

HAM

"What did you say, chief?" Pollo asked.

"I said that I know how Jed and the other three felt," the voice responded uneasily. "Tell me, Pollo, just what has gone wrong?"

Because telephone lines are not the most private things in the world, Pollo told a story about a prize calf named Fair of May, and another one named Evening Brook, both of which escaped— so the story went—from the pasture where they were being kept down on the farm. The escape had been accomplished in spite of two keepers, one named Juan, who had been on hand. The calves when last seen were believed heading north.

"You understand?" Pollo finished.

"I do, and it does not make me happy," his boss said.

"What are we going to do about it?"

"I have some farmhands who are not scared of those calves or the bull that they run with. We will put them on the job. While these calves are heading north, we probably could not find them. So we will get them when they reach the north pasture. They will probably go straight to their home shed. Station the farmhands at the shed. We will have a barbecue. Do *you* understand?"

"Fully."

"Good. By the way, have you any qualms about the bull I mentioned?"

"Doc Savage?"

"Yes."

"Not a qualm."

"Have you ever seen him?"

"No."

"That would explain the lack of qualms," the leader said dryly.

Chapter VII
THE LAST MINUTE

ARRIVING in New York, Ham Brooks was neatly groomed, correct in afternoon coat and striped trousers, and by far the best-dressed man who stepped from the plane at La Guardia field. He had wirelessed ahead to Miami, the stop, giving size, color, fabric, so that a tailor could furnish him with a complete outfit.

Monk wore the same suit which he had worn during the finding of the strange golden man in the sea, the torpedoing of the *Virginia Dare,* their long incarceration in jail. "If this suit was good enough for all that, it's good enough for New York," Monk insisted. Actually, he knew the scarecrow garment irritated Ham.

They strode through the airport terminal, and it was warming to be back. People stared at them, at their two unusual pets, Habeas Corpus and Chemistry.

But almost at once, Monk got a shock. He was passing the center of the terminal, where there was a circular dome and windows through which the afternoon sunlight slanted. The sunlight chanced to fall across a woman's right hand, particularly across a ring the woman was wearing. Monk's eyes protruded a little.

He touched Ham's elbow, whispered, "Turn around and walk back with me."

"What ails you now?"

"Take a good look at the ring on that dame's right hand. The one in the mink coat."

They strolled back, and casually examined the ring in question. "You notice it?" Monk whispered.

Ham nodded. He was startled.

There was no doubt but that the strange set in the ring the woman was wearing on the small finger of her right hand was a star. A black star. A star edged with red, which caught the light and sent it glittering.

Monk asked, "Does that star remind you of the one we saw in the sky the night the golden man got found in the sea?"

"Yes, it does," Ham whispered.

"I'm gonna brace her. Ask her about the ring."

Ham plucked at Monk's sleeve. "Better not. I happen to know who that woman is."

"Who?"

"Mrs. H. Courtney van Stigh."

"So what?"

"She has more social position than the King of England, and more dollars than Europe has soldiers."

"That's nice," Monk said. "We should get along great." He started toward the lady of social and dollar prominence.

"You'll get a coat of icicles," Ham warned. Ham had heard Mrs. van Stigh had a notable record for snobbery, so he was astonished when Monk approached the lady and said, "Beg pardon, but I'm interested in your black-star ring," and Mrs. van Stigh gave Monk a *friendly* smile. "Yes, that ring is my most precious possession," she said.

"Does the ring represent something?" Monk asked breezily.

"Oh, yes," she said. "The sea was his mother, and the night was his father. There was a black star edged by fire in the night, and an ectoplasmic light in the sea, and they were his guardians. The dark star is the symbol."

Then she glanced toward the clock on the wall, gasped something about missing her plane, and scampered off.

Monk was rooted to the floor.

"What the hell!" he muttered, finally. "She isn't crazy, is she?"

"Not," Ham told him, "that I ever heard of."

THEY took a taxicab. When the machine was moving, Monk said, "I remember somebody who said his mother was the sea and his father was the night."

"You and me both," Ham said.

"The man who was found in the ocean."

"Yes, I know."

"Suppose there's any connection?"

"How the heck *could* there be?"

Monk said thoughtfully, "Her voice got sort of strange when she started talking about the ring. She sounded kind of like a mother speaking of her new baby. And didn't you say it wasn't like the old heifer to condescend to even speak to a mere stranger?"

Ham nodded. "Particularly a mere stranger who looks like a bum," he added.

"Bum? Meaning me?" Monk became indignant. "Listen, why should an old moneybags like that high-hat *me?* I've got plenty of culture."

"The only trouble with your culture," Ham told him, "it's all physical."

They fell to quarreling enthusiastically, and soon felt better. Their squabbling—it was so fierce that the taxi driver looked infinitely worried—served them, like it always did, as a tonic; it got rid of the rather eerie sensation which had resulted from seeing the dark star ring.

It was good to be back. The cab was now bright; the interior was clean, fawn-brown; the radio was clear. The new superhighway up and across the Triborough Bridge was smooth. The sun glowed.

They were filled with that fine getting-back-to-God's-country feeling.

In this mood of rejoicing, they came in sight of Doc Savage's headquarters, which occupied the top floor—the eighty-sixth story—of one of midtown Manhattan's most spectacular buildings. The skyscraper was like a spike of gray ice probing up at the placid cumulous clouds.

"I don't know when I've been more glad to get back," Monk said. And he added hopefully, "Now, if we can just have some excitement."

Monk said that last as he was getting out of the cab backward, so that the man who came up behind him and put the hardness of a gun muzzle where it was unmistakable against the homely chemist's back, answered by asking, "How is this for a start?"

MONK stood there—he was half in and half out of the cab—and asked, "What do you want me to do, pal?"

"Get back in the cab," the man said.

"Then what?"

"Just sit there." The man showed the gun to the cab driver. "Look, hacker," the man said. "I think the thing for you to do is take a walk."

The cab driver thought so, too. His walk was a run. He headed for the nearest corner.

The man with the gun said, "I am going to go away. You two fellows sit here. If one of you wants to make a move, he had better first consider whether he is bulletproof."

Then the man put his gun in his pocket—he had not displayed the weapon prominently enough for pedestrians moving on the sidewalk to notice it—and walked away.

Monk and Ham were puzzled by the performance. But only for a moment.

Up the street, a sedan, black and inconspicuous, moved from the curb. In the back seat of the sedan were two men and blued steel. The windows were down.

"Machine guns," Monk croaked.

He did not add that they were army caliber and could cut through the taxi as if it was paper. Ham would know that. Ham's mouth was open, his eyes stark, both hands gripping his sword cane, which he had recovered in South America.

Ham said, "They tried to get rid of us in South America. Now they're trying the job again."

Monk's nod was hardly perceptible. "Think of something," he said hoarsely.

They could do two things. Stay in the cab, or get out. The only difference seemed to be one of getting shot while sitting, or while running. There was no protection; there was no time to reach, for instance, the entrance of the skyscraper. Monk and Ham watched the dark sedan.

There was—while they watched—suddenly blue-red flame under the front wheels of the approaching sedan. The flame came suddenly, was about ten feet across, approximately circular in shape, flat at first, but becoming tall, and with jagged petals like a monstrous red-blue rose that had blossomed. As the rose of flame grew tall, it lifted the front of the dark sedan until the car was practically standing erect on the rear wheels. Tires and tubes came off both the front wheels. One front fender detached and arose some forty feet in the air, twisting idly while it lifted, like a large black leaf.

There was a concussion that laid their ears back.

A second blast occurred sometime during the big one, but this one—it was not much more than good firecracker noise—was lost in the echoes that gobbled through the street following the greater blast. The smaller explosion took place on the sidewalk a few inches from the feet of the man with the long blue revolver. It caused smoke, about a tubful of smoke to begin, but this swelled to a roomful, and more, and more. It enveloped the man and his revolver.

In the smoke, the man screamed two or three times. His revolver popped loudly, adding blasting echoes to the discord. Then the man and his gun were silent inside the smoke, except for moaning.

In the taxi, Monk clamped both hands over his ears to muffle the uproar, and put on a grin.

"Sounds like Doc was around," he said.

THE dark sedan, having balanced on its rear wheels for a moment or two, fell back with a crash to the street, and the frame bent, and all four doors flew open.

The three men in the sedan—only one of the pair in the back seat still retained his machine gun—piled onto the pavement. They put their chests out and ran. They headed north.

By running north, they got behind the cloud of black smoke—this had obviously come from a smoke grenade—which had enveloped the man with the gun.

One of the trio in the wildness of flight veered over so that he got into the edge of the smoke. There was tear gas in the smoke. The man yelled. He rubbed at his eyes. Although suddenly blinded, he had the judgment to dash to one of his companions, so that he could be guided in his flight.

The three of them reached the end of the block. They had a second car—this was the machine the man with the long blue revolver had intended to use—parked there. Two of the three men—the one who did not have the machine gun, and the one who was tear-gassed—ran on to the car.

The man with the machine gun stopped. He waited. There was wind that had blown the smoke aside.

The victim of the tear gas had dropped his long blue revolver. He was down, squirming around on the sidewalk, distraught from blindness and from not knowing which way to flee.

It was obvious that he could be captured by anyone who cared to take the trouble.

The man with the machine gun made a fish mouth and braced the rapid-firer barrel against the corner of a building. His forefinger tightened. The gun poured staccato thunder into the street and made his body shake violently from head to foot.

The tear-gas victim on the sidewalk suddenly relaxed and a red lake spread around his body.

The machine gunner then ran to the car, which was already moving slowly. He climbed in. The car jumped ahead.

"You fix Ike?" the driver asked.

"I fixed Ike. He won't tell them anything!" Still wearing his fish-mouth expression, the man looked at his machine gun. "Smart thing is supposed to be to throw one of these guns away, ain't it?"

"Machine guns are hard to get these days," the driver said.

"Yeah. I guess I'll take a chance." The man kept the gun. He put it on the car floor boards. The car traveled fast and turned often.

DOC SAVAGE was a bronze giant of a man who somehow fitted in with the turmoil which had occurred—he had caused it—in the street. He appeared from the entranceway of the skyscraper, from which point he had thrown the explosive grenade and the smoke bomb.

Doc crossed the sidewalk, dived into the cab with Monk and Ham and began cranking up windows.

"Get the windows up," he said.

His tone was imperative without being loud or excited. He started the cab engine and meshed gears. He finished cranking up the front windows while spinning the steering wheel to bring the machine around in the street.

By this time the bomb smoke, with a high tear-gas content, had spread until it shrouded the entire upper end of the street. To trail the killers, they would have to try to get through the stuff.

The cab was not air-tight. Some of the gas came in, and, because it was potent stuff, even a small quantity rendered driving unsafe. Their eyes became blurred with agony and leaked tears.

The bronze man twisted the cab in to the curb. He said, "They must have got away in a car. Get a description of it."

He flung out and ran into a drugstore and entered one of a battery of telephone booths. He called police headquarters, dialing the unlisted number of the radio room direct, and gave them—he first identified himself, since he held a high honorary commission on the city police force—a description of the three killers, the scene of the crime, the direction which they must have taken.

Ham came in. "Man across the street saw the car. Light-gray coach." Ham named the make of car and gave the license number.

Doc Savage relayed that information to the police, using sentences that were short, conveying clear detail.

Then he went back to the cab, started the machine and drove carefully around the block, sounding the horn frequently because his eyes were stinging wetly.

Monk asked, "How did you get wise?"

"You notice a new newsstand across the street?" Doc asked.

"Didn't have time to notice anything."

"The newsstand proprietor is an observant ex-detective who lost both legs in an accident," the bronze man said quietly. "We have him on salary."

"You mean this sleuth in the newsstand is hired to stay there and keep his eyes open for what looks like trouble around the building? It's a good idea. This ain't the first time we've been waylaid near headquarters."

Doc Savage said, "The detective telephoned that four men seemed to be watching the place. Renny, Long Tom, Johnny and myself have been taking turns keeping an eye on the four."

Monk nodded. Renny was Colonel John Renwick, noted for his big fists and his engineering knowledge. Long Tom was Major Thomas J. Roberts, electrical wizard, and not as feeble as he looked. Johnny was William Harper Littlejohn, eminent archaeologist and geologist, and a walking dictionary of the largest-sized words. These three, with Monk and Ham, made up a group of five men who were associated with Doc Savage in his unusual profession.

Doc stopped the cab near the body of the man who had carried the long blue gun. There were two policemen and a crowd.

"He was hit twenty times," one of the policemen said. "He died as quick as they ever do."

Doc said, "We would like to examine his clothes."

The policeman agreed. "I imagine it will be all right, Mr. Savage. As soon as the morgue wagon gets here, I'll have them undress him inside it, and send his clothes right up."

Doc nodded. "Tell your homicide squad that four men attempted to assassinate my associates, Monk and Ham. We do not know why. This one got some tear gas, and could not escape. One of the others shot him, probably to keep us from questioning him."

"I'll tell homicide," the officer said.

Chapter VIII
WATCH RUTH DORMAN

SOME years ago when Doc Savage began the unusual career for which he had been trained, he had started equipping the headquarters which he now occupied on the eighty-sixth floor of the mid-town building. The establishment took in the eighty-sixth floor, and was divided in three sections, the first section being a reception room, a small chamber furnished with little more than a huge safe and a rather startling inlaid table of rare woods and some comfortable chairs. A much larger room was the library, packed with scientific volumes. But the largest section of all was a laboratory which, as was well known to men in advanced science, contained some of the most advanced equipment in existence.

In the reception room, Doc Savage waved Monk and Ham to chairs. "You two fellows disappeared following the torpedoing of the *Virginia Dare*. When the survivors were landed at Buenos Aires, we naturally expected you to be accounted for. But when we sent a cablegram to Captain Kirman of the *Virginia Dare*, we received an answer saying that you two had never been on his liner."

Monk and Ham both had open mouths. "You say Captain Kirman cabled that we had never been on the *Virginia Dare?*" Ham muttered.

Doc Savage nodded. "That is what caused the delay in finding you. We had no idea what had become of you. We finally put a worldwide detective agency to work trying to find you. Just a few days ago, they located both of you in that South American jail." Doc Savage's metallic features were composed, his flake-gold eyes expressionless. "Suppose you tell the complete story."

Monk said, "It's some story."

Ham said, "It's a story about a golden man they found floating in the ocean. It will sound kind of goofy."

"Proceed."

Ham went back to the beginning of the story. He did not use many words. Twice, Monk interrupted to bring in facts which Ham had overlooked.

"And we had never seen those men who tried to waylay us in front of this building a while ago," the lawyer finished.

Doc Savage had heard the story without showing any emotion that was visible. But there came into existence within the room a low, weirdly exotic sound that was, as nearly as could be defined, a trilling note that had no tune, yet possessed definite musical quality. Seeming to come into being from nothingnes, it rose and fell without giving the impression of emanating from anywhere in the room, and finally died away... a sound that was a small unconscious mannerism of Doc Savage in moments of mental stress.

The silence that followed lasted some moments. Then Doc asked for certain repetitions of the story, as if to verify points that he considered significant. "You filled a jug with the luminous water which had surrounded the *Virginia Dare,* but the jug was broken and the water lost?" he asked.

"Yes. The jug rolled off the table in our stateroom and broke," Ham explained.

"But you are not sure the ship was rolling enough to really tumble the jug to the floor."

"That was what puzzled us."

DOC SAVAGE'S expression did not change. "Did this unusual golden man make *any* prediction which did not come true?"

Monk answered the query. "Everything the guy predicted happened. The villa in Maderia being sold to the ship's physician, the ship being torpedoed, the rescue vessel showing up—all like he said."

"And the golden man knew you two by sight, although you had never seen him before?"

"Yes."

"You barely mentioned a Mr. Sam Gallehue," Doc Savage said. "Was there anything particularly outstanding about him?"

Monk's head shook a negative. "Naw, he was just one of these syrupy clucks that was so agreeable he got in your hair. Affected a phony English accent. Liked to hang around us, and run around after Captain Kirman."

"In other words, the kind of a man who cultivated the company of important people, whenever he happened to be?" Doc suggested.

"That's right."

Ham said, "Definitely a snob, is what I would call Mr. Sam Gallehue."

"Clever man?" Doc asked.

"Oh, no. Just a fawning dope of a guy."

Doc Savage got up, moved to one of the windows and stood looking out through the thick bulletproof glass. He asked, "This unusual person—the fellow you call the golden man—did he seem entirely willing to come to New York so that we could examine him?"

"Quite willing to come," Monk agreed.

"And it was shortly after he agreed that you began having your troubles?" Doc said in a tone that was half question and half remark.

"Eh?" Monk stared. "You think maybe *that* was why we were framed in South America?"

Without answering, Doc Savage slightly shifted the line of inquiry by stating, "This golden man said the sea was his mother and the night was his father, you say?"

Monk made an it-seems-goofy-to-me-too face. "And here's something else, Doc. When we got off the plane a while ago, we saw a woman that Ham claims is one of the big bombs in society around here. She was wearing a funny ring with a black-star setting. I asked her about it—"

Ham interjected, "Yes, and when he asked her, I expected Mrs. van Stigh to sick a chauffeur or a secretary on him. But instead, she said something about the sea being a mother and the sky a father and something about ectoplasm. She positively beamed on Monk while she said it."

Ham's tone implied that anyone who could beam on Monk must have something drastically wrong with their mental mechanism.

The bronze man made no comment. He turned from the window slowly.

Monk continued, "But to get back to what we want to know—who got us in all that trouble in South America? The first guy I want to see about that is Captain Kirman!"

"Captain Kirman of the *Virginia Dare.* You suspect him?"

"He's our bird," Monk agreed.

A buzzer whined softly, a red light flashed, and Doc Savage moved over to the inlaid table and touched a button which caused a television image to appear on a wall panel. The image showed the corridor outside, and a policeman with a bundle of clothing. Doc opened the door.

The policeman explained, "That man who was machine-gunned in the street—one of our homicide men knew him. He had a record as long as a giraffe's neck."

Doc said, "It might be a good idea if the police started picking up his known associates for questioning."

"We'll do that," the officer agreed. He put the bundle of garments on the table. "This is the stuff he was wearing when he was shot."

The officer departed, and Doc opened the bundle of redly-damp clothing.

The garments were on the cheap, flashy side. A billfold, containing four hundred and twenty-odd dollars, led Monk to remark, "A lot of green stuff for a mug like him to be packing around. Whoever he was working for must pay off."

The only written or printed document in the clothing was a slip of paper, coral-pink in tone, on which had been pen-printed in blue ink three words.

The words:

Watch Ruth Dorman.

While they were looking at the bit of paper, the buzzer whined again and the red light flashed—the gadget was a protective alarm which prevented anyone setting foot on the eighty-sixth floor without their knowing it—and three men entered.

The first of the newcomers was extremely tall and thinner than it seemed any man could be and still live. He wore, dangling from his lapel, a monocle that was obviously a magnifying glass. Staring at Monk and Ham, he said, "I'll be superamalgamated. An ultraauspicious eventuation."

Monk grinned. "I see you've still got the words, Johnny."

The second arrival was small, with a complexion that would have gone well with a mushroom cellar. He was Major Thomas J. Long Tom Roberts, the electrical wizard, and his appearance of feebleness was deceptive. Not only had he never been ill, but he could whip nine out of ten football players on an average campus.

The third man had fists. Fists that would not go into quart pails. His face was long, with a habitual funeral-going expression. Physically, he looked bigger than Doc Savage, although actually he was not. He was Lieutenant Colonel John Renny Renwick the engineer.

These three, all associates of Doc Savage, shook hands heartily with Monk and Ham.

"Holy cow!" Renny jerked a large thumb in the general direction of the street below. "The cops just told us there was a Fourth of July down there a while ago."

"We can't figure it out," Monk said.

Long Tom asked, "Where have you two lugs been? Why did you disappear for three months?"

Doc said, "Tell them the story, Monk."

Monk described the affair again taking more time and using more words than Ham had employed earlier in reciting the same details to Doc Savage. The bronze man listened intently, but Monk brought out nothing that Ham had not mentioned, so he made no comment and asked no question.

Renny looked at the sheet of paper from the machine-gunned man's clothing. "Who's Ruth Dorman?" He used his normal-speaking voice, which was loud enough to make bystanders instinctively want to put fingers in their ears.

Doc Savage passed the slip of paper to Renny. "You might start tracing it," he suggested. "Johnny and Long Tom can help you."

The big-fisted engineer nodded.

Monk and Ham had gone into the laboratory, where there were equipment lockers. They returned with supermachine pistols. These weapons, resembling oversized automatics, had been developed by Doc Savage. They could discharge an astounding number of bullets in a minute—either high-explosive slugs, mercy bullets, gas pellets, or smoke slugs.

"I'm ready to hunt Captain Kirman," Monk announced. "Wonder where we'll find him?"

Doc Savage said, "We can try the steamship line which owned the *Virginia Dare*. They may have information."

Chapter IX
DEATH BY IMPOSSIBILITY

THE building stood on Broadway, south of Wall. There were seven steamship lines listed on the bronze plaque beside the entrance, and *Intramarine Lines, 20th Floor,* was second from the top.

There was dark marble and indirect lighting on the twentieth floor, and wide double doors that admitted into a large room where many clerks and stenographers were at work. They made themselves known. Not more than a minute later, Doc Savage was shaking hands with a Mr. Elezar.

"Captain Kirman?" said Mr. Elezar. "Oh, yes. One of our most efficient commanders. Had a brilliant career. Went to sea at the age of ten, won first command before he was twenty-five. We were very sorry to lose him."

"Lose him?" Doc asked.

"Yes. Didn't you know? He has quit the sea. Oh, yes, indeed. Seemed broken up over the loss of the *Virginia Dare,* although he did not say so. Said he was just getting old, and thought he would like to try it a spell ashore. Ridiculous idea, too. He is no older than I am." Mr. Elezar looked to be about fifty.

"Is Captain Kirman now located in the city?" Doc asked.

"Oh, yes. Yes, indeed. Hardly two blocks from here. He has rented and furnished an office suite."

"Can you tell us what kind of business he is in?" Doc asked casually.

"Rare fish."

"You mean that he has become a dealer in rare tropical fish?"

"That's right."

Doc Savage nodded. "Thank you very much," he said. He reached out and took Mr. Elezar's hand and shook it, and, still holding the man's hand, turned it over and looked at the ring he had noticed.

"Unusual ring."

Mr. Elezar did not say anything. He seemed uncomfortable. Monk craned his neck and saw that the ring contained a setting which was in the shape of a black star with blood-red edging.

"An extraordinary ring," Doc Savage said thoughtfully. "Believe we have heard of another ring of this type."

Mr. Elezar pulled his hand away. He looked as if he was about to break out in perspiration.

Doc said, "Can you tell me about that ring?"

Mr. Elezar said, "I'm sorry, but Captain Kirman suggested—" He bit his lower lip. "I'm … er … I have no information about the ring. It … it's just a thing I picked up in a pawnshop. Yes, that's it. I got it in a pawnshop."

"Could you give me the name of the pawnshop?" Doc asked. "I would like to get myself a ring like that one."

Mr. Elezar seemed desperate as he put on an act of trying to remember, then said, "I'm sorry, but I can't seem to recall. It was one of those places on the Bowery. There are so many."

Doc Savage was silent as they rode down to the street in an elevator.

But Monk growled angrily. "Mr. Elezar and the ring," he decided, "will bear looking into."

HAM had expected Doc Savage to go directly to Captain Kirman's office, and he was surprised when the bronze man turned into a downtown telephone office.

"What now?" Ham asked.

Doc said, "When you got in trouble in South America, you say the commandant talked to Captain Kirman, and *he* said he did not know you?"

Ham nodded. Monk put in, "And that ain't all, Doc. Captain Kirman bribed the radio operator to fake a radio message from you that denied we were who we claimed to be."

"Are you sure it was Captain Kirman?"

"The man answered his description."

"That," Doc explained thoughtfully, "is the point."

The bronze man entered a telephone booth where he remained for some thirty minutes.

His expression was unchanged when he finally came out of the booth, but Monk and Ham got the idea he had learned something interesting.

"I was fortunate," Doc told them. "The commandant was in his office. However, the telephone connection to that part of South America could be improved."

"What on earth did you telephone South America for?" Monk demanded.

"To ask the commandant the location of the scar on Captain Kirman's head," Doc explained.

Monk's small eyes narrowed. "And where was it?"

"Under the left eye."

Monk exploded. "But Captain Kirman's scar was on top of his head"—Monk wheeled to stare at Ham. "Say, the commandant didn't talk to Captain Kirman at all. Captain Kirman didn't bribe the radio operator. It was that other cuss, the man who sold us the Spanish shawls that got us into jail."

Ham nodded gloomily. "I remember how the case of mistaken identity occurred. One of us asked the commandant if Captain Kirman had a scar on his head, and the commandant said he did have, and that it was the result of a mine fragment in the World War. Captain Kirman's scar came from that cause, and we just took it for granted the commandant had talked to Captain Kirman."

"Dang it, now we're without a clue!" Monk complained. "Captain Kirman was my suspect!"

Doc said, "There is the matter of that star ring Mr. Elezar was wearing. Judging from Mr. Elezar's confusion, the ring had some connection with Captain Kirman. We might still talk to Captain Kirman."

CAPTAIN KIRMAN'S office girl was a sensible-looking middleaged brunette. When she learned their business, she went away through a door, but came back shortly.

"Captain Kirman is on the telephone," she said. "He will see you soon."

Doc Savage moved over to examine some of the tanks of rare fish. Monk joined him. They peered at an array of tanks, filters, aërators.

Monk squinted at the fish. "They're kind of fancy fish to be so small," he remarked. "They worth much?"

Doc said, "Some of them probably sell for more than a hundred dollars each."

Monk gasped. "You mean that a fish an inch long will bring a hundred bucks?"

"Or more. Collector's items," Doc explained. "You take these two fish in this tank, for instance. They are *mistichthys luzonensis,* native of the Philippine Islands, where they are called *Sinarapan* by the natives. They are very small, rarely more than half an inch long, and they are rare because they occur in Lake Buhi, far in the interior of the islands, a place so remote that it is almost impossible to bring out any living species."

"Then they're high-priced because they're scarce?"

"Something like that. However, in the Lake Buhi district of the Philippines, they are so plentiful that the natives catch great quantities of them in nets and make them up into little cakes which they serve with their rice—"

A buzzer sounded and the office girl picked up the telephone. She was not, something about her indicated, a woman who had been an office girl all her life. There was a polish in her manner, a confident ease, that indicated she was a woman who had possessed money and social position. She put the telephone down.

She said, "You may go in now."

Captain Kirman's office was large and the windows were wide. The windows faced the bay, so there was a view of ships sailing, ferries drawing long white wakes after them, tugs working. In addition to the door through which they had entered, there were two other doors—one door on each side—which were closed.

Captain Kirman looked different. It was not the absence of his uniform—Captain Kirman seemed worried and strained. His face was not as ruddy as when Monk and Ham had seen him last.

And his voice was bluff and hearty after the fashion of an actor with stage fright.

"Well, well, well!" Captain Kirman said. "Imagine seeing you fellows. Imagine! This *is* a pleasure."

Monk took the captain's hand, and it was cool and clammy, like holding a live frog.

Monk said, "I never expected to find you in the fish business, skipper."

"Oh, it's a very profitable business," Captain Kirman said vaguely. "By the way, what have you fellows been doing with yourselves?"

"That," Monk explained, "is what we wanted to talk to you about."

"Me?" Captain Kirman seeming puzzled, absently rubbed the scar on his bald spot.

"Yes. You see, something happened to us in South America."

Captain Kirman said vaguely, "I did wonder what had become of you and your friend, Ham Brooks. You disappeared rather suddenly. I presumed that you had decided to stay over, or something. I missed those frightful quarrels you two used to have."

"We didn't stay voluntarily," Monk said.

"The hell!" Captain Kirman's eyes flew wide. "What do you mean?"

"We were jobbed. Framed. Somebody got us thrown in jail on a fake charge. Then, today, when we got back to New York, somebody tried to kill us."

"The same one who framed you?"

"We don't know," Monk said. "But we got some very large suspicions."

Captain Kirman passed a hand through his hair. He seemed to be growing pale. "Why are you talking to me about this?"

"Remember that golden man who got found in the ocean?" Monk inquired.

"Why—of course. Naturally."

"Recollect the black star that was in the sky just before he was found?"

"I—yes. Yes, I recall."

"Well," Monk said, "we want to ask you about some rings that have black-star settings. For instance, we want to ask you about one particular ring, worn by a friend of yours—named Mr. Elezar—"

He did not finish because a man cried out in horror in an office somewhere upstairs, cried out shrilly, "Stop him! He's jumping out of the window."

Doc Savage and the others, turning instinctively toward the window, were in time to see the body fall past.

THE cry from the office above, the cry to stop someone who was jumping out of a window, was not loud, but it had arresting quality of horror. It jerked all eyes to the window, so that all of them saw the form tumble past the window.

"A suicide!" Ham gasped. The dapper lawyer jumped to the window. There was no screen, but a glass shield across the lower part kept papers from blowing out. Ham leaned across the shield and peered downward. His voice became stark. "Look!" He pointed.

About ten floors below there was a ledge that was part of the architecture of the building. The figure they had seen fall past the window was sprawled out on this. There was no retaining wall to the ledge and, although the ledge was wide enough that the body could not very well have missed landing on it, there was nothing to prevent the victim toppling over the edge of the ledge, if much moving about was done. That would mean a fall of another ten floors to the street.

While they were staring at the body, it moved. The victim doubled one arm. A leg drew up, and the contorted figure turned half over.

"He's alive!" Monk gasped.

"If he moves, he'll roll off that ledge!" Ham breathed.

Captain Kirman said sharply, "We've got to do something. You get down there and see if you can reach the ledge. I'll telephone the police."

Captain Kirman snatched up the telephone.

Doc Savage, Monk and Ham rushed out of the office. As they passed through the reception room, the office girl gave them a bewildered stare. They did not stop to explain.

Doc Savage took the stairway down; Monk and Ham waited for an elevator. However, all of them reached the floor, ten stories below, at about the same time. Evidently that entire floor of the building was unoccupied. None of the doors was labeled with firm names.

**The body was lying there on the ledge—and there was
no doubt about its being that of Captain Kirman!**

Doc tried a door. It was locked. He put force into twisting and a shoving, and wood groaned and the lock tore out. Inside there was a large room, comprising most of that floor of the building. It had been in disuse for so long that dust was a layer over the floor. The windows across the room was huge expanses of soiled, uncurtained glass.

Monk looked out of a window. And always remembered how he felt. An eerie sensation. He later tried to think of the feeling as like the time Ham put an oyster down his collar, which did not describe it exactly, however. The man was lying there on the ledge, dead now. And it was Captain Kirman.

THEY stared at Captain Kirman's body, and it was impossible to believe. They had left Captain Kirman in the office ten floors above after they had seen the body here on this ledge. They had seen a body fall past the window. It had not been Captain Kirman. It could not have been. Captain Kirman had been standing in the room with them at the moment. But Captain Kirman was lying here dead.

Monk pulled in a deep breath so charged with astonishment that it whistled.

"He must have a twin brother," he said.

Ham reached for the window lock.

Doc Savage said, "Wait." The bronze man examined the window lock closely. It had not been touched recently. There was dust, and the dust had not been disturbed. No visible indication that the window had been opened for weeks. Doc scrutinized the floor, bending down so that the light slanted across the dust. There were the tracks they had made in the floor dust, but no others.

Ham said, "No one has been in or out of this place for some time." His voice was strange.

Doc opened the window. There was a layer of soot and city grime on the ledge. But there were no tracks. The only marks were a smear or two close to the body, where it had moved a little after it had fallen.

Monk, looking at the body, suddenly paled.

"What's the matter?" Ham asked.

"Remember that scar on top of Captain Kirman's head?" Monk asked.

"Yes."

"Look."

Ham stared. "The same scar on the top of this man's head."

This is Captain Kirman!

Doc Savage suddenly wheeled, raced back across the room, into the hallway, and took the stairs upward. He kept climbing at full speed, until he reached the floor where Captain Kirman's office was located. The climb did not greatly quicken his breathing, but his metallic features were strangely set as he entered the office.

The middle-aged, competent office girl glanced up. "Yes?" she said.

"Has Captain Kirman gone out since we left?" Doc asked.

She shook her head. "No." She made a move to rise. "Do you wish to see Captain Kirman again? Shall I announce you?"

"Never mind," the bronze man said.

Doc shoved open the door of Captain Kirman's private office and entered. The captain was not there. The window was up, the way they had left it, and nothing appeared to have been disturbed.

Going to the window, Doc looked down. He could see the body lying on the ledge, and Monk, who had climbed out and was standing beside it.

Doc went back to the reception room. He asked the office girl, "You are *sure* Captain Kirman did not leave his office?"

She stared at him for a while. She was puzzled. "Positive," she said.

The bronze man was quite motionless for a time.

Then: "Captain Kirman," he said, "is dead."

The woman seemed to tighten all over. "How?"

"By impossibility it would seem," the bronze man said.

Chapter X
BEAUTY AND A SPHINX

HAM BROOKS arrived in the office, his chest heaving and perspiration popping from the race up the stairs. He gasped, "Was Captain Kirman here?"

"Captain Kirman is the man lying dead there on that ledge."

Ham swallowed. He seemed to become stiff. He said, "That couldn't happen."

Doc turned to the office girl. "Did you hear any strange sounds from the office?"

She tried twice before she could answer. "You mean—after you men rushed out?"

"Yes."

"No."

"You heard nothing?"

"Nothing."

"And you are certain that Captain Kirman did not leave his office."

She nodded. "He was in there after you left."

"How do you know?"

The woman said, "I tried the door. It was locked. I wanted to ask Captain Kirman why you had rushed out in such a hurry. The door was locked. I knocked. He said he did not wish to be interrupted. I heard his voice distinctly."

The flake-gold of the bronze man's eyes seemed to stir with strange animation.

"The door was locked when you tried it?"

"Yes."

"It was *not* locked," he said, "when I came back a moment ago."

She stared at him. She continued to stare, much too fixedly. Then, rather slowly her eyes unfocused, and one turned off slightly to the right, and the other turned up, both showing whites. Her lips parted. Her breath came out slowly and steadily as if her lungs were emptying themselves to the utmost. While she was sagging, Doc caught her. He lowered her to the floor. Her eyes closed.

Ham asked, "Fainted?"

"Yes."

"Why?"

The bronze man did not answer. He put the woman on a desk. He went back into Captain Kirman's office. The other two doors from the office were still closed. He opened the one to the right. It admitted to a small closet. Doc examined the plaster walls of the closet, and found them solid, undisturbed.

The other door let him into another room, larger than the closet, which had one window. There were fish tanks in the room, and fish swam in some of them.

In one of the tanks a cloud of small, brilliant orange-black-blue fish dashed out of sight among water plants the moment the bronze man appeared.

Doc Savage looked at the orange-black-blue fish. He moved over to the tanks, peering into them. A few of the tanks were labeled, but most of them bore no markings. The orange-black-blue fish fled when he came close to them. Some remained motionless in the water and watched him with popeyes.

Doc looked around. Only two fish tanks seemed to be empty. Those two tanks had water and plants like the others. But no visible fish.

Ham came to the door. "What are you doing?"

Doc Savage did not answer immediately. Finally he said, "Looking at the fish."

Ham was puzzled.

"Fish can't tell us anything."

Doc pointed. "Two tanks seem to be empty."

WITHOUT commenting on this remark, Doc went back to the office where they had left Captain Kirman. Doc gave attention to the window, then put his head out and examined the walls of the skyscraper. Other windows were closed. Directly across, was the blank brick wall of a building which must be a storage warehouse, judging from complete lack of windows. The bronze man's gaze swept the vicinity, searching for staring faces at windows, but there were none. Nobody appeared to have witnessed the weird death.

Ham said, "This thing couldn't have happened!" And his voice was hoarse.

Doc went to Captain Kirman's desk. There was a long letter opener of ivory lying there. He picked up the opener and returned to the small room which held the fish tanks.

Doc went to the two tanks which seemed to hold no fish.

There proved to be fish in the tanks. When he thrust the paper knife down into the plants, tiny fish flashed into view, and fled madly around the tank, so swiftly that only close observation showed their presence until they again sought cover.

There seemed to be satisfaction on the bronze man's features as he replaced the letter opener on the desk where he had found it.

"Well?" Ham asked.

"Murder," Doc said.

"But how?" Ham demanded. "How did he get killed?"

The bronze man said, "We might call it a case of death by impossibility, for the time being."

Ham stared at him. But Doc's expression, as far as Ham could see, was one of unchanged seriousness.

"What … what do you mean, Doc?"

Doc Savage seemed not to hear the question. So Ham did not repeat his query. Ham was acquainted with the habit which the bronze man had of becoming conveniently deaf when he was asked something which, for a reason, he did not wish to commit himself by answering.

The telephone rang. Doc picked up the instrument. "Yes… Yes, speaking," he said.

Doc used Captain Kirman's voice.

Ham gave a violent jump, then looked sheepish, deciding his nerves must be going bad. But it was eerie to hear Captain Kirman's voice speaking in the room—or an imitation of the captain's tone and delivery that was of startling fidelity. Ham hurried over and pressed his ear close enough to hear what came over the wire.

Doc listened to a woman's voice say, "This is Elva Boone, captain."

"Yes," Doc replied.

"Listen, I've stumbled onto something," Elva Boone said. "I think it may be what we have been hunting for. I think your life may be in danger."

"That is interesting," Doc Savage said.

The girl—the feminine voice was young—asked, "Where is Ruth Dorman?"

Doc Savage—although memory must have

flashed through his mind of the phrase *"Watch Ruth Dorman"* written on the bit of paper in the pocket of the man who had been machine-gunned—did not hesitate. He said, "I do not know where she is just now."

"Can you find her?"

"Well—not immediately, I am afraid."

Ham was spellbound by admiration for the voice-imitating job. He had heard Captain Kirman talk a great deal while they were on the *Virginia Dare,* and he knew the perfect imitation of the captain's voice which Doc Savage was managing was uncanny.

Elva Boone asked, "Can you meet me right away?"

"Yes."

"Good. I will be at Ruth Dorman's apartment."

Doc Savage, without changing expression, said, "If I am in danger, it is possible I am being watched. Maybe it might be better if we did not meet at Ruth Dorman's apartment. Perhaps a place near there would be better."

"How about the drugstore on the corner two blocks down the street?"

"What corner would that be?"

"Eighty-sixth Street and Broadway," said Elva Boone.

"Oh—are you uptown now?" Doc asked.

"Yes."

"That's funny," Doc said. "I saw a woman a while ago that I thought—what are you wearing? A brown dress?"

"A gray suit," Elva Boone said.

"It wasn't you, then," Doc told her. "Well, I will be there in twenty minutes."

He hung up.

Ham said admiringly, "You used a nice trick to find out what she would be wearing."

THEY took a subway uptown. Because the subway was faster, and they happened to catch the rearmost car, whereupon they moved to the back, where there was privacy.

Ham said, "I had a last look at the office girl. She will be all right. Just fainted."

Monk muttered, "I wonder why she fainted."

"Guess it was just shock over finding out her boss had gone out of the window," Ham said.

Monk frowned at the dapper lawyer. "You think he committed suicide?"

"Captain Kirman?"

"Well—he was the dead man, wasn't he?"

Ham said, "When the body fell past the window, Captain Kirman was in the office with us."

"But the captain is dead on that ledge."

"A man can't be dead, and still stand and talk to you."

Monk rubbed his jaw, and felt of his necktie as if it was tight. It was a gaudy necktie, one he had chosen to offend Ham's taste. "Captain Kirman *did* talk to us, didn't he? He told us to get down there and keep the man from rolling off the ledge, while he got busy and telephoned the police. Isn't that what he said?"

"Something like that."

"Well, what happened?"

Monk looked uneasy. "Stop harping on it!"

"Well, how could a thing like that happen? A man can't be dead and still stand and talk to you," Ham said.

Monk said, "You remember that golden man they found in the ocean?"

Ham grimaced. "It will be a long time before I forget *him.*"

"Well," Monk reminded, "there were some strange things about him. He foretold the future. He knew things it didn't look like any man could know. He was unnatural. Spooky."

Ham stared strangely at Monk, but he did not say anything more.

There was a girl in a gray suit waiting in the drugstore at Eighty-sixth and Broadway so they decided she must be Elva Boone. She was a tall girl, and there was a curved delight about her that caused Monk to shape a whistling mouth of admiration, but no sound, and scowl sidewise at Ham.

There was actually more than prettiness about this girl. There was strength under her curves, strength of spirit and of will and of ability. She had dark hair. Her eyes were blue, like clear Christmas skies. Her mouth was a warm full-blown rose.

Monk strode forward and took the elbow of the girl in the gray suit before she was aware that he was in the neighborhood.

He asked, "You are Miss Elva Boone, I presume?"

The girl stared at them. She shook her head.

"I'm sorry," she said. "My name is Jalma Coverly. You have made a mistake—or you are crazy."

Monk looked foolish.

Ham burst out in a chuckle, Monk looked so foolish, while Monk grew red-necked and sheep-faced and peered at him malevolently. They were going to have trouble over this girl, both of them suspected.

Doc Savage turned partly away. He was good at ventriloquism, but no one is ever perfect at it, particularly when imitating an unfamiliar voice while at the same time getting a ventriloquial effect. Doc imitated Captain Kirman's voice, and made it low and excited. "Run, Elva! Run!" he said imperatively. "It's a trick!"

Fright flashed over the girl's face. She half turned in an effort to escape. Doc's hand leaped out and trapped her wrist.

"You gave yourself away," the bronze man said quietly. "You are Elva Boone."

Ham, his face getting sober, said, "We had better go somewhere and talk this over."

Elva Boone was glaring at them to cover fright. "You must be crazy!" she said.

Ham shrugged. "We might be. If we are, it would explain some of the things that have been happening."

THEY moved out of the drugstore before Doc Savage spoke, then the bronze man said, "Miss Boone, you have some information. We want it."

The girl was not impressed. "I'll tell you nothing," she said defiantly.

Doc Savage had no idea of the exact location of the apartment of the mysterious Ruth Dorman, although it must be somewhere within two blocks of this spot. The neighborhood was a section of large apartment houses. An area of two blocks radius would include thousands of apartments.

Doc addressed Elva Boone.

"We will go to Ruth Dorman's apartment and talk this over," he said confidently, as if he knew perfectly well where the place was.

The complete casual confidence in his voice worked. The girl was fooled, and she led them to Ruth Dorman's apartment.

There was one incident before they got to the apartment.

They met a policeman.

Elva Boone tried to have them arrested. "Officer, these men are kidnaping me!" she gasped.

Doc Savage drew the patrolman aside and produced from his billfold a card which identified him as a high-ranking police official. The patrolman examined the card, and in addition recognized Doc Savage, so he was satisfied. He grinned at Elva Boone and walked away.

The girl got the wrong idea of what had happened, for she had seen the billfold.

"You bribed him!" she said angrily.

Chapter XI
SISTERS

RUTH DORMAN'S apartment proved to be an eleven-room duplex that was a semipenthouse, with ceilings that were high, the furniture all period stuff, and good. On the library wall was a Persian animal rug that was typical of the apartment—it was a rug made in silk and silver, a rug which had taken decades to weave, and which was very old, and which had cost a small fortune even when first woven.

"Good taste," Ham said, glancing about appreciatively.

Doc Savage pocketed a tiny, ingenious metal probe with which he had picked the apartment lock. He moved through the rooms, searching, but found no one.

"Servants?" he asked Elva Boone.

She glared at him. "You should know. You have been watching the place for days!"

Doc asked, *"We* have been watching this apartment?"

"Yes!"

A trace of grimness came over the bronze man's face, and he turned to Monk.

Monk said, "Doc, if this joint is being watched, maybe Ham and I had better find out who is doing it."

But Doc Savage shook his head. "We will put Long Tom, Johnny and Renny on that job."

The bronze man found a telephone and got his headquarters on the wire. Renny, answering, said, "Holy cow! Doc, you remember that piece of paper you gave us to trace? The one with 'Watch Ruth Dorman,' written on it."

Doc asked, "Have you traced it?"

"Well, to some extent. It was a narrow piece of stationery of good quality, and we decided it was probably torn off a sheet of hotel stationery. You know hotels generally supply their stationery to the guest rooms in wide and narrow sheets. Well, we concluded this was a narrow sheet. The only trouble with the theory was that this paper was coral pink. The high quality suggested a swanky hotel, so we began calling the snazzy hotels and asking if their stationery was coral pink. It turned out to be the Royal Rex."

"How about the blue ink with which the note was written?" Doc inquired.

"The Royal Rex supplies blue ink to its guest rooms," Renny said. "Do you want us to go to the hotel? That's not the biggest hotel in town, but it comes pretty near being the most ritzy. I don't know how on earth we would find the person who wrote that note."

"Here is what I called you about," Doc said. He gave the address of Ruth Dorman's apartment. "It is possible someone may be watching this apartment," he said. "So you and Long Tom and Johnny come over here and search the neighborhood. But be careful."

"Have you found out what this is all about yet?" Renny asked.

"Not yet."

HAM came in from another room. He had been searching the apartment.

"A man lives here," he announced.

Elva Boone stared at him. There was surprise in her aquamarine-colored eyes. "And where else," she asked, "would you expect my sister's husband to live?"

Ham held his mouth open for a moment. "Your *sister's* husband?"

"Of course," said the girl.

"Ruth Dorman is your sister?"

"Yes."

"Go on."

She stared at him. "What do you mean—go on?"

Ham explained patiently, "We are after information. You have some that we need."

The girl compressed her lips, and did not say anything. Her manner indicated she did not intend to answer.

Doc suggested, "We might look in her handbag."

At that, the girl's lips parted, and she made a gesture of half lifting her hand, but she did not speak.

Doc found the usual woman-litter in her handbag—and one other article. The article was a pin of yellow gold with a setting in the shape of a black star that was edged with crimson. It was exactly the same kind of star that they had seen in the two rings.

Doc showed the girl the star. "What does this mean?" he inquired.

She would not answer.

An hour later, they had got nothing out of her except stubborn refusals to talk. Then the police arrived with Mrs. Ruth Dorman—alias the office girl from Captain Kirman's office. Mrs. Dorman was pale, but not hysterical. Her composure, as a whole, was good.

Doc Savage consulted the policeman in charge, asking, "What did you learn?"

The officer shrugged. "Practically nothing." He glanced sidewise at Mrs. Dorman. "I'm not sure but that this woman doesn't know more than she is telling, though. But she is an important person—or her husband is—so we can't just lock her up on suspicion."

"Important? In what way?"

"Money."

"She is wealthy?"

"Her husband is."

"Then why was she working as Captain Kirman's office girl?"

"Just to learn about fish, she says. She was interested in rare fish, and was working there to learn about them. Or so she claims." The officer frowned. "That was a little funny, too. Captain Kirman didn't know anything about rare fish."

Doc Savage was thoughtful for a moment.

"You mean that Captain Kirman was not particularly interested in rare fish?"

"Matter of fact, he didn't own those fish in the office, even the fittings in the place. Another guy had financed him."

"Who was Captain Kirman's backer?"

"Old codger named Benjamin Opsall."

"Have you learned anything about Opsall?"

"We haven't talked to him. Opsall's butler said he wasn't home. But we've inquired around. He is a rare-fish dealer, all right, one of the biggest."

"How about Mrs. Dorman's husband?"

"Fred Dorman is his name."

"What is his business?"

"Broker. Big business man. As dough-heavy as they come."

"How long has Ruth Dorman been married to him?"

"Little over two years."

"Children?"

"One. It's adopted. Boy. About five years old. He's away at boarding school."

That was about all the information the policeman could give. He departed.

Chapter XII
TRAIL TO THE WIZARD

WHERE Elva Boone got her two dueling pistols was something that forever remained a mystery—but she got them, and they were loaded. It nearly cost Monk his left ear to learn about their being loaded, the bullet missing the ear by no more than an inch or so. Elva Boone had refused to talk. Mrs. Dorman likewise had refused. It had become more and more obvious that both women were scared out of their wits—not frightened of Doc Savage and his men, but afraid of something else.

The mystery of where the guns came from was doubly confounding because, although Elva Boone had moved around a little, Monk and Ham had watched her. It was a pleasure to watch her.

But suddenly she was pointing two dueling pistols at them, which was no pleasure. The guns were short and blue. The girl's voice was elaborately calm. She said, "You men will get down on the floor and stretch out."

Monk then had the bright idea which he later regretted. He said, "Nobody ever keeps dueling pistols loaded while they're lying around the house."

Elva Boone, her voice like fine metal, said, "You wouldn't believe me if I told you these are loaded, would you?"

"No," Monk said.

The girl then pulled the trigger of the left-hand

gun, and it made such a shocking noise that a vase full of flowers upset on a side table. Monk squawked, dodged so violently that he nearly followed the vase in upsetting.

"The other one is also loaded," the girl said. She backed toward the door. "Ruth, you come with me," she ordered.

Mrs. Dorman put her fingertips against her teeth. She was pale. "But, Elva, is this wise—"

"Come on," her sister said grimly, "I have an idea."

Mrs. Dorman obeyed. The two women backed out. The door was slammed, and the lock clicked.

Ham said, "There's a back door!" and whipped through dining room, kitchen and storeroom, to get to the rear door. But as he approached it, he heard the lock clicking.

"They got here ahead of me," Ham roared angrily. "We're locked in!"

He rushed back, joined Monk and his eyes hunted for Doc Savage. "Where'd Doc go?" he demanded.

Monk pointed.

The bronze man had jacked up one of the window screens, and had swung out on the window ledge. There was hard concrete sidewalk and street more than twenty floors below. The building was not of brick, but of block-stone construction, with a space at the joints. But not much space. Hardly safe purchase for fingertips. Doc started up.

Monk moved over to the window—looking at the wall Doc was scaling, peering down onto the street—and had the feeling that his hair was standing on end. He knew Doc possessed fabulous physical strength. He had seen the bronze man do things that looked impossible. But that did not keep ice out of his veins.

The bronze man reached the roof. There was a small superstructure there which housed the elevator mechanism. The door was hasped shut, but not locked. He got inside.

The machinery of one elevator was operating. Doc stopped it.

TEN minutes later, when Elva Boone and Ruth Dorman hurried out of the apartment house—the elevator had stopped dead between two floors, and it had been necessary to send the building superintendent to the roof before it could be started again—Doc Savage, Monk and Ham were out of the building. They were at the far end of the block, waiting in a taxicab.

"That good-lookin' gal has got that pistol in her purse," Monk said grimly. "Notice how she carries the purse, her hand in it."

The two women headed in the opposite direction, walking fast.

Ham asked, "See any sign of Renny, Long Tom or Johnny? They should be here and watching this place by now."

Doc Savage pointed. "Notice the telephone lineman."

"Eh?"

"In the center of the street."

New York City telephone lines are carried in underground conduits which can be reached in most cases through manholes in the pavement, which accounted for the fact that the "lineman" was seated on the rim of an open manhole in the center of the street. A regulation telephone company truck was parked at the curb, and a protective railing and red warning flags had been erected around the manhole.

The "lineman" sat there with an acetylene cutting torch in his hand. He wore the kind of hood that welders wear, and he was going through the motions of welding something below the lip of the manhole.

Ham chuckled. "Long Tom, isn't it?"

Monk said, "That's a slick disguise he's thought up. I didn't even recognize him."

A cab cruised down the street, and Elva Boone hailed it quickly. The two women got in.

Doc said to the driver of their own machine, "Trail that cab—the one that the two women just got in."

The driver looked around. He was suspicious, and not afraid. He said, "What is this, pals?" in a tough voice.

"We're detectives," Monk told him, altering the truth a little.

That made it different, and the driver put the cab in motion. They proceeded to follow Elva Boone and Mrs. Ruth Dorman south and east to Central Park.

Doc Savage made no move to stop the two women. Monk and Ham did not question him as to his reasons. They had seen Doc do strange things before. They had seen him let a suspected person apparently get away, and lead him to the higher-ups.

"What about Renny, Long Tom and Johnny?" Ham asked.

Doc said, "They can stay where they are. If anyone is watching the Dorman apartment house, they may be able to spot whoever it is. Anyway, we have no means of communicating with them without attracting attention."

Monk eyed the bronze man. "What do you think is back of this, Doc? Don't it look as if it hitches up, in some way, to that golden man they found in the ocean?"

"Apparently it does," Doc admitted.

The taxi they were following moved slowly.

When the machine was in the park, the two women abruptly alighted and dismissed the cab. They walked for a while, seemingly doing nothing but strolling.

Doc and his men kept out of sight.

Without having done anything except stroll, the two women took another taxi.

"What was the idea of *that?*" Monk pondered. "Did they just take a walk to calm their nerves?"

Doc Savage said nothing.

ELVA BOONE and Mrs. Ruth Dorman ended their trip in front of a building of distinctly startling appearance. The structure was near the swanky Murray Hill section, one of the old brownstones. But fire escapes and every hint of ornamentation had been stripped from the face of the structure, and the building was painted a somber black.

The two women talked to their cab driver for a while. The driver shook his head—some money changed hands—and there was a little more conversation. The driver nodded.

When Monk glanced at Doc Savage, the bronze man was watching the two women through a small pocket telescope which Monk happened to know was powerful for its size.

Doc said, "They told the taxi driver they are going into the black building, then through an alleyway to a side street, where the driver is to pick them up."

Startled, Monk was about to demand how Doc had found that out. Then he understood. The telescope—Doc Savage was a skilled lip reader.

"Monk, you keep an eye on the front of the place, in case we were mistaken," Doc suggested.

Monk nodded. He waited until Elva Boone and Ruth Dorman had entered the black building, then got out of the cab. Doc and Ham rode around to the opposite side of the block. Doc said, "Ham, you stay in the cab, two blocks down the street, and watch for signals." Ham nodded, moved away in the machine.

A moment later, Doc himself was in the street, crouching back of a parked car for concealment.

Elva Boone and Mrs. Dorman had stepped out of an areaway. They seemed familiar with the vicinity, and glanced about for their cab. The hack was not there. The women waited for a few moments, obviously growing more nervous. It dawned on them that their cab driver had gotten the idea there was something wrong, and had decided not to have anything more to do with them.

Elva Boone and Ruth Dorman walked to a drugstore, where they ordered soft drinks. They sat at a table.

The drugstore had a side door. Doc got through the side entrance and into a booth without being observed. From that spot, he could watch the faces of both women, and, although it was impossible to hear what they were saying, he could read their lips without difficulty.

Elva Boone was talking energetically, driving home some kind of an argument which ended, "—so that we can keep you out of this, Ruth. The fact that you were in Captain Kirman's office when he was murdered—I'm convinced he was murdered—was unlucky as the dickens. But the police don't suspect you. Or if they do, they certainly don't suspect the real facts. You can tell your husband you were merely working there to learn about fish."

"I wish," said Ruth Dorman, "that we could tell the whole evil truth."

"We couldn't prove any of it, Ruth."

"I know. Only—"

"And *you* don't want your husband to find out about it."

Ruth Dorman shuddered. "No, Fred mustn't even guess."

Elva Boone said, "However, if you were smart, you would tell him."

"No, no! You know Fred—the way he believes. And the way he would feel about a thing like this."

Elva Boone frowned at her sister. "You were an idiot, Ruth, to get involved in it."

Mrs. Dorman nodded dumbly.

Elva reached over impulsively and squeezed her sister's hand. "However, I think my plan will work. Doc Savage and his two friends trailed us—trailed us right up to the Dark Sanctuary. They will think we went there, so they will investigate the place. Investigate it—that's what we want them to do."

Again Mrs. Dorman nodded.

Elva added, "Let's get out of this neighborhood. We've led the bloodhounds to the rat hole where we think they should do their digging. Now we can sit back and see what happens."

"I hope you're right, Elva."

"It can't hurt anything," said the positive young woman. "From what I've heard about Doc Savage, if anyone can crack this nut, he can."

The two women left the drugstore and hailed a taxicab. While they were doing that, Doc Savage stood where the sisters could not see him and signaled Ham, semaphore style, with a handkerchief.

"Follow them and RARHQ," Doc wigwagged.

Ham acknowledged that he understood. The code letters RARHQ meant, "Report to the automatic recorder at headquarters." In the bronze man's skyscraper laboratory was a gadget connected to the telephone wires which automatically recorded incoming calls together with whatever the caller said.

Chapter XIII
DARK SANCTUARY

MONK MAYFAIR was standing in front of an apartment house with a pencil and paper in hand pretending to be a newspaper reporter in search of material for a feature story about the strange things that apartment-house doormen see. Standing there, Monk could see the black building which Elva Boone and Mrs. Dorman had pretended to enter.

"Where's my pet hog?" Monk asked Doc Savage.

"With Ham in the cab," Doc explained. "Ham is trailing the two women."

Monk joined Doc, and they walked down the street. Monk said, "I asked that doorman about the black building. He says it's the Dark Sanctuary."

"The what?"

"Dark Sanctuary."

"Did he tell you what it is?"

"I asked him, but he said he didn't know. He said a lot of limousines and chauffeured town cars drive up there in the course of a day, though."

"The two women want us to investigate this Dark Sanctuary."

"That's why they led us here?"

"Yes."

"It ain't a trick, maybe? The dames didn't maybe hope to lead us into a trap?"

The bronze man remained silent on that point. As they approached the severely plain-black front of the building, a car was just pulling into an arched driveway which penetrated into one side of the building and out the other. The machine was a fifteen-thousand-dollar imported town car with chauffeur and footman in uniform.

Monk said, "Hey, they sure have the ritz around the place."

Doc headed straight for the door.

Monk was uneasy. "You figure on barging right into that joint, Doc?"

Doc Savage nodded.

By the way of preliminary precaution, Monk took his trouser belt up a couple of notches, so that he would not lose that essential garment if the action became brisk. He altered his necktie knot, tying in a knot of his own invention which was not fancy to look at, but which had the very good virtue that, if a foe grabbed hold of the necktie in a fight, the necktie would come off Monk's neck instead of choking him.

"Well, let's hope it's a keg of nails," Monk said.

The door was of some type of black wood, and the use of black coloring at the portal, together with the black coloration throughout, had achieved an effect of dignity. There was no effect of garishness about the place—nothing theatrical, nothing carnival. But it was impressive.

At the door stood a man in a black uniform, a uniform not completely black, but touched off with deep scarlet.

Monk stared at the scarlet touches on the uniform, and remembered the black star with the crimson edging.

Monk said to the doorman, "We are newspapermen. We have orders to get a story out of this place for our paper."

A forbidding expression came over the doorman's face. "Nothing doing, pal!" he snapped. He must have touched a button, because three other men, dressed like himself, and husky, appeared. The doorman said, "You two birds clear out."

Doc Savage's voice was quiet. "Possibly," he said, "this might make some difference." He displayed credentials which proved he was a police official.

The doorman hesitated. Finally he told one of the men he had summoned, "Go get Gallehue."

"What the hell is cops doing here?" the man asked.

"Go get Gallehue."

The man went away.

Out of a mouth corner, Monk said, "You hear that, Doc? Gallehue. There was a Sam Gallehue on the *Virginia Dare*. Reckon it's the same bird."

Still with no expression on his metallic features, Doc Savage turned to the doorman and asked, "You are sending for Mr. Sam Gallehue?"

"Yes," the doorman said shortly. "What about it?"

Monk said, "It's lovely. We're old pals."

Mr. Sam Gallehue thought it was lovely, too; at least he told them so effusively while he pumped their hands—Monk's first—and said, "Oh, how delightful. Quite. I'm so glad to see you, really I am."

Monk returned the handshake as enthusiastically as if he had hold of a dead fish and said, "This is the chief—Doc Savage."

Mr. Sam Gallehue additionally was delighted no end, he said. He had heard of Doc Savage, he added, and now that he was meeting the bronze man, it was one of the moments of his life. Really a pleasure. Would they have some cocktails? He consulted his wrist watch. There was a swell place around the corner which was especially nice at this hour.

Monk, with not too much tact—courtesy was not Monk's long suit—said, "It's this funny black building we're interested in."

Mr. Sam Gallehue blinked. "Beg pardon?"

"What kind of a joint is it, Sammy?"

"Joint?" Mr. Gallehue was horrified. He glanced about nervously. "Suppose we go to my private office," he muttered.

The private office was not black, but it was darkly wooden in tone. Nothing was gaudy, but also nothing was very cheap. The effect was one of rich dignity.

Sam Gallehue pulled out chairs and patted the seats as if to make sure they were soft enough for his visitors. But he did not look happy.

"I hope, I sincerely hope"—Gallehue was looking at Doc Savage—"that you are not here in your official capacity."

Doc asked quietly, "What would my official capacity be?"

"Or—by that, I mean"—Mr. Sam Gallehue ran a finger around the inside of his collar—"that I have heard you are a man who, and I can say so without exaggerating, is known extensively— known in the far corners of the earth I may truthfully say—as one who devotes himself, his energies and the services of his organization to righting what are considered to be wrongs."

Monk put in, "Then we're to take it there's a wrong around here you're afraid we might try to right?"

Sam Gallehue sprang up in alarm. "Oh, my! My, no!" He popped his eyes at them. "Surely, you're kidding me! Surely!"

Monk watched the man and thinking that this was the first instance, in the time that he had known Mr. Sam Gallehue, that he had heard the man disagree with anyone.

"Just what kind of racket you got here?" Monk asked bluntly.

Sam Gallehue paced over nervously and opened the door, looked out, then closed it. There was no one listening, if that was what he had wanted to find out. He faced them and opened his mouth, but, instead of speaking, walked over and got a drink of water. Finally, "You remember the golden man found in the ocean?" he blurted.

Monk blinked. "I'll say I remember the golden man!"

"You recall also," said Sam Gallehue, "that he was an... ah... shall we say—unusual person."

"There was plenty screwy about him."

Mr. Gallehue was displeased. "That is—blasphemy!"

"Blasphemy!"

"What the heck!" Monk scowled. "Who you trying to kid?"

Mr. Gallehue's tone became dignified and firm. "The golden man," he said, "is a person with powers beyond those of mortal ken."

The manner in which the statement was made, coupled with the quietly rich atmosphere of the room, was so impressive that Monk discovered himself glancing uneasily at Doc Savage, then at the floor. "You trying to tell us," Monk muttered, "that he's... he's—"

"No—not a supreme deity," Mr. Sam Gallehue said with effective dignity. "I have never put forth a flat statement on that point." He hesitated, then added solemnly, "It is my own personal conviction that such must be the case, and I did not arrive at such a conviction lightly, I assure you. In the beginning, I was a skeptic, like yourselves. But I assure you solemnly that I am no longer a skeptic."

Monk scratched his head. "I don't get this."

Mr. Sam Gallehue said, "In the beginning, I realized that this golden man from the sea was not an ordinary mortal. I was, I think, his first follower. The first believer. And I am now his business manager and backer."

"You put up the money for this place?" Monk indicated their surroundings.

"Yes." Mr. Sam Gallehue nodded for emphasis. "And for the Mountain Sanctuary as well."

Doc Savage, who had spoken almost no words, now entered the conversation. "You handle the money?" the bronze man asked.

"Yes."

"Do you charge fees?"

"No."

"Then how do you get the money?"

"Everything," said Mr. Sam Gallehue proudly, "is voluntary donation."

"Then this is a cult?"

"I do not like that word—cult," the other replied in an injured tone.

"But if we wish to be vulgar, we might call it a cult?"

"I— Yes."

Doc Savage stood up. "In that case, I believe we would like to talk to this golden man."

Mr. Sam Gallehue shook his head hurriedly. "I am sorry, indeed I am, but you will have to make an appointment, and I must warn you that it will be several days before you can expect an audience—if you are so fortunate as to get one at all."

Doc Savage's flake-gold eyes fixed on Gallehue intently. "Take us to him. And never mind announcing us in advance."

"I—" Gallehue was perspiring.

Monk put in a growled warning. "There's several things this golden wizard of yours better clear up. There's the mystery of who got me and Ham locked up in a South American jail. There's the question of how Captain Kirman was murdered. And there's more about Ruth Dorman and Elva Boone." Monk scowled. "How would you like for us to run you and your cult into jail?"

"I—" Gallehue shuddered. "Jail! You couldn't do that. We are not guilty of anything."

"You would have a chance in court to prove that."

Gallehue wiped his face. "I— Come with me," he said finally.

They followed Gallehue. Monk, walking close to Doc, muttered, "So my friend Gallehue brought the golden man to New York and set him up as a cult leader. Smart idea. They been makin' dough, too. From that limousine trade, they must be hookin' the big-money trade."

Doc said, "Mr. Gallehue."

"Yes."

"Do the members of your cult wear black star rings or pins as insignia?"

Gallehue complained, "I wish you would not refer to it as a cult."

"Do the members wear a black star insignia?"

"Yes. That is the way our—believers—identify themselves."

DOC SAVAGE had never seen the golden man before—Doc was *sure* of that—but the golden man arose from where he was sitting in a darkly dignified chair in a darkly dignified room and extended his hand and said, "I am very glad to see you, Mr. Savage."

Doc, amazed, said, "You know me?"

The golden man seemed not to hear the inquiry. He studied Doc for a few moments, then said in a deeply impressive, solemn voice, "Since that stormy night when you were born on the tiny schooner *Orion* in the shallow cove at the north end of Andros Island, you have done much good, and many things that are great."

Doc was floored, figuratively. Not by the praise—praise did not impress him, and it was always embarrassing—but by the fact that this golden man knew the exact place of his birth. It was astounding. Doc himself had known of no living man who had those facts. His five aides did not know. It was in no written record.

The golden man added, "You will be grieved to know your friend, Baron Orrest Karl Lestzky, is dying in Vienna tonight. He will be dead in another three hours, and, as you know, it will be a great loss, and very sad. Lestzky is one of the few great surgeons who really understands your new brain-operating technique, as I know you are aware."

Doc Savage, trying not to be impressed, *was* impressed. He made, without being aware of doing so, the trilling that was his unconscious habit, and there was amazement in the sound.

Doc asked, "You know Lestzky?"

"Only as I knew you—if he would walk into this room." The golden man seemed to be weary.

He leaned forward, took his face in his hands. He sat there. Doc watched him, studying him with rigid intentness.

"It is sad," the golden man said dully. "Very sad. I am tired in my soul."

Then he got up and walked out of the room. He said no more. The door shut behind him. They could hear his footsteps, heavy, for a time, going away. Then silence.

Doc got up and moved through rooms to the street exit, saying nothing, and left the Dark Sanctuary.

Monk followed. Monk didn't know what to think.

Chapter XIV
THE FISH MAN

BENJAMIN OPSALL met Doc Savage and Monk Mayfair on the semicircular driveway that was like a tunnel in the front of the Dark Sanctuary. A limousine and chauffeur stood there, and Opsall was walking back and forth, looking completely delighted with the world and with himself.

When he saw Mr. Sam Gallehue—Gallehue had followed Doc and Monk to the exit—Opsall dashed forward, saying, "Oh, there you are, Mr. Gallehue!" Opsall thrust a slip of paper into Mr. Sam Gallehue's hands. "I want you to have this!" Opsall exclaimed. "It's a small expression of my gratitude!"

Gallehue looked at the slip of paper, which was a check. The figures for which it was made out were large. Gallehue glanced apologetically at Doc Savage, then took Opsall's elbow, and the pair moved to one side.

From the corner of his mouth, Monk whispered, "String figures on that check looked like the tail of a comet."

Doc Savage studied Benjamin Opsall. Opsall had large moist eyes and a large moist mouth, and he was wide and solid. His skin was clear with health, drowned by the sun—or sun lamp—and, even without the limousine, he would have looked prosperous. Around fifty was his age.

The Gallehue-Opsall conference broke up when Sam Gallehue pocketed the check, then shook Opsall's hands and patted Opsall on the back.

Doc Savage said, so that only Monk could hear, "Trail this Opsall."

"Eh? Why?"

"He is the man who set Captain Kirman up in the rare-fish business."

"Oh!" Monk pulled in a deep breath. "I forgot that."

Trailing Benjamin Opsall proved unexpectedly easy, for Opsall came over to Doc and Monk. He grabbed their hands. "Two more *Believers,* aren't you? That makes you friends of mine." He laughed delightedly. "We're all friends in a wonderful peace, aren't we?"

"Let's hope so," Doc Savage said conservatively.

Opsall smiled at them. "Are you coming? Going?" He held open the door of his limousine. "Can I give you a lift?"

Doc Savage said, "That would be very kind."

The bronze man got into the limousine, and Monk followed. There were jump seats which folded down, and the chauffeur lowered one of these for Monk. Opsall climbed in, and the big machine got in motion.

Opsall proceeded to talk a blue streak. "I've been a *Believer* for over a month now, and I'm more sincere now than on the day I became one."

He effused for some minutes about the wonders of the golden man, and the spiritual benefits of being a *Believer.* There were financial benefits, too, he imparted—and the story of what was behind his joy came out. It seemed that the golden man had informed him several days previously that a certain European nation was going to confiscate the foreign property of an American company. This had happened on schedule, and the stock of the company had naturally tobogganed. Opsall, having sold a great deal of the stock short, naturally had made money from the debacle. "A cleaning!" he declared.

"This being a *Believer* must be profitable," Monk said.

"Oh, enormously." Opsall leaned forward and patted Monk's shoulder. "But, mind you, I would be a *Believer* even if there wasn't a damned cent of profit in it. By the way, would you gentleman care to drop in at my place of business for a spot of tea?"

"What sort of business have you?" Doc asked innocently.

"I deal in rare fish."

"Tropicals?"

"Yes. Maybe you might like to see my stock. It is one of the most complete in existence."

"That would be interesting," Doc admitted. Monk grinned.

THE Opsall rare-fish establishment was impressive, there being large showrooms with tanks containing species of aquarium fish—dwarf *gouramis, betta* fighting fish, and other bubble-nest builders; *platys, helleri,* and various types of live bearers, together with egg-layer types such as *cichlasomma meeki, neon tetras* and white cloud mountain fish. Opsall recited the names of the fish

MONK

rapidly, leading Monk to mutter, "Sounds like Greek to me."

"Your terminology on chemistry would sound as confusing to me," Opsall assured him.

Doc Savage asked, "Mr. Opsall, are you acquainted with Captain Kirman?"

Opsall looked up quickly. "Oh, yes."

"Known Captain Kirman very long?"

"Well, only a few weeks."

"Business associate of yours?"

"Not exactly."

"But you set him up in the tropical-fish business?"

Opsall nodded slightly. "May I ask why you seem so interested?"

Monk answered that question. "Captain Kirman died today. It was no natural death."

Opsall showed distress. "Damn it, he owes me—" He hesitated, then said apologetically, "I … I'm sorry that the first thing I thought of was the money he owes me. I suppose I'm vulgar and mercenary."

He gestured for them to follow him, and moved away. "We will go to my private office," he explained. "I'm distressed by this news. I need a drink."

They entered the private office, Opsall opening the door and stepping inside and turning to hold the door ajar for them.

"Some place!" Monk exclaimed.

"My private greenhouse," Opsall said. "I use it to grow plants to augment our displays of rare fish."

One wall of the office was glass, and beyond was a view of a small private greenhouse filled with colorful tropical and semitropical flowers. A second wall was a huge aquarium in which fish of all colors and sizes swam among water plants that were as exotic as the fish. The other two walls were ordinary plaster.

"I'll say it's some place!" a distinctly unpleasant voice informed Monk.

Men with guns—there were four of them—had been standing, two on each side of the door, and they now fanned out quickly so that, if necessary, there would be room for bullets.

"Señors, you are slow getting back," one said. He was a thin man with a scar under his left eye.

Opsall ogled them. "But I don't know you!"

"Hey, Doc!" Monk was pointing at the man with the scar. "Doc, this is that guy who framed me and Ham in South America."

Doc Savage remained silent, although he could have added another pair of the four men to the identified list. The pair had been members of the group who had tried to waylay Monk and Ham in front of the skyscraper headquarters.

The thin man with the scar went to a desk which stood in the center of the floor. When he turned, he had a tray and glasses. Water was in the glasses.

The man uncorked a bottle, poured a part of its contents into each of the glasses.

"This will only put you to sleep, Señors," he said. "Drink it. No harm. Good. *Mucho bueno.*"

Doc and Monk had caught the odor of the stuff. They knew what it was. Poison, which would be working slow if it took more than five minutes to kill them.

Doc Savage spoke three words in a strange language. The words translated into, "Hold your breath."

THE language was ancient Mayan, a vernacular spoken by the Central American civilization of Maya centuries ago, but now a tongue so lost in the civilized world probably no one but Doc Savage and his associates understood or could speak it. Doc and his men used it for communication without being understood by others.

Doc, after he spoke, and as if afraid of the menacing guns, lifted both arms slowly so that his hands were above his head. His arms were not straight up, and the right one was doubled and tight as if it was making a muscle. The bulge of biceps sinew swelled up against his forearm until there was crunching sound as a fragile container inside his sleeve was crushed. It was a small noise, and no one noticed.

He waited. The gas released from the container he had broken was odorless, colorless, potent—it would induce harmless unconsciousness with uncanny speed. And it had an additional quality of becoming ineffective after it had mixed with the air for slightly more than a minute.

Unfortunately, the anaesthetic gas did not first bring down the thin man with the scar. It was one of the others, and he was very susceptible to the gas, because it got him before the others had breathed enough to be greatly affected. The man caved down slowly.

The scarred man yelled. He fired his gun straight at Doc Savage's chest. Then he sprang backward, fleeing wildly.

The bullet knocked Doc back, although he was wearing a bulletproof undergarment of alloy mesh. That protection was at best an emergency one, and the bullet struck a blow greater than any fist.

Monk threw out a hand, clutched a chair, and hurled, all in one move. The chair hit a foe. The fellow reeled, upset, lay where he fell—either the chair had knocked him senseless, or it was the anaesthetic gas, for he had fallen where the gas should be strongest.

Doc got back his balance, then leaped forward, making for the thin man with the scar. The thin man fired his gun, but missed completely. Somehow that must have given him the idea Doc was bulletproof. He took to flight. The quickest escape route was through the glass wall into the greenhouse, so the man put his hands over his face and plunged into the glass wall. Glass broke, came down in jangling sheets.

That left only one assailant in the room. Monk made for that one. Monk's hands were big and hairy and hungry in front of him. The intended victim saw Monk, tried to escape. He was slow. Monk's fist made a sound like a fistful of mud falling on a floor, and the man walked backward, senseless, making waving movements with his arms, into the falling glass of the greenhouse wall.

The anaesthetic gas had by now become ineffective from mixing with the air.

Opsall still stood rigid in the same tracks he had occupied when it all started. The anaesthetic gas had not affected him—he must have been so scared that he was holding his breath.

REINFORCEMENTS arrived. Other men—they had been hidden in the greenhouse—joined the action. These men had kept hidden behind the flowers, the luxuriant tropical plants, in the little private greenhouse.

They leaped up, three together—then two more—and a sixth.

The man with the scar screamed, "Watch out—they let loose gas!" He went flat on his face, knocking over flowerpots.

One of the six reinforcements was a dark man with a weapon peculiar to South America. A bolas. Three rawhide thongs, tied together at one end, with iron weights on the free ends. A bolas, but one that was more compact than those used by pampas cowboys to trap the legs of cattle and throw them.

The man was good with his bolas. He took a

slow windup, the bolas weights whistling, then let fly. Doc saw it coming, tried to leap clear. His jump was about a foot and a half too short—one of the thongs went about his arm; then with lightning suddenness, both arms were tied to his chest by layers of rawhide. His strength, developed as it was, could not break the thongs.

The impact of the bolas, coupled with the loss of his arms for balancing, caused Doc to upset.

The bronze man, sprawling on the floor, rolled in a melee of upsetting flowerpots. A gun began crashing; its uproar was deafening. Doc rolled as best he could without use of his arms, until he was in a narrow aisle lined by crockery pots and long troughs which held plants.

There was no skylighting in the greenhouse. The flowers were cultivated entirely by fluorescent lighting, and the fluorescent tubes were glowing nests of rods in the ceiling.

Doc Savage, still on the floor, rolled over on his back, got a heavy flowerpot between his heels, and tossed it upward. He aimed at the fluorescent light tubes, at the nest of contacts at one end of a bank of them. The pot hit the target, and electric blue flame showered.

It was suddenly dark in the windowless place.

He had managed to short out the light circuit and blow fuses.

In the darkness, a man came charging across the greenhouse floor, upsetting things, groping and cursing. Pure luck led him to stumble over Doc Savage. Doc struck with a leg; the man yelled. Doc lunged, grabbed with both legs, scissors fashion, and got hold of the man. Using the enormous muscular strength of his legs, Doc hurled the fellow away, and there was noise of objects upsetting and the man howled in pain.

Bullets were going through things, making various kinds of racket. Back in the office, there was a fight, a violent fight between several men, one of whom was Monk. Doc listened to it while he struggled to get the rawhide bolas thongs loose from his body. Then Monk's angry roaring suddenly stopped.

A man puffed, "Gimme a knife or gun, somebody! The leg of the damned chair broke when I hit him."

The voice of the man with the scar came out shrilly over the uproar, demanding, "Have you caught one of them?"

"Yeah. The one they call Monk."

"Do not kill him!"

"But, hell—"

"Keep him alive!" yelled the scarred man. "If we fail to get Savage, we can use this Monk."

"I'm damned if I—"

"Take Monk and get out!" yelled the leader. "If Savage does not stop bothering us, we'll kill his damned friend."

A moment later, a new voice—it must have been a lookout they'd had posted outside—began howling that police were coming.

"Clear out!" shouted the scarred man. "Run, hombres!"

Doc seized another flowerpot with his feet. He did not throw it. He put it down. The distance was too great. There were too many of them and they had too many guns for him to tackle unless his arms were free. Some of them were still shooting, driving bullets at random, while others searched for those who were casualties.

"I thought there was supposed to be gas in here," a man said.

"There was," the leader growled. "I do not know what happened to it. Get a move on. The police are close!"

"What about Opsall?"

There was a moment of brittle silence.

"Knock him senseless," the leader said finally, "and leave him. He does not mean anything to us."

Doc Savage lay prone and helpless, struggling with the tangled rawhide, while they left, taking Monk with them.

Chapter XV
DECEIT

THE police were not very patient with Benjamin Opsall. They thought it was strange that the gang had staged the ambush in Opsall's private office in such an extensive fashion. They were inclined to wonder if Opsall had led Doc Savage and Monk into a trap.

"But it wasn't my doing," Opsall assured them. "Practically the last the leader of those men said was to knock me senseless and leave me, because I had no value to them."

Disgruntled policemen made a complete search of the vicinity.

While Doc Savage was waiting around for the police-made excitement to subside, he did one peculiar thing. He happened to find a revolver lying in the greenhouse wreckage. It was an ornate gun with elaborate pearl grips and some gold-inlay work on the barrel.

The gun was the one which had been carried by the thin man with the scar under his left eye. The fellow must have dropped it during the fight.

Doc pocketed the weapon. He did not say anything to anyone about finding it.

The police failed to locate Monk. They did find an eyewitness who had seen the homely chemist tossed into a car. The car had then departed the neighborhood at high speed. Monk had been unconscious at the time, the witness believed. He was also bleeding from the mouth.

Having done all they could do, the police departed.

After they had gone, Doc Savage left Opsall's rare-fish establishment, and found a telephone. He got in touch with his headquarters and found that Ham Brooks was there.

"Anything to report?" the bronze man asked.

Ham said, "Elva Boone and Mrs. Ruth Dorman went back to their apartment and Renny, Long Tom and Johnny are watching the apartment house. So far, they have not been able to discover anyone shadowing the place."

"Anything else?"

"Yes. Remember that steamship company official who was a friend of Captain Kirman's—the one who told us where Captain Kirman's office was located? I mean the fellow who was wearing the black star ring, and wouldn't tell us anything about it."

"I know who you mean."

"I got him on the telephone," Ham said, "and when he found out Captain Kirman was dead, he jarred loose with some information. Here's how he got the ring. At Captain Kirman's request, he had joined a kind of cult that hangs out in a building uptown called the Dark Sanctuary. Black stars with red borders are the insignia of this cult. That cult sounds interesting. The cult leader is a strange golden man. And the cult business manager is none other than our friend, Mr. Sam Gallehue. That's something, isn't it?"

"You say the steamship official joined the cult at Captain Kirman's request?"

"Yes."

"Why?"

"Captain Kirman wanted him to investigate the cult."

"Did Captain Kirman want it investigated secretly?"

"Yes, secretly."

"Why was Captain Kirman so interested in the cult?"

"The steamship man didn't know."

Doc Savage said, "Ham, will you come to Opsall's fish establishment? Meet me at a tobacco store a block south and a block east."

TWENTY minutes later, a dark-skinned man with curly yellow hair and a rather unhealthy cast to his skin, a lumpy left cheek and a nose with distended nostrils, approached Doc Savage at the cigar store a block south and a block east of Opsall's fish establishment.

"How do you like it?" the unusual-looking man asked.

"Good enough, Ham," Doc said.

Ham Brooks said, "I found this make-up stuff at headquarters. Not bad, eh? Wax in one cheek. Gadgets up my nose to make it flare. And skin dye."

Doc said, "You will watch Opsall."

"Where is he?"

"In his place of business. But be careful, Ham. Be careful with your trailing. But do not fail to follow him."

Something in the bronze man's tone impressed Ham.

"What are *you* going to do, Doc?"

The bronze man's voice took on grimness. "We are not making much progress in this thing," he said. "So it seems we will have to start some bombing operations."

Doc's first bombing operation came off without complications.

The bronze man crept into Opsall's rare-fish establishment by way of a rear window; eventually he managed to reach the semiwrecked private greenhouse without being observed. In the office, visible from the greenhouse, Opsall sat. Doc watched him. Opsall was straining his hair with his fingers and smoking a new white meerschaum pipe.

Doc tied a long string to the doorknob and kept hold of the other end of the string.

Then the bronze man got out the inlaid, pearl-decorated revolver. When Opsall's head was turned just right, Doc took careful aim, resting the gun on a flower trellis, and shot the meerschaum pipe out of Opsall's teeth. The gun report was deafening. But, if possible, Opsall's astonished howl was louder.

Doc then made some noise of his own. He fell down on the floor, out of sight of Opsall, and knocked things over. In his own voice, he shouted, "Drop that gun, you!"

In an imitation of the voice of the man who had the scar under his left eye, he yelled, "Get away, damn you!"

Doc then fired the gun twice more, kicked over a row of plant boxes, threw a flowerpot against the wall, hurled another at the ceiling. He drove a fist into a palm to make a loud blow sound. He groaned and upset a bench.

Slapping his hands against the floor, he made a fair imitation of a man taking flight. Then he jerked the string, causing the door to slam. He kept pulling the string, and it slipped off the doorknob. He hauled it in, rolled it up and thrust it in a pocket.

The whole thing had been a fair imitation of an attempt on Opsall's life which Doc had thwarted.

Some moments later, Doc arose to his feet. He

made himself tremble, and felt the back of his head as if he had been hit there.

Opsall approached empty-handed and frightened.

Doc demanded, "Which way did he go?"

"W-who?" Opsall gulped.

"The man who was trying to kill you."

"He gug-got away through the duh-door." Opsall swallowed. "H-how did you happen to tuh-trail him?"

Doc said, "Oh, I was keeping a watch on this place. Afraid those raiders would decide you knew too much, and send somebody back to kill you."

"W-which one was it?" Opsall asked.

"Hard to tell. One of them had a scar on his face, didn't he?" Doc exhibited the gun. "This is the gun that was dropped."

Opsall's eyes were about as wide as they could get. He was speechless.

Doc handed him the ornate gun. "You better keep this for self-protection," he said.

"Thuh-thanks!"

"Do you know of any other reason why they should kill you?"

"I—no. No, of course not!"

After assuring Opsall that he did not think the raiders would be back soon, Doc Savage left the building. He re-entered secretly at once by the back door, got into the basement, and found the telephone junction box. He tore the wires out, disrupting all telephone service to the building.

Then Doc Savage joined Ham.

"Follow Opsall if he goes anywhere."

"Right."

"If Opsall is mixed up in this," Doc explained, "he now has something to think about, and he will want to talk to the others about it. He can't telephone, so he will probably go to them. And wherever he goes, you follow him. Make your reports by shortwave radio."

"I'll be tied to his shoestrings," Ham said grimly.

RENNY RENWICK was sitting behind the counter of a candy store. Through the window of this store, he could watch the entrance of the apartment house where Mrs. Ruth Dorman lived, and munch chocolate cherries at the same time.

"I rented this job for the day," Renny told Doc Savage. "I have a car parked close to here, in case we need it. Johnny is around at the back of the apartment house. Holy cow, they got good candy here!"

"Is Long Tom still welding manholes in the middle of the street?" Doc asked.

"No. He has tapped the Dorman woman's telephone wires. He's listening in on that."

"Has he heard anything?"

"Nothing."

Doc Savage said, "It is time we started some action. Can you get Long Tom and Johnny?"

Renny grabbed a fistful of candy, then came around from back of the counter. "I'll fetch 'em."

Five minutes later, Renny was back with Long Tom and Johnny.

Doc gave instructions.

"Long Tom, you and Johnny watch a place called the Dark Sanctuary." He gave them the address of the establishment. "Long Tom, you tap the telephone wires as soon as possible."

"Want me to try to rig microphones in the place, so we can eavesdrop?" Long Tom asked.

"If you see a way of doing that, it would be a good idea," Doc admitted.

"Shall we watch for anybody in particular?"

"Two men. One of them is the unusual golden man who is the cult leader. I want to know what he does and where he goes. The other man is Sam Gallehue, the business manager of the cult. Report his movements, too."

"Report to the recorder at headquarters?"

"Yes."

"Where's Monk?"

"They got him."

"Who did?" Johnny gasped.

"The same scar-faced man who got Monk and Ham thrown in jail in South America."

Johnny and Long Tom departed, grimly silent, deeply concerned.

Doc Savage told Renny, "We will call on Elva Boone and Mrs. Dorman and see if we can get them to talk sense."

ELVA BOONE answered the doorbell of the Dorman apartment, then tried to slam the door, but Doc pressed inside. Renny followed.

"That was accommodating of you to lead us to the Dark Sanctuary," Doc informed the angry young woman. "Unfortunately, we did not get much information from the place."

The girl was startled. She hesitated, then shrugged. "I thought I fooled you," she said curtly. "You knew I was leading you there. So what?"

Doc said, "How about a complete story?"

"And a true one," Renny added.

Elva Boone glanced over her shoulder at her sister. Mrs. Dorman shook her head frantically. "No, Elva! We can't tell anyone!"

Elva Boone looked at Doc Savage. "We've been discussing you," she said. "We could use the brand of help you dish out."

Her sister gasped. "Please, Elva! If my husband ever found out—"

"Ruth, you fool, you're already mixed up in Captain Kirman's murder."

"But—"

Doc said, "Let's have the story."

Elva Boone hesitated, finally nodded. "My sister was married several years ago and thought she had divorced her husband," she said. "There was one child. Later she married Mr. Dorman, but she was a fool. She never told Mr. Dorman about being married before, because her first husband was—well, a trashy kind. Mr. Dorman is a snob, but my sister happens to be in love with him. Then she found she wasn't divorced. It was kind of a problem, and it bore on her mind.

"To bring the story up to date—a little more than a month ago, Ruth got all worked up over this cult that hangs out in the Dark Sanctuary. She became what they call a *Believer.* She was impressed. She actually thinks this strange golden man who is head of the cult is—well, not an ordinary mortal. In justice to Ruth, I'll have to say that it's hard not to think otherwise.

"But to make the story still shorter, Ruth told the golden man about her other husband, and her divorce she didn't get. She asked advice—and she got it."

"What was the advice?" Doc asked curiously.

"To make a clean breast of it to Mr. Dorman. The golden man told her that if Mr. Dorman wasn't man enough to forgive and forget, he wasn't man enough to be a husband."

"Good advice," Doc said.

"I agree. But it would have lost my sister her husband, as sure as anything. Ruth didn't take the advice."

"Then what?"

"Blackmail. About a week later. A man delivered a note from Ruth's ex-husband, demanding money, or he would go to Mr. Dorman with the story."

"Has Ruth paid anything?"

"Yes." Elva nodded. "She decided to pay. But I talked her into trying to ferret out who was at the bottom of the blackmail, at the same time. I helped her."

"How did you do the ferreting?"

"I suspected the cult, so I watched the Dark Sanctuary. I discovered another man watching it, and one day, I accosted him, and he turned out to be Captain Kirman. He told me that he, like myself, was trying to get evidence against the cult."

"You and Captain Kirman joined forces, I presume."

"Yes." Elva nodded. "Ruth went to Captain Kirman's office to work and help in the investigation whenever she had spare time. To tell the truth, about all she did was take care of the business while Captain Kirman was out investigating. But that was a help."

"Did you get evidence against the cult?"

"Not a bit."

"Why was Captain Kirman so interested in the cult?"

Elva Boone grimaced. "That's a funny thing. He would never tell us. But he was interested. *Very* interested."

Doc said, "Would you care for some advice about your sister?"

"I would welcome it," Elva Boone said fervently. "We're at our wits' end."

Doc asked, "Does your sister have an out-of-town relative she can visit in a hurry?"

"Why, yes. Our Aunt Lorna, in Detroit."

"She should visit Aunt Lorna."

"You mean—get her out of the way until this is settled?"

"Yes."

Elva turned to her sister. "Ruth, I think you had better do that."

They got Ruth Dorman aboard a Detroit-bound plane which left LaGuardia field at six o'clock that evening.

THE automatic recorder which receives messages in Doc Savage's skyscraper headquarters had abilities that were almost human. If a stranger called the bronze man's establishment, a mechanical voice from the device said, "This is Doc Savage's office, but no one is here at the moment. This voice is coming from a mechanical device. If you wish to leave a message, whatever you say will be recorded automatically, and Doc Savage will receive it upon his return."

After Ruth Dorman had been shipped off to Detroit, Doc Savage returned to headquarters with Renny and Elva Boone. He turned on the recorder to see what messages had been received.

There was a report from Ham. It was, "Watching Opsall's place. Nothing has happened. No sign of Monk. That is all."

The last message was from Johnny.

Said Johnny's voice, "Johnny reporting, Doc. Mr. Sam Gallehue left the Dark Sanctuary at five-twenty. He went to a large apartment building on Park Avenue. He has an apartment there. He is now in the apartment. The building is across the street from that snazzy club Ham belongs to. Long Tom is watching the Dark Sanctuary. He has tapped the telephone. No sign of Monk. That is all."

Doc Savage switched off the apparatus.

"Do you know some good actors?" he asked Renny.

"Actors?" Renny was puzzled. "Holy cow! What do you want with actors?"

"Do you know any?"

"Yes. Male or female?"

"Male. Men who will do a rather tough job if they are well paid."

"The actors I know," Renny said, "would play Daniel in a den of real lions for cash money."

"Get hold of three of them," Doc said grimly.

"What are you going to do?"

"Toss another bomb, and see what happens."

Chapter XVI
MURDER IS AN ACT

MR. SAM GALLEHUE, answering his door-bell himself, wore a long purple robe, comfortable slippers, and his fingers fondled a dollar cigar.

When he got a good look at his visitors, Gallehue nearly dropped the cigar on the expensive rug. He was not disturbed so much by the visitors as by the way they were holding their hats. They carried the hats in their hands in such a fashion that the headgear concealed shiny revolvers from the elevator operator, but allowed Gallehue a distressingly unobstructed view of the weapons.

"Invite us in, Sammy," one man said.

Gallehue went through the motions of swallowing a hard-boiled egg, then said, "Cuk-come in."

The two men entered and closed the door.

"I… I don't know you!" Sam Gallehue gasped.

"Sit down," said one of the men.

"But—"

"Sit down!"

Sam Gallehue sat down. His hands twisted together. He quailed involuntarily while one of the men searched him for a weapon and found none.

"What—who—"

"One more word out of you," one of the gunmen said fiercely, "and we'll knock about six of your teeth out."

Gallehue watched in silence as the men went to work. A little at a time, his expression changed. One of the gunmen kept a close watch on Gallehue.

The other gunman opened the window, shoved his head out and looked upward. It was quite dark outside.

"O.K., Gyp," the man said.

From a window above, a voice called down cautiously in the darkness. "All set?"

"Yes."

"Are you boys down below?"

"Yes."

"Did they get an apartment right under this one?"

"Two floors above that ledge, nine stories below us," said the gunman. "Go ahead and drop the wire down to them."

A moment later, a thin wire with a weight on the end sank past the window. The gunman reached out and steadied it in its descent. "All right," he said finally. "They caught the end of the wire down there. They'll make that end fast to something in the room."

From the night overhead, the voice whispered, "Now we better tie the dummy on this end of the wire, eh?"

"Go ahead."

"How is Gallehue dressed?"

The gunman turned around to look at Gallehue—the cult manager had become practically as pale as he could get—then wheeled back to the window. "He's wearing a purple dressing robe."

"We ain't got nothing like that up here to dress the dummy in."

"What kind of clothes you got?"

"A blue suit."

The gunman withdrew his head again, and prowled around the apartment until he found Gallehue's closet, from which he dragged a blue suit. "Put it on," he ordered Gallehue.

"But—"

"Put it on!"

When Gallehue had drawn on the blue garment with shaking fingers, the gunman went back to the window once more.

"All set," he called upward to his companion. "He's got on a blue suit now. Put the blue suit on the dummy, so everything'll be cocked and primed."

"O.K."

The gunman, whispering upward, gave full instructions about how the murder was to be committed.

"When you hear Doc Savage in this apartment, toss the dummy out of the window, so it will land on the ledge below. Doc Savage will see it fall past the window, and see it on the ledge. The boys downstairs will have the end of the wire, attached to the dummy, and they'll give it a jerk or two to make it look as if the dummy is about to fall off the ledge. Savage will rush down there to save the dummy. As soon as he is out of the room, we'll knock Gallehue on the head and toss him out of the window, and his body will land on the ledge. The boys downstairs will then haul the dummy back up out of sight—and Doc Savage will have another impossible death to puzzle about."

"Right."

THE gunman withdrew his head, and stepped back to eye the window appraisingly. "There should be more light outside," he remarked. "But the man upstairs will yell that somebody is about to commit suicide, and that'll get Doc Savage to look at the window, so he will see the dummy fall past."

Gallehue tried two or three times to speak, and

finally croaked, "Yuh-yuh-you're going to *murder* me?"

"Them's orders."

"W-who gave such orders?"

The gunman laughed in a way that made Sam Gallehue's hair seem to move around on his scalp. "You poor fool. You put a lot of trust in your pals, don't you?"

"I don't understand what you mean," Sam Gallehue said.

"Didn't it ever occur to you that someone else might want the split you've been getting?"

While Sam Gallehue was getting paler, the doorbell rang. The two gunmen looked at each other. "Doc Savage," one whispered. "He's about due here."

The other gunman jammed his revolver muzzle into Sam Gallehue's ribs. "Don't let on we're here," he snarled. "If you let out one peep about us, we'll blow you to pieces."

The two gunmen then moved into an adjoining room. They left the door open a crack, so that their weapons still menaced Gallehue.

The doorbell rang again. Sam Gallehue admitted Doc Savage. Gallehue was wet with perspiration, afraid to try to make a break. Doc Savage stepped into the apartment. Big-fisted Renny followed the bronze man.

Doc eyed Gallehue. "Is something wrong?" the bronze man asked.

"I—no," Gallehue croaked. "No, nothing is … is—"

Doc Savage's flake-gold eyes moved over the room, then he approached a chair. He took hold of the chair, as if to change its position.

Gallehue suddenly broke.

"Two gunmen!" he shrieked. He pointed at the side door. "In there!"

Doc Savage hurled the chair at the door which concealed the two gunmen. The chair hit the door with a crash, Doc Savage following it. The gunmen, however, got the door shut before Doc reached it. They did not fire their revolvers.

"Renny!" Doc rapped. "Head them off! The hall!"

Renny raced for the hall.

The bronze man himself hit the door with his shoulder. It crackled. The third time he slammed his weight against it, the lock tore out of the door, and he plunged through.

There was the pound of running feet. Angry words.

Mr. Sam Gallehue staggered over to a chair and was a loose pile of paleness in it. He did not entirely faint, although he held both hands against his chest over his heart.

It was fully five minutes before Doc Savage and Renny returned to the room.

Both men looked disgusted.

"They got away," Doc reported.

"Thu-thank goodness!" Gallehue gasped.

"What were they doing here?" Doc asked.

"They were gug-going to murder me."

"How?"

Mr. Sam Gallehue told them how the murder was to have been committed. He told them exactly what had happened in the apartment, and what had been said, and nothing more.

DOC SAVAGE and Renny Renwick, leaving the apartment house half an hour later, were somewhat silent, as if disappointed. At the corner, three men joined them, two of these being the gunmen who had menaced Sam Gallehue, and the third man their companion who had carried on the dialogue from the window overhead.

Doc Savage said, "Renny recommended you as very good actors, and he did not exaggerate. You did an excellent job."

Doc paid them.

"Thank you, Mr. Savage. I believe we put it over, all right. Gallehue was completely fooled." The actor hesitated and looked uneasy. "But what if he reports this to the police?"

"Both Renny and myself are honorary police officials," Doc explained. "So we can explain it, if necessary. What you were doing was actually a piece of detective work."

The three actors, satisfied with themselves and the pay, entered a taxicab and drove away.

Renny said, "Doc—that business about the dummy body—are you sure that was the way Captain Kirman was murdered?"

"As positive as one could reasonably be," Doc said.

"How did you happen to solve Captain Kirman's murder? It looked like an impossible death—a body falling past a window, and the body turning into that of a man who was standing in the room with you."

Doc said, "You recall that a room adjoined Captain Kirman's office. The killers were hiding in that room while we were in the office. Captain Kirman knew they were there, but he did *not* know they were going to kill him, so he gave no alarm."

"How'd you figure that out?"

"The fish."

"Eh?"

"There were two tanks in the room which contained very timid fish. These fish had been recently scared. It was a reasonable surmise that they had been scared by the killers of Captain Kirman hiding in the room."

"But how did the killers get out of the small room after they threw Captain Kirman's body out of the window, and their colleagues in a downstairs office hauled the dummy off the ledge? They didn't leave through the door. Mrs. Dorman was in the outer office."

"Probably stepped to the window ledge of the adjoining office—or climbed a rope ladder. It was not difficult, probably. And no one would have seen them because the building opposite was a warehouse which had no windows."

"How come Mrs. Dorman didn't know the men were there?"

"Captain Kirman must have sent her out on some small errand to get her away. Or he brought the men in when she was out. Or they sneaked past her somehow. There are several ways."

"Holy cow!" Renny sighed and eyed his big fists. "Well, that's one danged mystery cleared up—all but *why* they killed him. But we didn't get any concrete results with our gag we pulled on Gallehue, did we? You think he is guilty."

"We scared him, and we deceived him."

"But he did not act guilty."

A long, thin piece of shadow, and a small shapely one, joined them, and Johnny's voice said, "Miss Boone and I got the Gallehue telephone tapped. It's hooked onto a recording device, so that any calls Gallehue makes will go on to a record."

"Good," Doc Savage said. "Johnny, you continue watching Gallehue. If he leaves his apartment, trail him."

"Right. You want me to keep in touch with you by radio?"

"Yes."

"What do you want me to do?" Elva Boone asked. "I'm beginning to like this excitement."

"Come with me and Renny," Doc told her.

"What are we going to do?" she inquired. "Another bomb?"

"Yes, another bomb," Doc agreed. "If we keep it up, the law of averages should bring us some kind of a result."

Chapter XVII
THE EMPTY BUSHES

THE night sky was a dark path for ponderous black clouds that slunk like marauders, almost scraping bellies against the higher buildings. The air was so heavy that one was conscious of breathing it; it was like perfume without odor. Street traffic was listless and made vague discontented murmurs, while far down in the bay a steamer embroiled in some harbor problem kept hooting long distressed blasts mingled with short excited tooting.

The Dark Sanctuary was a swarthy mass of dignified masonry. Next door, however, leaped up an apartment house with lighted windows that were many bright eyes in the murk of a depressing night.

Doc Savage and Renny and Elva Boone located Long Tom Roberts in the shadows.

Long Tom asked, "Any trace of Monk yet?"

"No."

Long Tom said grimly, "The place is as quiet as a grasshopper in a hen yard. There were some lights at the windows, but they all went out about eleven o'clock, and a lot of men left. They looked like servants and attendants, because they all wore uniforms. The golden man is still in there."

Doc Savage said, "Keep an eye on the place. In about twenty minutes, you should get a radio call from me. If you do not, use your own judgment."

"You mean—if we don't hear from you, bust into the place?"

"That might be the best idea."

Doc Savage entered the lighted apartment house next door to the Dark Sanctuary. He talked awhile with the doorman, and showed his police credentials. Eventually he was conducted to an empty sixth-floor apartment.

A few minutes later, Doc Savage swung out of the window of the empty apartment and went down a thin silk cord which was equipped with convenient handholds. The end of the cord was tied to a collapsible grapple, and the grapple was hooked around a radiator pipe.

A slowly descending shadow, he reached the roof of the Dark Sanctuary, then searched rapidly. All skylights and roof hatches were steel-barred, and locked, he found. He had hitched to his back with webbing straps a pack of some size. He shoved a hand into this, felt around, and brought out a bottle.

The contents of the bottle hissed and steamed when he poured it on the ends of half a dozen skylight bars. He waited about five minutes, then grasped the bars one at a time and broke them apart without much effort. The acid he had used was strong stuff, and he was careful in replacing the bottle in the pack, because it would eat through flesh as readily as through steel.

The glass panes in the skylight were large, and it was not much trouble to remove one near the edge. He hooked another silk-cord-and-collapsible-grapple device over the rim of the skylight, then went down into darkness.

He searched.

The Dark Sanctuary was empty except for the golden man.

The golden man was asleep in a second-floor room, sleeping placidly, snoring a little.

Doc uncorked a small bottle and held it under the sleeping man's nostrils. After a while, the snoring became more loud and relaxed. Doc reached down and shook the figure, to make sure the golden man was now unconscious.

DOC SAVAGE made another quick search of the building in order to make certain no one else was there. The most impressive part of the place, he discovered, had been shown to him on his previous visit.

From the back pack of equipment, Doc Savage removed a tiny radio of the so-called "transceiver" type which had both transmission and receiving circuits in a space little larger than that of a camera.

"Long Tom, report in," he said into the microphone.

From somewhere in the street outside, Long Tom Roberts advised, "All quiet out here, Doc. Renny and Elva Boone are here with me. What shall we do?"

"Keep a watch on the place," Doc said. "Warn me if anyone comes."

"Right."

Into the radio, Doc said, "Ham, report in."

Ham's voice, rather faint, said, "All quiet."

"You are still watching Opsall's tropical-fish place?"

"Yes."

"Opsall has not gone anywhere?"

"No, he is still there. He sent someone out, and they came back with several men in work clothes. I presume they are workmen he hired to straighten up the damage to his office and greenhouse."

"Report any developments at once."

"I will."

Doc said, "Johnny, report in."

Johnny's voice—he never used his big words when speaking directly to Doc Savage—said, "All quiet here, too. Gallehue has not stirred from his apartment. He has made no telephone calls."

"You report any developments, too."

"Right."

The bronze man left the receiving part of his radio outfit switched on and placed the instrument on a table near the head of the bed on which the unconscious golden man lay.

Opening the pack, he spread the contents out on the floor. There were chemicals, various instruments used in diagnosis, and lighting equipment.

He put up the light reflectors first. They were clamp-on style type, and when he switched them on, the fuse immediately blew. He found the box and substituted a heavier fuse. There was an enormous amount of intense white light.

There was a deceptive quality about his movements, for they seemed slow, although actually he was working at high speed. He laid out instruments and chemicals.

The portable X-ray was one of the first instruments he used. That and a fluoroscopic viewer so that it was unnecessary to take photographs. Probably fifty times, he shifted the X-ray about the golden man's head and body. He took blood samples and put those through a quick analysis; he did the same with spinal fluid. The fact that the golden man was under the influence of an anaesthetic handicapped to some extent the checking of the nervous condition.

Nearly two hours later, he finished with his diagnosis, and studied the notes he had made. He seemed to be making a complete recheck.

Finally, with the same sure and unhurried movements that had characterized his diagnosis, he mixed three different batches of chemicals. He administered these, two in quick succession, and one later, with hypodermic needles.

He went to the radio. "Long Tom," he said.

"Yes."

"Everything quiet?" Doc asked.

"It seems to be," Long Tom replied over the radio. "Some guy is throwing a masquerade party down the street, and there are a few drunks stumbling around the place."

Doc Savage got reports from Ham watching Opsall, and Johnny at Gallehue's apartment. Neither man had anything to announce.

"It is vitally important that I am not to be interrupted for the next two or three hours. If anyone tries to enter the Dark Sanctuary, stop them. Use any means you have to, but stop them."

"I take it you're about ready to toss the next bomb?"

"About."

"Nobody will get in there," Long Tom said.

During the two hours following, there was no one but Doc Savage in the room where the floodlights made intense glare, and Doc was glad of this, because what happened in the room was not pleasant to see or hear. Doc's metallic features were inscrutable in the beginning, but toward the last they changed and his neck sinews turned into tight strings of strain and his cheeks became flatly grim and perspiration crept out on his bronzed skin.

He was busy most of the time, at first being in great haste finding stout sheets and blankets and ripping them in wide strong sections which he folded into flat bands that were as strong as canvas straps. With these he tied the golden man. The bed was strong, but he made it stronger by removing a heavy door from its hinges and placing it on the bed and arranging a pad of quilts, then lashing the golden man to that.

By then the golden man had become hot, feverish, moist with perspiration. He twisted restlessly. He made muttering noises. His condition grew rapidly more delirious. His body twitched uncontrollably and at times strained against the confining straps, the effort making knots of muscle crawl under the skin of his arms and legs like animals.

When his screaming became loud, Doc Savage applied a gag.

There were hours of that, until past midnight, when the golden man became quiet, except for some nervous shaking in his hands. Eventually he opened his eyes.

He said, so very weakly that it was hardly understandable, "It was the agent at Lisbon. No one else knew what plane I planned to use."

"All right," Doc Savage said. "Everything will be taken care of."

He gave the golden man something to make him sleep, and the man slept.

A CLOCK somewhere was finishing striking two o'clock in the very black night when Doc's radio receiver began hissing, indicating one of the short wave transmitters used by his aides had come on the air.

Ham's voice said, *"Doc!"* excitedly.

The bronze man leaped for his radio, but before he reached it, Ham said wildly, "Those workmen who went into Opsall's place—they weren't workmen. They've grabbed Opsall! They just carried him—"

Ham's voice stopped. There was a report—it might have been a gunshot, a quick blow, or someone might have kicked the other microphone. Then there was a loud, metallic gnashing that indicated the microphone had been dropped, and other noises that were made by feet, and by the radio being kicked about.

"Now—slam him one!" a voice grunted. "But watch out for that sword cane!"

There was a blow, then silence.

"Ham!" Doc said sharply.

He heard a voice, evidently belonging to a man who had put Ham out of commission, say, "What the hell is this box thing?"

"Must be a radio," another voice said.

That last voice, Doc Savage was positive, belonged to the thin man with the scar under his left eye.

The first speaker growled, "We'd better put the radio out of commission." There was a crashing, and the radio suddenly went off the air.

Almost instantly afterward, Long Tom Roberts was on the air demanding, "Doc, what had we better do about that? They got Ham, it sounded like."

Doc Savage asked, "Is your car close?"

"Parked about half a block away. I can get—"

Then Long Tom's voice also stopped. It ended instantaneously, with a lifting snap to the last word that indicated intense alarm. Followed fully half a minute of silence.

"Long Tom! What happened?" Doc asked.

When Long Tom's voice did come, it was a yell of warning at Renny. "Renny!" he roared. *"Renny!* Watch out for those guys! They're not drunks!"

Not from the radio, but from the street outside came the sound of six shots, very closely spaced. From the street in front of the Dark Sanctuary.

Doc Savage lunged for a stairway and went down in long leaps. The uproar in the street was increasing. It must be very loud, in order to penetrate to his ears in such volume. A supermachine pistol turned loose. The unusual weapon belonged to either Renny or Long Tom, of course. It made a sound that might have come from a great airplane engine.

Doc reached the front door of the Dark Sanctuary and flung the door open.

Renny dived inside almost instantly. He had Elva Boone in his arms—under one arm, rather—and he dropped her and put a fresh magazine into his supermachine pistol. He aimed into the street. The gun made its great bullfiddle roaring, the recoil shaking Renny's fist.

Doc shouted, "Where's Long Tom?"

Renny, his big voice an angry rumble, said, "They grabbed him. If it hadn't been for his warning, they would've got me, too."

"Who?"

"Remember we said there was a drunken party in progress down the street? Well, they weren't drunks."

Elva Boone said, "The drunks proved to be plenty sober, and they were watching *us.* They got all set—and then they closed in."

RENNY finished emptying his supermachine pistol into the street, then did something that was rare with him—he swore. "It's no use," he said.

Doc Savage looked through the door. Two trucks were in the street. Huge ones. Van bodies, with sheet steel inside, apparently, and solid-rubber tires that bullets would not ruin. And bullets could not touch the motors, because both machines were backing down the street. They came slowly, angling toward the door of the Dark Sanctuary.

Doc said, "They have prepared for this. Renny, take the girl. We may manage to get away by the back door."

Renny growled some kind of a protest—he was never anxious to retreat in a fight—and in the middle of his muttering, there was an explosion from the back of the building. Wood crashed. Then men ran and a voice said, "Get those masks on! And fill this place full of gas!"

"They've blocked the back door!" Renny rumbled.

Doc said, "Try the roof!"

Half up the first flight of stairs, Doc heard charging feet in the hall above. There was a rear stairway; men had rushed up by that route to head them off.

Doc wheeled, went back. He found the entrance switch—the master switch which controlled all current in the building; it was the type which mounted the fuses in blocks that could be pulled out—and yanked out the fuse blocks, and ground them underfoot, rendering them useless.

He started back through the darkness, and met a man.

Doc whispered, "Did Doc Savage go this way?"

"Oh," said the man. "I didn't know you were one of us—"

Doc struck him with a fist. Because it was too dark to depend on repeat blows, the bronze man hit very hard at the middle of the body. The man doubled. Doc grabbed him around the neck and used fists some more. The fellow was wearing a gas mask, and the mask came off and skittered across the floor.

Upstairs, there started a great bear-bellowing which, with blows, rending clothing, cries that denoted various degrees of agony, indicated Renny had gone into action.

Along with that noise, there was a quick series of mushy explosions that were undoubtedly gas grenades.

Renny's fight noise stopped as suddenly as it had started.

"Is he dead?" a voice asked.

The voice was muffled and unreal, indicating the speaker was wearing a gas mask of a type that permitted conversation to be carried on.

"Don't think he's dead," another voice said. "I banged him over the head with a gun, that's all."

"Keep him alive. Put him in one of the trucks."

"What about the girl?"

"Put her with him."

Upstairs, there was an anxious voice shouting, "They've done something to the golden man! He's dead! There's floodlights rigged up in his bedroom, and all kinds of instruments scattered around. He's lying here on the bed, dead."

Doc saw faint ghosts reflected from flashlights and heard feet going up the stairs to the golden man's bedroom.

"Hell, he's only asleep!" They had evidently examined the golden man more closely.

"But you can't wake him up!"

"Well, he's unconscious, then. He's got a pulse. Take him out, too."

"Want him put in the trucks?"

"Yeah—put him in the trucks."

DOC SAVAGE withdrew quickly, moving back until he was beside the man he had knocked unconscious. He found the gas mask where it had fallen on the floor, and placed it beside the senseless man, then ground a foot on the mask to give the impression that it had been ruined in a fight.

By now, the gas had started penetrating to this spot. The bronze man's eyes stung; it was tear gas. Doc brought out of a pocket a transparent hood, air-tight, which he drew over his head. Elastic at the bottom held the hood tightly about his neck. It was a contrivance that served as temporary gas mask, waterproof container, or other uses, as need required.

He heard pounding feet approach, and a man calling, "Bill, what happened to you? Where are you?"

Doc Savage stepped through a nearby door and waited there, hidden.

A lunging flashlight beam appeared, and located the man senseless on the floor.

"Bill!" The man with the flashlight dropped beside the form on the floor. "Damn the luck!" he said.

Doc Savage lifted the rim of his transparent hood until only his mouth was exposed. He asked, imitating as closely as he could, one of the voices he had heard upstairs, and making the voice sound far away, "Is Bill alive?"

"Yeah. Just knocked out. Broke his gas mask."

Doc said, "Roll him in something so the gas won't hurt his eyes. Use a rug. Then get some of the men to help you carry him out to a truck. Keep him wrapped up so the gas won't get to his eyes."

"Right," the man said.

The fellow hurriedly rolled the unconscious Bill in the rug. The rug, an eight-by-ten size, made a compact covering. Then the man dashed away to get help in carrying the burden.

Doc came out of his hiding place and unrolled the rug, lifted the unconscious man and dumped him into a closet. Returning to the rug, Doc grasped one edge and rolled it about himself. Then he waited.

Very soon, men arrived and laid hold of the rug. Doc was tense all the while he was being carried—but luck was with him, and the rug did not unroll.

He heard a man join them, cursing the fact that they had found silken cords dangling from a forcibly opened skylight, and another silken cord from the roof up to a window of the apartment house.

"Savage escaped that way," the man snarled. "It looks like we shook an empty bush."

Doc, still inside the blanket, was dumped into a truck.

Sounds told him that the golden man was placed in the other truck.

There was noise of a police siren, followed by perhaps twenty pistol shots. After that, the trucks rolled rapidly and the police siren did not follow. On the truck floor, Doc bounced quite a lot.

Chapter XVIII
THE SHOCK CURE

AFTER the truck had rumbled along for ten minutes or so, a man dropped beside Doc Savage and began tugging at the rug. "You come out of it, yet, Bill?" the man asked.

Doc made his voice weak and different and muttered, "Go 'way! I'm all right. Lemme alone!"

He knew by then that it was intensely dark inside the van body of the truck. He moved impatiently, growled again, "Lemme alone! You wanna bust in the face!"

The man who had come to him growled something about an ungrateful so-and-so, and went away.

Someone shouted at the driver, "Damn it! Is that as fast as this thing will go? The town will be alive with cops looking for us in another ten minutes!"

"Keep your shirt on," the driver snapped back. "We're driving out on the wharf now."

A wharf, Doc decided, meant a boat. He hastily unwrapped the rest of the rug, but remained where he was, holding the rug about him.

The truck stopped, the rear doors were thrown open, but practically no light penetrated. The night was amazingly dark.

"Unload and get everybody on the boat," a voice ordered. "Make it snappy. Don't show any lights."

Doc Savage threw the rug down. He fished hastily in his pockets, found a pencil, and began scribbling on the interior of the van body. He wrote by the sense of touch alone, printing at first, then using longhand because that was faster.

To further insure his message being found, he located a crack and stuck the pencil into it, leaving it there.

"Bill?" somebody demanded. "You able to move?"

"Lemme alone," Doc growled. "I'm coming."

He climbed out of the truck. There was not enough light to distinguish faces, but he could make out, faintly against the river water, the outlines of a boat. It was a power cruiser, evidently

near eighty feet in length. The vague impression of it indicated speed.

Doc walked aboard and felt around until he located a lifeboat. He discovered there was a canvas cover over the boat. He unlaced that and climbed in.

He heard another conveyance drive out on the dock. The driver of this car had switched off his lights and was guided by a lighted cigarette which a man waved in a small circle. It was a passenger car.

Sam Gallehue's voice spoke from the machine. "I've got that one called Johnny," Gallehue said. "How did it come out?"

"We got everybody and everything but Doc Savage."

"How did he get away?"

"Through the roof. The police were coming, and we had no time to follow him."

"We've got all of his men now?"

"Yes. They're all aboard."

"That ain't so bad," Sam Gallehue said. "We'll keep his damned men alive for a while and try to use them for bait in a trap that will get him."

Mr. Sam Gallehue was evidently a versatile individual; previously he had given the impression of being a rather timid man who was overanxious to agree with everyone, a man who was inclined to fawn on people. The Sam Gallehue who was talking now had snakes in his voice.

DOC SAVAGE judged that the big boat made in excess of thirty knots while it was traveling down the bay and out through the channel—the channel lights kept the bronze man posted on their whereabouts—to the open Atlantic, and thirty knots must be cruising speed, because the motors were not laboring excessively. The boat was probably fast enough to outrun a naval destroyer, if necessary.

No lights were shown.

Before things had time to settle down, Doc left his lifeboat hiding place. He moved along the deck. Twice, men passed him, but he only grunted agreeably and stepped aside to let him pass, since it was too dark for recognition.

A little rain began to fall. There was no thunder, and, best of all, no lightning. The rain was small drops, warmer than the sea spray which occasionally fell across the deck like buckshot.

Doc took a chance.

"Where'd they put the golden man?" he asked a shadowy figure on deck.

"Stern cabin," the figure said. "Who're you?"

"Bill."

"How's the head?"

"'S'all right," Doc muttered.

There was no one at the door of the stern cabin, and no one in the corridor outside, although the corridor was lighted. Doc Savage took a deep breath, shoved open the door as silently as he could, and entered. He closed the door behind him, and kept going.

The one man in the cabin—he was the thin man with the scar under his left eye—stood at a bunk on which the golden man lay. He half turned. His mouth flew open, so that his jaw was loose and broke under Doc's fist, although Doc had intended only to render him senseless. The man fell across the bunk. Doc lifted him off and put him on the floor.

On the bunk, the golden man's eyes were open. He asked, "How much longer is this mess going to last?" His voice was still weak.

Doc turned one of the golden man's eyelids back to examine the eye. "How do you feel?"

The other grimaced feebly. "Terrible."

"The treatment you underwent tonight accounts for that," Doc explained. "But with your constitution, you will be all right in a few days."

The golden man shut his eyes for a while, then opened them. "Treatment?" he asked.

Doc said, "You had amnesia."

"Loss of memory, you mean?"

"Amnesia is not exclusively loss of memory," Doc Savage explained. "In your case, however, it did entail the misfortune of not being able to recall who you were, what you had been doing, or anything about yourself. But it also included a semidazed state, in which condition you could not rationalize thought processes. That sounds a little complicated. Your trouble was partly amnesia, and partly a form of insanity brought on by physical shock. Mental derangement, we can call it."

The golden man breathed deeply. "I seem to remember having an awful time earlier tonight."

Doc said, "That was the treatment. You underwent what is sometimes called the shock treatment for mental disorder."*

"Could shock have brought on my trouble?"

"Yes."

"Then I guess it happened when the bomb went off in my plane."

Doc Savage asked, "You remember everything that has happened?"

The golden man nodded.

---

*The method of treatment for insanity to which Doc Savage is referring is well known to mental specialists under various names and methods. One of the most widely used being the treatment of insanity by inducing high fever in the patients—a sort of kill-or-cure process which, as less stringent methods are developed, is gradually falling into disuse.

"Suppose you give me an outline of the story," Doc said. "And try to compress it in three or four minutes. We may be interrupted."

The golden man lay still, breathing deeply. "My name," he said, "is Paul Hest. I am chief of intelligence for"—he looked up slyly—"let's call it an unnamed nation, not the United States. We learned that an American liner, the *Virginia Dare,* bringing refugees from Europe, was to be torpedoed. The torpedoing was to be done by the U-boat of another nation, disguised as a submarine belonging to my country. The idea was to build up ill feeling in the United States against my country."

Doc nodded slightly, but said nothing.

Paul Hest continued, "We wanted to warn the *Virginia Dare,* and at the same time lay a trap for the submarine. We could not radio a warning to the *Virginia Dare,* because the message would have been picked up. So I flew out by plane to drop the warning on deck. But there was a bomb in my ship. A counter-espionage agent put it there. I think I know who it was—a man in Lisbon. But that is not important. What is important is that the bomb blew up, and the shock gave me amnesia."

Doc Savage reminded, "You were found floating in the sea, naked."

"I guess I came down by parachute and took off my clothes so I could swim."

Doc said, "I understand there was a strange black star-shape in the sky above you."

"Yes, I remember that faintly. It was just smoke from my plane, after the explosion. The star shape was—well, an accident."

Doc said, "There was also a glowing material in the water. It followed the *Virginia Dare* after the liner picked you up."

The golden man smiled faintly. "That happens to be a war secret of my country, so I can tell you only in general terms what it was. It was a substance which has the chemical property for glowing, like phosphorous, and which is also magnetic, in that it will cling to any metal, providing that metal is not nonmagnetic. It is a substance for trapping submarines, in other words."

"The glowing material," Doc said, "can be put in depth bombs and dropped near submarines, and it will then follow the sub and reveal its location. Is that it?"

Nodding, Paul Hest replied, "Yes, that is it. I was carrying bombs of the stuff to use on the sub that intended to torpedo the *Virginia Dare.* I told you we intended setting a trap for that U-boat."

Doc Savage listened intently. Someone was coming down the corridor.

Paul Hest said, "I imagine the star and the glowing stuff—and my crazy talk about being born of the sea and the night—was kind of eerie."

The footsteps stopped at the door and the door opened and a man entered.

DOC SAVAGE had moved and was standing behind the door; he pushed against the panel and shut it instantly behind the man who had come inside; then Doc put his hands on the neck of the man, all in one fast chain of motion. The struggle between the two of them made them walk across the floor in different directions for a few moments, then Doc got the man down and made the fellow senseless.

"Better finish that story in a hurry," Doc told the golden man.

Paul Hest shrugged. "What else do you want to know? After the plane explosion, I was goofy. I couldn't remember a thing about myself, although I had no difficulty recalling some information. I had heard of you and your men, of course, and I knew a great deal about you—I have a complete dossier of yourself and your men in the files at headquarters. I studied your methods, too, which accounts for the great knowledge of you which I recall having displayed."

Doc said, "Numerous times, you showed you knew things that apparently no man could have known."

Paul Hest smiled faintly. "The intelligence departments of most leading nations know things that apparently no one could know. I happen to have a prodigious memory—Or did I say that? Anyhow, that accounts for my knowing your men, knowing you, knowing about your friend who was to be killed in Vienna—that was a projected political murder of which we were aware months in advance. As for knowing the *Virginia Dare* was to be torpedoed, naturally I was aware of that, and I also knew what ships would be in the vicinity. We had arranged for an agent of ours on the steamer *Palomino* to fake a distress call from the *Virginia Dare* in case the ship actually was torpedoed, which accounts for my knowing the *Palomino* would turn up for the rescue that night. My agent used gas on the *Palomino* radio operator to get the fake S O S into the captain's hands. Remember?"

Doc Savage said, "Did Sam Gallehue actually think you were a—well, shall we say a wizard?"

Paul Hest nodded. "I believe he actually did. At any rate, he was quite sincere in taking me to New York and setting me up as a cult leader."

"Gallehue was sincere?"

"I believe so."

"But Gallehue has staged all this," Doc advised. "He got Monk and Ham consigned to a South American prison, so he could get hold of you. He hired men to try to kill Monk and Ham.

And he has been fighting us tooth and nail."

Paul Hest grimaced. "I said he was sincere—I didn't say he was honest."

"Did Gallehue start the cult with his own money?"

"No, it was Opsall's money."

"Did Gallehue start the cult as a method of getting information which he could use to blackmail the people who became so-called *Believers* in the cult?"

Paul Hest considered. "I don't think so. I think Gallehue was sincere. A crook, but sincere. The cult was making a lot of money. It was a gold mine. Why should Gallehue resort to blackmail?"

Doc Savage was silent for a while.

"If anyone comes in," he said, "you act as if you are out of your mind. Make them think you knocked these fellows unconscious." Doc pointed at the pair on the floor.

Chapter XIX
THE CRASH

THE big boat was still plowing along in complete darkness. One man was at the wheel, and the binnacle enclosing the compass presented a small wedge of light in front of him.

Doc Savage, moving up to him casually, asked, "Where did they put the prisoners?" in a low, guttural voice.

"Fo'c's'le," the man said gruffly.

Doc moved around beside him, reached out as if to take the wheel, but instead took the man. The man was bony and not overly strong, and Doc crushed him against the wheel, holding the throat clamped shut against any sound, until he could locate nerve centers at the base of the skull. Pressure there, while not as quick as a knockout, produced more lasting senselessness.

Doc put the limp figure on a cockpit seat, and pulled a blanket over him, so that it might appear the fellow was asleep.

Holding his watch close to the binnacle, Doc read the time. There were other instruments which flooded briefly with light when he found a panel switch. He noted the boat's speed off a log that read directly onto a dial. He did some calculating.

Later, he changed the course, veering it sharply to the left, then straightening out the craft so that it was headed toward a destination of his own.

His flake-gold eyes strained into the night, searching.

He left the wheel briefly to search the helmsman he had overpowered. Of the stuff he found, he took a gun, cartridges, two gas grenades and a pocketknife.

It took a long time, and he was showing signs of intense strain—before he picked up a light. It was a bit to the starboard far ahead. He watched the light, counting the number of seconds between its flashing.

The wheel had a locking screw which would clamp it in any position. He set the course carefully, locked the wheel, and walked forward.

A man was sitting on the forecastle hatch. He wore oilskins, judging from the slashing noise when he moved, and he was disgruntled.

"Everything quiet down below?" Doc asked.

"Hell, yes," the man snarled. "What the devil do they want to keep a guy out here for? In this rain! Everybody in the fo'c's'le is tied hand and foot, anyhow!"

Doc Savage said, "Here, let me show you something," and leaned down until he found the man's neck.

A moment later, Doc got the forecastle hatch open. He listened, then dropped the guard's unconscious body inside, and followed.

"Monk!" Doc said in a low voice.

A gurgle answered him. Monk sounded as if he was gagged.

Doc felt around until he found Monk's form. He cut the homely chemist loose. "Get circulation back into your arms," Doc ordered. "Then cut the others free." He stabbed the blade of the knife into the bunk mattress and pressed Monk's fingers against it. "Use this knife. You able to do that?"

"Sure, Doc," Monk said with great difficulty.

Doc said, "When the boat hits, jump over the bow and swim ashore—all of you."

THE boat hit the beach at a speed of about thirty knots, which was nearly thirty-four miles an hour, and the beach was sloping sand, so that the craft crawled up a long way before it stopped. In spite of that, the shock was violent enough to bring crashing down everything that was loose and throw Doc Savage, who was in a braced state of semiexpectation, against the wheel so hard that the spokes broke out and he was forcibly relieved of his breath.

Doc had located in advance the button which controlled the boat siren. He sent a hand to this as soon as he could manage, but the siren remained silent; the circuit had been disrupted somewhere. Neither would the lights work.

It seemed to Doc that the first real sound after the crash was Monk's elated howl from the direction of the bow.

"We're off, Doc!" Monk bawled. "We're off the boat!"

Doc Savage was relieved, and sprang for the rail himself.

Then the searchlights came on. They blazed on as he gained the rail. They plastered upon the boat a light as white as new snow, and spread a calcimine glare over the sea. Searchlight beams came from five directions, X-ing across each other at the grounded boat.

Three of the searchlights were from State police patrols on shore, and two from coast guard boats on the sea nearby.

Doc tossed the tear-gas bombs on deck for good measure, then dived overboard. He swam ashore without trouble.

A State policeman put a flashlight on him, then asked, "You're Doc Savage?"

"Yes."

The cop said, "The New York police found a message written inside a truck in pencil. It said to plant an ambush at four places along the coast of New Jersey, Long Island, Connecticut and the Hudson River. You are supposed to have written that message."

Doc admitted having written it.

The State policeman picked up a riot gun. "Come on, gang," he said to his brother officers. "Some of them birds may try to swim ashore."

DOC SAVAGE had been standing at the window of the coast-guard station, watching Sam Gallehue and his gang being loaded into police cars.

Long Tom and Johnny came in.

"I'll be superamalgamated," Johnny declared. He dropped in a chair. "Opsall just broke down and confessed. That sure surprised me."

Doc asked, "Opsall was doing the blackmailing?"

Johnny said, "Yes, Opsall admitted the blackmailing. He worked it as a sideline, and Gallehue didn't know anything about it. Opsall had a man or two working in the Dark Sanctuary, and had a microphone or so in the place. He gathered his information that way."

Long Tom interrupted, "You know what set them against each other, and caused the blowup, Doc?"

Doc suggested, "Our so-called bombs?"

Long Tom grinned faintly. "That's it. You made Opsall think Gallehue had sent a man to kill him, and that set him against Gallehue. You made Gallehue think Opsall had tried to kill *him*. The result was the blowup—Gallehue went wild and grabbed Opsall and everybody else he could lay hands on. He was heading for a spot up on the Maine coast where he had fixed up a summer layout for his cult, as near as we can make out."

Johnny said, "Right now, he's headed for assuetudinous statuvolism."

"What's that?" Long Tom asked.

Renny said, "Another word for jail."

THE END

INSIDE THE FICTION FACTORY by Will Murray

The legendary publishing house of Street & Smith was formed when writer and compositor Francis Shubael Smith and accountant Francis Scott Street partnered to take over the *New York Weekly* in 1855 on a dare. They soon branched out into dime novels, where heroes like Nick Carter, Buffalo Bill and Frank Merriwell helped make their fortunes. The firm of Street & Smith eventually grew into one of the largest publishing houses in the world.

After the death of Francis S. Street in 1883, the company fell into the hands of the Smith family. Francis S. Smith passed away in 1887.

In 1905, they built a seven-story red-brick office building in the Chelsea district of Manhattan, near Greenwich Village. It was said to be the strongest New York structure yet built, and a mirror of the Popular Mechanics Building in Chicago. By this time, dime novels were on the way out. Pulp magazines were the latest vehicle for popular fiction.

Shadow and *Doc Savage* editor John Nanovic remembered:

> Street & Smith were six buildings in a row, interconnected with steps between the buildings. The front building had editorial and executive offices on the sixth floor, composing room on the seventh floor, and some editorial offices on the fifth floor with rolls of papers. Paper rolls were everywhere because Street & Smith was a printing

The Street & Smith Building

house more than a publishing house.

Set at the corner of Seventh Avenue and 17th Street, the address was 79-89 Seventh Avenue. A double set of marble columns marked the public entrance.

Science-fiction writer Frederick Pohl painted a marvelous word picture of the physical plant:

> The Seventh Avenue side was the new building, but it was filled mostly with presses and binding machines that actually manufactured their magazines; when the presses were going, which was usually, their thudding rocked the building.
>
> The editors were housed on the 17th Street side, and to get there you entered on Seventh Avenue and made your way through doors and passages, up a step or two and down a few as you passed from one building to another... There was a time clock at the employees' entrance on 17th Street, and they all had to punch in and out like any Ford assembly-line factory hand.
>
> The building had a hydraulic elevator. To make it go up and down, the operator had to tug on a rope outside the car itself. The building had long since been declared a hazard by the fire marshal, and so smoking was prohibited everywhere in it.

Getting to editorial was like threading a maze.

"It's a long and dangerous route," remarked Harriet Bradfield, columnist for *Writer's Digest* and contributor to *Love Story Magazine.* "Beware! You pass by the high heaped rolls of paper that next month will feed the giant rollers on a lower floor of the building. And you feel awfully insignificant and adventurous, beside such a mountain of future reading matter."

"Quartered oak was the motif," wrote Quentin Reynolds in *The Fiction Factory,* "and each office held the tall, cumbersome roll-top desks considered to be the last word in office furnishing in 1905. The place was immaculately clean."

Visitors described it as a beehive of activity. Denver author Albert William Stone visited Street & Smith in 1926:

> The Street & Smith building is several stories high, and crammed from basement to roof with visible and audible evidences of the great publishing business housed in it. You hear the linotype machines clatter and the presses rumble continuously. Busy young men and girls rush about, flitting from floor to floor and from door to door, pencils behind their ears and stuck in their hair, green shades over their eyes, ink stains on their fingers. Great motor trucks are backed up under immense shelters at one end of the building, and bales of magazines are being loaded into them for transportation to railroad shipping points.

"The loading dock was busy all day," remembered *Air Trails* editor William Winter, "perhaps

Street & Smith's book warehouse

more so than the *Times,* with big flatbeds constantly unloading rolls of paper. Production was fantastic, extremely well organized. It was massive, believe me."

Street & Smith was rightly called "the uncontested Ford of magazine publishing." For a time, a beehive was the company trademark. Albert William Stone's description continues:

> A pleasant-faced woman seated behind a desk in a cubbyhole at one side of a square, boxed-in room containing for furniture only a settee or two, spoke my name into a telephone transmitter. In a moment she smiled at me.
>
> "Do you know the way over to the *Western Story* office? No?" She called, and a boy appeared. "Take this gentleman to Mr. Blackwell's office, please."
>
> The boy conducted me through halls, down corridors, into offices from which arose the busy clatter of typewriters, up short flights of steps and down others, and finally into a big room filled with desks whose surfaces were fairly plastered with manuscripts. It was a formidable array of contributions; I recognized them instantly as such, to be sure. And they were being read by a small army of young men and women—those individuals we writers know as "readers."

The interior was such a labyrinth that a visiting memory expert had to backtrack for directions before he could navigate back to the street.

Many visitors recorded their impressions for posterity. No matter the era, it seemed eternally the same.

Doc Savage cover artist Robert G. Harris first entered those doors in 1931.

> It was very early in the morning when I eagerly arrived. I never had seen a publishing plant before, and the thrill of seeing all this mass production of magazines, with the clatter and din of press, binding machines, and the over-all glorious smell of printers ink was a bit of heaven to me.

On his first visit, Isaac Asimov was struck by "the piles of magazines... permeated with the heavenly smell of pulp paper."

Henry Kuttner dropped by in 1939:

> I made an appointment with John W. Campbell, Jr., editor of *Astounding* and *Unknown,* to whom I'd previously sold a few

The "small army" of readers

A corridor at Street & Smith

his first tale of Speed Dash, the Human Fly:

> Arthur Scott was the editor of *Top-Notch.* As he subsequently told me, he read my story and shook his head, walked over to his office window on the seventh floor of the building, looked down at the sidewalk to see for himself how impossible the story was—and made a startling discovery. The Street & Smith office building, built of stone, had curved recesses cut along the border of each block, and as these stones were fitted together, they made indentations. Scott reached his hand out the window, and nesting his fingertips in the indentations, felt the sudden surge of enthusiasm which comes with an editorial discovery.
>
> "By George, a man *could* climb the building, if, of course, he was young, strong, and cool-headed."

yarns. The sanctified atmosphere of age hangs over the ancient brown block of a building which houses Street & Smith. The elevator was an enlarged version of the Iron Maiden.

The receptionist took my name and asked me to wait, so I sat down in a Victorian anteroom and looked at the mellow paneled walls. I wished I'd bought a frock coat to wear. I felt entirely too brash and modern—a Saroyan at King Arthur's Court.

Fredrick Pohl recalled his first appointment with Campbell:

> A boy appeared and beckoned. "I'll show you the way," he said, and led me past vast circular rolls of paper five feet long and four feet high. We passed the doors of innumerable offices, from which emerged the clattering of typewriters, and the voices of editors, writers. My guide ushered me into one of the offices, and I decided I must be in the wrong pew.
>
> It was frugally furnished. The desk was littered with papers. John Campbell got up from the swivel-chair behind the desk, shook hands, and asked me to sit down.

Pulp historian Sam Moskowitz recalled:

> Each editor had a partition smaller than a prison cell and one window on the Seventh Avenue side of the building. The offices were cluttered with filing cabinets, a roll-top desk, galleys and manuscripts. Everything looked like it had been there since the building was opened, including the typewriters and telephones. Sometimes the editor would walk the visitor back to the exit, so they wouldn't get lost and wander through the canyons of rolled paper. Even the immediate area of the building was dingy, commercial and uncomfortable and it was always a relief to enter the subway or walk hastily back to a more familiar area.

The red-brick building, which Lester Dent once described as being "the color of stagnant blood," helped Erle Stanley Gardner to close the sale of

Thursdays were payday. Writers eager for checks began congregating early. *Love Story* and *Doc Savage* editor Daisy Bacon reminisced in her memoir, "The Golden Days of the Iron Maiden":

> On fair days they lounged against the marble pillars, smoking and talking shop. If the weather was stormy, they pulled back into the white-tiled hallway and onto the stairs, some even climbing

Daisy Bacon in her office

Street & Smith's in-house printing presses

them when the checks were late and they were in a hurry to get to the Chemical Bank around the corner before closing time.

No matter how many were waiting, nothing ever disturbed the equilibrium of Louis, the elevator operator, known affectionately to all the regulars as "Louis the Fourteenth." Louis would accept only so many passengers at a time for his steel-trellised cage, which was popularly known as the "Iron Maiden," and which rose and fell with maddening slowness.

"I think the 'lift' went click-click," recalled William Winter, "and I seem to remember a short, dark man who may have worked the gate, but it clicked in front of a main door to each 'factory' floor, each green, dark, like rising to an appointment with the electric chair, repeated six times to the top."

"On the rare occasions when the checks were going to be too late for the bank," continued Bacon, "some who had skipped lunch would slip down to Liggett's for a cup of coffee. Liggett's lunch counter was where, over a ham on rye, more gossip about the state of magazine publishing could be heard than ever appeared in the combined columns of *The News, The Mirror* and *The Journal-American.* More seemed to be known about our magazines than we knew ourselves! Every editor of importance was known by name and it was usual to discuss rumors of changes over lunch."

After hours, writers and editors repaired to Gately's for a drink. Nearby on Eighth Avenue was Halloran's, the restaurant where Henry Ralston and John Nanovic developed the concept of Doc Savage.

Thirty presses were in use. S&S ran four Hoe presses 24 hours a day, each capable of producing 12,000 magazines an hour. Some of their top sellers, such as *Western Story* and *Love Story* magazines, were published every week and sold 1,000,000 copies a month. It was said that the Fiction Factory produced 44 miles of magazines a month just in the year 1934.

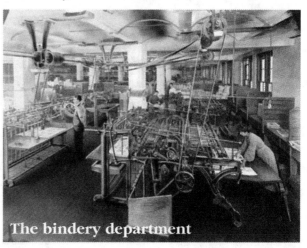

The bindery department

44 MILES of Magazines

FOUR TIMES AS HIGH AS THE STRATOSPHERE RECORD

IF the world's demand for Street & Smith magazines, in any one month of the year, was assembled in a single pile it would form a column more than 44 miles high. The space used for the illustration is not large enough to show relative proportions.

This great pillar of fictional literature would be more than 4 times as high as the highest recorded flight into the stratosphere.

The unofficial "high" for stratosphere flights is held by the Soviet Republic, whose intrepid airmen have penetrated the skies for nearly 12 miles.

The U. S. Navy balloon recently pierced the clouds for nearly the same distance which is now generally accepted as the official record.

In this mammoth pile of publications are stories of every conceivable type. Action, Adventure, Crime Detection, Romance, Sport, Mystery—no matter what sort of reading you like you'll find it in the great Street & Smith group of magazines.

"The bindery was on the ground floor of the huge old building, the print shop on the top," noted Nick Carter-writer Richard Wormser. "Between, the Smiths stored tons upon tons of paper and us."

The proofreading room was also on the top floor. According to William Winter, "…they had a big room, green eye shades, were very good, and stepped out of Dickens."

The art department occupied the top floor of the second building. Elderly William "Pop" Hines ran it. Like Louis the elevator starter and Frank Hatton who ran the pressroom, he was a fixture. Legend had it the S&S building super had worked there for over 50 years.

But the mail room was the busiest office, according to Daisy Bacon.

> During the years when Street & Smith published anywhere from twenty to twenty-five titles, we received hundreds of thousands [of manuscripts] which Station 'O' of the New York Post Office delivered in spite of wrong addresses or no addresses at all and with only the good-natured kidding that "this Bacon must run a correspondence school."

By the Great Depression, and the heyday of *The Shadow* and *Doc Savage Magazines,* the building had begun showing its age.

> For more than thirty years the presses had been roaring day and night, and the building was in a permanent state of jitters. It vibrated from top to bottom. The roll-top desks and the heavy-paneled quartered oak were still there, but time had not been kind to them. The corridors were stacked with heavy rolls of paper and bales of returns. There were back numbers and old books all over the building. Ormond Smith hated to throw anything away.

Not everyone disliked the factory atmosphere. "I would arrive at the office and go over plots with John Nanovic," Walter Gibson recalled, "then we would set up an appointment with Mr. Ralston. This took place in an elegantly paneled office that dated back to dime-novel days. The thirty-year-old brick building, once classed as 'the greatest printing house in the world,' had begun to show the strain of the high-speed presses, but the rhythmic vibrations that accompanied our conferences were something of an inspiration."

New management came along in 1938, and tried to spruce up the aging exterior.

Fred Pohl recalled: "Just before Christmas of 1938, Street & Smith invested in a big electric sign to go by the entrance; it cost so much, the employees were told, that there would be no Christmas bonus that year."

After World War II and its paper shortages shrank the firm's pulp line to a small group of digest-sized magazines, editorial offices were moved to the modern Chanin Building on 42nd Street and Lexington. With the move imminent, Harriet Bradfield waxed nostalgic about the grand brick edifice late in 1943:

Street & Smith's reception room

"On 42nd St.," lamented William Winter, "it was like working for General Motors, the color, innocence, and fiction almost totally gone."

In 1947, the pulp division was moved back to the old red brick fortress. Harriet Bradfield painted a final portrait of the soon-to-be-obsolete Fiction Factory:

If you used to take manuscripts to the editors when they were down in those offices before, you'll sniff the familiar scent of printer's ink with a little feeling of being right where you belong. The presses and the binders still rumble. The old cage-elevator creeps and creeps. But now you will find the editors all on the fifth floor. They are walled off on the west side, all freshly painted—with a sign in front of the *Western Story* door threatening *"non toccare si murore."* (Hope I got that right.) It's supposed to mean "Don't touch on pain of death," or so Jack Burr says. Remember the huge rolls of paper that used to hedge in those offices in the old days? Not a roll in sight, today.

There is something solid and dependable about the old Street & Smith Building, which has communicated itself to the magazines published there. The presses on the lower floors shake the very air, until it seems sometimes as if a job in that building would be fine preliminary training for a life at sea. But no one appears to mind the vibration. The golden oak paneling of the big square reception room is as firm as the day it was set in place. And the waiting room behind the reception desk echoes its air of dignity. The founders of the company look down from the heavy frames on the wall. And the massive directors' table holds current copies of all the Street & Smith magazines.

This waiting room with its elaborate rug might have served as the model for Doc Savage's skyscraper reception room. Doc's gigantic office safe no doubt was inspired by the S&S safe where manuscripts were stored in the event of fire. The arrangement of adjacent buildings thrown together unquestionably begat The Avenger's Greenwich Village headquarters, with its identical layout.

In describing the modern new digs, Harriet Bradfield couldn't help but evoke the staid old stand:

It took a map or an experienced guide to get you into Editor Burr's cubbyhole down in the labyrinths of the old Street & Smith place. The new office seems nearly as complicated to find, with left turns and right turns, and a jaunt through a library where all the ancient publications of the company are lined up.

Writer H. Wolff Salz contrasted the old with the new early in 1944: "The new Street & Smith editorial layout occupies a floor of the Chanin Building, and the S&S reception office looks like you're coming into a svelte advertising agency. Modern furniture, thick rugs, high wide mirrors and a beautiful blonde."

Not everyone saw it that way.

Printers' union issues eventually caused production to be relocated to the old Fruhauf Trailer Plant in Elizabeth, New Jersey. The remaining pulp editors also moved out to 775 Lidgerwood Avenue.

Shadow radio writer Alfred Bester received an invitation to visit John W. Campbell there.

"I was delighted to accept the invitation despite the fact that the editorial offices of *Astounding* were then the hell and gone out in the boondocks of New Jersey," recalled Bester. "The editorial offices were in a grim factory that looked like and probably was a printing plant. The 'offices' turned out to be one small office, cramped, dingy, occupied not only by Campbell but by his assistant, Miss Tarrant. My only yardstick for comparison was the glamorous network and advertising agency offices. I was dismayed."

In 1949, the pulps were abandoned by Street & Smith. All but *Astounding,* which is still published today as *Analog.* Street & Smith celebrated its one hundreth anniversary in 1955. In 1960, it was purchased by the Condé Nast Publications. The name continues today only as a series of Street & Smith sports annuals.

"S&S was a mighty place," recalled William Winter. "While Bill Barnes was an element, I was part of the flow of that company during two great transformations, as one of the world's greatest and richest empires survived and adjusted to a rapidly changing world. For example, *Life* and pictures relegated that old pulp giant into a Roman if not Grecian glorious past."

Lester Dent (1904-1959) could be called the father of the superhero. Writing under the house name "Kenneth Robeson," Dent was the principal writer of *Doc Savage,* producing more than 150 of the Man of Bronze's thrilling pulp adventures.

A lonely childhood as a rancher's son paved the way for his future success as a professional story-teller. "I had no playmates," Dent recalled. "I lived a completely distorted youth. My only playmate was my imagination, and that period of intense imaginative creation which kids generally get over at the age of five or six, I carried till I was twelve or thirteen. My imaginary voyages and accomplishments were extremely real."

Dent began his professional writing career while working as an Associated Press telegrapher in Tulsa, Oklahoma. Learning that one of his coworkers had sold a story to the pulps, Dent decided to try his hand at similarly lucrative moonlighting. He pounded out thirteen unsold stories during the slow night shift before making his first sale to Street & Smith's *Top-Notch* in 1929. The following year, he received a telegram from the Dell Publishing Company offering him moving expenses and a $500-a-month drawing account if he'd relocate to New York and write exclusively for the publishing house.

Dent soon left Dell to pursue a freelance career, and in 1932 won the contract to write the lead novels in Street & Smith's new *Doc Savage Magazine.* From 1933-1949, Dent produced Doc Savage thrillers while continuing his busy freelance writing career and eventually adding Airviews, an aerial photography business.

Dent was also a significant contributor to the legendary *Black Mask* during its golden age, for which he created Miami waterfront detective Oscar Sail. A real-life adventurer, world traveler and member of the Explorers Club, Dent wrote in a variety of genres for magazines ranging from pulps like *Argosy, Adventure* and *Ten Detective Aces* to prestigious slick magazines including *The Saturday Evening Post* and *Collier's.* His mystery novels include *Dead at the Take-off* and *Lady Afraid.* In the pioneering days of radio drama, Dent scripted *Scotland Yard* and the 1934 *Doc Savage* series.